THE THIRD PATIENT

THE THIRD PATIENT

George B. Mannis

Rutledge Books, Inc. Danbury, CT

Copyright © 1999 by George B. Mannis

ALL RIGHTS RESERVED
Rutledge Books, Inc.
107 Mill Plain Road, Danbury, CT 06811
1-800-278-8533
www.rutledgebooks.com

Manufactured in the United States of America

Cataloging in Publication Data
Mannis, George B.

The Third Patient

ISBN: 1-58244-056-5

1. Medical novels.   2. Physicians. United States -- Fiction.

Library of Congress Catalog Card Number: 99-65199

Doctors are men who prescribe medicines of which they know little, to cure diseases for which they know less, in human beings of whom they know nothing.

— Voltaire (1694-1778)

ONE

Wednesday morning, Feb 17, Philadelphia, PA

I'M IN THE MIDDLE OF A BEAUTIFUL DREAM, SMILING IN MY SLEEP. IT'S a sunny day, and I'm skiing down a mountain blanketed with fresh white snow. A young, gorgeous, velvet-skinned woman approaches me, and we exchange meaningful glances. First we play follow the leader, then I brake my skis to a perfect stop to chat with her. She smiles, white teeth through thick lips and tanned face, and compliments my skiing, my coordination, my muscles. I slowly feel the hairs at the nape of my neck shiver and I'm ready to make a move, inquire about her after-ski plans when the phone rings. Heart thumping ferociously, I fumble for the receiver in the darkness, my eye catching the green fluorescent display on the clock. Two forty-four. My wife Irene, who is lying next to me, continues to sleep peacefully.

"Hello?" I clear my throat.

"Dr. Holden, I'm sorry to wake you up but . . . " the man hesitates.

"It's okay. What's up?"

"This is Steve Denker at the emergency room. We have just

admitted a lady with jaundice and confusion, and we're not sure how to proceed. She's not your patient, but I understand that you're on call for the Gastroenterology Division."

I can't put a face to the name or the voice, so I think Denker is maybe a rotating resident, spending the month of February in the ER.

"Whose patient is she?"

"Nobody's, or at least we don't know yet. She apparently lives alone. Was brought in by the medics. No file. Nothing. We just know that her name is Dorothy Alberts."

I sit up in my bed, scratching my face.

"Has Dr. Chandler taken a look at her?"

Dennis Chandler is the fellow, a physician in specialty training. He's supposed to examine the patients first, write down admission notes and then call the attending physician. It's the traditional way to train young doctors in a particular specialty. Also, if the fellow happens to be sufficiently smart and independent, he just might wait until morning before alerting the sleeping attending specialist.

"No. There is a note here that Chandler has left town to attend a wedding, and that you should be called first."

I remember now. I gave Chandler the day off. Didn't think much of it because lately I haven't been getting too many calls.

"Right. Well, what have you got so far?" I'm back in bed, leaning on my elbow. I'm still not sure whether I have to get up and drive to the hospital. Maybe I can give instructions over the phone and crawl back under the warm, inviting blanket.

"Classical hepatic failure, Dr. Holden. All the signs and symptoms, a textbook case par excellence. Tremor, jaundice, fetor hepaticus, high blood ammonia levels, the works. We started intravenous infusion, and are giving her oxygen, lactulose, steroids, the usual. She doesn't look good, though."

I don't like the sound of it. Hepatic failure is often fatal, especially when in advanced stages. Liver transplant is the only possibly life-saving treatment in severe cases, but the risks are considerable. Very often the patient is too sick for any kind of surgery.

I get up, walk to the closet and start looking for a clean white shirt. I turn on the lights. Irene groans and turns to the other side, apparently sound asleep. I know that if Danny breathed a little louder in the next room, she'd be on her feet in a millisecond. I'm still holding the phone.

"Any idea about the cause?" I ask.

"Nope. Alcohol, probably, but we really don't know. She can't talk and there's no family to answer questions. No medical history."

"Sounds like I'd better come down and see what's going on, huh?"

"Yes, Dr. Holden. I agree completely."

I sigh and continue to dress. It would be nice if Denker told me that everything was under control and that I could come later in the morning. But Denker didn't, and I know I have to go immediately. I take a look at my warm bed and head to the bathroom. I wash my face with cold water, towel off, put on my winter coat, gloves and hat and exit into the freezing wind. I have to drive slowly, as the roads are slippery from the recent snow. Of course, the expressway is empty and I make it to Lincoln General in less than fifteen minutes.

* * * * *

In the emergency room, the usual chaos. People screaming, crying, pain, blood, death. Several victims of car accidents. Gunshot wounds, lost limbs. Nurses running, doctors shouting orders, phones ringing. Welcome to civilization in a free, trigger-happy society.

I put down my coat in the nurses' station and look around, hoping to attract Dr. Denker's attention. At six foot one, with dense brown hair covering my scalp, I'm an easy target to spot. People tell me that with my large ears, partially covered by hair and with my tiny mustache I look like Clark Gable. But my brown eyes are more friendly, this according to Irene one week into our honeymoon. I don't agree with most of these flattering descriptions, but then I may be too critical.

I know many of the staff members in the emergency room, because I visit this place very often. Too often. Anytime somebody bleeds into their gut, I'm down here with my scope trying to find the bleeding spot. When I was in training, just a few short years earlier, I spent many tumultuous sleepless nights here.

I see a thin, bespectacled unshaven young man in a white coat approaching. Now I recognize the face. He was a medical student in my department, but we had little contact because I wasn't the attending physician that month.

"Hi, Steve," I say and shake his hand, "let's see the patient."

Steve seems relieved that I remember him. We walk together and enter room number 8. There are two patients in the room, separated from each other by a white curtain. From the door, I can see the yellow-tinted face of Dorothy Alberts. We approach the bed. A nurse is changing the infusion fluid and removing the air bubbles from the intravenous line. Mrs. Alberts is middle-aged, slightly overweight and despite her illness has a pleasant face. In younger and better days, I bet she occupied the thoughts and fantasies of many men. Now she is breathing loudly, and seems to stare blankly at the ceiling, mumbling incoherently. She doesn't respond to the sound of her name but screams when I poke her skin with my neurological pin. She's hooked to several monitors, wears an oxygen mask and has two lines inserted in her blood vessels—one venous and the other arterial. She is also restrained to her bed with tight bandages, so that she doesn't pull out the lines in a fit of disoriented frenzy.

I examine the patient carefully for several moments. All the signs are unmistakably those of serious liver failure, but I wonder whether the onset was sudden or slow. I'm looking for skin marks or rashes that might suggest a lengthy, chronic problem but see none. No evidence of alcohol related changes either.

"What's this?" I ask Steve. Steve bends forward, his slim figure throwing a long shadow on the white sheet. I point to a long scar on the patient's left ankle. It's about four inches long, and looks quite recent. It has very smooth edges and is straight as an arrow. These cuts were obviously made by a top-notch fully trained board-certified plastic surgeon.

"I don't know." Steve has obviously missed it.

I remove the sheet from the right ankle and look at the dark, swollen skin. I don't see any scars.

"What do you think this is?" Steve asks.

"Oh, it looks like some sort of a biopsy." I look closer. "Yes, it could be sural nerve biopsy."

This is a surgical procedure where a small piece of a nerve is cut and examined under the microscope to try and diagnose the cause of nerve disease.

There's a sudden piercing scream from an adjacent room, and I feel my chest tightening for a second. Then I hear a little voice, a boy or a girl, yell "no, no, please . . . " and it's the pleading 'please' that wrenches my gut. Then there's a sudden eerie silence, and I notice that Steve is following the same outside distraction, the color draining from his face. I look again at Mrs. Alberts.

"She must have suffered from some sort of neuropathy," I continue, "any more information on her previous diseases?"

"She was too confused to give us any history."

"Hmm. What about lab results?"

"Jaundice is severe. Her bilirubin is 33, transaminase 4080, pro-time 17%."

These numbers tell me that a large portion of the liver is destroyed, and that deadly bleeding could occur any moment. People can recover from such extensive damage, but chances aren't particularly good. The outcome often depends on the cause of the illness.

"And another thing," Steve continues, reading from a crumpled piece of paper he digs out of his pocket, "her blood glucose was very high. Five-oh-seven. We put some insulin in the infusion."

I nod. If she's diabetic maybe the long nerves going to her feet have been destroyed, a condition called diabetic neuropathy. The patients don't feel a thing at the bottom of their feet, step on hot or sharp objects, and before you know it the foot has to go. Usually, one doesn't need to cut a piece of nerve to diagnose this nerve disease in a patient with diabetes. You just listen to the patient tell her story, test her for sensation with a hammer, pin or cotton wisp and you have your diagnosis.

"What's that?" I point to a small brown bottle on the table next to the bed. There is a white label on it with indecipherable scribbling.

"This is a bottle of her medications which the medics found in her bag," Steve says. "There were four different pills in it, but I only identified two of them. One is Valium, the other Dyazide. I guess she didn't sleep well and had hypertension."

I open the bottle and empty its contents on the small round table. I have no trouble recognizing the yellow, heart-shaped 5mg Valium tablet and the red-white capsule of Dyazide. The third pill also looks familiar. It is white and rhomboid.

"This is Glucotrol," I tell Steve.

"Oh, good. That confirms it then. She is diabetic," Steve says and jots something down on his crumpled paper. Glucotrol is used to control blood sugar in diabetic patients, the kind that develops later in life.

The fourth pill is a white-blue capsule. I pick it up, sniff at it, hold it up in the air, then turn it to see both sides. All I see is the word "Gother" engraved on it. Gother is a pharmaceutical company, but I don't recognize the pill.

"We searched in the PDR," he says, "but it's not in there."

Steve must be reading my mind. PDR, short for Physicians Desk Reference, contains the names and pictures of all the pills sold in the US. It is published just for occasions like this.

"That's strange," I mutter.

I look at the list of treatments given to Mrs. Alberts. Steve prescribed all the right measures to reduce bacterial toxins in the gut, through enemas and antibiotics. When the liver stops functioning, all the toxins continue to roam freely in the blood, eventually accumulating in the brain and causing confusion and coma. I'm standing there, scratching my head, looking for something clever to add, but come up empty.

"Uh, what's the cause of this liver failure?" Steve asks, "I mean, if it's drug induced, could dialysis work?"

I can tell that this kid's head is screwed on the right way. Many drugs can cause liver disease, but most of the time the effects are minor and transient. Often, the only measure required is discontinuation of the responsible drug. This case is different. This is serious liver destruction and more drastic measures are required.

"It's a good idea, but dialysis can make her situation worse by inducing electrolyte imbalance," I say, "so I wouldn't do it unless I knew that the offending drug is still in the blood stream."

Steve nods and looks at the patient pensively.

"She's slipping, I think," he says. "When I first saw her, she was more combative and agitated, and also more alert."

"Well, nothing more we can do at this stage. Her body will have to fight the toxins and the liver will have to heal."

I look at the nurse who comes in to check the monitors. She's moving slowly and I can see she's tired and continues to function on inertia alone, and dozen cups of coffee.

"Steve, let's transfer her ASAP to the intensive care unit. Get a renal consult to check her kidneys, a neurologist to closely follow her mental situation and get somebody from the surgical team to check if a liver transplant might help. Oh, and see if somebody in the pharmacy recognizes the fourth pill."

Steve writes down my orders, says something to the nurse and we leave the room. The tumult in the ER has all but died down, and the nurses and doctors are laughing over steaming cups of coffee. I try to look for the little kid who screamed earlier but I'm not sure where to look. I realize that there's nothing I can do even if I find him or her.

I look at my watch and yawn. It is twenty after four.

"I'll be in the section head's office if you need me," I say.

"Fine."

I take the elevator to the ninth floor, and enter the office of the head of my department, Dr. Arthur Scott. His is a much larger office than mine, and it has a sofa. I lie down on the sofa and after a few moments I fall asleep. I try desperately to return to the skiing dream but I can't.

TWO

A LOUD THUD, AND I JUMP UP OFF THE SOFA AND LAND ON MY FEET. DR. Scott has just dropped a heavy briefcase on his desk and is now staring at me, squinting through his thick glasses. He is a beefy mountain of a man, huge hands, large protruding stomach, enormous ego. He has lots of experience and when it comes to dealing with complex clinical problems he has no equals. He's one of the most highly sought after consultants for the high and mighty in our society, those who can afford his services. He's the one who hired me but our relationship has had its ups and downs. Recently we have been getting along just fine, mostly because he doesn't stick his nose into my business any more than is absolutely necessary.

"Sorry, Paul," he says.

"That's okay," I lie, "I have to get going anyway."

"You can shave in my bathroom," he says, and opens his briefcase. As head of a section he has a private bathroom attached to his spacious office. I feel the stubble on my face.

"There are some new razors you can use," he tells me and removes a packed folder from his briefcase and flops it on the desk.

I shave and comb my hair, and when I finish I cross his office again on my way out. He's on the phone now and I wave to him.

I walk across the hall to my office. My secretary, Carol, a young freckled red-head is already here, filing away some documents. A few days earlier she let me know that she found a "great new boyfriend" and I can see that her energy level has picked up several notches. One more proof that we're all nothing more than slaves to our hormones. Just when I get behind my desk the phone rings. Steve Denker is on the line.

"Dr. Holden, Mrs. Alberts's daughter arrived and she wants to talk to you."

"Where is she?"

"We're here in the intensive care unit."

"How's the mother doing?"

"Not much change. Perhaps slightly more alert."

"I'm on my way."

I hang up and look at the large clock on the wall. It is 7:45, which is when I normally arrive at work. In the outer office I ask Carol to call the clinic and tell them I'm going to be late.

The intensive care unit is a suite of twelve patient rooms on the sixth floor. The control room has several monitors for each patient, and nurses move about to check the green fluorescent screens. The most seriously ill patients are admitted here and the atmosphere is always solemn and dreary.

There is a large waiting room for patients' relatives adjacent to the intensive care unit. Green chairs, dark green carpet, beige wallpaper, landscape paintings, all very sedate. As I enter the waiting room, Steve Denker and a young woman approach me. She extends her hand and looks me straight in the eyes.

"Nice to meet you, Dr. Holden. I'm Lydia Alberts."

She's in her early twenties, slightly overweight with a pretty face. As she emerges from her heavy dark-blue coat, I watch her dark hair, bushy eyebrows, green eyes, a pleasant attention capturing contrast. Underneath the coat I notice gray pants with spots of splashed mud. She seems anguished and tired, as if she spent the night on the road. She looks like a typical college student, and her chubby countenance can perhaps be ascribed to late night pizza parties in the dormitories.

"Nice to meet you, Lydia," I say, and motion for them to sit down.

"I came as soon as I heard," she says. "Mom's neighbor, Donna, called me at school. She said mom was acting strange, shaking, not making any sense. Mom refused to call the doctor. Finally, at around one thirty Donna called the medics and they brought mom to the hospital."

"Where do you go to school?" I ask. I'm surprised at her deep cracking voice, which somehow doesn't fit her looks.

"Yale. Third year law."

Steve looks at me, to see if I'm impressed but I don't show him that I am.

"Is she going to make it, Dr. Holden?" she asks and purses her lips.

"It's hard to say. The odds are somewhat against her because she waited very long to get medical attention. The outcome also depends on the cause, of course."

Her eyes get misty, and I wonder if she's going to ask me to be more specific about the odds. She doesn't. Either she thinks I don't know or maybe she doesn't want to know.

"Well, what is it then? I mean, what caused her liver failure?"

Steve gives a little cough but says nothing. I speak.

"We're still running some tests. We don't have all the information. In the meantime, we are doing all we can."

I try to sound warm and encouraging, but I find myself

giving her the standard routine lines. She looks at me intensely, as if searching for some hidden meaning.

"Perhaps you can help us here," I say, folding my arms across my chest. "I'd like to ask you a few questions."

She nods, and I peer into her green eyes.

"Does your mom live alone?"

"Yes. My dad died in a car accident a couple of years ago."

"I see. Now, what do you know about your mom's health status?" Steve pulls out a note pad and is holding his pen poised.

"She was fairly healthy until her fiftieth birthday about three years ago. She was then diagnosed with diabetes and high blood pressure at the same time. The doctor gave her some pills and she felt okay. She went on a diet, special foods and everything. She lost some weight, not much, but at least she didn't need insulin shots."

Steve is writing feverishly, then he takes his eyes off the pad.

"Do you know why she was taking Valium?" he wants to know.

Lydia looks at me, like, why is he asking questions and who's in charge here? She decides to answer.

"I guess sometimes she had trouble falling asleep."

Steve gives me a look, and I think he wonders whether I'm going to accept this answer. I have no problem with the Valium, so I ignore him.

"Did your mother suffer from sensation problems in her feet, like tingling, pins and needles?"

"Yeah, I think so . . . but I'm not sure. Mom never complains or talks about her medical problems."

"What about alcohol? Does she drink?" I ask.

"Never. She hates it." Lydia says this with a loud voice that makes Steve stop writing.

That takes care of that. Alcohol could not have caused her liver disease. I'm scratching my chin.

"Last thing. Do you know of any surgery to remove a piece of nerve from her ankle?"

"Yeah, I think she was participating in some kind of a study. As I said, mom doesn't like to talk about her diseases, and since I don't live at home, you know, she doesn't want to worry me over the phone."

I stand up.

"Thanks a lot, Lydia. As soon as we have some information we'll let you know," I say, and look at Steve who is studying his notes.

"Oh, by the way," I ask, as I shake her hand, "do you know the name of your mom's doctor?"

"Sure. He's the one who diagnosed her diabetes. His name is Dr. Melvin Kraft. His office is in Springfield, I believe."

"Thanks. We'll try to get in touch with him," I say, and turn around.

I walk into the unit, pull out Mrs. Alberts's chart and start reviewing her most recent lab results, while Steve takes Lydia to see her mother. The numbers in the chart tell me that her fluid and electrolyte situation is well balanced, sort of, but that her liver damage is still very extensive. I go to examine Mrs. Alberts, just as Lydia and Steve are coming out. I don't see any real change in her condition. Her belly is still swollen and tight as a drum, and the coma is just as deep, perhaps slightly deeper. I walk out and from the corner of my eye I see Lydia talking to Steve and looking in my direction. I wouldn't bet any money on her mom making it.

THREE

Today the clinic is busy and tiring. I spend more than an hour on my first patient, an old man with many liver complications related to alcohol abuse. When I'm finally done with him, I see Joanne, the clinic secretary, approaching me. A Dr. Kraft is on the line, she says. She has told him that I was busy, but this Kraft insisted that it was urgent. I walk into the conference room and pick up the phone. On my way I notice the waiting room is covered wall to wall with patients.

"Dr. Holden," Dr. Kraft says, "I need to talk to you."

"I know, I wanted to discuss Mrs. Alberts with you."

"Not on the phone," he says. I look at my watch.

"Where are you?" I ask.

"I'm rounding on my patients now, but with any luck I should finish by lunch."

It's almost ten o'clock, and I figure I have to see at least ten more patients. There's no way I can see all of them in two hours. But I know I have to talk to this Kraft fellow.

"Are you familiar with Gusti's?" I ask.

"I know the place."

"Then let's meet there, say, at twelve?"

"I'll be there."

I move into high gear and dispense with most patients in a hurry. The last three patients I decide to leave for the fellows and residents. I rush down the elevator and out to the street. My white coat is flying as I dash into Gusti's.

Gusti's is a combination coffee shop and bar, just around the corner from Lincoln hospital. It's frequented by employees of the hospital, mostly nurses and doctors. I walk in and scan the crowded round tables in the middle and the bustling booths that line the windows. There are no table cloths and the napkins are paper, but the place is clean and the pasta is better than in most fancy downtown Italian restaurants. I don't know Dr. Kraft, and I don't see anybody responding to my inquiring gaze. After awhile, one of the tables becomes available and I sit down. A few moments later a short young man in his late thirties, with a pleasant open face and sticky brown hair, drops in a chair at my table.

"Hello. I'm Mel Kraft. Nice to meet you." He has a soft voice and a limp moist handshake, and avoids any direct eye contact. I expected somebody much older.

"I came straight here. How's she doing?" Mel continues.

"Same. No improvement."

Mel shakes his head nervously.

"Damn. I should have never let her join that clinical trial."

He sees my reaction of surprise.

"You don't know?" he asks.

A young waiter comes by our table and describes at great length their list of esoteric lunch specials. When his song and dance is over, we ignore the specials. I order angel-hair pasta with marinara sauce and Mel orders a tuna fish sandwich.

"What clinical trial?" I ask.

"Oh, they're trying this new drug for the treatment of diabetic neuropathy."

"What's the name of the drug?"

"Neurovan. It supposedly prevents the late complications, you know, the foot ulcers."

I have only a vague recollection of this new drug.

"Who are they?"

"Gother. I don't know all the details of the clinical trial. All I know is that the patient has to take one capsule of Neurovan every morning for one year. Then there is some sort of a nerve biopsy at the beginning and end of that one year. That's about it."

Bingo. The fourth pill.

"So you are one of the investigators in the trial?"

"No. No," Mel raises his voice. "I may be listed as co-investigator, I'm not even sure. My senior partner, Roy Tarrow, is the principal investigator. What I sometimes do is mention the trial to some of my patients. If they like the idea and decide to volunteer, they go to Roy and he enrolls them."

I take a sip from my water.

"So you think this trial caused the liver problem?" I ask.

Mel takes the napkin from under his utensils and wipes his brow.

"Don't you?"

I shrug.

"Neurovan has caused some liver disease in patients before. I don't know if anybody became this sick, though," Mel says. He blurts his words fast, as if he isn't sure whether he'll get enough time to finish his sentences.

"Well, we shouldn't completely ignore other possibilities. When was the last time you saw Mrs. Alberts?"

"Oh, maybe a month ago. I checked her sugar levels, adjusted the diet a little bit and that was it. A routine visit."

The food arrives. Nervously, Mel takes a huge bite from his sandwich. He's looking at his plate the whole time.

"Did you check her liver functions during her last routine visit?" I ask.

"No. There was no reason to. Roy does it as part of the clinical trial. If something were wrong, I would have been notified."

Mel continues to eat rapidly as if wild coyotes are eyeing his catch, shaking his head and muttering to himself.

"She is such a wonderful lady. Always polite. Always cheerful. Despite her diabetes. Despite losing her husband in a terrible car accident."

Mel takes a big sip of water and gulps it down, making a loud sound. He then picks up his knife and stares at it blankly while talking.

"And her three children. She is so proud of them. The oldest, Milo, is some sort of a psychologist or philosopher, teaches out in Los Angeles, I think. The second son, David, is a journalist and the little girl is a law student at Yale."

I'm impressed how well Mel knows his patients and their families. He seems to belong to the almost extinct breed of authentic and ideal family practitioners. To know the inner workings of one's patients is the first and most important step in the healing process.

"And did you know? Dorothy writes poetry. She once showed me one of her poems. I'm no artist, but, I tell you, very powerful and moving stuff."

"What does she do?" I wonder.

"I believe she has a degree in English literature, but because Hank, her husband, was a well-to-do banker, she has never really worked full time."

Mel finishes his sandwich, while I have barely finished spraying Parmesan cheese on my pasta.

"God, I hope she makes it," Mel sighs deeply, still fidgeting with the knife.

His concern sounds earnest and real, but the fact that he was the one to send her to that clinical trial must weigh heavily on his conscience.

My cellular phone rings inside my coat pocket. It's a nurse from the intensive care unit, and she tells me to get there stat. I get up and look wearily at my full plate. I give Mel the "we gotta go" nudge and I walk in long strides towards the exit with Mel marching closely behind. Gus, the owner, waves at me when I run by him and I give him the palms up, shoulder shrug "what can I do?" sign.

FOUR

WE'RE BOTH BREATHLESS BY THE TIME WE ARRIVE AT THE INTENSIVE CARE unit. As we approach the station, I immediately spot Steve Denker and Mrs. Alberts's daughter, Lydia. When Lydia sees Mel Kraft, she tears off and hugs him, teary eyed.

"She's getting worse, and they're seriously considering a liver transplant," Steve tells me.

Mel is still hugging Lydia, as he says, "I know they'll do everything humanly possible."

"I need to go in and talk to the surgeons," I say and Lydia nods.

I enter the central monitoring station. As is usual in such emergencies, several physicians are milling around. I see the kidney specialist, the neurologist and two liver transplant surgeons. The head of the intensive care unit, Dr. Carey, is reading Mrs. Alberts's chart. Donald Carey, wide-faced and sad-eyed, is one of the best in the business, with more than twenty years of experience. When he notices me, he comes over.

"Paul, I saw your orders in the chart. Everything was done just right. I had nothing to add. This whole thing developed remarkably quickly and aggressively. The liver just stopped functioning. Obviously, we don't know the cause, though it does look like a severe drug reaction. Ernie thinks that there still is some chance with a transplant."

One of the nurses approaches and hands us a purple printout of the lab report. Dr. Carey and I look at it together. All the tests for viral disease are negative. Also, there's no evidence that her body produced antibodies that could destroy the liver.

I shake my head. Dr. Ernest Callahan, the head of the transplant division joins us. He is young and energetic, his high wrinkled forehead contributing to the sincere countenance that he exudes.

"We put her on the list," he says, "we just need to find a donor. Paul, any clues on the cause?"

"It looks more and more like a drug-induced problem," I say.

Steve comes in and overhears my last comment.

"Probably doesn't matter at this stage. Other than a new healthy liver, nothing will reverse it now," Carey says and rubs both his eyes with the back of his hands.

And I add, "we still need to learn more about that investigative drug, Neurovan, because this may not be the last case."

Ernie joins me as we go into the patient's room to examine Mrs. Alberts again. She's breathing laboriously now, her lips are purple like violets and when we pinch her foot all she does is utter a short hoarse grunt and nothing else. She seems to have slipped into deepening coma, and I relate this to Ernie.

"We'll give it a shot." Ernie's talking about the new liver.

We leave the room and approach Lydia Alberts, who's pacing in the waiting room. Mel Kraft is hovering over us.

"It's not looking good, but we'll try our best," Ernie tells Lydia. "If we're lucky we'll get a donor real soon."

"If mom's lucky, you mean," Lydia says.

Ernie gives her a warm, encouraging look.

"The list. How big is it?" Lydia asks.

"Sorry?"

"I mean, what's mom's place on the list? How many people ahead of her?"

"There's only one other person with her blood type, size and so on who is waiting for a liver. This other man has been waiting for more than a week."

"Does it matter how sick a person is?" Lydia persists and Ernie takes another close look at her.

"In terms of the list? Of course it does. I'd say, your mom and that man are about equally sick at this time."

Ernie takes her hand, squeezes it in a friendly gesture, then turns around and leaves. I stay a moment longer.

"Ernie's the best," I say, "she's in good hands."

I clasp her arm and she puts her head on my shoulder, sobbing.

I wait until she collects herself, and then I take her to the nearest chair. She sits down, covering her face.

"I'm so afraid. I hate hospitals," she says.

I'm on a chair next to her.

"I know," I say. "My father had cancer surgery here last year. I hated coming to this place, even though I worked here."

Lydia wipes her eyes with her forefinger.

"At least when my father died he was never in the hospital. He died quickly."

"How did it happen?"

"Some drunken kid hit him. He was walking on the sidewalk, and the car swerved in his direction. He had just come out of a flower shop, where he bought irises for my mom."

I turn my head away, ever so slightly. But she's perceptive.

"I thought you guys must be used to all that life and death

stuff," she says softly. I get into this long explanation, I don't know why.

"When I deal with patients I am insulated by the huge wall that I have erected around me. But as a patient or relative, I'm just as vulnerable as the next person. It's a humbling experience for a physician to have a family member get sick."

"How is he doing now?"

"My father? He's okay, I suppose. But with cancer you never know, at least not initially. It may be hiding its ugly face somewhere."

We sit in silence for a few moments.

"I'm sorry but I have to go now," I say and stand up.

Lydia nods.

"I'll see you later," I say and leave.

It's getting late in the day. I still have to perform several gastrointestinal procedures that afternoon and patients are waiting.

On my way to the elevators Mel Kraft runs after me. Accompanying Mel is a dark young man whom Mel introduces as David Alberts, Lydia's brother. Of medium height, David has a strong chin, deep brown eyes and there's a gap between his two front teeth. His dark thick hair is curly and unkempt.

"David just got here, Dr. Holden. I hope you don't mind answering some questions for him," Mel says.

"Of course. Unfortunately, right now I have patients. . . "

"Sure, Dr. Holden. I'll give you a call some time next week, if you don't mind," David Alberts says. He gives me his business card, which has his name written on it, a Washington address and a description of his profession as journalist, freelance writer.

"Just one question, Dr. Holden, please," David clears his throat, "do you think that this investigational drug caused all that?"

This isn't the first question that I would have asked.

"It's possible. Unfortunately, we know so little about this drug that it would be inappropriate for me to speculate."

Mel and David turn around and depart.

I go upstairs to perform my first endoscopy of the day, the inserting of a tube into the patient's nose down to the stomach to check if there's an ulcer or cancer lurking in the darkness. I just hope to finish the clinic fast and go home to sleep.

* * * * *

It's almost seven o'clock when I arrive home, earlier than usual. I go straight to the kitchen, where Irene is feeding Danny, our eighteen months old son. Danny makes facial grimaces as he's spitting the food out, spraying it in all directions. Irene has endless patience and I admire her for it.

Even at the end of an arduous day with a toddler Irene seems fresh and bubbly. Indeed, the task of nurturing and caring for our son seems to have invigorated her. Irene has just turned thirty, and our three years of marriage were nothing but constant bliss. With one exception: we've tried to have a second child but so far, no cigar. I can't understand why because all the tests are just fine. We were told to be patient and we don't have much choice in this matter.

"You look tired, Paul," she says.

"That's because I am. But you look lovely," I say and kiss her on the neck, just underneath the ear. Irene is of a petite frame and has long wavy brown hair. She has an open, smiling face anchored around an almost classical Greek-type nose, slightly upturned at the tip, and bright soft eyes. Her pale complexion, long neck and gentle rhythmic motions remind me of an antelope.

"Your food is ready," she says, shoving a spoon in Danny's mouth, "just nuke it, it's cold."

I do as I'm told, and then I drop into a chair.

"You left in the middle of the night. What was all that about?" she asks.

I look at her, then I stick my fork in the mashed potatoes.

"I had one sick lady in the ER. Jaundice, liver failure, confusion. They are looking for a liver. Hope she gets one soon."

Irene wipes off some baby food that Danny has tossed at her face. She does it with little emotion, as if waving away an annoying mosquito.

I tell her briefly what has happened. I mention the sick lady and her family, her concerned physician, everything. I explain that the liver failure is maybe induced by a drug, but I'll be damned if I know which.

"Her disease progressed very quickly," she comments. Irene is a nurse, with experience in the intensive care unit. Over the past two years, she took time off to raise Danny. I need to keep her medical interest alive by giving her details on my more interesting patients.

"I know, and I'm troubled by it."

"Alcohol?" she asks.

"Probably not."

"Poor kids. Losing both parents in such a short time must be awful," she says.

"The mother is still alive," I remind her.

"From what you tell me, barely."

I'm chewing on a large piece of hamburger, so I just make a face like she's got a good point.

"Anyway, is this investigational drug any good?"

Still chewing, I shrug my shoulders.

"With all the protests of animal-rights groups, we're being forced to use human beings instead of guinea pigs," she continues.

Danny refuses to eat any more, and Irene puts a spoonful of his baby food in her own mouth.

"Hmm, yummy," she coos, barely resisting the urge to spit it out. Danny is watching her with great interest, but when offered another spoonful of food he turns his head away.

"He's probably too tired to eat," I say. Irene gets up and puts him in his crib, conveniently parked next to the kitchen table.

"So, do you think that we have?" she says as she sits down.

I'm just about ready to introduce a new piece of beef in my mouth.

"Have what?"

"Do you think that people have turned into guinea pigs?"

"No, of course not. All new drugs must be tested extensively in animals before they're shoved into a human body."

"Are you sure?" she asks.

"Reasonably so."

"You know, anyway, there are very few really new drugs out there. Most of the drugs tested are just new versions of old drugs. Very little new added value."

"Are you quoting something you read or did you just make it up?"

"I must have read it somewhere. Don't you agree with that?"

I'm too tired to argue with these sweeping generalizations.

"There are many new life-saving drugs and you know it."

She gives me an oblique look.

"Listen, just imagine you're getting one of your monster headaches, you're reaching for the cabinet and there's nothing you can take for it," I say.

"Okay, okay."

I lean back in my chair and wipe my mouth with a napkin.

"What if it's that investigational drug?" she asks. Once Irene sinks her teeth into something, she doesn't let go easily. I listen, because she has a good horse sense about these things.

"What do you mean?"

"What if this drug caused that liver failure? What are you going to do about it? Don't you need to warn the other patients who may still be taking it?"

The thought has crossed my mind, but I'm in no mood to figure out exactly what to do, if anything.

"I'll do something tomorrow," I promise. Irene looks at me, as if about to say something, but I guess my tired look stops her from pushing further.

I get out of the kitchen and crash on the couch in front of the television. Across the room I look at my computer, my ticket to many exciting trips on the information super-highway. I'm tempted to take another ride, but am too exhausted. Within minutes I'm sound asleep.

FIVE

THE ALARM CLOCK GOES OFF AT 6:00 A.M., AND THE LOUD SOUNDS OF Berlioz's Symphony Fantastique permeate the air. The transition from sleep to wakefulness isn't pleasant for me, a sense of discomfort and confusion. Something is bothering and weighing heavily on me, but I'm not alert enough to remember. I sit up, knuckle-rubbing my eyes for a long moment. Finally, I do remember. The patient. The liver. The drug.

I get up slowly and walk out to the living room. A few warm-up exercises, then the treadmill for 20 minutes. Then a long shave in the shower. Constantly thinking, analyzing, taking stock of my life.

I'm a relatively junior faculty member at the Lincoln Medical School, only five years out of training. At 37, I'm doing what I have always wanted to do. Since my first year in medical school, when I dissected cadavers in the large Anatomy halls of Johns Hopkins in Baltimore, I had always dreamt of this. I've become an expert in my field, gastroenterology, and I take care of patients in a stimulating intellectual environment. Sheer satisfaction. Sick patients getting better, colleagues respecting me, beginning to publish in top medical journals, giving lectures. The life of an academic physician. The future should be more of the same. Moving up the invisible professional ladder, which would one day culminate in a tenured position and, with some luck, chairmanship of a department. More knowledge. More respect. More money, though money is secondary. I suppose I'm still an idealist to the core.

Despite relentless self-reminders that Mrs. Alberts is just another sick patient in a busy hospital, I'm nevertheless troubled by her illness. Rules about disease progression have exceptions, and her course is clearly such an exception, faster deterioration than anything I can remember ever witnessing. Is there something about this new drug that is different? Is there something about Mrs. Alberts tissues and metabolism that is different? Irene's comments from the night before also start to sink in. Are there other patients out there in imminent danger of becoming gravely ill and possibly dying because of this new drug?

I'm toweling off when the phone rings. It's Steve Denker.

"Hi. I hope I didn't wake you up."

"Are you kidding? At this time?"

"I decided to call and give you a progress report. Mrs. Alberts is stable. Mental status perhaps better, she was more combative this morning but responded a little better to pain. Just as I went to call you, I heard that there may be a suitable donor in Harrisburg. I think Ernie is going there on a chopper to bring in the liver."

"I thought there was another person ahead of her?"

"Apparently Mrs. Alberts is now number one."

"Good," I say, though I realize it isn't that good for the other patient.

"Oh, by the way," Steve is choosing his words carefully, "Dr. Kraft stayed here until midnight and then he showed up this morning before six. What's wrong with this guy? Do you suppose he's scared of being sued by them or something?"

"Possibly. I think he may be operating under the assumption that when the family likes the doctor, it isn't likely to sue, even if he screwed up."

"But, actually, he hasn't done anything wrong, has he?" Steve wonders. "I mean recommending a clinical trial to a patient isn't negligent, is it?"

Still in my underwear, I'm now in the kitchen, pouring myself a glass of not-so freshly squeezed orange juice. I'm carrying around the portable phone.

"You're probably right, unless he's not telling the truth about when he saw her or spoke to her last time, what exactly did he recommend, and so on."

I want to eat breakfast and go to work, but Steve obviously needs to get some things off his chest. So I'm waiting.

"The way I see it," Steve says, "the drug company may be sued. The partner of Kraft, what's his name, Tarrow, who actually followed the patient for the study may also be sued. Especially if she dies."

It's late and I'm getting antsy.

"Listen, Steve, you should worry about saving the patient, not this lawsuit business. Chances are there won't be any."

I shove two slices of white bread in the toaster, and press down the lever.

"C'mon, Paul," Steve chuckles, "a university professor, a journalist and a law student watch their mother get sick, maybe getting a liver transplant, maybe dying, all that under cloudy circumstances, possibly due to some new untested drug, and there won't be tons of questions asked?"

Before I can answer, Steve yells, "Shit, I'm late for my morning report. Talk t'ya later," and hangs up.

Steve could be right. I know that everything is possible in this litigious environment. There are certainly too many frivolous lawsuits against physicians, but then there are also, unfortunately, many dishonest and incompetent physicians who don't care enough about what happens to their patients. Not much different than many other professions.

I reflect on these issues and on Steve's remarks while drinking my morning coffee. Am I being sucked into something that I'm not ready to handle yet? I wonder whether general public health issues, like the safety of our clinical trials, are really my personal responsibility? Nah. For now, I'm assuming that the Gother Company, together with the FDA, are doing their best to protect all patients.

I finish breakfast, put on my suit and walk to my car, briefcase in hand. It's already 7:30, and since my seminar for fourth year students is scheduled for 8:15, I have to hurry. In the driveway, I hear the phone ring inside the house. Irene is still sound asleep which means that she must have had another rough night with Danny. I hesitate for a moment and then decide to run inside. The phone stops ringing just as I grab the receiver. After a few seconds it rings again and I pick it up.

"Dr. Holden?" a familiar voice of a woman, but I can't place it.

"Speaking."

"Dr. Holden, this is Lydia Alberts."

"Oh, hello." I put down my briefcase.

"I just heard that there might be a liver for mom."

"Yes, I know. That's great news."

"So. . . does she have a prayer?"

"Without the transplant she will almost certainly deteriorate." Lydia hesitates.

"There's another thing. I . . . we . . . that is, my brothers and I think it's important to get to the bottom of all this. We want to know why this happened to mom. Could anything have been done to prevent it?"

I am silent for a while, remembering Steve's speculations on a lawsuit.

"Dr. Holden, are you still there?"

"I'm here. Your questions are legitimate, but how I can be of any assistance? I saw your mother for the first time only when she was already very sick."

"I know, but we need a physician. Somebody who knows about liver disease. Mel is okay, but he's no expert. He's also too nervous. I can't think of anybody better than you."

I can hear her swallow hard a couple of times.

"Please come with me to see Dr. Tarrow. I have an 8:30 appointment in his office at Merion hospital. If I go alone, he'll treat me like some demented child, and I won't accomplish anything."

It all sounds perfectly reasonable. In fact, I have planned to find out more from Tarrow about the drug.

"I'll be there, Lydia."

I call my office and tell Carol to cancel the seminar. Just then Irene walks by, in her nightgown, yawning and removing her long brown hair from her face. She has a petite body, with just the right amount of padding in the critical places.

"Why are you canceling? Where are you going?" she wants to know, from the kitchen.

"I am going to pay a visit to Dr. Roy Tarrow, you know, from that Alberts case."

"Really? How come?"

"Oh, I just thought I might learn something useful about that drug, something that might help Mrs. Alberts."

Irene passes near me, coffee cup in hand, and gives me an encouraging smile.

"Good, Paul, good!" she says, "and don't forget to ask if other patients are still at risk."

I kiss her, exit the house and get into my beige Ford. Approximately half an hour later, I turn right off Lancaster Avenue, and moments later park my car in the open parking lot for visitors at Merion hospital.

* * * * *

The sign on the brown door reads: "Dr. Roy Tarrow, Internal Medicine, Diabetes and Endocrinology."

There's a bell next to the door, but the door isn't locked so I just walk in. I find myself in the waiting room. It has about a dozen chairs, plush azure carpet and contemporary art work on the walls. A nice and agreeable place to wait for an unpleasant encounter with the doctor to discuss one's failings of the flesh. Lydia is already there, seated. When she sees me, she comes over and, to my surprise, gives me a long and tender hug and then plants a little kiss on my cheek. I look into her green eyes but they appear red now, an unmistakable sign of sadness and apprehension. Her state of mind fails to hide her good looks, though. Together with her green blouse, black slacks and small simple earrings, she somehow manages to look both vulnerable and sophisticated.

Before we can exchange a single word, the inner door opens and a stout, balding man wearing a white coat emerges. He has a gray patrician beard that almost entirely covers his thin lips. He walks briskly in large determined strides, his beer belly bouncing ahead of him as he moves. He goes straight to Lydia with great gusto and I worry that he might bump right into her. But he stops in time, extends his arms and grabs her hand with both of his. I notice a large purple ring on his right hand.

"Ms. Alberts. I am so sorry about what happened. What an unexpected shock."

Dr. Tarrow speaks in a brassy affected voice, with a tinge of southern drawl.

Lydia nods and thanks him in a faint voice. He then turns to me, and I find myself staring into ice-cold blue eyes.

"You must be Dr. Holden. Ms. Alberts mentioned last night that you would accompany her."

I shake his hand, while giving Lydia a look, like how dare she be so presumptuous. She stares at the floor, innocently.

"Please, come in. We can talk in my office."

We go inside. Soon we find ourselves in a suite consisting of several examining rooms and a large office right next to the entrance and the waiting room. We enter the office and I look around.

This is a typical office for a practicing physician. Large desk, a few chairs, computer, diplomas on the wall. Scanning the diplomas I find out that Dr. Roy Anthony Tarrow went to Penn State for his undergraduate studies, to Emory for medical school and University of Pennsylvania for residency and fellowship. He is board certified in Internal Medicine and Endocrinology.

Dr. Tarrow sits behind his desk. Lydia and I sit in chairs in front of the desk. I notice that Tarrow's chair is higher than ours. Tarrow obviously wants to enjoy his home court advantage.

He speaks first, looking at Lydia.

"I was so shocked to hear about your mother's illness. I considered her a fairly healthy person, though I knew her for a relatively short time. She was, as you know, Dr. Kraft's patient, and he thought she was perfect for the Neurovan study. Of course, she was diabetic, had the beginning of nerve damage from the diabetes, and she also had high blood pressure. But she never had any liver problems, or else I wouldn't have put her into the study."

"How do you know?" Lydia asks.

"That she had no liver problems? Well, we tested her liver functions through numerous blood tests before enrolling her in the study. Everything was perfect. The protocol is very clear about the need for these tests."

"How long has she been in the study?" Lydia again, and now she pulls out a notepad and pen. Tarrow is shifting in his chair.

"I have her chart right here." He picks up a folder from the corner of his desk. He puts his reading glasses on, while turning pages in the chart.

"Here. Her first blood tests were done on August 11. She received her first dose of medication on Aug. 31. She also had blood tests in September, October, once every month in fact. Her most recent test was January 27, and it was normal. What's today . . . February 18? She was due for her next test February 25. It's all here."

He puts the chart down and stares at us above his glasses.

"What other tests have been done every month?" Lydia wants to know.

"Whatever they put in the protocol. Blood count, kidney function, routine stuff. This is very common practice with an investigational new drug," he says.

Seems like a good time for me to chime in.

"As far as I know, you don't routinely perform liver tests quite so frequently, even with a relatively new drug. Was there any reason to suspect that this drug might cause problems?"

Tarrow turns to look at me.

"Look, I just follow the protocol. The protocol is written by the drug company docs and I make sure that we follow it to a tee. Obviously, there was some concern about the liver, or else they wouldn't have insisted on checking it that often."

"Some concern?"

"Well, yeah. A few patients had mild liver problems, but I

understand they all recovered. Look, maybe you should talk to the physicians in the company."

"Do you have any patients now in the study with abnormal liver functions?"

"Just one. She is fine, though. We stopped the drug when the enzymes reached a certain level, and they quickly returned to normal."

Lydia continues to take notes.

"I understand that the protocol calls for a nerve biopsy?" I ask.

"Two," Roy says, "of the sural nerve. One in the beginning and the other after one year of taking Neurovan."

Taking a piece of nerve from around the ankle, even though done under local anesthesia, is no picnic.

"What are the clinical endpoints?"

"I guess Gother has devised some sophisticated method to look at the individual nerve fibers under the microscope."

I was involved in clinical trials with new drugs several times before. As a fellow I used to examine the patients and enter the results of my examinations into a case report form. When recruiting patients into a new study, I also described the studies to patients and asked them to sign an informed consent form. In it, all the possible risks and benefits to the patient are described in detail.

"What does the consent form say about the liver?"

From Roy's deepening furrows on the forehead and reddening ears, I can tell that he is getting irritated. By now he must be wondering what exactly are we doing there and what right we have to ask him all these questions.

Dr. Tarrow controls himself. He picks up another document and reads it silently for a few moments.

"Here. It says that approximately five percent of patients can experience liver test abnormalities. All tests return to normal when the drug is stopped. There is no mention of jaundice or liver failure, certainly nothing about confusion or drowsiness."

He offers the document to me. I skim through its three pages quickly. A lot of little details. All tests and procedures are spelled out, number of visits, nerve biopsies, everything. Many findings from previous studies are listed. The liver and the five percent are there too. At the bottom, I notice three signatures. Mrs. Dorothy Alberts. Dr. Roy Tarrow. Dr. Gerald Lennox. The title of Dr. Lennox, director of clinical research at Gother Inc. is underneath his signature. Next to Gother's name I notice their address in Berkeley, California.

Lydia looks up from her note pad.

"For every bad drug effect, there's always the first time," she claims.

"Yeah, that's true. Every time somebody takes a new drug, there is the risk of the unknown. Unexpected things are always unexpected."

Dr. Tarrow stands up and walks over to Lydia. He's signaling that the meeting is just about over.

"And don't forget. If it makes the blind see and the lame walk . . . huh? That's something, huh?"

"Right now my mother can't see or walk," Lydia says dryly.

We're all standing up now.

"Do you know, Dr. Tarrow," she asks, "if my mother was on the Neurovan or on the dummy pill?"

"How could I?" he responds. "It's a double-blind study. I don't know which patient gets what, and the patient doesn't either. In fact, neither does the company. The code is broken only when the study is over."

"How about emergencies?" asks Lydia.

"Well, yeah . . . "

"Do you have the code, somewhere?"

"I suppose so, but opening it is out of the question."

"What the hell is that supposed to mean?" Lydia yells and moves closer to Tarrow, and for a moment I think she's going to smack him right on the nose. Tarrow retreats, looking dumbfounded.

"Listen here . . . uh . . . Ms. Alberts. I have never done this kind of thing before. I need to check with the company. . . I'll call them later . . . "

"Bullshit," Lydia shoots back, "Dr. Holden needs it for my mother's therapy, and if you . . . "

I put my hand on her arm. She's shaking.

"I think, Dr. Tarrow, that this situation requires some special handling. I am sure the company will agree with this decision," I say.

Tarrow seems to falter. "I think it's in a special envelope in our closet. I'll have to ask Rhonda about it."

After Tarrow leaves, we start pacing across the room.

"Stubborn little bugger," she says, and I can't help but smile at her feistiness.

"The Gother people must have scared him to death. They don't like to break the code because it can influence the results," I explain.

A few moments later Roy comes back, holding more than a dozen envelopes. He drops them on the desk and starts shuffling them around.

"Let me see. She was patient number 004, so where is the envelope . . . ah, number 004."

Roy separates that envelope from the others and puts it in front of him. He then calls Rhonda and has her return the other envelopes to their hidden place in the cabinet. Finally, he opens the envelope bearing the numbers 004. He has quick and abrupt puppet-like movements, and I find following them quite tiresome.

"Neurovan," Tarrow says.

He looks at me.

"There you have it. She was on Neurovan. What good does that do?"

"Well, for one, we won't be wondering about this anymore. And we'll limit the search for other causes. As for her treatment, there's little choice now. She'll get a liver as soon as a donor is found."

"Okay, everybody satisfied now?" he asks.

The buzzer on the phone rings. A high-pitched woman's voice is heard through the speaker phone.

"Dr. Tarrow, there is a Dr. Lennox on line two. I told him you were busy but he said it was urgent . . . "

Through the gray tinged beard, I notice that Tarrow's face and neck become crimson. Lydia and I exchange glances, like, talk about timing.

"I'll be right with him," Dr. Tarrow says tersely to Rhonda over the intercom. He then turns to us, his face full of professionalism.

"Ms. Alberts, I'm sorry about your mother. I know how concerned and upset you must be. Believe me. All doctors involved in drug development do their best to prevent such things from happening. I have already reported this serious event to the company. They will then report it to other investigators, to the FDA, all the other patients."

As he turns to me, Lydia says, "I want a copy of the protocol, the consent form, and my mother's chart."

Tarrow looks at her as if she just asked him to take off his clothes and make loud gorilla sounds.

"Ms. Alberts, that's impossible. These are confidential documents. But, tell you what. I can ask the Gother people."

Lydia suddenly straightens up, fire in her eyes.

"Dr. Tarrow, my mother is dying under some questionable circumstances. I can make one phone call and two lawyers would show up here with a formal request and then you would have no choice. I have the right to understand exactly what happened, and if I can't do it with your cooperation, I'll do it without it. Don't fuck with me, Dr. Tarrow."

Tarrow looks at the blinking light on the telephone. His high forehead is covered with beads of perspiration. Finally, he grabs the chart, the consent form and the protocol and hands them to Lydia.

"Rhonda will copy these for you. I have to go now."

We all shake hands and Lydia and I leave the office. As the office door closes behind us I can hear Tarrow say, "Oh, hi, Gerry. Sorry to keep you waiting."

While Rhonda is copying the documents, Lydia and I sit silently in the waiting room. We can hear the muffled sound of Tarrow's voice on the phone. Once in a while we can make out some words. Two elderly ladies and a gentleman are seated there in silence, reading newspapers. After several minutes the internal door opens and Rhonda shows up with the requested copies. Her high heels click as she walks, and the people in waiting raise their heads in unison, perhaps anticipating to be called in. As Rhonda is handing Lydia the papers, and with the door open, I can hear Tarrow yell at the top of his voice, "What the hell could I have done?"

Rhonda smiles apologetically, obviously used to her boss's temper tantrums.

We thank Rhonda profusely and leave. We don't speak until we're in the parking lot.

"Sorry about my outburst and my crude language," Lydia says.

"That's okay. It's understandable." I am still thinking about the call from this Dr. Lennox. He must have been very eager to talk to Tarrow, because it's only a little after six a.m. in California.

We keep walking until we reach my car. It's cold and thin fog is rapidly descending on the parking lot.

"By the way," I say suddenly, "you can call me Paul."

She smiles for the first time since I saw her yesterday.

"Paul, would you please review these for me and tell me what you think?"

"No problem. I assume you're going down to the hospital now?"

She nods.

"I'll see you there."

Through the thickening fog her body becomes a dark blur. Still, I can see her cat-like green eyes glistening.

"Paul, what do you really think about the transplant? Have you ever seen people who were as sick as mother recover?"

"Many times. The only unknown factor is this drug. All we can do at this time is hope for the best."

Lydia gets misty eyed. I stand awkwardly near her, papers in hand. She suddenly comes closer and plants a kiss on my cheek, the second one this morning, and a little longer, I think.

"Thanks Paul. I'll see you at the unit."

She turns around and runs off. I enter my car and turn on the engine, waiting for it to get warmer.

I leaf through the protocol. On the last page, I notice two phone numbers. One belongs to the medical monitor of study number 95-18, Dr. Gerald Lennox. The other to a clinical associate from Gother Inc. , a woman by the name of Dara Lyons. She is also listed as a monitor for the study.

Both numbers are in the 510-, San Francisco area code.

I move my car out of the parking lot and drive onto Lancaster Avenue towards City Line. Traffic is light. I hesitate for a moment, then pick up my cellular phone and dial Dr. Lennox's number. It rings a few times and then a click.

"Dr. Lennox speaking."

"This is Dr. Paul Holden, Gastroenterologist at Lincoln Hospital, Philadelphia."

Silence.

"I'm calling about a patient I admitted two days ago to our hospital with liver failure. Apparently she was participating in one of your clinical studies, with a drug called Neurovan."

Still waiting.

"Hello, Dr. Lennox?"

"Yes. I'm listening. We have been notified about the case through Dr. Tarrow, the investigator at the Philadelphia site. How can I help you?"

A cab suddenly pulls in front of me and I have to slam on the brakes.

"I was wondering if you could give me more information on Neurovan and its effects on the liver."

"Everything we know is in the investigator's brochure and consent form. Have you seen those?"

I wasn't supposed to see them, and I don't see any reason to cause more trouble for Tarrow. Yet.

"No."

"Seven percent of patients on Neurovan developed liver function abnormalities, that is, enzyme elevations on a blood test. All were mild. No symptoms. No jaundice. No hepatic coma."

Lennox sounds like he's reciting from some written, rehashed material, possibly handed to him by the Gother public relations office.

"So this is the first case where Neurovan caused serious liver disease?"

Long pause, and I get twangs of uneasiness in my stomach.

"To my knowledge. Also, keep in mind that half the patients in our trials are assigned to drug and half to placebo. We still don't know whether your patient was on Neurovan or not."

"Why not? Don't you think that's important information?"

"It may well be, but we feel that breaking the code can jeopardize the rest of the study. The FDA won't believe that the study was conducted in the correct double blind fashion, if we break the code too many times."

I feel that the man is trying to appear accommodating without cooperating, a form of passive-aggressive obstructive assistance. I think maybe it's time to stir the pot a little.

"I see. Well, I happen to know our patient's assignment."

"You do? How?"

"Dr. Tarrow told me."

"He doesn't know the code. He is also blinded to the treatment."

"Well, he does now."

I can hear Lennox smacking his lips.

"You mean he broke the code?"

I'm now on the expressway and traffic is flowing quickly. I can still hear Lennox surprisingly well. I notice that Lennox doesn't want to know whether the patient was in fact assigned to take Neurovan.

"Of course. We need to know if dialysis or other therapy might be indicated."

He's still not asking me about the code, but I need to move on.

"Did you say that all cases of liver problems you had reversed to normal?"

"Yes."

"And how long did it take before functions returned to normal?"

"No more than a few weeks."

"What's a few? Two, three, ten?" I press.

"Oh, I'd say the longest recovery lasted six weeks."

"Did you have any case as serious as this one?"

"No. This is the worst."

The hesitation in Lennox's voice is growing, and it occurs to me that maybe his superiors restrict the number of out of school tales he can deliver, if any.

"What kind of pathological changes do you see in the liver with Neurovan?" I still don't give up.

"I probably shouldn't try to describe it in any detail because, frankly, I'm not an expert. I understand there was cell necrosis in the center of the lobule, without effects on bile ducts."

This is common to drug-induced liver disease, but could be other things.

"So you do have human data? I thought this was your first case."

"First case of hepatic failure. As I said, we did have some cases of mild damage, and the investigators decided to perform liver biopsies."

Now I start wondering whether Dr. Lennox is not only instructed to conceal information but also to confuse and mislead. I decide to leave alone the issue of patients with serious problems. For now.

"What about the FDA? Don't you have to notify them on something like this?"

Despite the distance and the noise of the rumbling engine, I can hear Lennox take a deep breath.

"Frankly, Dr. Holden, I don't think this is a particular concern of yours. This is a company decision. For your information, we always follow all the rules and guidelines set by the FDA."

It's time for me to change the topic once again. I have nothing to gain by annoying Lennox at this early stage of the game.

"Okay, I understand. By the way, how are the studies coming along? Does Neurovan work in diabetic complications?"

"We think so, but we don't have all the results yet."

I'm approaching the downtown area and Lennox is fading rapidly.

"Dr. Lennox. You've been very helpful. I'm sure we'll be talking to each other in the future."

"Thanks for the interest, Dr. Holden."

I hang up just as I enter the Lincoln Hospital parking lot. As I walk from the car to the hospital, I'm deeply concerned about one fact. According to his own admission, Dr. Lennox is not a liver expert. Why doesn't he bother, not even once, to ask me about my opinion on the cause of the liver problem? After all, I am a liver expert. Doesn't Lennox want to know how safe or unsafe his drug really is, or does he already know?

SIX

THE DAY GOES BY SO FAST THAT I HAVE VIRTUALLY NO TIME TO THINK about Gother, and the unfortunate crossing of paths between Neurovan and Mrs. Alberts.

By the time I get home it's past eight o'clock. Danny is just finishing his dinner, and when he sees me he goes, "dada, dada." I lift him up in the air and he smiles and giggles, but at the same time shows clear signs of concern about the danger of a sudden pull by gravity. I bring him down and we sit on the couch and I start reading to him a book about the zoo. I point to the pictures of various animals and make the appropriate sounds. Irene is sitting nearby and reading the newspaper, cracking up at the sounds I make.

In between my barking and howling I tell her about the visit to Tarrow, Lydia's plead for help and the conversation with Lennox. She agrees that something just doesn't seem right. Lennox is too defensive, but is it him or is he following strict instructions? And then there are still the bigger issues. Are patients being told the truth about potential risks of an investigational drug? Has Gother done everything possible to prevent Mrs.

Alberts's severe liver disease? Have they learned from Mrs. Alberts's case, so that this serious event would not be repeated time and again?

I let Irene handle Danny, while I pull out the consent form and Mrs. Alberts's chart from my briefcase. I sit in front of the computer, start my favorite software organizer, and then open a new file which I call Neurovan. The Pentium II 350 mHz chip performs all this in a blink of an eye. This is where I am going to enter my findings and thoughts about the case.

The consent form mentions the five percent incidence of liver abnormalities, and some other minor complaints such as headache, nausea and so on. Nothing serious or alarming is mentioned. Every case of liver disease seems to be reversible. It takes me less than ten minutes to realize that a patient signing up for the trial hasn't the faintest idea that one day she might end up in the hospital, yellow, comatose, tubes stuck in every orifice, waiting for liver transplantation as a last measure to possibly save her withering life.

It takes me longer to examine the chart of Mrs. Alberts. It has information on all the visits, examinations, complaints, her medications. Blood tests of liver functions were performed every month, just as Dr. Tarrow has described. Something attracts my attention. The latest blood test in the chart is from December 21. I recall Tarrow claiming that the last test he had performed was on January 27, and that the results were normal. I look everywhere but can't find the results of this test in the chart. I make a note to check the test from January 27 and close the chart.

Irene is carrying the sleeping Danny to his bed when the phone rings. I'm next to it so I pick it up after one short ring.

"Hello, Dr. Holden, please," a woman says in a low voice. She has either a severe case of laryngitis or she is whispering.

"Speaking."

"Dr. Holden, I haven't got much time. My name is Dara Lyons and I work for Gother. I wonder if we could get together tomorrow . . . "

I remember her name from the Neurovan protocol as one of the monitors.

"I am sorry, but I don't think . . . "

"I work on Neurovan, you know, and we understand that you have a patient . . . "

"Of course, yes."

"Well, I'd like to meet you tomorrow. I'll be in Philadelphia."

"Meet me? Why?"

I hear some loud booming noises. She could be calling from an airport.

"About the patient in Tarrow's site. Gerry, that's Dr. Lennox and I are leaving now on the red-eye to the east coast. We're meeting with Tarrow at ten. If you could come to the Four Seasons at seven, that'll give me enough time to shower and change."

I'm not sure yet if she wants to kick my ass or kiss it.

"I spoke with Dr. Lennox today . . . "

She interrupts me, speaking very quickly, swallowing her words.

"I know. Listen, it's essential that we meet. Human life may depend on it. Please, just tell me how to recognize you . . . "

It all sounds so strange, but she seems earnest enough.

"I'm six one, long hair, boyishly handsome . . . "

"Dr. Holden, that's very funny but I'm really in a rush . . . "

"Well, except for the handsome part it's sort of true . . . "

"Okay, never mind. The lobby at seven. I've got to go."

A click. I'm still holding the receiver when Irene walks in. I tell her about the bizarre call. She hugs and kisses me for a long time. She looks nice with her brown wavy hair flying in front of her eyes.

"You'd better drop the whole thing. It's a waste of time."

I look at her stunned, then I realize that she's just teasing me and then we both laugh.

"You have been talking to too many young women for your own good, Paul," she sighs.

"You're right. I don't want to get involved in this horrid case. Let someone else worry about the poor slobs entering into clinical trials with Neurovan. I refuse to discuss the case any longer or meet with anybody remotely connected to it, and that's final."

Irene puts her arms around me and kisses me. Again.

"Oh, shut up. You're too much of an idealist for that to be true."

She's leaning on me and then she pulls me slowly by the hands until we reach the bedroom. She hits our bed first and I land on top of her. She pretends for a moment that I'm too heavy for her, but then she stops talking and becomes totally focused on the task at hand. She makes love the same way she does everything else: thoroughly, competently, slowly, passionately, savoring every second and every angle. Afterwards, we fall asleep in each other's arms.

SEVEN

Friday AM, February 19, Philadelphia

THE LOBBY OF THE FOUR SEASONS HOTEL IN DOWNTOWN PHILADELPHIA is a busy place at seven o'clock in the morning. The first things that I notice as I enter the hotel through the main double doors are the picturesque Chinese vases replete with a resplendent assortment of multicolored flowers. Behind them is a garden-like patio which includes a few charming mini-palms. The lobby is long and relatively narrow, with the usual array of sofas and couches found in every elegant city hotel. To the right is a posh restaurant that serves a breakfast of coffee, juice, and muffins for some twenty dollars. Businessmen in dark suits, briefcases in hand, hustle to find a table in that restaurant, eager to spend their company's money on this lavish perk.

I look around, trying to figure out who this Dara Lyons might be, but there's nobody there who even remotely resembles my imaginary picture of her. In fact, other than the young, long-legged, model-like brunette sitting in the corner, reading Time magazine, there are no women there. After a few moments the place gets busier, and more women mill around in the lobby. I think that some could have been Daras, but apparently aren't because they ignore me. I sit down and wait. Ten, twenty minutes. I start to wonder how an intelligent man like me can be so gullible and impulsive. Finally, at seven thirty, I get up, walk out through the double doors and head towards the parking lot. Close to the lot, I suddenly hear a woman's voice behind me.

"Dr. Holden, please continue walking straight. When you get to the Franklin Plaza, please get into the coffee shop and get yourself a table. I'll join you there."

The voice seems hurried, but pleasant enough, and I continue my casual stroll. In the Franklin Plaza I find the coffee shop and get a booth in a quiet corner. A moment later, the brunette from the lobby of the Four-Seasons, long-legs and all, slips into the booth on the other side of my table.

"I'm sorry, Dr. Holden. I needed to watch you for some time before deciding to trust you."

I look at her closely. She's twenty-five, maybe twenty-six years old. Pretty, tanned face. Soft skin. Hazel eyes. Full mouth. High cheek bones. Her brown hair is long and frizzy, and she keeps tossing her head to remove the locks from her face. Other than some dark bags underneath her eyes, courtesy no doubt of the red-eye special, she could easily be a cover girl for Glamour or Elle magazine. She appears fidgety and tense, as she folds her legs underneath our table and kicks me in the shin in the process.

"So you think you can trust me?"

"Yes."

Maybe it wasn't such a bad idea to come downtown after all.

"How can you tell?" I ask.

She tries to smile, but all she can muster is a forced grin.

"I have my ways," she says. "By the way, you were telling the truth about your looks on the phone."

"No, I wasn't." She looks at me quizzingly.

"I'm actually six foot three."

She laughs, but her laugh is strained. We both order coffee, juice and danish, the continental breakfast business special.

Dara keeps throwing nervous glances around her, searching for something in the faces of other customers. After apparently being satisfied, she rests her arms on the table and brings her face within inches of mine, speaking in a very soft voice.

"Dr. Holden, I have less than thirty minutes to talk to you. I'm supposed to meet my boss, Dr. Lennox, for breakfast. We have been notified by Dr. Tarrow about this very sick lady. He gave us your name as the attending liver specialist, and I felt I had to talk to you. I needed to talk to somebody."

"What is it exactly that you want to tell me?"

She takes a deep sigh.

"I don't know where to start. This drug, Neurovan, has a lot of problems. For one, it probably doesn't work. We have looked at our interim data, you know, in the middle of the big study. Nothing. Then some consultant convinced our management that nerve biopsy is the way to prove that it works. So now we have been chopping nerves out of patients' legs. But . . . "

She brings her mouth closer to my ear, so close that I'm tickled by the hot air she's blowing.

"But . . . no one knows how the hell to measure what's happening in the nerve. You know what I mean? No one can tell if the drug works because the measurements are so inaccurate, you know. One so-called expert thinks he sees something, the other sees something else. They're not even sure what name to give to the things they think they see."

She stops as the waiter brings our meal. I slowly pour some cream into my coffee.

"I don't get it. Why is your company doing this? Why would they perform painful and expensive procedures like nerve biopsy if they can't measure drug benefit?" I ask and take a sip of cold orange juice.

"Because when we started, the consultants promised it could be done. A Dr. Roger Lacoste, from St. Louis, who knows some people at the FDA, practically guaranteed it to our president. But, you know, Lacoste isn't even a pathologist. On the other hand, some company experts told our top brass that it simply wasn't going to work. All our management sees, breathes, and smells are green dollar signs. Profits is all they think and care about and aren't willing to listen to any opposing views. It's the bottom line, stupid."

She grabs an apricot danish and tears off half of it. She offers me the other half and I take it, pondering.

"Do you get it? You tell our management that Neurovan is the best thing since electricity and sliced bread and they love you. If you tell them it sucks, you're toast."

"What did you tell them?" I ask.

"Who cares about me? I'm just a clinical associate, the lowest level on the totem pole. Maybe Lennox tried to protest in the beginning, you know, but at the end he just does what he's told. He likes to keep things close to the vest, and sometimes he can be so scary."

She's talking fast, as if in a race to say the most words in a limited amount of time. I look into her eyes, trying to read her thoughts through her incessant rambling. Despite her sincere demeanor, I find her story too incredible. It simply makes no sense for the company to proceed with a project that is doomed to fail, throw all that money down the drain. It's madness all right, but whose?

From her body language I can tell that she isn't through. And I can't figure out why she is telling me all this.

By now Dara is getting all worked up as she speaks,

breathing rapidly and moving back and forth in her bench. Somehow, she manages to keep her voice low.

"You must wonder why I tell all this to a liver expert. Well, liver is our biggest problem. There's a rumor about a case of liver disease and jaundice in Belgium, no. . . maybe Austria. I don't know if it's true, because I'm not involved in European trials. Anyway, they keep very close tabs on this type of information. But I did hear that they don't think that Neurovan did it. They blamed something else, I don't know what. So the consent form stays the same. You know what that means, don't you?"

Before I have a chance to respond, she races on.

"People who take this drug don't know what's going to happen to them, that's what it means. They can't possibly understand the risks they face."

I put my fist under my chin, listening. These are serious charges. She goes on, barely catching her breath.

"We had a consultant tell us it was just a matter of time before somebody died from Neurovan-induced liver disease. Guess what? We thanked him, paid his honorarium, and never invited him again."

"Who was it?"

"Axelrod."

"Ira?"

She nods. Ira is one of the best in the business, the grandfather of liver experts. But he has a confrontational style, an unwavering belief in the truth of everything he says, so some people are turned off.

"Are you sure that there were no other reasons for not inviting him back?"

"Like what?"

I shrug, and she makes a face like get real, I'm giving you

everything you need to know. I say nothing and bury my face in the coffee mug.

"You have no idea about the pressures. We have committees discussing liver safety, but no one dares open his or her mouth. Everybody is a yes-man, no dissenters allowed. No individual thinking. And another thing . . . "

In mid-sentence she suddenly stops, and I turn to look at her. Her facial expression startles me. She's pale as a sheet, her mouth dropping. Her gaze is fixated on something inside the restaurant and I look in that direction. A man wearing a dark suit approaches our table. Dara rises to her feet, but not without leaning on the table as she does.

"Dr. Holden, please meet Dr. Gerald Lennox," she says.

EIGHT

Quickly on my feet, I am also brandishing a big smile.

"Dr. Lennox, thanks for joining us. A pleasure to meet you."

Dr. Lennox shakes my hand while staring at Dara. I point to the empty seat next to her.

"Would you join us for breakfast? We just started ourselves."

Lennox hesitates for a moment. I take another look at Dara, whose face is still desperately searching for some blood flow. Finally, he sits down. Dara and I do the same.

"The line in the coffee shop at the Four Seasons was so long, you'd think they're giving out free breakfast. I left a message with the concierge, but he told me you walked out in this direction."

Lennox looks at Dara. The color on her face is slowly coming back, but her finger tips are still trembling.

"For some reason, men remember pretty women," Lennox continues with a dry smile.

"Dr. Lennox," I say, "we just got here ourselves. Ms. Lyons has very kindly just started filling me in on your company's products. Very impressive. But my real interest is drugs and their effect on the liver. Ms. Lyons suggested that I ask you about the technical details associated with Neurovan."

Dr. Lennox orders the breakfast buffet. While he talks to the waiter I examine him closely. He is in his late 40s, slightly overweight though quite muscular, graying temples, silver rimmed glasses, round face with a healthy ruddy complexion. He seems reserved and on guard, but there's nothing frightening in his expression. I know looks can be misleading. Lennox turns to me.

"Dr. Holden, we came here earlier this morning to find out more about the patient and the circumstances of her hospitalization. I can assure you that we'll do everything we can to prevent similar things from happening in the future. We know Neurovan can cause mild changes in liver function, but this case is so extreme and unusual that we seriously question if it's related to Neurovan."

He has a staccato speech, the mannerism of a well rehearsed speaker.

"I see. Then you must have another explanation for it."

"I do. There are many reports on the combination of Glucotrol and Dyazide causing severe liver disease. If she took Tylenol and a glass of wine in addition to these two, the danger of liver disease increases dramatically. And, you know, Dr. Holden, close to a thousand patients received Neurovan to date, and the safety record is excellent."

Lennox speaks slowly and confidently, as if it's impossible to doubt any of the facts. I listen intently, but at the end I'm not sure what Lennox really believes. I know that these lines were delivered many times before. Maybe he's trying to steer Dara to the right direction. When Lennox finishes, and without waiting for me to comment, he excuses himself and saunters towards the large buffet area.

Dara puts her hand on my arm as soon as he disappears from our view. She has long tender fingers, and the nails are red.

"Thanks, Dr. Holden. That was very sweet of you. Unfortunately, it won't help. I am sure they'll fire me when I get back."

"You can't be serious."

"Oh, yes. Lennox, and especially Barnes, his boss, will question me to death about why I met you, how I met you, what we talked about. You don't know our chairman, Richard Walnut III. Neurovan is the jewel in the crown, his gold mine. He'd stop at nothing to get Neurovan approved for marketing."

I'm listening to her warily, and serious doubts begin creeping into my mind. About Dara, about her story. On balance, most of what she told me makes very little sense. I have heard of greed and ambition, but to spend millions on an unsafe drug that doesn't work is beyond belief. In fact, I mull the situation over and conclude that I don't believe her. I'm a little bothered, though, because I can't figure out why she'd make up such a story.

Lennox returns with a plate covered with an omelet, bacon and hashbrowns. As he sits down, he looks at me first, then at Dara, searching for something, but we just smile. I'm getting the itch to leave. I don't want to get mixed up in the internal political struggles at Gother, nor am I going to learn anything new about Neurovan.

"I'm sure that Dr. Tarrow will fill you in on all the details of Mrs. Alberts's disease. If you need more up to date information, don't hesitate to call on me," I tell Lennox.

I motion to the waiter, giving him the "check please" sign. Dr. Lennox stops my arm in mid air.

"Dr. Holden, allow me to take care of that."

I shrug my shoulders, like suit yourself.

"Thank you."

We stand up and I give him my parting comment.

"Good luck with Neurovan. I hope you succeed in finding the cure for diabetic complications, but, please, no more Mrs. Alberts."

No need to antagonize the guy. We shake hands. Dara remains seated, pensive and detached.

"Dr. Holden, do you think that Mrs. Alberts will recover?" Lennox asks suddenly.

He is very formal in his manners, a stiff stick in the mud.

"It's possible, though I'm afraid the odds are against her."

"I see," Lennox says. I think for a second that maybe there's a slight sadness in Lennox's voice, some grain of compassion, but Lennox switches immediately to his more circumspect, business-like demeanor.

"Thank you, Dr. Holden. We'll keep you informed, and if you don't mind we may contact you again should the need arise."

I nod, turn to Dara and shake her hand. Her pretty eyes are sorrowful. She squeezes my hand, perhaps for an extra second, and just says, "thanks for coming, Dr. Holden."

I leave them and walk to the parking lot, getting strong images of Lennox chewing Dara out. It's drizzling and I am walking very fast. I get to my car wet, confused and exhausted, and sink in the seat. Then I realize that it's only eight o'clock in the morning.

* * * * *

I sit in the car for some time, trying to make sense out of the situation, trying to sort out the events, to separate fact from guesswork and speculation.

Some facts are clear. A relatively young woman develops serious liver disease. Before she was hospitalized she had taken three drugs that could have caused the liver disease. The liver changes may not be typical for two of the drugs, Glucotrol and Dyazide, but I'm not sure about the combination. Also, Neurovan is known to have caused mild liver function changes in five to seven percent of diabetic patients studied. In other words, some fifty to seventy patients out of one thousand will have some degree of liver damage.

I lean back in my seat and close my eyes. If Dara's story is true, then something is wrong with that Gother Company. But . . . what if she's wrong . . . what if she's lying, for whatever reason . . . what if she misrepresented the facts, exaggerated or took information out of context . . . she seems earnest enough, speaks with great passion and eloquence . . . the way she got scared when that Lennox fellow showed up . . . who knows?

It's all too strange and confusing. I need some evidence before plunging into what could be a messy quagmire. Patience! Let's see how events play out and if Dara's story is somehow corroborated, then, and only then, I'll dive in.

Having reached a sensible decision, a reasonable plan, I feel better about the whole thing. I feel resolute. The cobwebs seem to have cleared.

I arrive at the hospital feeling relieved and refreshed. I stop at the intensive care unit, where I run into Dr. Carey. He's in an animated conversation with one of the young surgeons on call. As I approach them, I hear the words of the surgeon:

"There are three rules to follow in life: eat when you're hungry, sleep when you're tired and never screw with the pancreas."

I laugh, and so does Carey. Carey and I walk away and carefully review Mrs. Alberts's chart. Her condition is slightly improved. There are short periods when she is more awake. I know that temporary improvements occur frequently, but may mean little in the overall prognosis. The situation is still grave, but all hope is not lost.

From the unit I go upstairs to my office. It's time to dictate letters to the physicians who sent patients to me for testing. I try to immerse myself in the task, but Dara's pale face when Lennox shows up fails to leave my mind.

NINE

THE FIRST TEST OF MY WAIT-AND-SEE POLICY COMES ABOUT LATE IN THE afternoon. I have just reported the results of an endoscopy to an old patient of mine, Alex Taylor, a lawyer with stomach pains. I saw a small shallow ulcer and prescribed the usual medical treatment. At the end of the session Alex asks my opinion on a dilemma he's facing. He's a diabetic and occasionally feels tingling in his feet. The physician who takes care of his diabetes recommended a new drug, which can only be obtained by participating in a clinical trial. The name of the drug is, and Alex pulls out a small piece of a neatly folded paper from his pocket, . . . uh . . . uh . . . Neurovan. What do I think?

My mind races. Here I am, forced to take another bite from the apple I thought I'd tossed away because it was rotten. I look in Taylor's chart to check the identity of his diabetes specialist. There it is, in the top right corner of the letter: Roy Tarrow MD. After a long pause, I tell Alex that I'm not sufficiently familiar with the drug, but this being a new drug he'd better read carefully all the information given to him, especially the consent form. A small white lie that just might do the trick until I know more.

Just as I'm about to leave work Lydia Alberts calls from New Haven. She had to go back to school for one day to take a final exam. I wonder how she could prepare herself for a test with her mother so gravely ill. Lydia is in a surprisingly good mood, and hearing some noises in the background I ask her where she's calling from.

"I'm here with some friends at the bar. It's happy-hour," she chirps and laughs. "I just finished taking my exam and we're here celebrating."

She then wants to know what's new.

I tell her about Dara and Lennox and our little meeting. I paint in broad brush strokes, avoiding most of the detail. I tell her the company seems reasonable, it's trying to prove that the drug works, and there's a difference of opinions on the possible side effects. I don't mention all of Dara's concerns or the other questionable case in Europe. Finally, I tell her about my decision to concentrate on my work at the hospital. Of course, I'll continue to take care of her mother, but that's the limit of my involvement with Neurovan.

Despite the merry noises surrounding her she turns somber.

"I understand. But I have a problem, and it has to do with my brother David. He's a writer, you know, free lancing. He wants to write a bunch of articles about the whole thing, mostly about clinical trials, about what patients know when they enroll, how the safety of the patients is protected, and so on. What do you think?"

"Sounds interesting."

"He is very close to mom. He's her boy. He's having a hard time coping with her disease. We all suffer, but he's devastated. In the unit he was calm because he was in shock. Afterwards he just fell apart."

She's in a very talkative mood.

"David just doesn't know when to quit. He'll write and probe and investigate and question. He really hopes that you can guide him. Review the stuff he writes, you know, especially all the medical terms. He also wants to talk to the company, and that's another thing you can help him with."

Now she's talking slowly, as if in a trance. I am not sure any more whether the neurons in her brain are still wired in the proper direction.

"You know, Paul, what else I think? I think he'll file a lawsuit. He'll sue everybody because he's getting angrier by the day. I know he likes you and counts on your helping him. But if you can't help him he might sue you too."

I sit down, incredulous. The sounds of inebriated laughter over the phone are surreal.

"Sue me? For what?"

"Oh, I'm not saying he will. He's just pissed off at the entire medical establishment because of the treatment mother has received. From Mel, Tarrow, you know, the hospital, the unit, everybody."

"We're doing everything possible to save her. She may recover," I say softly.

"What can I say, David is a melancholic, a depressive sort of fellow. He is getting ready to face the worst."

"I see. Lydia, where do you stand in all this?" I ask. She giggles, and I hope that she's just had her last drink for the day.

"Moi? I'm not involved in his work, but I share his desire to get to the bottom of this. You know I like you and I'll do everything I can to leave you out of it altogether."

Another pause, a giggle, a noise that sounds like a burp. She then continues.

"So when he calls, you'll be ready. Just listen to him. What have you got to lose?"

My decision from earlier this morning seems more distant and irrelevant by the moment.

"Well, Lydia, thanks for the information and advice. I appreciate it."

"You're welcome. Good bye, uh, Paul Holden."

She utters these last few words in a singing voice. She's drunk now, but I have no doubts that the story about David is accurate.

Before leaving the hospital I go to check on Mrs. Alberts. I am not on call for this weekend and one of the other docs in the department will be responsible for her. To my delight, Mrs. Alberts is doing somewhat better. She responds with mumbles when I talk to her, and occasionally opens her eyes. Her blood tests are unchanged, though, and I know that a long uphill struggle is still ahead.

Once out of the unit, I start to relax and think about the upcoming weekend. I need to get away in a big way. I call Irene and tell her to get ready because we're about to go skiing in the Poconos. She understands and agrees, no questions or arguments. On the way to the mountains we drop Danny at Irene's sister, Ellen. Ellen watches us with stupefaction, because we are usually not the spontaneous types. In the car, Irene and I listen to music and sing silly songs at the top of our voices. It's close to midnight when we arrive at our hotel, tired but in high spirits. Never once do I think about last week's events and I fall asleep within seconds of hitting the pillow.

That night, however, I can't escape from reality altogether. I have an eerie dream. It's pitch dark, and I am sitting on a grave in the middle of a huge, sprawling graveyard. Strange people walk by and lay wreaths on the grave. Once in a while, one of the people stops to stare and point at me. I'm especially distressed because two women who point at me look remarkably like Lydia and Dara. Lydia comes so close with her pointing finger that she pokes me in the shoulder, and then she whispers, "spineless," and from the other side Dara breathes into my other ear, "coward."

They are wearing white transparent gowns and they start a dance macabre on the grave, slowly swaying as the wind is blowing and raising the gown above their thighs. I want to look at them, but I can't, because my head is turned in such an angle that only the name on the gravestone is visible. In the beginning it's too blurred but soon I can make out the letters. It simply reads: "Justice."

That dream shakes me up but I'm determined to enjoy myself this weekend. The weather is perfect, and Irene and I ski almost incessantly. We eat well, appetite stimulated by the fresh air, engage in plenty of horse-play on the snow and in the evenings we read to exhaustion. All in all we enjoy a spirited and jaunty vacation.

We miss Danny, but Ellen informs us that he's doing well and that he doesn't miss us. I return home invigorated and ready to tackle anything and anybody.

*   *   *   *   *

Back at work, the morning doesn't start very well. Mrs. Alberts had a setback. Her road to recovery was rudely interrupted. She had a bleeding episode which led to worsening of her mental status. The search for a liver donor proceeds in high gear. On top of this, there were many admissions over the weekend, including some very sick folks. I make rounds with the house staff, spending many hours examining the patients, and reviewing their histories and treatment programs.

I eat lunch on the run, a turkey sandwich I pick up at the cafeteria and carry to my office. I am in my office, ready to sink my teeth into the sandwich when the phone rings. Carol is downstairs at lunch, so I pick up the phone myself.

Dara is calling from a pay phone. She is in tears and too upset to talk. Finally, she tells me that about an hour earlier she was fired.

TEN

I MANAGE TO CALM HER DOWN SO THAT SHE CAN TELL ME WHAT HAS happened. On her return from Philadelphia, all of a sudden she wasn't needed for the Neurovan project. She might be needed for another program, an anti-depressant drug, currently in early clinical development.

"Who talked to you?" I ask.

"Lawrence Barnes, vice-president of clinical research. He's Lennox's boss."

"What exactly did he say?"

"Something to the effect that my handling of the Neurovan project wasn't up to speed . . . the project is moving sideways . . . they want people on the project with deep commitment, believers, not dissenters . . . I'm too junior for this project . . . they are transferring me to work on some third-generation anti-depressant . . ."

Her speech is halting and her distress palpable. In Philadelphia she blurted out her words like a machine-gun.

"So they haven't fired you?"

"Well, no, not yet. But the transfer is a first step. Next step I'm out the door with a boot mark on my ass."

I don't know if she's cloaking something, or just suffering from the sky-is-falling syndrome.

"So Lennox told Barnes about our meeting?"

"What else? I don't think that Lennox wants to kick me out, but maybe he has no choice. Also, uh . . . Barnes and I have, how shall I say, a somewhat complicated relationship. Perhaps he's trying to punish me for more than one digression. Who knows?"

"How come it wasn't Lennox who delivered the news to you? I thought you reported to him."

"He is conveniently out of town today. I guess Barnes couldn't wait for Lennox to get back tomorrow."

"Maybe Lennox didn't have the guts to do this to you?"

"Maybe."

I am chewing over all this, but am still somewhat puzzled by something.

"Listen, Dara. If Barnes wants you out, he can fire you right away. Why transfer you first and then fire you?"

"I don't know. Maybe they're afraid of me. That I'll be angry and blow the whistle on them to the FDA. With time, my information will become obsolete and the threat will disappear."

I can hear her put more coins in the pay phone, while constantly talking.

"I don't know, maybe they're hoping that I'll quit on my own. They'll probably cut my salary, I don't know yet. Listen, Paul, they'll punish me, I'm telling you. This is an unforgiving organization."

The forces dragging me into the Neurovan affair are gaining strength. Maybe it's time for me to grab the bull by the horns, instead of evading him. For all I know, this Barnes fellow may have done all that to Dara for good reasons, and maybe this is related to some "complicated relationship" with Barnes, but too much of what she told me, and what I saw and heard on my own, starts to fit together.

"What are you going to do now?" I ask.

"I don't know."

She hesitates.

"I'm scared, Paul."

"Scared of what? I mean, I hope you can keep your job . . . "

"Paul, I know you'll think I'm paranoid, but one time when I was in Barnes's office, he got angry with someone over the phone, and I heard him mutter something like 'I'm gonna get Lucca on this' in such a tone that I didn't know what the hell to think."

"Who's Lucca?"

"I don't have a clue, Paul, but . . . "

This is too weird. I hope she doesn't lose her mind over all this.

"Listen, Dara, hang in there," I say, "I'll see what I can do."

Before hanging up I take her home phone number. I don't know why I think I can do something for her or that I have the first clue as to where to begin. Maybe I'm just being nice to a desperate woman, maybe old-fashioned chivalry is alive and well after all.

I don't have any more patient care responsibilities this afternoon. Instead of working on letters and scientific manuscripts, I decide to go home early.

Irene and I chat for a long time, kicking around all the recent events. While every single episode can be explained away somehow, the totality of the picture is getting more disturbing by the moment. We are tossing around questions for which we have no plausible answers.

My experience with drug companies is limited, but overall quite good. Hard working scientists, trying to crack many hard medical nuts. Through their work, we have antibiotics, vaccines and effective treatments for many diseases from headache to high blood pressure and high cholesterol. I have my doubts about their marketing and selling tactics. Everybody knows that promotional claims are often exaggerated, but I have to believe that the FDA watches over them carefully. Also, not all companies are created equal. Some are better than others. Gother is a medium-sized company and other than that they are the makers of some anti-cancer drugs, antibiotics and contraceptives, I know very little about them. If Dara's story has any truth to it, I obviously still have a lot to learn.

Irene feels sorry for Dara and angry at her company, but she can't see how I can possibly help her. She suggests that I call my liver expert colleagues to find out what they know about Neurovan. As an alternative, she proposes to call the FDA but I hesitate. Once I call the Feds, I lose my ability to be an impartial observer and investigator of the truth.

Irene has baked a wonderful chocolate-almond cake and we're nibbling on it, while sipping Colombian coffee in the living room. On the television screen a gaunt older man with thick dark eyebrows is talking. In the background is a chessboard, with only a few moves having been made from the starting position. I turn the volume up.

"Chess is a game of strategy. In the beginning the armies that face each other are identical. The rules are the same for both sides. The players have to move the pieces on the board, each taking his turn, and the one whose strategy is better will win the game. And to play winning strategy you need cunning, patience and deter-mination. I can watch your moves on the board and know more about your character than if I ask you to tell me the story of your life. The reason? Moves don't lie. Only people do."

The man speaks slowly in a mesmerizing tone and it dawns on me that he's describing my own situation. We have never agreed to sit down to a game, Gother and I, but a few moves were made and I can't stop now. First move, Mrs. Alberts gets sick. My move is to take her on as a patient. Kraft tells me about their investigational drug—their move. The visit to Tarrow—my move. Dara's call—their move. My going to meet her at the hotel—my move. She calls me again to tell me about the transfer—their move. Now I figure it's my turn to move in this giant chess game.

I guess it's not my turn after all. It's Gother's. Their move comes in the form of a phone call later that afternoon.

"Dr. Holden, what a pleasure to talk to you," I hear an unfamiliar deep voice. "My name is Lawrence Barnes, and I'm with the clinical research group at Gother."

"Oh. Nice to talk to you, too. In fact, I had a delightful meeting with members of your group last week."

Usually I mean what I say, and say what I believe, but maybe this time there's a grain of sarcasm in my voice.

"So I heard, Dr. Holden. In fact, that's the reason I'm calling you. I'm in charge of all our diabetes and cardiovascular programs here, and I'm concerned about the case of liver failure we had in Philadelphia. Dr. Lennox was very impressed with your expertise and we wondered if you could help us with this situation."

So this is Dr. Lennox's boss, the guy who was responsible for punishing Dara. He sounds nice and warm, speaks very slowly and confidently. I feel flattered.

"Of course," I hear myself saying, "I'd be delighted. How exactly can I help you?"

"We are having an internal meeting tomorrow, discussing the liver situation with Neurovan. We'd like you to participate."

"Tomorrow? I'll have to check my calendar . . . "

"We already have. Sounds like this is possible. No clinic patients."

I am getting angry at Carol, but I know she's right. I left myself plenty of time to work on my scientific manuscripts this week.

"If you agree, Dr. Holden, we'll book you on an early flight tomorrow morning. First class, of course. Tickets will be delivered to you tonight. You'll be here in time for a noon meeting. We've reserved a suite for you at the Fairmont. We'll put you on a plane back to Philadelphia on Wednesday morning."

"Sounds fine," I say, slightly overwhelmed by the flurry of activity. The Fairmont is possibly the best hotel in San Francisco. Irene is standing by my side, a puzzled look on her face.

"Of course, there will be an honorarium involved. What is your usual fee for such consultations?"

I've never had such a consultation job. I know that my boss, Dr. Scott, receives fifteen-hundred dollars for similar activities.

"Well, usually . . . " I mumble.

"Actually, there is nothing usual about this. This is such a short notice. Is five thousand dollars acceptable?"

Irene, who is now sticking her ear in between my ear and the receiver, walks away so that her shriek won't be heard.

"That would be fine," I say.

"Well, that settles it. There will be someone meeting you at the baggage claim area upon your arrival. Looking forward to your visit, Dr. Holden."

"Same here. See you tomorrow."

I hang up wondering if this man always gets what he wants. Probably.

Irene looks at me with eyes wide open, biting her knuckles.

"Wow," she utters, "that sure is a nice chunk of change for a day's work."

Specialists like me in academic institutions are paid decent salaries, but not as much as doctors in private practice. Such honorariums would, if received often enough, lead to substantial improvements in our life style.

"These companies swim in dough," Irene says.

"They must also be extremely worried about something. It's amazing how somebody at Barnes' level gets into all these details about flights and hotel. Is it the drug or is it me they're worried about?"

"Probably both," she says.

I call Dara and tell her about my flying out to San Francisco to meet the Gother scientists.

"They're trying to butter you up," she says immediately, "the oldest trick in the book. They'll wine and dine you and pay you exorbitant sums of money. Most people fold and turn from objective scientists into company advocates."

"Won't happen to me," I promise. It doesn't come out quite as convincing as I hope, though.

"Aha," she says.

"Listen, Dara. I need the names of the major characters in that Gother place. I need to know where their center of gravity is."

She gives me the whole list. Lennox reports to Dr. Barnes. Dr. Barnes is a vice-president, lots of industry experience, little science. A manager—administrator. He reports to the head of clinical research, a senior vice-president by the name of Dr. Leonard Ramsey. He and Barnes are buddies, alike in so many ways, old industry hacks. They know everything there is to know about clinicals, they know everybody at the FDA, they saw every possible side effect, every drug reaction, every drug profile; nothing is ever new to them in the drug development business. Owning many thousands of Gother stock options, all they care about is the company's stock going up, so that they can cash in their options and retire with tons of money. The president, and Ramsey's boss, is Dr. Carter Dell. He's relatively new to the company, but has already established himself as a dictator with a bad temper. Nobody likes him, and everybody is afraid of him.

"That's very helpful," I say when she finishes. I write it all down, and later I will enter this information into my computer.

"I guess you won't have enough time to meet me," she says.

"Maybe I will. They said nothing about dinner tomorrow night."

"Oh, don't worry. There will be dinner in a fancy restaurant. Trust me. I won't be surprised if Dell shows up. By the way, are you staying at The Fairmont?"

"Yes. Is that the usual guest house for Gother?"

"Only for VIPs."

"Dara, I do want to talk to you. I'll call you when I get a chance. I hope we can get together."

Irene stands nearby, listening, making a face, but says nothing.

I call my secretary Carol and tell her about my trip, and she confirms that this will cause no serious problems. In one clinic, where I have to supervise the fellows in training, there are usually enough attending physicians so my absence shouldn't be too painful. I have covered for others in the past.

"I don't know if you can dance in two weddings at the same time," Irene says.

"What do you mean?"

"You're either on Dara's side or on Gother's side. Neither will trust you for too long, you know."

"I need more information before choosing sides," I say. Irene shrugs and goes to the kitchen to make us dinner.

After supper, I play with Danny until late. Danny is wide awake and in a good mood, and so am I.

I sleep better that night than I have in a long time. The alarm goes off at five-thirty, and I jump out of bed wide awake and full of energy. The plane tickets are under the door, as promised. It occurs to me that I've never given my address to anybody from Gother. They obviously have their ways of finding out.

Driving to the airport I whistle the march tune from the opera *Aida* along with the radio. My first class seat is wide and comfortable, and I have two glasses of champagne before we take off.

ELEVEN

Tuesday, February 23, Berkeley, California

As I enter the luggage claim area in the San Francisco airport, I see the sign. It is printed in large letters and has my name on it. The elderly man holding the sign wears a blue uniform and his black shoes are sparkling. He introduces himself as Ralph. He takes my bag and I follow him to a long black limousine.

I sit in the back seat and look around. The deep leather seats are beige and the carpet is dark gray, all squeaky clean. The radio is tuned to the all-news station, and copies of the San Francisco Chronicle, Wall Street Journal and USA Today are strewn on the seat next to me. The TV is on CNN Headline News. When Ralph notices that I'm staring at the bar he says, "please, help yourself, Professor Holden."

I look out through the shaded windows. It's sunny, and trees are swaying in the wind, and unlike the East Coast, there is no snow in sight. I open the window and take a whiff of the warm California air.

We drive north on route 101 and after a few moments I see the signs for Candlestick Park. Ralph tells me that he has been with

Gother for more than 20 years, that it is a nice company, and that he is looking forward to retiring next year. He'd have more time to visit his sons who have all moved back to the East Coast.

We pass all the exits to downtown San Francisco and get on the Bay Bridge. Once off the bridge, we turn north and soon find ourselves in Berkeley. A few moments later I see the big gold-on-blue sign of "Gother Inc." The driver turns into a long, winding driveway lined with maple trees. We are in a largely secluded area, a stone's throw away from the bay.

I get out of the car and stretch my legs, trying to get used to my new surroundings. I face several buildings connected by curved, rambling open-bridges, giving the entire campus a web-like appearance. Each building is painted with a different color. Ralph takes my suitcase and places it next to me. He starts talking.

"Gother, is a midsize pharmaceutical company. This is our U.S. headquarters and here we do animal research, drug discovery, manufacturing, clinical research and marketing, all from this one central location. Each building was given a name, based on dominant color of its facade, be it the tiles or the window panes. The administrative building, where all the top executives resided, was named, the. . . white building."

Ralph is rattling off all this information as if reading from some invisible prompter. From his little pause at the end of the sentence I have to assume that maybe white is not the most appropriate color for the executives, at least not in Ralph's mind.

I look at a drab straw yellow building near the edge of the campus.

"That's the animal facility. The tawny building next to it is the discovery institute."

Ralph points to a building with bright blue window panes around the corner from where we stand.

"This is the clinical research facility. That's where we're going."

Ralph picks up my suitcase, but I put my hand on his arm.

"Thanks, Ralph. I can take it from here."

"Sorry, but I have my instructions, Professor Holden," he rebuffs me and picks up my luggage.

"This way," he says and starts towards the blue building.

I enter the building, and find myself in a spacious lobby. On one side I notice windowed panels displaying various boxes of drugs manufactured by Gother. I'm impressed by the sheer number of drugs Gother has on the market, including a first rate antibiotic ointment. In the center of the lobby, two security guards are sitting behind a large desk, glued to three TV monitors. The clock behind them indicates the time: 11:38.

Just as I sign my name in the visitors book, Dr. Lennox appears. He grabs my hand with two hands, all smiles, as if our previous breakfast meeting in the Philadelphia coffee shop was the epitomy of friendship.

"It's so wonderful of you to come on such short notice," he says.

"It's good to be here."

We walk through long corridors, lined by cubicles and offices. White walls, light-blue carpets. All very quiet, very sterile. People reading, writing, talking to each other in hushed voices.

"This is the clinical research building. The other buildings are for basic research, including discovery, toxicology, drug metabolism. If we have some time later, we can arrange for you to visit everything." Lennox explains in a cheerful voice, and for a moment I think I'm visiting some tourist attraction, the White House maybe.

We cross a bridge to an adjacent wing of the building. Past the bridge and around the corner, we enter a conference room. The sign outside reads, "Executive Conference Room."

I enter the large room ahead of Lennox. Beige walls, checkered carpet. A long mahogany table, which could comfortably accommodate at least twenty people, is in the center. The swivel chairs are covered with ugly, faded-red leather. At one end of the conference room hangs a large screen, at the other sits a slide projector. On the walls, paintings of trees, meadows and sailboats in the ocean. I'm slightly disappointed. A Renoir, or perhaps a large Rubens would be more fitting for the ambiance. Along the wall, credenzas are covered with neatly arranged sandwiches, salads and drinks. Light lunch served in an environment of serene opulence.

A few people are already in the room and Lennox starts introducing me to them. Most are junior scientists involved in animal research related to new drugs, especially Neurovan. Two young women are introduced as research associates working on Neurovan, and I wonder which of them is Dara's replacement.

I'm surprised to see a familiar face. Dr. Eric Dayton, a well-known liver expert from Vanderbilt is also here. I don't know him well, just a few polite exchanges at scientific meetings. Eric smiles when he sees me, and I figure he too is happy to see a friendly outsider.

There's a printed sign on the table with my name on it and I sit right behind it. This also happens to be next to Eric, so we engage in small talk and wait. After a few moments we are handed copies of the agenda. The meeting will concentrate on Neurovan and the speakers are to describe data from animals first, then humans. Effect of the drug on diabetic complications will be presented in detail, as well as its human safety record.

Dr. Lennox approaches and hands me a two-page document.

"Here is our confidentiality agreement. We need you to sign it before we can start."

This is a standard procedure done for experts who consult

several pharmaceutical companies at the same time. By signing that paper I promise not to breathe a single word to anybody about what I am about to hear. I sign without reading it and hand it back to Lennox. He tears off the second page of the document and returns it to me, for my files.

At precisely twelve o'clock, several people enter the room. Two men, entering first, are laughing hard and one of them, a short, mustached man has his arms around the shoulders of the other, a slightly taller and younger man with thinning hair.

After the introductions I learn that the shorter man is Dr. Leonard Ramsey, the head of clinical research. He has brown, piercing eyes emerging from under bushy eyebrows, thin lips under a thin mustache, and a strong chin. His hair, brown with gray streaks, is cut very short as if glued to his ball-like round scalp. His ears are disproportionately large and seem to move and flail as he speaks, as if his skin is attached too tautly to his jaw. I look at him and wonder what happened to the theory that in order to be successful in corporate America you have to be tall with gray hair and TV charisma. But Ramsey's deep voice and calm demeanor give him an undeniable aura of authority and I think that maybe he'd do okay as a radio talk show host.

The taller man whom he was hugging when they came in turns out not to be a Gother employee. He is Dr. Roger Lacoste, a diabetes expert from St. Louis. Dara has mentioned his name to me, but I've never seen him before.

As this entourage enters the room, a stocky man walks directly towards me. I stand up, as Dr. Barnes grabs my hand and squeezes it with fervent vigor.

"Dr. Holden. I'm Larry Barnes, we spoke yesterday. I'm so glad you could make it. I hope your flight was satisfactory."

He has a firm handshake, and he never stops looking in my eyes as we exchange pleasantries, as if trying to read my soul.

Dr. Ramsey joins us and without much ado cuts directly to the chase.

"Dr. Holden, I'm Len Ramsey. I don't go to every meeting on every drug. Neurovan is the most important product for our company. I've been told time and again that this is a breakthrough treatment of diabetic complications."

Ramsey gives Barnes a look, an unmistakable signal that Barnes should not screw up on this one. I remember Dara mentioning the friendship between these two, and I'd hate to see the look that Ramsey reserves for his enemies. Dr. Lacoste, who is listening, nods when Ramsey looks in his direction, I'm not sure why. Ramsey doesn't mince his words.

"We cannot allow one severe case of jaundice, unfortunate as it is, which may or may not be related to Neurovan, to derail our march forward. At the end there will be no doubt whatsoever that Neurovan is safe and effective."

He smirks self-importantly underneath his razor-thin mustache and then he turns away to sit at the head of the table. Lacoste sits to Ramsey's right and Barnes to Ramsey's left. Lennox slides quietly into the empty chair next to Barnes, who is sitting erect as if he has just swallowed a broom, anticipating Ramsey's words. Nobody says anything, but everybody seems to know his or her place. I watch with interest as the orchestra is getting ready to play under the guidance of an invisible conductor. I'll have to wait and see what kind of music they produce.

Ramsey puts on his reading glasses and looks around, searching for something. From all directions, people try to hand him a copy of the agenda.

He takes one from Barnes, and Barnes nods, beaming. Ramsey calls on the first presenter.

It's a fellow from the marketing department. Young, energetic, vigorous and enterprising, Joe Lansing discusses the great medical need for therapies in the diabetic complications field. He is tall and under his shirt I can see his bulging chest and arm muscles. He wouldn't look out of place in a baseball or football uniform. His large head with closely cropped hair sways and bobs as he speaks, adding spunk and fervor to his animated delivery. He has dozens of fancy colored charts and he often uses words like "product line," "franchise," and "situation." Towards the end, he starts showing some data on early clinical trials, without giving any critical detail. I look at Eric and he smiles, like, why is a salesman talking science he obviously doesn't fully comprehend.

Next is a presentation on animal data. Dogs were used to demonstrate that the progression of eye complications in diabetes could be halted with Neurovan. It turns out that dogs also developed serious liver problems when given Neurovan. I jump in, asking about doses used in dogs and humans, because it appears that the drug caused liver problems at doses below those that appeared to help the eye disease. There's a commotion, as nobody seems to have the pertinent data at their fingertips, but everybody tries to come up with some answer.

Finally, Dr. Lacoste, not a known liver expert, makes the irrelevant comment that it all depends on how much drug got into the tissue in question, and that, anyway, many drugs cause similar damage to the liver. He implies that looking at a slice of liver under the microscope doesn't help determine the cause of the damage. I say nothing, just watch, listen and take copious notes.

At exactly one o'clock we adjourn for lunch. Dr. Barnes walks over and invites Eric and me to join him for lunch, upstairs, at a private dining room. Ramsey and Lacoste join us, as does the young marketing guy, Lansing, but Lennox is not present. He's apparently having lunch with the scientists in the conference room. It appears that two classes are formed. The ruling class members are served crab chowder and grilled salmon while team

B members have to satisfy their appetite with cold tuna sandwiches and cole slaw on paper plates.

Lunch is pleasant enough. The Gother people try to make all
the guests feel at home. Ramsey gives us a brief history of the
company and describes its assets with great detail. Gother is larger than I thought, with annual sales in the four point five billion
dollar range. Ramsey seems jovial and amiable as he speaks, but
his dagger-like stare has an intimidating and daunting effect.

The marketing guy, Joe Lansing, sits next to me during
lunch. Joe turns out to be a funny and gregarious character with
lots of amusing stories. He's bubbling with excitement and his
confidence about Neurovan's success makes me wonder
whether I'm over-reacting to the liver problem. Joe tells me that
the company's field representatives are flooded with calls from
patients requesting this "miracle drug" and that Neurovan
might soon be approved for sale in several European and South
American countries.

At precisely two o'clock we march back to the conference
room, and the meeting resumes. Lunch makes us all more relaxed
and the meeting becomes less stiff and formal.

Dr. Lennox is the next speaker and he talks about the results
of human clinical trials, with special emphasis on safety. He says
that eight percent of patients taking Neurovan have developed
some liver problems. I dig into my memory bank and withdraw a
figure of five percent stated in the consent form at Tarrow's office.
The number seven-percent came up in my phone conversation
with Lennox. All this immediately cools my earlier positive reaction to Lansing's exuberant tales. I just make a note in my book
and say nothing.

Lennox then proceeds to mention the Alberts's case, and I
extend my antennas to their full length. He gives the facts of her
illness accurately, but at the end he concludes that her problem is

probably not related to Neurovan. Instead, he argues, it's the combination of all three drugs that did Alberts's liver in. He claims that Alberts is the only case of jaundice or coma for a patient possibly taking Neurovan. Possibly, he says, because she could have been taking a placebo.

I'm dumbfounded. I thought that Mrs. Alberts's assignment to Neurovan, not placebo, has been established. I say so into a deafening silence. Lennox hems and haws, avoiding any eye contact with me. Finally he agrees in principle, but makes the implausible distinction between Tarrow's opening the code and the company doing it. The company hasn't done it yet, he claims. From the corner of my eye I see Barnes nodding vigorously in approval, and Lennox seems to have gained a few chips in his boss's bank. I recall that Lennox lacked any curiosity about the code when we spoke over the phone, but it's hard to believe that Tarrow has never mentioned it to Lennox or to somebody else from Gother.

"It is useful for you to remember two things," I stand up for emphasis, looking Ramsey straight in the eye, "odds are that Neurovan is the culprit, at least partially, and that sooner or later a patient will die. In fact, several will die. I don't have the slightest doubt about this, because I've seen this before with other drugs."

Ramsey's eyes stab me as I speak, and I turn to Dayton for support. Dayton agrees completely, but he's more circumspect and less willing to commit himself.

"We need more information before the full impact of the liver problem can be assessed," he says, but from the way he says it I know he's just trying to kiss ass, I'm not sure why.

Lennox then gives details of all the clinical studies underway. Long and complicated studies, thousands of patients followed for years. Nerve biopsy is supposed to be the best method of measuring diabetic changes in patients with diabetic nerve damage.

He yields to Lacoste, who peppers us with lots of technical details about the nerve disease. I'm struck by how little concrete information is available on Neurovan's benefits to patients, and how zealously Lacoste supports everything associated with Neurovan. But Lacoste is a smooth talker with considerable skills, and it's not difficult to see why he is liked so much within these halls.

There's a long pause when he finishes. Ramsey finally speaks, and he's addressing me.

"Paul, I'm sure you can appreciate how open we are in discussing our results. We value your comments, but with time you'll realize that your fear and gloomy projections are unfounded."

And Barnes adds, "we shouldn't fall into the trap of being too pessimistic about it all."

I suddenly remember something that Dara mentioned during our breakfast encounter. I try to choose my words carefully.

"Dr. Lennox, is Mrs. Alberts the only serious liver patient in your studies?"

Lennox is back in his seat and I can hear the collective wheels of Gother's brass turning. Before he has a chance to open his mouth Barnes chimes in.

"Yes, Dr. Holden, just this one and only case."

"And you've studied three thousand and . . . "

"Close to four thousand," Barnes continues, raising his forefinger in the air, "and we have just one case. That's what I mean when I talk about premature and exaggerated gloom."

I smile and Barnes leans back in his chair, satisfied. But, Dara said . . . a rumor about a case in Austria . . .

"This includes Europe and the United States, right?" I persist, but I'm speaking in a matter-of-fact tone, so they have no reason to be alarmed or concerned.

"That's correct, Dr. Holden."

I nod, as if my questions are over, and scribble Barnes's

repartee on my note pad. Barnes and Ramsey exchange quick glances, a quick flicker that I doubt anybody else notices, but there's no visible change in their expressions.

Slowly, Ramsey puts on his glasses and looks at the agenda, which has reached its final item. Before he can say anything, perhaps adjourn the meeting, the phone on the wall rings. It's a particularly loud ring, and several people are startled. One of the Gother scientists, who sits closest to the phone, picks up the receiver. He mouths something into the receiver, then looks up, motioning in my direction. I give him the "do you mean me" sign and he nods. I get up, walk over to the phone, and bring the receiver to my ear. It's Dr. Donald Carey from the unit and he gives me some bad news.

"I see," I say to Don, "thanks. I'll talk to you later."

I put down the receiver. All eyes are on me.

"Mrs. Alberts has died," I say.

And Ramsey says, without missing a beat: "The meeting is adjourned. Thank you all."

Once the meeting is over, and everybody has dispersed, Dr. Barnes approaches me.

"Perhaps, we can talk about all this over dinner. We reserved a table at the Stouffer's, just across the street from your hotel. I hope you can make it."

Before I can respond he says:

"Great. We'll meet you in the lobby at 7:30. Ralph will take you to your hotel right now so that you can freshen up before dinner. By the way, if you're interested in touring our campus, Gerry will be delighted to take you around. I'd love to do it myself, but I'm expecting an important phone call."

Lennox, who is standing near by, looks up and nods.

"I'd love to," I say, and Barnes says, "done."

I look for Dayton but he isn't there. After shaking a few hands

I'm taken to the lobby where Gerry and I start our tour. For the most part we walk past hundreds of offices, where, as best I can tell, the most engrossing activities are drinking coffee and chit-chatting in the hallways. I'm impressed, though, at the large number of projects and the large number of people devoted to every single project. I'm told it's all because of the regulations imposed by the FDA. Every single word or page that has to do with an investigative drug is subject to scrutiny and auditing. The regulatory group, whose job is to interact with the FDA, and the legal group, seem especially large.

From the office building we move to the animal housing facility. I can hear the barking and howling of dogs getting louder as we move closer in. A large brown German shepherd wags his tail at me and cries softly with his large brown eyes as I pass by his cage. I put my fingers through the cage holes, and the dog licks them with great gusto. All the dogs are waiting to be fed some new chemical for a few days or weeks, after which they are killed to determine the effects of the chemical. It's a cruel world, where the well being of one species is dependent on sacrificing another. Since most chemicals never see the light of day as drugs anyway, most of the killing is a sad waste. I wish there was a more humane way to develop new drugs.

From there we go to the manufacturing plant, where we don masks, aprons and gloves as we watch up-close how powders are being made in huge containers. In another large hall we observe the compressing of powder into tablets and in yet another, the finished tablets are packaged into neat colorful blisters, and then into boxes, the boxes we buy in the pharmacy. I'm impressed by the clean and sterile environment, and even Lennox seems to enjoy this change in his routine.

We're back in the white office building, and in the distance I see a small figure of a young woman, her back turned to us as she's hurrying away. I'm not positive but I could swear that it's Dara. She seems to have bolted out of the corner office, the one we're about to pass. I peek inside the office as we do, and there I see Larry Barnes. He's holding a phone, and his feet are propped on the desk, soles pointing at us as we stop for a split second at the door. I take a quick glimpse inside. A large office with heavy furniture, and in the corner a small round table next to a sofa, and on it two empty wine glasses. Behind the desk, a typical personal computer and printer. Barnes cups the receiver and turns to me, feet still on the desk.

"Come in, Paul, come in." He gives me the "it won't take long" signal as he's pointing at the phone.

Gerry and I enter the office and sit on the sofa. As I look around, I'm struck by something unusual about this office, and it takes me a few moments to figure what it is. Other than a neatly folded copy of The Wall Street Journal in the corner of the desk, there isn't a single piece of paper in the entire place. I make a comment about this to Gerry, who whispers in my ear.

"Yep. He's the one-minute manager par-excellence. When Barnes gets a memo or a letter he either tosses it or sends it to his direct reports. He uses the internal e-mail system quite a bit, though."

Meantime, Barnes is holding the phone and listening, face turned up towards the ceiling. Ever so often he grunts into the receiver, without opening his eyes. While waiting, I take a good look at this man. He is a muscular man in his early 50s. He has square shoulders, which support a huge oval head covered with sparse black hair with gray sideburns. Relative to the enormous head, his eyes are wide-set, beady lusterless ponds which are constantly shifting. Between them, like a shriveled potato, is planted a large bulbous nose, visibly hirsute on the inside. While not exactly handsome, I suspect that his soft velvety bronzed skin, his cheerful manner and his deep booming voice make him an attractive target for women who don't have the pleasure of working with him. Also, his financial status and stylish wardrobe are hardly impediments in that regard. He wears a perfectly tailored navy-blue suit which has European design written all over it. A conservative red-blue striped tie matches his suit. All in all, he reminds me of a well dressed younger version of Anthony Quinn.

A click, and Barnes is off the phone.

"So, Paul, what do you think of our little zoo out here, huh?" he thunders.

"Impressive, very impressive."

"You bet'ya. And this is only the beginning. Wait five-six years and then you'll really have something to see. We'll be number one, Paul, mark my words."

"That's great," I offer, "if you can do that with all the brutal competition around."

"We thrive on competition, Paul," he says and raises his fist up in the air, "we all work hard, we have a bunch of great prospects in the pipeline, new scientists standing in line to join us, we have dozens of experts scouting the land for new compounds from other companies, the whole nine yards, my friend, the whole nine yards."

Barnes gets up from behind his desk and approaches us, extending his hand to me.

"Anyway, I'm glad you got a glimpse of our operations. We'll have a chance to talk some more tonight at dinner."

I thank him and we leave his office. I am struck by the fact that Barnes never addressed Lennox, acting as if Lennox doesn't exist. We stroll slowly down the corridors, and I wait for Lennox to say something, but he is pensive and mute.

"Some character, this Barnes fellow," I remark.

"At his previous company, his nickname used to be 'the boa'," Lennox says.

"The boa?"

"Because he used to slowly squeeze people under him until they became limp and depressed, or until they managed to escape."

"Hmm. Does the boa have a family?"

Lennox shrugs.

"He has no children. According to one story he left his wife of more than twenty years, on the same morning that she was diagnosed with amyotrophic lateral sclerosis."

I shake my head. This is a fatal disease, also nicknamed Lou Gehrig's disease. We are walking down the stairs now, and I can see the lobby in the distance.

"How long have you been with Gother?" I ask.

"Almost ten years."

"What did you do before coming over here?"

"I was on the faculty at Stanford. Associate Professor of Medicine."

"Are you an endocrinologist?"

"Yes. Diabetes is my shtick."

We turn the corner of the hallway. Occasionally somebody would pass us and say hello to Gerry, but he is too self-absorbed, staring at the floor as he walks.

"So, what made you switch from Stanford to a drug company?"

Lennox shrugs and grimaces.

"I needed more money to take care of some family matters."

His body language tells me that maybe he thinks he made the wrong decision by coming to Gother, and I decide to leave the subject alone. Anyway, we're now in the lobby and Ralph is already waiting. While shaking Lennox's hand, I can't help but notice that he looks sad and tired.

"Again, sorry about Mrs. Alberts," he says like he means it.

"It's very bad, though not unexpected. She has. . . had a very nice family."

"I'm sorry I can't make it to dinner with you tonight. I have to take care of my girls," he continues.

"I'm sorry too," I say.

Ralph and I march towards the limo and I sit in the now familiar surroundings. The little television is on, but I find the local news boring and meaningless and flip the switch off.

The more I learn about the Gother organization, the more positive my vibes are about this Lennox fellow. Compared to Barnes and Ramsey, the polished, smooth and ruthless political animals, Lennox seems downright civilized and human. But then I remember how much Dara feared Lennox, how evasive he was on the phone the first time and that maybe he's hiding another liver case, so things aren't that simple. They never are.

But Lennox's last words stay with me for some time. I know he was trying to communicate something to me, but I'm not sure exactly what or why.

TWELVE

THE FAIRMONT HOTEL IS A HUGE MAJESTIC BUILDING HUGGING THE corner of California and Mason streets atop Nob Hill. At the front I'm greeted by dozens of flags waving in the breeze above the pillared entrance. Inside, a uniformed bell-man takes me through the lobby, which is furnished in an old world style of burgundy couches and chairs. Brown streaks climb up the dozens of round golden columns, and the carpet is a dark red punctuated by dragon-like black stripes.

My suite is commodious and neatly decorated, with fine attention to details A basket of fresh fruits and a bottle of champagne adorn the coffee-table in the living room. From my window I see the bay, and the two bridges that span across it. The Golden Gate Bridge is engulfed in thick fog.

I'm tired and slightly jet-lagged but I decide not to sleep. Instead I jump into the shower. With warm water streaming on my head and body I feel refreshed and alert, as I try to ruminate over the events of the day.

Though I have anticipated her death, I feel sad about Mrs. Alberts, and I can't help thinking of her grieving family. I'm particularly sorry that I couldn't be there when she died, perhaps to offer support and comfort to the family.

The meeting itself offered me a fascinating glimpse of the inner workings of a giant company. I can't put my finger on it, but I felt ill at ease during the entire event, at the attention I received. The Gother people tried hard to be accommodating, yet for some reason I kept thinking of their white building as a zoo housing dangerous animals. Why does a non-scientist marketing person, Lansing, the hyena, full of fire in the belly, present complex scientific data? Is this what all companies do? I doubt it. The clinical data on Neurovan's benefits to diabetic patients are dubious, yet Lacoste is very excited. Lacoste, the eager beaver, is a zealot, and I don't trust zealots. Barnes could well be a boa, and Ramsey reminds me of a rat. It was all carefully planned and crafted, like a well rehearsed performance, and maybe that's what made it artificial and peculiar. But there's nothing particularly alarming or puzzling in what was said or done. I can't confirm a single fact from Dara's story.

Still wearing a towel, I call my hospital. It's close to nine on the East Coast and I don't expect any of the senior staff to be at work. Steve Denker, the emergency room resident happens to be in the intensive care unit and we chat for a few moments. Mrs. Alberts died peacefully, he tells me. She slipped into a coma and never recovered. Her family was there, as was Mel Kraft, and they all left a short while ago.

"They asked about you," Steve says.

"If you see them again," I tell him, "have them call me tomorrow night. I'll be back home."

"Any news about this Neurovan drug?"

"Not much, but it's getting interesting. I'll tell you when I see you."

"Okay."

I hang up and then call Irene and tell her about the events of the day. She listens quietly and wishes me continued pleasure at dinner. She also mentions that David Alberts and Mel Kraft have called. They didn't leave any messages. There was also a message from Carol at the office. Somebody from the FDA had called me, and as I listen to Irene I wonder whether they could have already heard about the patient's death. After exchanging a few syllables with Danny, I hang up.

There's a sudden loud knock on the door. I put on my robe.

"Who is it?"

"It's me, Dara. Open up."

I open the door and she sneaks in quickly, looking behind her into the empty corridor.

"There are always some Gother people in this place. You can't be too vigilant," she says.

She looks at me, at my red robe and wet hair and starts laughing.

"Caught you by surprise. I'll wait here. You can change in the bedroom," she giggles.

She wears a white turtleneck, a tight black skirt and black stockings. Underneath her sweater her nipples are visibly erect. Her hair is strung in a ponytail, and her eyebrows are painted dark, and I realize that without the dark bags under her eyes, she's easily one of the most stunning women I have ever met.

I put on my tie and suit and go back to the living room. Dara is seated in the deep couch, the bottle of champagne is open and she has a full glass of the bubbly in her hand. She motions for me to take the other glass she filled.

"Let's drink to us, and to justice. May the just ones win."

She's in a jovial mood, gone is the distress from our recent phone conversation. We touch glasses and drink. I am close to her and I notice how delicious she smells. She observes my inhaling and absorbing the aroma.

"It's called Cosmic Tease," she says.

"It's very nice," I say. I can't tell whether this is the real name of her perfume or she's just teasing me. A warm wave rushes up my chest and neck.

"So what's new at work?" I ask.

"Too early to tell. For the time being I'll work on that antidepressant drug. But I think they're watching me."

"What do you mean?"

"Just a feeling. My new office is as far away as possible from my old office and from the Neurovan group. One of the secretaries told me that my old files were locked and transferred to central records. That's a guarded area, and you need a gazillion signatures before they let you look at any documents there."

She takes a deep breath before continuing.

"And there are cameras everywhere, turnstiles that require identity cards, the works. You'd think we work on an advanced version of the A-bomb or something."

She takes a sip from her glass and holds the champagne in her mouth for a long time before gulping it down.

"Oh, and another thing. They took away my password, so now I only have a limited access to the files on our computer network."

I'm listening and thinking, all the while trying to look away as she folds her long legs, showing a little thigh in the process.

"Do you still think that they're going to fire you?" I ask.

"Very possible. For now they don't want to rock the boat, because I may cause them trouble."

She picks a grape from the fruit basket and starts nibbling at it very slowly.

"So, tell me, how was the meeting today?" she's curious.

I tell her briefly about the events of the day. Off the bat, I express my concern about Lacoste's zeal.

"He's a hired gun. He's involved in analyzing the tissues from the patients. He has a huge operation and he makes millions— and I am not exaggerating— millions from this work. Do you think he'd come out and say that the drug doesn't work or that it has any safety problems? Get real, Paul."

I can't argue with her logic.

"I am also troubled by the constant change in the percentage of patients with abnormal liver lab tests. It was five percent first, then seven, now it's eight. What the hell is going on?"

She takes another sip from the champagne.

"That's simple, Paul. As new patients enroll in studies, more patients get into trouble. What did they say about serious liver disease, like jaundice and death?"

I sit next to her.

"They only mentioned the case I knew, Mrs. Alberts. She died today, you know."

"I heard about it just as I was leaving work."

I don't ask her how she heard about it.

"The rumor about the other case is getting stronger," she says, "I told you in Philadelphia. It happened in Vienna, Austria. The patient is a diabetic kid, fifteen or something. He has jaundice and I think he's still fighting for his life, but I honestly don't know what's going on. They try to blame some other drugs he took."

"It's what they're trying to do with Mrs. Alberts's case," I remark.

"I know."

"They didn't mention any Austrian cases."

"Did you ask them directly about it?"

I look at her, raising my glass to my lips.

"I didn't want to expose my sources."

She thinks about it for a moment.

"So they said absolutely nothing?"

"I asked whether Alberts was the only case and they all said yes. I asked does that include the US and Europe and Barnes said yes. I had the feeling that Lennox was about to say something but I'm not sure. In any case, they stood by their one case."

She let her head drop on the back of the sofa, her face looking up at the ceiling.

"I've just realized something," she says.

"What's that?"

"You don't believe me. I mean it's my word against the word of a multi-billion company. Who are you gonna believe?"

I look at my watch.

"I have to go," I say, "they're meeting me at the lobby now. What are you going to do?"

She looks at me, brown eyes wide open, playful innocence.

"Could I stay here?" she asks.

This doesn't sound like a good idea, but I need to talk to her some more. I hesitate and she notices that.

"I don't want to run into the Gother brass downstairs," she adds rapidly.

"What are you going to do here?" I'm stalling.

"Nothing. Read. Watch TV."

I have to leave.

"Okay. But don't answer the phone and don't order room service," I say.

I don't think that Irene would be happy to hear Dara's voice in my room. I also don't need nosy hotel employees.

As I leave she sends me a kiss across the room.

I feel much better in the cooler elevator. The heat in the room was becoming unbearable.

*   *   *   *   *

In the lobby, I meet Dr. Ramsey and Dr. Barnes. They greet me warmly and we all walk down the block to Fournou's Ovens restaurant in the Stouffer Stanford hotel. I am told that this is one of the city's finest restaurants and that it derives its name from the huge oven it contains.

To my surprise, only Joe Lansing, the fast-talking marketing guy, joins us for dinner. I wonder what happened to Dayton and why he wasn't invited.

The restaurant is at the bottom of a winding stairway. We have the best table in the restaurant, just the right distance from the oven. The grilled lamb, the house specialty, is delicious, but the wine, a 1985 red Burgundy called Chauvenet Corton "Dr. Peste," a bottle of which sells for several hundred dollars, is simply out of this world.

Lansing may well be one of the most entertaining men I have ever met. He has stories from his travels, mostly abroad. Speaking with what to my ear sound like perfect Swedish, Japanese, Italian and German accents, he spits one funny tale after another. His brown turtle eyes seem dull when he's listening, but when he is in his element, they sparkle. Barnes and Ramsey prove to be good audience, as they encourage Joe with slaps on the back, though their laughter is muted and reserved. I laugh harder that night than any other in recent memory.

As dinner progresses, I am getting tired and the wine loosens me up completely.

By the time we're drinking the fourth bottle of wine, the Gother people start talking shop. Ramsey is asking about international sales of a drug for asthma, and Joe responds,

"Sales suck. Those international creeps couldn't sell water in the Sahara desert."

Barnes looks at Ramsey.

"If that's what domestic marketing thinks of international, I wonder what domestic thinks of R&D."

"That's easy," Joe shoots back, grinning. "They think that the only thing coming out of research are nerds at four o'clock in the afternoon."

I look at Ramsey and Barnes, who laugh unperturbed by Joe's remark. Joe is getting red and sweaty in the face, and his voice grows louder.

"One thing about clinical research. You have abundance of fresh meat there, young soft beef, if you know what I mean."

Ramsey makes some faint hand signals for Joe to stop, but Joe is the only one around the table who doesn't notice it.

"That leggy model, what's her name, from the Neurovan group . . . uh . . . Dana, no . . . Dara. That's it. Dara. Boy, she's a sin waiting to happen."

The table is shaking slightly, as Barnes kicks Joe in the shin. I can feel the vibration around my ankle.

"I haven't seen her today. Usually she comes to these meetings."

"She's been assigned to a different project," Barnes says matter-of-factly, throwing glances at Ramsey.

"Really?" Joe persists.

"She was needed on the Protizelam project," Barnes continues, shifting in his chair.

"I met her in Philadelphia. Seemed like a competent person," I decide to volunteer a cautious opinion.

"Interesting," Barnes says, "I didn't realize that."

I open my mouth but decide to shut it right away. I always learn more by listening than by talking.

Joe takes a huge swig from his glass of wine. He's now at the stage of drinking where he's not going to be stopped or denied until he has fully expressed his views.

"That's too bad," Joe says to Barnes, "I mean that she's in another group. You can't fool around with her anymore, can't pinch her ass anymore."

Barnes smiles awkwardly, but the alcohol levels in his gray matter also exceed the decency limit.

"Yeah, but I bet she misses it more than I do," he chirps.

Ramsey leans forward, looking sternly at Joe and Barnes.

"Enough, guys. I still want to talk business with our friend Paul here."

Joe and Barnes sit quietly, and I'm surprised that Ramsey is stronger than the alcohol. Ramsey turns to me. He has to wait for the waiter to finish delivering the coffee.

"Paul, Larry and I talked about it earlier. We would like to retain you as an exclusive consultant."

I find it difficult to concentrate after all the drinking.

"What do you mean, exclusive?" I ask.

"What we really mean is sort of a full time consultant. We know that you currently have a full time job, but we want to be able to talk to you and consult you any time it becomes necessary."

"And, of course, you'll be precluded from consulting other companies," Barnes says. "It's only logical," he adds, "because we'll pay you a regular salary."

The bill arrives and Ramsey puts his credit card on top of it without looking.

"Of course, you'll have to think about it. It may mean more frequent travel to the West Coast."

"I'm not sure if my hospital and medical school will allow that," I mumble.

"Usually there's no problem. Most schools favor ties with the pharmaceutical industry. The exchange of ideas is healthy."

What he means is the exchange of money for ideas, but it

sounds okay to me. Ramsey and Barnes stand up. Ramsey pockets the credit card and we walk upstairs towards the lobby, then turn underneath the arch leading to the hotel's yard and step into the cold air of California Street. My headache, slowly getting more throbbing, welcomes the fresh air. We walk to the lobby of the Fairmont, my hotel, where we say our good-byes.

"Let me know what you think about our offer," Barnes says, "and if you decide to accept, you'll find our offer very generous."

Joe cracks his final joke, we all laugh and I turn towards the elevators.

When I enter my bedroom I find Dara in my bed, reading. Her sweater and skirt are neatly folded on the chair. I sink in the couch, exhausted.

"What are you doing in my bed?" I ask.

She puts down the newspaper.

"Reading. Why?"

"You know what I mean. You took off your clothes."

"Not all of them. It is more comfortable this way."

I realize I'm getting nowhere in a hurry. And I'm almost falling asleep, despite the throb in my temple.

I start taking off my jacket and shoes.

"So? How was it?" she asks.

"It was fun. They offered me full time consultancy."

She whistles.

"We pay a hundred and fifty grand for such things. They must be scared shitless," she suggests.

I close my eyes. My head is spinning.

"This is strange, very strange," I remark. "Didn't you tell me in Philadelphia that the last consultant who told them that somebody might die from Neurovan was never asked to come back?"

"Why, is that what you told them today?"

"Precisely."

She just sits there pensively, pulling the blanket up to her neck.

"Dara, I think you should go home now."

"You're sending me out in the middle of the cold, dark, scary, night . . . "

"Oooh, you're afraid that they are gonna send Lucca after you?" I'm giddy and not completely in focus. But I remember the comment she made to me on the phone.

I look at her and she suddenly trembles.

"Paul, promise me never to make fun of this Lucca thing. It's so eerie."

She makes a grim face, but I don't pay too much attention.

"Whatever, Dara. You can stay."

I stand up, barely. I try to concentrate for one last moment.

"Listen, Dara. I'll need a few things from you when you get a chance. I need all the clinical documents on the patient with jaundice in Austria. And I need all the lab data obtained on Mrs. Alberts from the time she enrolled in the study. Can you do it?"

"It won't be easy, I told you. I lost my access rights."

"I know you can do it."

"I'll try."

"Good girl," I mumble, "you'd better go now to the other room."

She gives me a naughty smile exposing big white teeth, and lifts the blanket on the side of the bed where I'm standing. Underneath it I can see her tight stomach and firm thighs, separated by white underwear. Or maybe she wears nothing. I am too tired to tell the difference.

"I'm sorry, kid. This just ain't your day," I mutter. I take off my pants and slide into bed, without getting close to her. I'm sound asleep before I can count ten sheep.

THIRTEEN

I GET UP AT FIVE O'CLOCK TO CATCH THE EARLY NON-STOP FLIGHT TO Philadelphia. I look around, remembering last night's events, but Dara is gone and for some reason I feel a little disappointed. I go to the bathroom, shower and get dressed, but I'm still a little groggy. Just as I'm about to leave I notice a white piece of paper taped to the chair in the bedroom. Underneath the logo of the Fairmont hotel is a short paragraph, written in a rounded feminine handwriting. Despite the cobwebs, I read it smiling. "Once-in-a-lifetime opportunities only come once-in-a lifetime." It is signed Dara, with the letters "ara" enclosed in a large "D". I know she's right but there's a nasty, adventurous part of me hoping that she's dead wrong.

I make it downstairs to the lobby at 5:30. Ralph is already waiting, wearing his uniform and his shining black shoes.

During the flight to Philadelphia I mostly nap. When awake, I ponder the situation and examine my options.

The Gother people gave me a big warm embrace, but I have to wonder if it wasn't more of a bear hug. The importance of Neurovan to the company is obvious, and that seems to cloud their judgment. Honest people, let alone dishonest people, can be driven to do dumb and dangerous things in the name of unabashed greed. Do the Gother brass really believe that Neurovan is a superb drug, or are they all playing the old political game, putting their personal ambitions, their desire for short term financial rewards, ahead of patients' lives. Has the entire organization turned into one single mind, lacking principles but sharing goals? And all is done through methodical, thorough indoctrination. Even if somebody knows some unpleasant truth, there's nothing to be gained by telling it. Messengers get shot. The yes-men phenomenon becomes a surrogate for self-preservation.

I have to accept their offer. If I don't, I'd be cut off from the process and become irrelevant. But I can't allow myself to be driven by money and self-interest, to be brainwashed, to become a part of the collective, synchronized, unified mind that is called Gother. Dara is living proof that it can be done. I don't know yet about Lennox.

I arrive at my office after 4 p.m. to check my mail and messages. The first phone call I make is to Dr. Horatio Rubelli from the FDA. Rubelli is still in his office when I call. He introduces himself as the associate director of the Endocrinology and Metabolism section. He tells me that liver disease is a common problem with many drugs that their group reviews and that my name came up as a possible member of their advisory committee. This committee is responsible for approving new drugs for sale in the US.

"What exactly is involved?" I ask.

"We have about five or six two-day meetings a year. You'll be expected to attend these, after having read materials we send you in advance No honorarium, only travel expenses."

It all sounds interesting and I decide to accept on the spot.

My boss, Dr. Arthur Scott, wanders in. He saw me walk by and decided to say hello. We haven't seen each other for a few days. I welcome this opportunity to talk to Art about Neurovan and Gother, because I need his cooperation on the consultancy offer.

I tell him about Gother, the anti-diabetic drug they have and their concern of liver toxicity. I don't mention my own concerns, but I do mention their interest in an exclusive consultancy arrangement.

Art is surprisingly supportive.

"I had a similar arrangement with Anvers years ago," he tells me. "Worked like a charm. I helped them get an antibiotic through the FDA and they really appreciated it."

He winks, and rolls his fingers in the universal sign for cash.

"Only one thing. We'll have to cover your clinics and teaching duties. Give me sufficient notice so we can shuffle our forces."

Art leans against the wall, staring at me squarely.

"Why are you really so interested in all this?" he asks.

I sit on the edge of his desk.

"Let's say that I'm just a curious sonofabitch."

Art throws me a glance and grins.

"You must be one of those poor souls who went to medicine because you wanted to do detective work, diagnose obscure diseases, only to find out that all the new imaging gizmos make your skills obsolete."

"Guilty as charged."

He gives me an encouraging look and then turns serious.

"Be careful. These companies are big, strong and they mean business. Your only hope is to be smarter."

I tell him about the FDA advisory committee. Art looks puzzled.

"That's strange. I would've expected them to contact me before making their choice."

He shrugs his shoulders.

"Probably someone else that the FDA trusts has recommended you. Perhaps another liver expert who couldn't accept. Ah, what the hell."

Arthur waves his hand in the air and leaves.

I sit down to make my other calls. David Alberts isn't home. Dr. Mel Kraft is in his office.

"Oh, Paul, thank goodness you finally called," he says, "I've been looking for you all over the place."

Mel sounds excited.

"What's up?"

"It's about Mrs. Alberts. I looked at my notes from her last clinic visit. Turns out that her blood pressure was too low that day and I decided to see what happens if I stopped the Dyazide."

I jump to my feet.

"What are you saying? That when she came down with liver failure she wasn't taking the Dyazide?"

"Yes. But that's not all. At the same time she also ran out of Glucotrol and I gave her a new prescription."

"So, what about it?"

"The pharmacist told me that she never picked up the new pills."

So she wasn't taking either of the two other drugs that could have caused the liver damage. I can't believe my ears.

"Are you sure?" I snap. I'm getting suspicious of everything and everybody.

"Positive. My notes are clear. The pharmacist called me today. He has known Mrs. Alberts for years, and when he heard that she was sick, he checked his records."

"But when we met at Gusti's you told me that the visit was routine . . . "

"I remember. I was so distraught about the whole thing . . . look, I'm really sorry."

I remember something.

"Wait. . . but the bottle of pills she had with her in the hospital? It contained Dyazide and Glucotrol."

"That's the bottle she carried around to show doctors what she was prescribed. She wasn't good at remembering names. Think about it, Paul. Patients normally keep pills that they routinely take in separate bottles so that they know when to take what."

Suddenly it all makes sense. She had only four pills in the bottle that I found, four different types of pills.

"You know what that means, Mel, don't you?"

Mel hesitates.

"Neurovan is the only thing that could have caused her death, isn't it?" he finally says, slowly.

"You're damn right," I am suddenly very angry, because I feel I should have had this information all along.

"Does anybody from the Alberts family know about this?" I ask.

A pause.

"Yes, I told Lydia. Then David called me to confirm. I think he was looking for you."

"What about Tarrow?"

"Not yet. He's been so bad tempered recently that I decided to wait for the right moment."

"And anyone from Gother?"

"I didn't tell anybody."

A sudden thought.

"By the way, Mel, is the information on your patients computerized?" I query.

"Everything," he says proudly. "Our office has been like this from the beginning. I can even dictate a note into my computer while I'm making rounds in the hospital."

"What about Tarrow's office?"

"Same thing. We share the same computer, though we each have our own terminal."

"Now, about the clinical trials. Is all the information on the patients collected on paper report forms or is it entered directly into the computer?"

"I'm pretty sure it's entered into the computer, and sent directly to Gother. Why do you ask?"

"I need you to check something for me. Mrs. Alberts had a blood test on January 27 but I can't find the report. Could you find it for me?"

"Uh . . . I can try. Are you looking for something particular?"

"Not really. The routine stuff."

He'll probably guess that I'm after the liver results, but there's no need to spell out every detail for him.

"Okay."

I decide that I've heard enough.

"Okay, Mel. Thanks for the information. We'll just have to see what happens now. Bye."

I hang up.

All of a sudden I realize why I'm furious as hell. I'm mad because a woman died from a drug, and the people who made the drug enjoyed dirty jokes and excellent wine last night. Worse. I was there with them. The worst part, I'm about to make lots of money from the people who made the drug, and I'm going to make the money because Mrs. Alberts died. That's exactly why I'm so angry. But I have to keep taking their money, or else more patients are going to die.

* * * * *

On the way home I pick up a few egg rolls, and two orders of super-spicy kung pao chicken and shrimps with honsu sauce from our favorite Chinese restaurant and Irene and I have a quiet dinner in the kitchen. Danny is tired and falls asleep.

I tell Irene about my trip in great detail. She agrees that if I want to get to the bottom of this and make a difference, I have to accept Gother's offer and become their consultant.

"As long as you don't do it for the money, it's fine," she says.

"They might think so, but I'm not," I assure her.

"Are you also gonna try to fool me?" she asks, smiling.

"You'll know they bought me for real when I stand up in a public forum and proclaim that their drug is wonderfully effective and safe," I answer.

"I'll remember that."

"Irene," I add, "if you see me behave strangely, as if I sold my soul, make sure to tell me."

"I will," she says.

"Did you have time to see Dara?" she asks.

"She came to my room and we had the greatest sex I've ever had in my life," I say and start laughing.

"You're funny," she says dryly, her gaze centered right in my eyes.

She can be jealous, my little wife.

"No, I met her briefly in the lobby of the hotel before we went out to dinner," I say finally.

She'll have a hard time believing that Dara came to my room at night, lay in my bed half-naked and nothing happened. I could barely believe it myself.

"I asked her to get me some documents and she said she'd try. She now works in a different part of the building, so it may be difficult."

When we finish dinner, we read our fortune cookies. Mine reads:

"It is not who is right, but what is right, that is important."

FOURTEEN

Thursday, February 25

DAVID ALBERTS IS ALREADY WAITING IN MY OFFICE WHEN I ARRIVE. HE has a colorful tie, some sort of horses leaping over hurdles, and the gap between his teeth gives him an unintended Letterman-like air of frivolity. I tell him that I only have a few minutes before my patient rounds. David gets straight to the point.

"Based on all the available information, I've concluded that my mother died because of a Neurovan induced liver toxicity."

He takes out a small notebook and opens it.

"One, Neurovan is known to cause liver damage. And we know she wasn't on the placebo. Two, all the other possible causes have been ruled out. No viral disease, no alcohol. And three, it turns out that she had stopped taking the other two drugs well before she got sick."

He looks up from his book.

"There are two issues here. We want to be compensated for what happened. That's why we'll file a lawsuit. And, also I want to write a series of articles on this subject. I want to investigate the practices of these companies when they run clinical trials. I'm especially interested in what the patient knows when he signs that form. I want to know how informing that consent form really is."

I have no reason to object or argue. He obviously had all this planned while his mother was still alive. David swallows hard and continues rapidly,

"Could anything have been done to prevent her illness and death? Can they predict who's going to get a liver problem? Will a new patient entering the study know about my mother's death?"

All good questions.

"I hope you can help me," he says, "I'm talking about the articles. The lawsuit we can handle. Of course, you'll be asked about your experience with mother's disease, but that's all."

I look at my watch and David jumps to his feet. He hands me a tiny tape-recorder.

"If you don't mind, anytime you have new information or thoughts about the subject for my articles, just spit it into this little gizmo."

He smiles broadly. "It's a small present from Lydia and me. By the way, she worships the ground you walk on."

"She's an okay kid," I mutter, "she called me the other day from some bar . . . "

"I know," he says, "she asked me to apologize for her. When upset, she sometimes drinks too much. Next thing you know, she's way off her diet."

I smile.

"She's a fit girl. A little dietary indiscretions are okay."

"Well, yeah, but sometimes she gets into trouble. She gains weight, next thing you know she needs to increase her insulin."

I wipe the smile off my face.

"I didn't know she was diabetic."

"Oh. I thought she told you . . . "

"No."

"Damn. She's not going to be happy about my blabbering . . . "

"Don't worry. I'm used to dealing with confidential information. How long?"

"Since she was fourteen."

"Any complications?"

"As far as I know, only occasional tingling in her feet. But I'm sure I don't know everything."

"Who's her doc?"

"Kraft used to be when she lived here. Now she sees some diabetes specialist up in Yale."

We walk together to the elevators. I change the subject.

"By the way, have you hired a lawyer already?"

"Yes. Jeffrey Lund. Heard of him?"

"Who hasn't? He's one of the best in town."

"That's what they say."

The elevator door opens and we enter. There's no one else inside.

"Who is the lawsuit against?" I ask.

"The company, Gother, Drs. Ramsey and Dell, their medical monitor Lennox and his boss, Barnes, and the two physicians here, Kraft and Tarrow."

I am puzzled about one name.

"I am surprised that Mel Kraft made the list. He seems to be so close to your family," I remark casually.

David shrugs.

"He is. We just do what the lawyer tells us."

Down on the first floor we shake hands and split. David heads to the exit and I walk towards the internal medicine ward, hands tucked in the pockets of my white coat. In one of the pockets I feel the tiny taperecorder that David has just given me. I don't like it, and I doubt if I'll ever use it.

Three fellows, two residents and four medical students are already there, waiting for me. The medical students are interested and eager to learn. The residents are tired from an all night call and want to sleep. And the fellows are bored, because they think they know everything. By the time we're done seeing all the patients, four hours later, the students have had enough and want to eat. The residents are still tired but more appreciative, and the fellows show more respect. I tried to show them that they didn't and couldn't know everything. One needs humility if one intends to swim in the vast and deep-ocean called medicine.

* * * * *

It's late in the afternoon, and I am about to finish an important chunk of my paperwork. I set aside some time to call Barnes. But before calling to accept Gother's offer, I decide to get a second professional opinion and call my colleague and liver expert, Eric Dayton down in Nashville. We haven't spoken to each other since the San Francisco meeting.

Eric is there, and is his usual pleasant, cooperative self. I can picture him sitting and smoking his cigar. When I tell him about the consultancy offer, Eric doesn't hesitate.

"I wouldn't do it," he says.

"Why not?"

"Paul, you'll be signing a pact with the devil. Once they start paying you, you have no freedom. You'll have to toe their party line, your objectivity gone."

Eric speaks slowly and sounds like somebody who's been there before.

"Think about it," he adds.

"What do you think about Neurovan?" I ask.

"That anti-diabetes drug? I think it's dangerous. It's probably toxic to the liver. I also suspect that it doesn't work."

"Did you tell this to the Gother people?"

For the first time Eric takes his time answering.

"No. What's the use? They wouldn't listen to me anyway. They've got Roger Lacoste peppering them with rosy pictures of cure and salvation. They think that somehow the liver thing will disappear like magic, or that they can raise enough doubts about it to confuse the issue."

Eric is right on the facts, but I don't agree with his conclusion.

"Eric, if you don't tell them truthfully what you think, and I refuse to accept their offer, they'll find someone else. The outcome will be the same. I can do a lot more when I'm part of the project than if I'm completely out of it."

Eric has obviously thought about all that. I sound more and more like I'm trying to convince myself.

"You're an idealist. The odds are that they'll change you before you change them. But, hey, if you have the time and the will, go for it. Just don't say I didn't warn you."

"Thanks, Eric," I say and hang up. I figure that the die has been cast and there's no going back.

Larry Barnes is in his office and he takes my call immediately. After the usual pleasantries, I mention the Gother offer.

"I've got a coupla questions, Larry."

"Shoot."

"Tell me again what my obligations are."

"Very simple, Paul. We have a drug that affects the liver and you're a liver specialist. You can help us design proper patient monitoring procedures, when to measure what, how to figure out the mechanism of liver effect and so on. We also expect you to help write documents to regulatory agencies, and perhaps even present our results in person to them."

This doesn't sound too complicated.

"What if my opinion is different from the company's?"

"That's to be expected. We are dealing here with science, not religion. But since you're the expert, I can't imagine why your opinion shouldn't prevail."

Sounds reassuring, though not really an answer to my question.

"Okay. Can you fax me the contract?"

"You'll have it in ten minutes."

There's something pleasing about Barnes's efficiency.

Minutes later, the contract arrives. Overall, it's more than reasonable, just as Barnes has promised. I can terminate it any time, but can't work for another company for at least one year after termination. Some travel, domestic and international, and I may be required to assist in their clinical program. The priority of my responsibilities at the hospital and medical school is acknowledged. My annual fees would total $150,000, paid in equal monthly sums. I'm also eligible to receive Gother stock options as a bonus.

That evening I discuss the situation with Irene, for the umpteenth time. There are really no new issues. She hopes that I don't get too tired from the travel and the extra work, and I reply that if not now, when? I'm young and full of energy. She remarks that we might have more money but less time to enjoy it, and I say that we'll have to find the time.

I have a long list of facts, events and thoughts to enter into my computerized Neurovan file. Indeed, I have to open some new files, one for each Gother person I have met. I also search for information on Gother from several Internet sources, but find nothing remarkable. It's after midnight when I finally fall asleep.

*   *   *   *   *

In the morning I fax the signed contract page to Barnes, who is at work before six o'clock. Barnes is his usual business-like self when he calls back.

"Well, we're happy you agreed to help us. Let's talk about the first thing we want you to do," he says.

"Okay."

"We have a meeting with a regulatory agency on Tuesday, in ten days. We'd like you to be there. I'll have Lennox contact you about the details."

"A meeting? Where?"

"In London," Barnes says.

* * * * *

Lennox calls me less than ten minutes after I have officially accepted, and gives me a rundown of the upcoming activities.

"Next Wednesday evening there'll be a rehearsal of the presentations to the British Committee on the Safety of Medicines, known as the CSM. The meeting will take place in Dallas, Texas. A few months ago, we submitted a written document required for drug approval in the United Kingdom. In it we described our data on the efficacy and safety. After reviewing our data the CSM asked some questions about Neurovan, and we will answer their questions at this meeting. If they like our answers, the drug will be approved for sale in Britain."

He stops for a second and deadpans,

"Our president, Dell, and also Ramsey and Barnes will get huge bonuses. I won't be surprised if Dell will have an orgasm, or as we say here dollargasm."

I chuckle. Lennox surprises me with his sense of humor, though it is of the gallows variety. His openness is also refreshing, and I think maybe our less than perfect first encounter is all but forgotten.

Lennox goes on.

"I'll send you a complete agenda of the meetings. You don't have to present anything, but you should be ready to answer questions about the liver, which are bound to come."

Sounds easy enough.

"I am going to fax you some information you may not have seen yet. By the way, do you have a fax machine at home?"

"No."

"I've been instructed to tell you to buy one and send us the receipt. Make sure you buy the best machine out there. Money is no object. This will facilitate communication."

"Okay. Anything else?"

"See you in Dallas on Wednesday."

* * * * *

Next, I have a very short meeting with my boss, Dr. Scott. I don't know why, but recently Art has been smiling more pleasantly when we meet. I surmise that perhaps the rumors of Art's affair with a nurse in the clinic are true after all.

Sitting back in his swivel chair, his huge hands folded in front of him, Art agrees to relieve me of my teaching duties for the month of March, which is about to begin next Monday. Clinics, rounds, lectures only if I'm available. No problem. Plenty of eager staff. I know that one day I'll have to repay everybody. In fact, Scott makes that point clear.

He asks me again about the liver toxicity of Neurovan. I tell him what I know, which isn't anything new, and how the company has been dealing with it.

"Could be serious. But things aren't always as they seem. Let me tell you how I think you should proceed. Feel free to ignore it."

Art leans back, his massive body wrapped around the chair, covering it completely.

"If nothing else, the managers in a pharmaceutical company are shrewd political animals. When dealing in political and scientific issues, remember that less is more. Don't say anything unless you're one hundred percent sure about the facts and all the possible ramifications. If you feel like saying something antagonistic or unpalatable, phrase it carefully and try to do it in the form of a question. This diffuses the situation somewhat, and intelligent people will understand what you mean."

Art stares down at me, checking the impact of his words. Pretty basic stuff, but Art is a clever man with plenty of experience.

"Don't get angry. Don't get defensive. Even if you've been lied to, even if people are clearly using you. The world belongs to the well informed who keep cool. Write down everything you see and hear, but don't show it to anybody. Finally, when giving opinions never put anything in writing if you can help it."

At this stage I'm accepting Art's paternal attitude gladly. I thank him and promise to keep him informed. Art walks around his desk and gives me a friendly pat on the back. He then turns more earnest.

"Paul, as you can see, I am doing my best to be supportive. Eventually, though, the work will pile up and I'll have many disgruntled physicians and you'll have colleagues turned into enemies. All I can guarantee is support for one month. What's today? The 26th. Let's say to the end of March. After April first, I expect you to be one hundred percent back, unless you have a fantastic, tangible reason to continue."

I nod and we shake hands. I return to my office elated. This is almost a mini-sabbatical, one full month to concentrate on the Gother project, uninterrupted.

FIFTEEN

I GET HOME EARLY AND SIT IN FRONT OF THE COMPUTER, TRYING TO devise an action plan. A lot has happened since the phone call from Steve Denker at 2:44 a.m. ten days ago. I have a long list of questions for which I need some answers.

First I call Dr. Roy Tarrow. I haven't talked to him since our visit to his office and I wonder if he has any new information.

Tarrow is in his office, and he's still in a foul mood, just as Mel Kraft found him a few days ago.

"Why should I tell you?" Roy barks at me.

"You don't have to," I say calmly.

"Listen, first you come here with the Alberts daughter, asking me all these fucking questions, and I give you everything you want. Next thing I hear is they're about to sue my ass. So whose side are you on?" he continues to yell.

"On the side of justice. Right now it's also your side," I respond.

"How come?"

"Because if they sue you, they'll need an expert witness to testify on your handling of the liver problem, and that expert just might be me. To the best of my knowledge you haven't done any-thing wrong. Yet. So you gain nothing by screaming at me."

I can hear the synapses clicking inside Roy's skull.

"I didn't have to tell them. Gother knew."

"What d'you mean?"

"They broke the code themselves, before I did."

"Are you sure?"

"Yes."

"Do you have it in writing?"

"No. Lennox called and told me. In fact, that's what he called me about when you and the Alberts girl were here."

So they knew all about it from day one! When I called Lennox from my car, Lennox claimed that the code hadn't been broken. Same story, same denial, during the meeting in Berkeley. That's why Lennox never asked me for Mrs. Alberts's treatment group.

I hold the receiver between my jaw and shoulder and type in: *Lennox lied about code breaking.*

"What do you know about the other case?" I ask.

"What other case?"

"I was under the impression that there was another patient with jaundice," I say softly.

"I have no idea what you're talking about."

"Hmm. . . a sick patient in Europe. . . " I try again.

A long pause. I can hear his breathing.

"Nope. Don't know. Lennox reassured me that there were no other cases. That's good enough for me."

I don't find it hard to believe that Tarrow isn't the inquisitive type.

"By the way, how many patients do you still have in the Neurovan study?"

"Eleven. Almost all have finished."

"I hope there are no more cases of jaundice," I say.

"Hey, shit happens, and it's no one's fault. Just bad luck."

"Nothing we can do about bad luck."

I remember one more thing.

"Roy, can you send me Mrs. Alberts's lab results from. . . " I double-check the date in my book, "January 27?"

"Why do you need it?"

Tarrow is becoming tiresome.

"To confirm that her liver functions were normal four weeks before she became sick."

"I told you they were," Tarrow bellows.

"I remember you did. Unfortunately, they were missing from the chart you gave us."

"Maybe you haven't looked hard enough."

"I doubt it."

"I'll tell Rhonda to mail them to you, if she finds them," Tarrow says and hangs up.

"Thanks," I mutter to the dialing tone.

I don't plan to hold my breath until Roy Tarrow sends me the results, which means that it's up to Dara or Mel to find them. Dara. She should have found something by now.

I try calling Dara at home. It rings for a long time and I almost give up, but she picks up the phone.

"What's new?" I start.

"Who's this?"

"It's me, Paul Holden."

"Oh, hello, Dr. Holden, how are you?"

"Fine. So what's new?"

"Not much. The usual."

I can sense a strange frost in her voice, despite the distance.

"Everything okay?"

"Yes."

"Any luck with the things we talked about?"

"What things?"

What's wrong with her?

"Well, there was the January 27 lab results for Mrs. Alberts. . ."

"Liver functions were perfectly normal. I got that straight from Dr. Lennox."

"Hmm. And the Austrian case?"

"The what case?"

"Dara, you know, that. . . "

"Dr. Holden, I don't know what you're talking about, but I'm sure that if you called Dr. Lennox, he'd give you all the information you need, especially now that you've become a full time consultant. . ."

What's going on? Suddenly I get it: her phone is tapped!

I have to think quickly.

"I must be wrong. There are so many drugs I'm consulted on . . . I must have gotten my facts mixed up. Sorry about that."

Pretty lame, but that's the best I can do.

"Listen," I proceed, "maybe this is not a good time to talk . . . "

"Well, I told you all I know. If you need any further information feel free to contact Dr. Lennox . . . his number is . . . "

"I have his number. Thank you and good-bye."

I hang up and spend the next several moments in total bewilderment. What have I gotten myself into? Now that they know about the ties between Dara and me, they'll cancel the contract, they'll fire Dara . . .

The phone rings and I lunge to pick it up immediately.

"Paul. I'm sorry about that. . . but they tapped my phone . . . "

"Are you sure?"

"Pretty sure. I mean, I've strong reasons to believe that they did it."

"Like . . . "

"Paul, trust me. I know who I'm dealing with."

"I see." What else can I say?

"Anyway, Paul. I'm calling you now from a friend's house so we're okay. About Alberts's lab results. I did get them and they all looked normal to me. I can fax them to you, if you still want to see them . . . "

"Please, do. And the Austrian patient . . . "

"This is the strangest thing, Paul. Can't find a thing. Not a single record. As if the wind just carried all records into the ocean."

"This is strange."

"So, I understand you've taken our consultancy job?"

She's her usual self again, jovial and friendly.

"Correct. Give the good old grapevine another gold medal," I say.

"I also heard rumors that you might become a member of the FDA's advisory committee. Is this true?"

The word about the inner workings of the FDA sure spreads fast to this company.

"We have our ways. Our connections. People know people. People talk. Members on advisory committees talk." She's reading my mind.

"So what did your big honchos think about it?"

"Oh, that's simple. They were expecting it and that was part of the reason for hiring you."

What is that supposed to mean?

"Don't you see? To get Neurovan approved, they need somebody to explain the liver problem. What can they do? They go through consultants. If they find a somewhat friendly consultant, they try to buy him off. Money, travel, computers. Anything goes."

She talks like she's got a lot of worldly experience and common sense.

"But what if the consultant is negative?"

She doesn't have to think about this one.

"You mean, if he's slightly negative and about to become a member of a key FDA committee? They neutralize him. They try to buy him off. If he stays negative, he'll have to excuse himself from discussing Neurovan at FDA meetings. But there is always the chance that he'll turn around and become positive, because of the perks they shower on him."

"So," I say slowly, "part of the reason for hiring me was to neutralize me as a possible adversary at FDA hearings?"

"Exactly," she says.

"But even if I become positive about their drug, I still have to excuse myself during advisory committee discussions of Neurovan?"

"Of course, but then you still can help them in all the other countries. Remember, the US is less than one third of the world market for this drug."

"So you knew this all along?"

"No, I really started putting it all together in the hotel, when you mentioned the consultancy position."

The logic of everything she says is quite compelling. She continues to read my mind.

"You're not surprised, are you? People use other people for their own evil goals. It's how you react to it that matters. You do what you have to do."

Before hanging up I remember something.

"Do you have a personal computer in your office?"

"Of course, everybody does."

"And can you access it, say, from your computer at home?"

"Actually, what I have is a laptop that belongs to Gother. It has a modem and I can access my computer at work from any place. I had to return it, though, when I was taken off the Neurovan project and I haven't received my new one."

"And can you access data from ongoing clinical studies?"

"It depends. For most studies, once data have been checked and cleaned, it's fairly easy, but only active members of a team get the password. I lost mine the moment I was moved."

I hesitate.

"What number do you dial to get in?"

"510-717-1484, but, as I said, you need a password."

"Can you get me a password?"

"Hmm. . . I suppose I could try. . . In any case, I'm not asking you why you need it."

"What was your previous password?"

"TATALINC. I have no idea what it means and why they gave me this one. Be careful, Paul."

"Thanks, kid," I say, "I'll do what I have to do."

She says nothing for a moment.

"Paul, when will I see you?" she asks. Her voice is velvet and I think I can smell her perfume through the phone line. My mind races.

"Any way you can make it to Dallas?"

"Yes, if you send me a plane ticket."

"I'll see what I can do," I say and hang up.

I decide that Dara is okay, after all.

*   *   *   *   *

In the afternoon, the fax from Dara arrives and I see immediately that she was right. All the liver tests on Mrs. Alberts are smack in the normal range, nothing unusual or strange about the numbers. The date is clearly marked and the information is in the correct box in the form: January 27. Maybe Tarrow was telling the truth, and maybe there is a simple explanation why the results are missing from Mrs. Alberts chart. None comes to mind, though.

SIXTEEN

THE FOLLOWING WEEK STARTS OMINOUSLY. A PHONE CALL FROM MIAMI, Florida greets me upon arrival to work. A Dr. Andrew Weissberg, specialist in endocrinology and diabetes calls to ask my advice. He received my name from Dr. Dayton, a classmate of Weissberg at Tufts Medical School. He speaks in a slow, deep, earnest voice.

"I understand from Eric that you have a special interest in drug induced liver disease. I have a young woman here, who is participating in a clinical trial with a Gother drug called Neurovan. She was admitted on Friday with jaundice and slight confusion. Her situation is pretty stable now, but she's not out of the woods yet. Seen anything like this before?"

I'm not sure where to begin.

"I'm sure she's been seen by your local liver expert. What does he think?"

"It has all the hallmarks of drug induced liver damage. Because she apparently drinks moderately, this could be the result of some combination of alcohol and the drug."

"Anything else remarkable about her history?" I query.

"Nope. She's been in the study for three months. All her liver tests were normal until that day when she showed up in my office yellow as a lemon. Other than insulin, she takes nothing."

"Did you break her treatment code?"

"I was advised by the company docs not to do it unless it was an emergency. Should I?"

"I'm not in the position to advise you on this. This is totally your call."

I then briefly describe my experience with Mrs. Alberts, and explain that when I first saw her she had already been disoriented and confused.

"Tell me, Dr. Holden. I have fourteen more patients in this study, and I'm getting nervous. Should I remove any of them from the trial?"

"Hard for me to say. Have you talked to anybody from Gother?"

"I spoke to Gerry Lennox. I don't know if you know him. . . "

"I do."

"I told him the whole story. I had to fill the usual form about whether I thought it was a Neurovan induced liver problem, and I put down yes. Lennox wasn't too pleased and suggested that I withhold judgment until more information becomes available."

"Did you ask him whether you should discontinue the other patients?"

"I did. He didn't feel it was necessary, because the studies were almost over, and the risk to the liver decreases over time."

"I guess you've got your answer."

"But what do you think?"

I take my time in answering.

"Are you asking me whether you should discontinue your patients from the clinical trial? I don't know. But I can tell you one thing. I wouldn't let my mother join such a trial."

A pause.

"I hear you, Dr. Holden," he says and hangs up.

I enter the information on the new patient in my computer. I begin wondering if it's time to check with the FDA, find out what they know about Neurovan and the liver. The FDA is an interesting place when it comes to giving or receiving information. If I call Rubelli, and ask him about recent reports on liver changes from Gother, he won't tell me because that's confidential information. But Rubelli might smell something fishy and call the company, and this could create problems for me. I decide to postpone that call until I'm good and ready.

Next, I call Dr. Roger Lacoste, in St. Louis. I want to learn more about this guy, who seems to play such a pivotal role in the Neurovan saga.

Dr. Lacoste is with a patient, but when he hears who's calling, he comes to the phone.

"I caught you at a bad time," I say.

"Nonsense," Lacoste retorts, "now is as good a time as any."

"Let me tell you why I called," I start, "I have been asked to help Gother with the CSM hearing in London, and I want to know more about the diabetes part of the drug."

"Shoot."

"Do you think that the drug will be approved for sale in Britain?" I ask him.

"Does a bear shit in the woods?"

"I take it as a yes."

"You bet'ya."

"Why?"

"Why? I'll tell you why. We have finished two studies with more than three hundred patients, showing that the pain in their feet improves with treatment. The tingling too. What else d'you want?"

"Placebo-controlled trials?" I ask.

Most sophisticated countries, certainly England, require very careful controls in clinical trials. Without them, any positive results may be due to chance alone.

"One of them. The second wasn't."

"If memory serves, pain in most diabetics gets better on its own, over time. That is, when the nerve gets sicker and dies, all sensation is lost, right?"

A pause.

"That's true, and that's why we're doing the nerve biopsy study. We want to show that with Neurovan treatment, new healthy nerves are formed."

"I see. When will you have the results of these biopsy studies?"

"Oh, we're almost there, just a few weeks left. We should have the data ready for submission to the FDA by summer. We expect the advisory committee to approve it by this summer, early fall."

Now he's talking about my committee.

I notice that Lacoste keeps saying "we," as if this is his compound and his company.

"You seem very optimistic. Things don't usually move so fast at the FDA," I say.

I can hear Lacoste chuckle.

"Neurovan happens to be a breakthrough product, unmet clinical need. Also, we have good connections with the cotton-pickin' FDA reviewers, very good connections, if you know what I mean."

"We all have colleagues that work closely with the FDA . . . " I say.

"Right. That's exactly what I mean," Lacoste says with oozing sarcasm, laughing loudly as he finishes.

I don't know exactly what he means, but it sure doesn't sound like a topic for a long distance phone conversation.

"Coming back to the CSM meeting, do you think we have

enough data for approval without the biopsy data?"

"Piece of cake. Remember, there's no other treatment for this condition. We made sure that the patients and their doctors swamp the CSM with calls and requests."

Here we go again!

"How?"

Lacoste chortles.

"There are ways, my friend. Just ask our good friend from Gother marketing, Joe Lansing. He'll give you a crash course on the subject. You'll be amazed what determination, money and connection can do in this world."

"I can hardly wait," I say.

Lacoste is still giggling.

"Remember, my friend, those CSM reviewers aren't exactly cotton-pickin' rocket scientists, you know. Also, don't forget our good safety with Neurovan. That's your puppy."

"You mean the liver? I'm not even presenting," I remark.

"Doesn't matter. Just answer their friggin' questions, calmly and confidently. The incidence of the problem, how all patients recovered, how we perform frequent blood tests, you know, the whole nine yards."

Lacoste's confident nonchalance begins to unnerve me.

"What if they inquire about the jaundice cases, and the death?"

"They won't," Lacoste shoots back.

"How can you be sure?"

"You can't ask about what you don't know, right?"

"What d'you mean?"

"How will they know to ask about these cases if we don't tell them they exist? Huh? Look, you know what your problem is? You worry too much. And you analyze too much. Relax. Everything is fine."

"Excuse me," he continues, as he is apparently talking to someone else. Then he gets back to me.

"I have to go, Paul. The patient comes first, you know."

I hang up, having received an education. Lots of food for thought. Lacoste isn't even surprised to hear about other jaundice cases. He must be aware of them, the Austrian and the Miami patients, or else he would have corrected me. But if he's right, and the drug works miracles . . .

In the evening, I set out to check out Gother's computer systems. After dialing the number that Dara gave me, I can hear the sound of modem connecting, and on the screen I'm asked to type in my password. I type: "TATALINC" and wait. A blinking message in red, accompanied by a high-pitched beep, appears: "Access Denied." I try again, with the same result. After the third trial, the screen goes blank, and I'm disconnected. For an hour I try redialing and using different order of letters in TATALINC, but the results are always the same: "Access denied." I turn off the computer. I knew this wasn't going to be easy. I have to be patient and learn more about Gother. The upcoming meetings in Dallas and London are becoming more interesting by the minute.

SEVENTEEN

THE VENUE THAT GOTHER CHOOSES FOR THE REHEARSAL MEETING IS THE Loew's Anatole Hotel in Dallas. A mammoth, fortress-like brown building; two wings, huge ballrooms, several restaurants and shops, a fitness center reached through a plush backyard—this is a mini village. If one has to get stranded in a building, this would be one of my top choices.

The rehearsal is scheduled to begin at seven, over a light dinner. I arrive at the hotel early and decide to relax in the bar. Roger Lacoste is already there and he waves me over. He's sitting at a small round table in the corner, facing a television set. On the screen, there's a basketball game on. The mute button is also on, so one can watch the game without listening to the incessant yammering of the loudmouth commentators. It happens to be my favorite way to watch sports on television. I approach Roger, we shake hands, and I sit next to him.

Roger is in his late 40s, with thinning hair and long sideburns, gray short-trimmed beard and mustache, pointy nose and large protruding ears. His brown eyes move perpetually, exploring and searching for acceptance and respect. He has built a fairly solid reputation as a scientist, though recent mediocre work has tarnished it somewhat. He also had been rumored to be more and more in the pockets of the large drug companies. A case in point was his involvement with Neurovan and Gother.

I order a Black Label on the rocks, and Roger asks the waiter for a refill on his Jack and ginger.

"Should be an interesting meeting," I start the small talk.

"Nah, boring as a Sunday sermon," he says. I raise my eyebrows.

"You'll see. The repetition will just kill you. And those cotton-pickin' companies stick every word from the presentation on the goddamned slide."

"So how long have you been involved with Gother?" I ask.

"Oh, a couple of years."

"How are their scientists?"

Lacoste holds his nose.

"Some are pretty decent, but most of them are incompetent."

"Really?"

"Cotton-pickin' amateurs, that's what they are. See, they know very little about diabetes or its complications. For that matter, they know very little about anything else. What do you think, are they any good with the liver?"

I haven't given it much thought, but he may have a point.

"I suppose that's why they have consultants."

The waiter returns with our drinks.

"I heard that you've become an exclusive consultant for Gother," he says. Roger's shifty eyes follow mine, trying to read my thoughts.

"You probably wonder how I found out? I have my ways . . . "

He tosses his hand in the air, signaling omnipotence.

"I would never do that, not in a thousand years!" he exclaims.

He notices the surprise in my eyes.

"Why should I? There are other companies with similar, or for all I know, better drugs, who may benefit from my experience."

"So, how do companies know that you don't tell their secrets to other companies?"

"They don't. I sign confidentiality agreements, but who's going to enforce them? You recommend to company B the same protocol you recommended to company A."

"And what if you're wrong, and neither of these compounds works?" I wonder.

Lacoste bursts into laughter, and takes one big swig from his drink.

"That's life. In the meantime, between my job at the hospital and the friggin' drug companies, I'm taken care of, thank you."

He looks at me with an irritating smirk. I just sit there shaking the ice against the glass.

"What exactly is it you do for Gother?" I ask.

Roger leans over to whisper in my ear.

"I read all the nerve samples they send me. We then analyze the data. I'm the heart and brain of their operation. I am the pentium chip of their computer."

He leans even closer. His beard is now tickling my ear.

"I have all the samples. I control them. If they want them, I don't have to give them anything if they don't say 'pretty please'."

"How come?"

"They figured they couldn't do it themselves. Their cotton-pickin' lawyers and managers practically signed it away."

Roger makes a cup-holding gesture with his right hand.

"I got them by the balls, my boy, by the balls."

I am amazed by Roger's story. I'm even more astounded as to why Roger is telling all this to me. He looks at my face.

"You don't believe me?" he asks.

I make a face, like why should Roger be concerned if I believe him or not.

"I'll show you."

"That's okay, I believe you. No need to get carried away."

"Who's getting carried away?"

Roger calls the waiter.

"Waiter, get me a phone, and one more of these," he points to his already empty glass.

The waiter walks away, and in a few moments returns with a phone and Lacoste's drink.

"Roger, it's okay. I believe you. No need to prove anything," I say again, louder this time. From the corner of my eye I see on the screen: Michigan 54, Illinois 51.

But Lacoste doesn't hear me, and he's getting more excited by the minute. He hands me the phone.

"Here, you dial," he says.

I try to protest but Roger insists.

"510-616-6543. Did you dial?"

I listen. Two rings and then I hear,

"Carter Dell speaking."

I hand the receiver to Lacoste. He holds it up in the air between us, so that I can listen to the exchange.

"Roger here," he says.

"Roger, how are you?" inquires the president of Gother.

"Fine. Just fine. Everything is just moving along. But I need a small favor."

He cups the receiver so that Dell can't hear.

"Paul, what should I ask for?"

"What?"

"Just say something. Anything. How about a nice trip to a vacation spot, huh?"

I can't believe what's going on. Roger speaks into the receiver.

"Carter, I am writing a paper now about the endpoints we're using in our study. But it's been so hectic here that I need to go somewhere quiet for a few days to finish the job. I was thinking of . . . "

He rolls his eyes, looking at me from the corner of his eye.

"Aruba. And I would need a new laptop, you know, so that it doesn't take forever to write."

My jaw drops. I realize that Lacoste has a nerve, literally and figuratively. I'm just waiting for Dell, the omnipotent president of Gother research, to stop this nonsense at once.

Roger holds the receiver next to my ear. The first thing I hear is a deep, throaty laugh.

"Roger? Since when d'you call me about such trivial stuff? Sure, Roger, there's no problem. Do what you have to do. I hope Barnes didn't screw up."

Lacoste is doing the cup-thing with his hand, looking at me triumphantly.

"No, Larry's been super. I just needed a quick decision. Allison will love the weather in Aruba. The hot, windy climate does wonders for her skin."

"Great. Say hello to her. Make sure you stay at the new Marriott. Actually, the Hyatt is also very comfortable."

"I'll do that, Carter."

"And good luck with the CSM in London. You know how badly we need this."

"I'll do my best. Just a moment, Carter." He palms the receiver and turns to me. His eyes are glistening with excitement.

"Paul . . . ask for something . . . anything . . . you'll see how easy this is."

"No, Roger, I'm fine."

"Anything . . . there's gotta be something you need or want . . . quick."

Roger is shimmying in his chair, smirking, intoxicated with power. I start wondering if it might be contagious because I have this sudden impulse, a wild idea. Dara.

"Do you know Dara Lyons, their research associate?" I ask Roger. My head starts spinning.

"The leggy brunette? Sure."

"She was taken off the project, against her wish. Ask Dell to put her back on the Neurovan project."

If Roger is curious why I make this request, he hides it well. He actually seems to like my idea, maybe because it gives him a chance to screw around with other people's lives. He's on a power trip.

"Carter, one more thing. One of your best research associates, Dara Lyons, was taken off our project. She has been extremely helpful to us, and she's one hell of a scientist. My group likes her a lot. Can you put her back on the project?"

A short pause.

"Consider it done. Starting next Monday, she's back. I don't know why Lennox would do such a dumb thing. Anything else?"

"That's it, Carter. Thanks."

Roger hangs up and motions to the waiter to take the phone away and bring him another drink.

I don't have much time to digest this bizarre event because at that moment, into the bar stride Dr. Barnes, Dr. Lennox and a group of Gother employees. Joe Lansing is there too. He walks over to me, grinning, and gives me a friendly pat on the back and a firm handshake. Then we all walk upstairs to a meeting room and begin our rehearsal.

On the way up, I stop at the men's room. As I'm washing my hands, I hear a click emanating from my jacket. I put my hands into the pocket and pick up the tape recorder. I completely forgot about it. For some reason, the record button is pressed and the red light is on. I stop it, rewind, and press the play button. From the tiny loudspeaker I can hear Lacoste's voice. His words come out loud and clear.

"I got them by the balls, my boy, by the balls."

I push the stop button.

*   *   *   *   *

The rehearsal for the CSM meeting is held in a suite transformed into a meeting room. Central large desk surrounded by a dozen or so chairs and long windows with curtains drawn to darken the room for better viewing of the slides. There is coffee and pastries on the counter, as well as several cans of soda.

All the attendees take their places. Barnes sits at the head of the table, Lacoste to his immediate right, Lansing to his left.

Barnes makes an opening statement. He reminds everybody that Neurovan is the number one product of the company. Following its approval, Gother will be in a position to build a franchise in the diabetes field. He then adds:

"This train is at full speed, and before reaching its final destination it will crush all the skeptics and the ignorant out there. And to get the job done we have convened a winning team, the A-team. Roger is a world class leader in the diabetic complications field, and Paul is a first rate liver expert. And this is not all. As you know, our team also includes three British experts in the field of diabetes, and another British liver expert."

This is the first I hear about a British liver expert joining us.

"These experts are important, because the CSM prefers to get its information with a British accent," Barnes says.

"Today we're going to hear Roger's presentation, Mark is going to talk about animal studies and Gerry will give us the liver situation. I have read a transcript of our British presenters and we'll all get to hear it during our final rehearsal in London."

Barnes clears his throat and motions with his hand. A slide appears on the screen.

"So here is the plan. Osgood, our manager in the UK gives an introduction. Professor Farley, from Birmingham, will give a presentation about diabetes and neuropathy. How prevalent it is, how terrible a disease it is, no other treatment and so on. Next, Prof. Lang, from Hammersmith, will present his own experience with Neurovan. He'll show how all his patients got better without any liver problems whatsoever."

Barnes scans the somber faces in the room, and detects no burning desire to speak up.

"Next, we go to Roger, and our overall efficacy results. Finally, Gerry will give our excellent safety record, including the liver. Mark will not present his animal data unless somebody asks him specific questions."

His eyes rest on me.

"Paul, you and the British liver girl, Mosby, will be present at the hearing to answer questions. In the final rehearsal we'll decide who's going to answer what and how."

Barnes looks around.

"Questions?"

He glances at Lansing.

"Joe?"

Joe jumps to his feet with amazing agility considering his size. In one quick motion he's near the screen, flashing the remote control for the slide projector.

"Just a few words of reminder, Larry."

In the next few moments he gives us all a lesson in optimism and enthusiasm. Fancy colorful slides, exquisite artwork. There are so many millions of diabetics in the world, and so many have this terrible affliction of the feet called neuropathy. All of them are desperate for some treatment, and will try anything. Luckily, we have a winner, he declares. He lists some twenty countries that are currently considering Neurovan for marketing approval. The sales projections are staggering. By the time all these countries approve it, sales will top two billion dollars. UK is the key, because if it's approved there, he expects a domino effect of approvals in many other countries. Joe sounds and acts very convincing. The enormity of what's at stake couldn't have been stated any clearer.

He's followed by Roger Lacoste, who gives the clinical presentation. Well organized, clear and coherent, it's probably one of the most brilliant talks I have ever heard. What Roger was able to do with the meager available data is nothing short of spectacular. I finally understand what enormous oratorical talents Lacoste possesses, and why the Gother people accommodate every whim of his. Only problem is, of course, that the results are quite weak and scientifically not convincing. The single controlled study looks positive for the drug until one appreciates the small magnitude of improvement in pain and the fact that many patients decided not to finish the study for a variety of reasons. The results can possibly be sufficient for small and unsophisticated countries, but the CSM in Britain will never fall for it. But if anybody could sell this lemon as a brand new Cadillac, Roger Lacoste is the man.

By contrast, Mark, the animal toxicologist speaks in a shrilling voice and is confused, disorganized and erratic. Gother must be hoping that this presentation never sees the light of day.

Next is Gerry Lennox. He describes in detail all the good things about Neurovan's safety record. It has no effect on the kidneys, on the heart, on blood count, glucose and so on. He speaks slowly, like a ho-hum college professor, resting his voice for long pauses to collect his thoughts. As I'm listening to him, I figure that this style of speaking is just perfect for Gother's purpose. They don't want to attract too much attention to the liver problem. He finishes by declaring that the liver situation is manageable and reversible and that the number of patients affected can be kept to a minimum by the comprehensive monitoring system they have put in place. Once he is done, Lennox walks to his chair and sits down. That's when I speak up.

"What about the jaundice cases and the one death?"

Barnes looks at me as if I were his beloved dog who suddenly turned on him and bit him in the knee cap.

"What are you proposing, Paul?" Barnes asks calmly, like haven't we been through this before?

"I think you should come out clean on the serious liver disease that you've encountered, that's all," I say, just as calmly.

Lennox is about to say something when he notices the right hand of Barnes rise ever so slightly above the desk, signaling for him to keep quiet.

"It's not a matter of coming out clean, Paul," Barnes says, "it's just that we can't report on something that hasn't been fully verified. What's more, we are required to present only information that had been submitted in writing to the CSM in advance. We can't spring on them, out of nowhere, information that hasn't been fully evaluated."

I'm on my feet.

"What hasn't been verified about the Philadelphia case?" I ask.

Barnes just looks at me and continues in a composed voice. I can't tell for sure if he's getting irritated but it's a safe bet that he's not happy.

"We don't know several things. Did she or didn't she take the other medications? When did she stop taking Neurovan? Was she an alcoholic? We don't have the final pathology reports either."

"What about the Austrian case? And the Miami case?" I ask.

There's no mistaking Barnes's irritation now.

"What are you talking about? I don't know anything about these cases." He's now looking at Lennox, who is the apparent cause of his irritation.

Lennox clears his throat. He has the worried look of a dog who soiled his master's favorite oriental carpet, and I can't help but feel sorry for him.

"I'm not sure what you mean exactly . . . " Lennox starts, but Barnes interrupts him at once.

"Dr. Holden, you seem to be in possession of some information that we're unaware of."

Barnes is now focused on me like a laser beam, and suddenly we're all formal again; no more "Larry" or "Paul" talk.

"Where did you hear about this so-called Austrian case?"

Obviously, mentioning Dara is out of the question.

"I assume, Dr. Barnes, that it was in the information package that you sent me."

Barnes and Lennox throw a glance at each other.

"I would imagine that if it was in the package we would have known about it," Barnes mutters, and looks around the room.

"Anybody else hear about an Austrian case?"

Silence.

"Well, must be some sort of misunderstanding, Paul. By the way, Gerry, do we have any studies in Austria?"

"I believe that our European partners have chosen a site in Vienna for study number 11, but I'll have to check."

Barnes leans back in his chair.

"Please do that. Now, did you say something about a Miami case?"

"Yes, I got a call from a colleague at the University of Miami about a jaundiced patient there in a Neurovan trial."

Barnes turns to Lennox.

"Gerry?"

"We just heard about it the other day, and we're looking into that."

For some reason Barnes seems to be satisfied.

"Good. Any other comments?"

Barnes now turns his attention back to me, interjecting finality into his tone of speech.

"Paul, we'll look into all that. If we must report it, we will."

Joe Lansing, the marketing man, chimes in, ignoring the finality.

"We shouldn't report information that's incomplete. It's going to kill the product in other countries. And what if it turns out that there are perfectly good explanations for these cases? What if Neurovan was definitely not involved?"

Barnes listens patiently and then declares,

"We'll see how our British colleagues advise us on this matter."

Barnes is clearly trying to end the discussion, delay the confrontation and placate me. But I'm still not sure how it all works. Safety of patients should come first, and if in doubt, assume the worst. I decide to test the limits of Gother's patience. Maybe I'm emboldened by my earlier encounter with Lacoste.

"I don't think you understand," I say, "we need to come clean on all the serious cases associated with Neurovan. I refuse to be party to any of this cover-up, Larry. You want more information, fine. More time to fully understand all the factors involved in the liver problem, fine. But don't give me that bullshit about the Philadelphia case, the alcohol bit or the other medications."

I speak softly in a measured voice, but the tension around the table is palpable. Barnes responds, and as he does I understand what it means to be a top notch non-emotional practical managing machine in a tough dog-eat-dog place like the pharmaceutical industry.

"Paul. You're right, of course, and we value your opinion a great deal. That's why you're here. We'll discuss it. We just need more time for a careful review, that's all I'm saying."

He's oozing sweetness and reconciliation, yet he speaks in a determined voice. He's deflated the wind out of my sails, and I have nothing further to argue.

Lennox looks at me with his sad eyes, and I think I can detect a new deference for me and my position. Lansing looks at me as if I was some actor who suddenly forgot his lines and deviated from the script. Joe must be thinking that my indoctrination is incomplete, and he has more work with me than he had anticipated.

I just nod and lean back in my chair, closing my eyes.

Barnes asks for any final comments about any of the presentations. Other than some minor wording changes and two typographical errors in Lennox's slides, everything is picture perfect.

We adjourn after Barnes announces with a wide grin that he's very pleased with the meeting, and that the next rehearsal will take place in the London Marriott the day before the hearing at the CSM.

Once done, we all take the elevator to the top floor for a dinner at Nana's. It's nice and warm in the restaurant, and the view of the lit skyline of Dallas is spectacular.

The atmosphere is loose and pleasant, as if the earlier exchange at the meeting never took place. Business is business, but this is dinner. I sit between Lacoste and Lansing, and after a few drinks we are all laughing, mostly at Lansing's jokes.

Joe tells the group some interesting facts about himself. In college he played football, and then made it to the first team of the Los Angeles Rams as a tight end, but was cut after one year due to a nagging knee injury. After football and before joining Gother, he was some sort of an assistant in the Reagan presidential campaign. After the campaign, he worked as a talk-show host on radio. He counts among his acquaintances several actors, including Arnold Schwarzenegger. He knows every world expert in the diabetes field, and has amusing personal anecdotes about each. He even went out on a date with the daughter of one of the most prominent Austrian diabetes experts. Luckily, he quips, he performed well, or else Gother would have lost Austria.

As he was talking, he was moving his large, beefy hands and scratching his short hair.

"Larry, you remember the story. This Professor Kunz told me he had two tickets to the Vienna opera, but he couldn't go. His daughter wouldn't go by herself and would I do him a favor and go with her? Would I? Are you kidding? One word from him and Neurovan is approved in Austria on the spot. I would have stuck my . . . uh . . . hand in a tiger's ass in Africa if he had asked me to. So I go to the opera, some German boredom, but I manage to stay awake, barely. Then we go to dinner, and I take her home on the subway. We have a great time. In the morning, when I am ready to leave, who shows up? The big professor, drunk, with a blond babe on his arms. The professor stops, gives me a bewildered look and says," and here Joe switches to do his German accent,

"I zee you had a vanderful time . . . and I say, yeah, the singing was excellent, the screaming was great too, and he says, no, I meant with my daughter Lilly, and I said, yeah, so did I. He's confused for a second, then he looks me straight in the eye, points at the blond babe and says, just forget you ever saw this woman, and I said, what woman? And left."

Everybody laughs, and Barnes asks,

"When did you say Neurovan is going to be approved in Austria?"

"Any time now," Joe says, and Barnes says, laughing,

"I hear that the head of the CSM in London has a very nice gay son," and Joe screams,

"No, please, Larry, there is a limit to my commitment to the company. Let's send Don from the Oncology group."

Lacoste is laughing so hard that he bangs his hands on the table.

The meal came and went, but this light banter continues for a long time. Finally, we say our good-byes and it's close to midnight when I return to my room.

Moments later, while I'm in the middle of brushing my teeth, the phone rings. It's Lennox, and he wonders if I'd like to join him for a drink downstairs.

I look at the neatly folded blanket over fresh-smelling sheets and at the golden wrapped chocolate mint on my pillow and realize that I'm tired as hell. But I know I must go, I have no choice.

EIGHTEEN

I ENTER THE MIRAGE BAR, AT THE LOBBY LEVEL OF THE HOTEL, AND survey the place. It's a large room, full of couches and round tables, all facing an elevated podium. The band must be on a break because there are several musical instruments dispersed about on the stage. The place is very dark, with faint light coming from one of the lamps in the corner. Squinting in the dark, I finally spot Lennox, who is seated on a couch in what appears to be the darkest nook in the bar. He's sipping from a glass, which he immediately informs me is a single malt Oban Whiskey. I sit down in a chair across the table. Despite the darkness I can tell that Gerry doesn't look well. His eyes are red and tired, his complexion pale and his shoulders are bent forward. Though he has a muscular physique, he looks weak and beaten.

I order a double martini. Lennox speaks without looking at me.

"I don't know if I can go on," he blurts.

"What do you mean?"

"It's a torture. I have to lie every time I present our data. And after the meeting Barnes just chews me out for not being more decisive, for not anticipating the concerns that you raised. He knows about all the cases we have."

"You mean about the other jaundice cases?"

"Sure."

"So there is an Austrian case?"

Gerry takes another swig and just stares blankly into the air.

"I really can't get into specifics here . . . "

"But, Gerry, I'm your consultant, for crying out loud . . . "

"I'm in enough trouble as it is. Paul, don't make me talk about that. I'll tell you anything and everything. But not that."

"Why?"

"Because of these stupid marketing people and our top management. Dell. And the CEO too, Walnut."

He turns to me, and starts laughing.

"You guys in the academic ivory towers, you don't have a clue as to what's going on in the real world. Money. Money. Tell me, what's more important, life or money?"

Lennox is beginning to lose control, and his speech becomes slurred.

"Life, of course."

"Wrong," he thunders, "wrong. Money. See, my name is on all the protocols. If something happens to a patient in our studies, who do they sue? Who goes to jail? The medical monitor. Who's the medical monitor? It's me. Do you get it, Paul? Do you get it?"

He puts down his scotch, and removes his glasses. Despite his emotional state, he seems coherent all of a sudden.

"I'm the one who's responsible before the law, but I don't get to decide on what's reported to patients or health authorities or even consultants. If I say I want to report the jaundice cases, they try to convince me that this is going to hurt registration, and it will hurt sales, and Walnut is going to get pissed off. So what can I do?"

I say nothing. I know Lennox isn't finished yet. He hangs his head on his chest.

"And poor Dara. She was just as upset as I was, but I couldn't tell her. I was her boss, and I was supposed to be a role model of company loyalty."

I remember Dara's description of Lennox as being the introverted silent type. This conversation proves that he's at wit's end.

"Why was she taken off the case and threatened to be fired?" I ask.

Lennox looks up at me.

"It's so complicated. She and Barnes have a weird roller-coaster type of relationship. There were rumors that he came on to her, harassed her, and she threatened him. I don't know, something's going on. And then she came on that trip to Philadelphia without getting all the necessary permissions. At least, that's what I heard."

I'm getting confused.

"So why did she make the trip?"

"She wanted to talk to somebody on the outside. She wanted to talk to a liver expert without anybody else from the company present. I told her she could come only if she cleared it with Barnes. When she showed up for the flight I assumed she did."

I have the feeling that Gerry's pain is genuine, but I'm not sure how much I can tell him about Dara's involvement. I also see no reason to tell Lennox that Dara will be returning to the project.

"So when we had that breakfast in Philadelphia, you weren't angry at Dara?" I ask.

The four person band gets on the stage and starts tuning their instruments.

"Only at first, but I couldn't talk to you in front of her. Remember, that was our first meeting, and the phone call we had earlier wasn't particularly friendly."

I nod in the darkness.

"I had no choice but sing the party line. Anyway, when we returned from Philadelphia, Barnes had his excuse to punish her. A liver case like that was very sensitive and they tried to avoid junior people finding out about it. He also must have been pissed off at her for some other reason."

Despite my sensation of heaviness and fatigue at the end of a stressful and long day, my anger is starting to build up. I don't think that Lennox is making all this up.

"So why doesn't he just fire Dara?"

He shrugs.

"I suppose he still hopes to somehow get in her pants."

The visual image of the gorilla-like Barnes trying to make out with this beauty queen raises my blood pressure further.

"Gerry, listen to me carefully because I really need to know the truth," I start.

Lennox straightens himself and looks in my direction. He seems fully alert, and less tired than he did when I came in. Our little conversation must have lifted his sagging spirits.

"Is there any reason to believe that Neurovan is a good drug and, in fact, it may help suffering diabetics?"

Lennox folds his arms across his chest.

"In my opinion, no. Despite what Lacoste has been telling everybody. See, there's nobody on this planet who knows the data better than I do. If the data could complain they would scream 'rape' at the top of their lungs. Lacoste raped the data to fit his theory."

"How exactly did he do that? Don't you have internal checks, quality control, that kind of stuff?"

The waitress stops by our corner and we order more drinks.

"He's been given too much leeway. He gets to decide what and how to analyze. For example, he makes the rules as to what patient's data should or shouldn't be included in the analysis. He decides how to define the endpoints. And, of course, he interprets the data and puts all the right spins on the information."

"And the FDA? They just let him do that?" I ask.

Lennox gives me a look like, you poor child, you're so naive.

"The FDA sees the data only at the end, and, believe me, not too many brain surgeons work for the FDA. Lacoste has many friends within the FDA. In fact the chief reviewer received his training in Lacoste's department, a fellow by the name of Aftaz."

The band starts playing a loud rock song. The singer has a pleasant voice, but the volume on the loudspeakers is too high and we have to raise our voices to continue the conversation. I'd like to believe him, but logic, at least my logic, tells me that a company can't be that foolish and ignorant.

"So, what next, Gerry?"

"Two things," he shouts over the music, "I want to stop Neurovan from killing more people and I want to nail the bastards at Gother, especially Barnes and Dell. What about you?"

By now, Lennox is talking like a fighter about to enter the ring.

"I want the same, Gerry, but you're taking a bigger risk. I have another job, you know."

"I may lose my job in the process, but I may lose it anyway when the drug officially fails. What can I do? I simply can't go on pretending that everything is honky-dory. So either I fight and maybe win, or I just quit and look for another job."

"How much time do we have to do something?"

The waitress comes back with our round of drinks and places them on the table.

"The next key meeting where Neurovan could get approved is in London. I doubt that the Brits will approve it. I believe we have some ongoing negotiations, arm twisting, bribing, God knows what. Belgium and Austria are next, and we're working on the experts there. The U.S. of A. is the big enchilada. We have to stop Neurovan before we submit the data to the FDA."

I mull this over for some time.

"But if the data are lousy, the FDA will turn down your application and that will be the end of the story," I say.

Lennox stares at me with genuine pity.

"Paul, you still don't get it. We own the FDA. They helped us with the protocols. On their part, they are dying to approve something for diabetic patients because of all the pressure from patient groups. And then there's good old reliable Aftaz."

I can't believe the FDA part of his story. Maybe stress has made Lennox paranoid beyond control.

"And the advisory committee will recommend approval if the data are lousy?" I ask.

"Any hint of something will be sufficient. We own them too."

Lennox leans closer to me.

"How do you think you got on the committee?"

I've heard this innuendo before.

"How?"

"Let's just say that it took a couple of phone calls. That's all."

The music suddenly gets louder, and it becomes impossible to talk. After a few moments, the music gets softer again.

"It's getting late," I say, "there's plenty of thinking that we both have to do. We'll talk some more in London."

Lennox stands up. His cheeks are ruddy and he's grinning with delight.

I also rise to my feet and we shake hands vigorously for a long moment. Just then the band finishes their song and a strong light floods the stage and illuminates the entire bar. I freeze. Barnes and Lansing are seated two tables away. They are laughing, no doubt to some of Joe's stories.

Gerry and I walk to the exit together. Before leaving I look back into the still lighted room. Barnes and Lansing are watching us intently, and as best I can tell they're not laughing anymore.

NINETEEN

Thursday, March 4, Dallas

IT'S ONLY 7:00 IN THE MORNING BUT THERE'S ALREADY A LONG LINE AT the lobby restaurant, the most convenient breakfast place in the hotel. As I'm moving through the line, I notice that somebody is waving to me from one of the tables. Joe Lansing is flinging his long arms in the air, inviting me to his and Barnes's table. I walk in and sit down.

We exchange greetings and I order my usual light breakfast. Coffee and orange juice are already on the table. Both men are friendly towards me, but Barnes seems more somber than usual. Lansing is wearing a green Polo short-sleeve shirt and I can't help noticing the huge tree-trunks he has for arms. Barnes is as spiffy looking as ever in his perfectly tailored suit and red, striped tie. I watch as he tries to cut the sausage in his plate with his fork. He finally succeeds and shoves a huge piece of pork into his mouth.

"So what did you think of the meeting yesterday?" Barnes asks me.

"Very interesting," I say, "I hope you didn't mind my candid comments."

At this point I realize that from now on I can't afford any more blowouts that might separate me from the Neurovan project. I have to be careful about preserving my relationship with these people. But I can't be too smarmy either.

"Not at all," Barnes says, without looking up, "we need to discuss all issues openly. We are one team now, and if we're to win we have to work together."

Joe clears his throat.

"So what do you think? How bad is the liver situation?"

I pick up my orange juice glass and take a slow sip. They are both looking at me with great anticipation.

"It's hard to say, Joe," I start, "it all depends. If your clinical benefits are compelling, you'll do okay. But if they're not, and more people get serious liver disease, then you're in trouble."

I'm not telling them that to overcome the liver problem their drug will have to perform miracles. Unless amputees make it to the national Olympic team, they don't have a chance to pass it by my FDA committee.

Barnes is pondering my answer as he stabs a new piece of sausage with his fork.

"Is there anything we can do to eliminate the liver problem?" he asks.

Fair question.

"Have you tried to test patients more frequently?" I offer, "say every two weeks instead of every month?"

Joe shakes his head vigorously.

"We can't sell a drug if the patient needs a blood test every two weeks," he exclaims.

I think to myself that they can't sell a drug that kills patients even if they test them every month, but I say nothing. I don't understand how they let a salesman get involved in discussions about safety.

"We really trust you, Paul, to take care of the liver problem. We'll all do very well if you do."

Barnes is now rearranging the hash browns in his plate.

"I saw you and Gerry had a long talk last night," he says casually.

"We were just relaxing," I smile.

"He has been very distraught lately. With his wife gone and all that, he hasn't been himself. And I don't think his analyst has been much help either."

I'm not sure where Barnes is going with that, but I play along. I guess he's trying to tell me that Lennox is mentally unstable.

"We all have our ups and downs," I remark.

"He's a good man," Barnes says, "but these days I would not take anything he says seriously. When somebody is depressed, the most trivial event becomes a catastrophe. You know, 'the sky-is-falling' syndrome."

"Isn't it his job to worry about the safety of drugs he works on?"

"To some extent." Barnes gaze is fixed to his plate, as if the answers to the mystery of the world, the clues to the meaning of life, lie there. "But he should leave most of the worrying to his superiors. We are more experienced, and we know what we're doing."

"I hope he gets better," I say.

Barnes gives me a puzzled look but says nothing.

There's silence for a few long minutes. I'm struck by how quiet Joe Lansing has been so far. No stories, no jokes. He obviously isn't a morning person.

"What do you think of Lacoste?" Barnes asks suddenly.

"How do you mean?"

"Is he a reliable scientist?"

Joe is watching my expression, so I try not to change it.

"I don't know. He seems to know what he's doing, I understand he published quite a bit . . . "

"Why did you ask him to bring Dara Lyons back to the project?" Joe asks.

There is nothing unpleasant or threatening the way he asks this, both with sphinx-like faces, casual. But they are not fooling me.

"Actually, it was Lacoste's idea. He feels that she was helpful for their group," I say softly.

Barnes keeps looking for something in his plate, staying expressionless.

"Dara Lyons. How well do you know her?"

"We had a nice breakfast in Philly. Just like this one. That's all," I smile.

If they tapped her phone, they know I'm lying, but I have no choice.

"She's a good kid." Barnes goes on, as if he hasn't heard me. "Emotional sometimes, even hysterical occasionally but, basically she's a good kid."

He seems to be talking to nobody in particular. I notice now that from the corner of his eye Barnes is watching my reaction.

"Did you know she was arrested once? Big fight with her husband. Threats. With a loaded gun."

"No, I didn't know that."

"They're divorced now, of course. Point is she's not very stable, if you know what I mean. Just keep that in mind."

"I suppose you can't always be sure about the mental health of employees you hire," I can't resist that. He's trying to send me a not so subtle message about the people who contacted me, so I have to needle him back.

He looks at me, surprised. He then smiles, for the first time this morning.

"Good point, Paul. Incidentally, I didn't hire them."

There's a lull in the conversation, and I jump back to the previous topic.

"Why exactly have you given him all that responsibility?" I ask.

"To whom?"

"Lacoste. Didn't you ask me about his scientific skills?"

Joe and Larry look at each other.

"Right. Uh . . . it's a long story, Paul," Barnes says, "one day we'll tell you. Maybe."

And Joe shakes his head and says, "yeah. Maybe."

We finish our breakfast without further conversation. When we're done, Larry says to me, "thanks for your help. We'll see you in London next week."

"Looking forward to that," I reply.

"Be safe, in your travels," Barnes says, and the way he says it sends a shiver down my spine.

We part and I go upstairs to my suite to get ready for my flight home.

On the plane I spend most of the time writing down what I think are the key events of the meeting. We have only a few short months before thousands of patients start getting exposed to Neurovan, if it gets approved anywhere. At the same time, Dell, Barnes and Ramsey, the salesman Lansing and the crooked scientist Lacoste should be punished. The real challenge is to do all that and preserve Gerry Lennox's job.

My plan is clear in its goals, but the execution is tricky. The timing is crucial. If I blow the whistle right away, say, by sabotaging the meeting in London, we may achieve less in the long run. Lennox will get fired, I'll be dropped as a consultant, and the clinical trials and registration efforts will merrily go on. If we wait until it gets to my committee at the FDA, more patients may develop jaundice and die. This should be our worst case scenario, our fall-back plan. But we need something faster. Unless we get smarter, we will never accomplish our goals. And I depend entirely on Dara and Lennox, the two people with all the inside information, the two people that Barnes portrayed as unstable and flaky.

*　*　*　*　*

When I arrive home Danny is running around chasing a small brown golden retriever.

"What's that?" I ask Irene, as she greets me with a long kiss.

"That's Rusty. I thought a dog would be nice for Danny. He'll develop faster."

"The dog or Danny," I quip, but she just gives me the "don't be silly" look. We have talked about having a dog for a long time, but I had hoped to be part of the search for an appropriate pet.

Danny is screaming "dada, my doggy" when Irene and I sit in the kitchen to drink tea.

I give her a detailed report of my trip, the talks with Lacoste and Lennox, and the rehearsal itself. I even play back the tape with Lacoste's remarks. When I tell her about Lacoste asking Dell to put Dara back on the project, she frowns and looks at me suspiciously. I shrug, and make an innocent face, like it was just to see how far Lacoste would go.

She sits quietly for a few moments, fist under chin, trying to make some sense out of all this. I can see her blue eyes and raised eyebrows through strands of wiggling brown hair.

"Let me see if I can summarize it. Lacoste is a fraud and a jerk, the company people are greedy and unscrupulous, except for Lennox who seems like a decent fellow. And you . . . "

She looks at me with smiling eyes and grabs my hand.

"And you are a damn fool who wants to save the world. But at least you're not doing it for nothing."

I smile and hold her hand.

"So who can you trust in that group?" She isn't done. She's methodical and likes to put one brick on top of the other in a logical way.

"Lennox is probably okay," I reply, "but despite all his bravado talk after a few drinks, I know he can't afford to lose his job. He also refused to confirm or deny the Austrian patient story, so I know his loyalties are split, at best. And Dara delivered on all her promises."

I should have known better than to interject Dara's name into the conversation. Irene has only one major flaw, and that's jealousy. Casually, Irene removes her hand from mine.

"Dara . . . " She rolls the "r" slowly, as if trying to understand the profound meaning of the name, "Dara, what does she look like?"

"Oh, she's in her late fifties, weighs at least 250 pounds and has a big mole right here," and I point to the center of my nose.

Irene gives me a mock slap on the wrist.

"Must be a real beauty, you sonofabitch," she laughs, and I think maybe she's gotten more trusting over the years.

"Do you still need her?" she asks.

"Yeah, I think so. I really don't want to use Lennox unless I absolutely have to. I'd hate to see him lose his job. Keep in mind, though, whatever I do, there's no easy way to stop this drug from hell."

Irene grabs Danny who just flew by chasing the dog, and puts him on her lap.

"I need to get into Gother's computer system," I say.

"What?"

"I thought I told you. I need to see what it is that they do there. First hand. In great detail. I don't want people sending me preselected information. There's some funny stuff going with one of the lab reports on Mrs. Alberts. I also need to know how many really sick patients they have, what they tell the FDA and what their internal memos show, everything."

Rusty is pulling Danny's sock off, and Danny thinks that's hilarious.

"How are you going to do that?"

"I need to get a password or two. We shall see."

Irene is pensive for a moment. Finally, she says,

"I hope you know what you're doing. Just don't break the law, d'you hear me?"

"Don't worry, honey. If nothing else, all the investment in our fancy computer will finally pay off."

Irene runs off to deal with a screaming Danny and a barking Rusty and I sit in front of the computer and turn it on. For a long time, I type in a summary of the Dallas experience, and then I add a few entries to the "actions" file. The title of my action plan is "heads will roll." Finally, I try one more time to enter the main computer at Gother using the phone number that Dara gave me. I try her old password, TATALINC, try to rearrange it in a hundred different ways but again, no cigar.

TWENTY

SATURDAY NIGHT IRENE AND I GO TO A BIRTHDAY PARTY. MEL KRAFT HAS apparently turned forty, and he decides to celebrate it. Since Danny was born we haven't gone out as much as we used to, so we accept a last minute invitation from Phyllis Kraft. I am surprised at the invitation, because I met Mel for the first time only a couple of weeks ago and I didn't know that we're that friendly. Phyllis tells Irene that Mel invited some colleagues I might know, as well as some members of the Alberts family. I tell Irene to accept, but that I reserve the right to bail out if the conversation drifts to the subject of Neurovan and the liver. I need a break and Irene knows it.

The Krafts live in the Norristown area, near the turnpike, in an old colonial-type house. It's one of the coldest days of the winter, and after slipping and sliding on the icy driveway, we reach the door of the house. Phyllis opens it for us, and we're immediately ushered into the living room, where we find a dozen or so people huddled around the crackling fireplace. Mel is playing bartender and Irene and I grab glasses of Chardonnay even before we have a chance to say hello. Glass in hand, Irene by my side, I search for familiar faces. It's a relatively small room, and we're all in pretty tight quarters, rubbing and pressing against one another as we move about, like some gathering of teenagers at a disco.

I don't have to look too far. Lydia is practically inches away, and when she sees me she throws her arms around me and kisses me as if I was her rescuer from a deserted island. I introduce her to Irene, but Lydia smiles and says hello to her without breaking eye and body contact with me.

"Paul, how are you?" She's on her tiptoes, trying to reach my ears with her mouth and speak over the background noise.

"Fine," I smile. My right hand is searching for Irene's, but all I do is grasp thin air.

"Long time no see," she continues.

"I know. How have you been?"

She lost a few pounds since I last saw her. She has her hair tied in a ponytail behind her head, and in her white open blouse and dark brown skirt she looks more attractive than I remembered.

"Okay. And you?"

"Can't complain."

In the corner, I spot a tall, bespectacled gentleman, giving some sort of a sermon to a group of spellbound listeners. He has a long, tanned face, graying hair, and the chiseled features of a movie actor. He has a finely grained pipe stuck in the corner of his mouth, and it emits a most delicious aroma. Lydia notices my interest in the gathering around the man.

"Have you met my brother Milo?"

"This is your brother?"

"Yeah. Why are you so surprised?"

My conversation with Mel at Gusti's is coming back to me.

"This must be the philosopher from the West Coast," I say.

She looks at me, then at Irene.

"Come, I'll introduce you."

Irene and I follow her. We get closer, but Milo is in mid-speech, and Lydia stops.

"It's really simple," Milo says softly, "when we compare creationism to evolution, it's not that one is wrong and the other right, in absolute terms. The problem is that we try to compare religion and science. Evolution is a fact understood by every scientist. There's no doubt as to its correctness. Creationism is a faith, accepted by the religious believer. It cannot withstand any scientific scrutiny."

"But what do you think? Have my ancestors been monkeys?" A woman asks. She's leaning on Roy Tarrow and I presume that this is his wife.

"Please don't take it personally, my dear lady, but I'm afraid that the ancestors of all of us have been monkeys. This is as certain as the earth revolving around the sun."

"This is blasphemy," the lady fumes.

"How so?" Milo inquires patiently.

"Since God created all of us, he must have done it at one time, just as the Good Book says. Saying that different animals were created at different times, is like saying that God couldn't have created all the creatures on this planet. Is that what you're saying?"

Milo smiles.

"No, Ma'am, this is what you've just said."

Lydia jumps in at what seems an opportune time.

"Milo, Milo!" she interrupts him.

Milo turns in her direction.

"Milo, I want you to meet Paul Holden. And this is his wife . . . uh . . . Irene."

Milo's eyes light up in recognition.

"Oh, of course, you took care of mom during her last illness."

We shake hands. He is in his early thirties, but his soft blue eyes exude worldly intelligence and patience way beyond his years. He takes Irene's hand and kisses it in the best European old-time tradition. Irene is visibly delighted.

"Milo spent years in Germany and Austria," Lydia tries to explain.

"I assure you, Irene, that I reserve this ancient habit only for the most beautiful women I encounter," Milo says, and Irene is melting before my very eyes. Milo looks at me innocently and winks.

"Looks like you acquired another admirer," I smile.

"You win some and lose some. I think before you came I lost that God-fearing woman over there," he tilts his head in the direction of Mrs. Tarrow.

David Alberts suddenly pops out of nowhere and gives me a warm welcome.

"Finally, I get to see all the Alberts clan in one place," I say.

"Recently, we have been meeting too often under not-so-pleasant circumstances," Milo says.

"So what's new, Dr. Holden?" David asks. He's the most intense of the three and he's trying to get to some point.

"Not much."

"I hear your consulting job with Gother is quite extensive and all consuming."

"Yeah. I'm learning a lot about the industry and the drugs they make," I say.

"Good," David says, "I hope you can put it all to good use when I'm done with my investigative reporting. You know, I've made great progress."

Irene and I exchange glances. My face repeats what I have said. I'm in no mood to talk shop at this time.

"Great. Let me know if you need help."

Lydia tugs at David's elbow.

"Leave Paul alone, David, he's here to enjoy himself."

David smiles and puts his hand on my arm.

"Sorry, Paul. Didn't mean to . . . "

There is now a circle of people surrounding Milo, who is puffing calmly on his pipe. Mel and his wife Phyllis, Tarrow and his wife, Lydia, and David are all there, as well as a few other people I don't know. Milo turns to Irene.

"So, Irene, what have you been doing for the soul recently?"

"Nothing, I'm afraid. Just raising my little Danny."

"You call this nothing? Yours is the most sacred work on earth. Passing on one's genes is relatively easy. Its passing on what we call memes, that is, life's experiences, survival tips and achievement advice to our children, this is the pinnacle of our accomplishments."

From across, I can hear Tarrow's wife mumble something to the effect that Milo talks too much, but I take an immediate liking to the guy. Irene's eyes are glistening and I can tell that she likes him too.

"So what exactly is it that you do?" she asks.

"Mostly, I teach and write."

"What do you teach?"

"All that brainy stuff that we hated when we were young. Philosophy. Thinking. Logic."

"Your students are very lucky," Irene tells him.

"Only when I'm having one of my good days, and these happen less frequently every year, I assure you."

She's drinking every word of his like it's the last drop of water on earth.

"And writing?" she persists.

"I've published a couple of books."

"A couple? How about seven?" Lydia pipes in.

"What kind of books?" Irene wants to know.

"Okay, I'll give you some titles. *The Ignorant Expert* is one. *As a Matter of Fact* is another. *Think or Swim* is another."

"That's fascinating," Irene says and we all nod approvingly.

There's a pause in the conversation. David raises his hand.

"Since we're all gathered here, I'd like to read to you one of my mother's poems. I think it's the last poem she wrote. It's called 'Will There Be Dawn?'"

There's a palpable hush in the room. David pulls out of his jacket a neatly folded piece of paper. He unfolds it, and starts reading in a rhythmic soft voice.

> "Younger is better, they all say and know
> Vigor. Smile. Sunshine. Green meadow.
> No more shooting ache at the tip of the toe
> Only bright eyes with visions galore."

David licks his lips and continues.

> "But, alas, the sun is almost down below
> Arid rain turns the grass hazy-yellow
> Muscle and tendon are pulling no more
> Stomach is throbbing like never before
> My eyes are cloudy hued like lawn,
> And I'm so tired and heavy, will there be dawn?"

As his voice dies away, there's a murmur of approval and respect. David folds the paper and tucks it back into the pocket of his jacket. He knuckle-dries his eyes and turns away, and Lydia hugs him warmly. From the corner of my eye, I notice that Tarrow wheels around, and slowly drifts away, without a word.

We stay for a long time, mostly enjoying the company of the Alberts's family.

I have the feeling that Mel is trying to communicate with me, tell me something out of the earshot of the others, but he either never musters the courage to do it, or never finds the right opportunity.

When its time to leave we say our warm good-byes to Lydia and Milo. Milo again kisses Irene's hand and she again shows her delight by giggling and feigning embarrassment like a teenager. David and I shake hands for a long moment. I comment how lovely and touching his mother's poem was and he nods his thanks. I ask him to show me the poem. He digs it out of his pocket and hands it to me. I unfold it and read the neatly typed lines again silently.

"It's wonderful," I tell him when I'm done.

"You can keep it, if you like," he says.

"Really?"

"Sure. This is a copy. I have the original in her notebook."

"Thanks. I really appreciate it."

I fold it and put it in my pocket.

"You said this was her last poem," I remark.

"Yes, the last complete poem in her book, number 88. I forget the date, but I think she wrote it two to three weeks before her final admission to the hospital."

"Very interesting," I say.

In the car, on the way home, we drive quietly. I am thinking about a perceptive and talented lady who died prematurely, and Irene's probably thinking about taking philosophy as a second career.

TWENTY ONE

Monday, March 8, London

IT'S MONDAY MORNING, AND THE DOWNPOUR AT HEATHROW AIRPORT IS approaching torrential proportions. When the British Airways Boeing 747, flight 218, touches down, visibility is close to zero. I sit with the tip of my nose brushing against the window, but I can't see anything. Not a building. Not another plane. Nothing. The plane finally stops at the gate and I wonder how on earth the pilot was able to find it.

Despite the relatively quick flight, less than six hours from Philadelphia, I am sleepy and tired. It's a relief to see my name on a board held by a short man in a gray uniform. It is the local Gother driver, who promptly grabs my suitcase and takes me to the parked car. The journey to downtown London takes more than an hour and a half, thanks to the vicious rainstorm. By the time I arrive at the registration desk of the Marriott hotel it's almost 10 a.m. and I'm exhausted. The room is quite small but I don't care. After a brief shower I lie down and fall asleep immediately. I want to be ready for the first rehearsal meeting, which is scheduled for 3 p.m.

Less than an hour later, I suddenly jump up in my bed, startled, as if somebody had just whacked me on the head with a hammer. It takes me several moments to realize that the phone is ringing. I am on my back staring at the ceiling, recovering, for a few moments before picking up the phone.

"Hi, Paul," Dara says.

I try to clear my throat, but no sound comes out.

"Paul?"

"Huh?"

"Did I wake you up?"

What a dumb question, I think, as I'm trying to clear my head.

"What do you think?" I manage to growl.

"I am so sorry . . . I was hoping we could grab a bite before the rehearsal . . . "

"Okay," I mumble and hang up.

I fall asleep again. This time I sleep peacefully and wake up on my own, but I'm still confused and disoriented. I remember something about a previous interruption but can't remember who or why. I splash cold water on my face for a long time, then I get dressed and leave my room to go straight to the lounge, where light fares are always available. Gerry Lennox and Dara are seated on the sofa near the entrance. As soon as I enter the room, they both rise to their feet. Lennox shakes my hand. Dara brings her face close to mine as if to kiss me, but thinks better of it and extends her hand to me.

"Sorry about the unscheduled wake-up call," she says, smiling. She wears a yellow, colorful blouse and long blue pants, tight as a drum. Her soft brown hair is combed into a long braid, which bounces around as she moves her head. Tired and all, it didn't take me a long time to relive my mixed emotions during our previous meeting in San Francisco.

"So it was you? I must have sounded awful."

"For a moment I thought I dialed the London zoo by mistake."

I smile.

"Any particular cage?"

"Yeah, the buffalo or rhino."

"Thanks. Would it have killed you to say the lion or tiger?"

We all laugh and sit down. I notice for the first time that she has one of those free, open and contagious laughs, which bring on cute thin laughter wrinkles at the corners of her eyes.

Lennox reaches into his jacket pocket and pulls out a long white envelope.

"Before I forget, I was asked by my management to hand you this," he says solemnly.

I take the envelope, puzzled.

"What is this?"

Lennox shrugs.

"All I know is that this is some token of our appreciation."

"Looks like a check to me," Dara ventures.

I hold it up against the light for a moment, then insert it into the inner pocket of my jacket. It all feels awkward.

"Whatever this is, thank your management," I tell Lennox.

We sit there for a moment, munching on grapes and biscuits. Just then, Larry Barnes walks in and approaches us.

Impeccably dressed as always, he's moving about like a leopard, quick and muscular. To me he seems alert and in robust health, endless stamina.

"Hello, Paul, so good to see you. Did you have a nice flight?"

"Good to see you, Larry. Very good, thanks."

Barnes addresses me, ignoring Gerry and Dara.

"Good. Good. We need you in top shape for this meeting."

Roger Lacoste appears at the entrance and Barnes turns to him.

"Hi, Roger."

"Hi, Larry. Hi, everyone."

Roger is wearing a flannel, checkered shirt and blue jeans, looking relaxed. He examines the rest of the group.

"This rehearsal is informal, right?" he asks.

"Sure, Roger. You know me, I just like to dress," Larry chuckles, and pats Roger on the back.

"When did you get here?" I ask Roger, sinking into the inevitable small talk.

"Allison and I came on Friday. She just loves to fly the Concorde and she loves London. So we spent the weekend sightseeing."

Barnes is listening with attention.

"Next time you should bring Irene, Paul. Does she know London well?"

"I'm sure she'd love to come." I don't remember ever mentioning my wife's name to Barnes.

Barnes looks at his watch.

"I think it's time. We'd better go. Our conference room is down the hall."

"I'll be right there," I say.

I go straight to my room and open the envelope I just received from Lennox. A check falls out, and a note is clipped to it.

The note reads, "Paul, welcome to the team that'll bring Neurovan to the market. This is a small bonus for your efforts." It is signed by Dr. Leonard Ramsey. The check reads, "pay to Dr. Paul Holden the amount of $25,000 only."

* * * * *

We are in the final rehearsal before the all-important CSM meeting. Dr. Ramsey sits at the top of the large desk and the rest of us are randomly spread around it. In addition to the by-now familiar Gother group—Drs. Barnes and Lennox, Joe Lansing from marketing, the animal expert Mark, and Dara—there is also a local contingency. I am next to Lacoste and observe the Brits as they march in together. Alan Osgood is the general manager of the company in London. Flabby and balding, with a strong Irish accent, he appears pale and nervous. This is hardly surprising, given what's at stake. I find out that even though the local company is called Gother UK, part of the larger Gother Inc., sales and profits stay in England, and local salaries and bonuses are determined by local performance. Neurovan has the potential of being the number one product in Britain, well before its expected approval in the USA and the rest of Europe. Professor William Lang is in his early 60s, tall and trim with gray locks of hair collapsing almost down to his shoulders. Professor George Farley looks gaunt, and with his wide-open, blue eyes he has an unmistakable air of arrogance about him. I'm not sure if it reflects his general sense of superiority or whether it is directed specifically at the American group. Farley, who is from Birmingham, is a past member of the CSM, and this is the main reason that he was invited by the Gother people. He's supposed to talk about diabetes in general and offer helpful hints about the proceedings and the best way to respond to questions. The liver expert, Dr. Mosby, turns out to be Eleanor Mosby, a woman in her 40s, a heavy set square-framed motherly type who gives me a friendly look as we're introduced to each other.

As soon as everybody is seated, the meeting starts. Ramsey gives his by now familiar speech about the importance of the event, and how this A-team was assembled, the best minds getting together for the best product, and how the rest of the week should be spent building a winning spirit and presenting to the CSM a well-oiled machine. Farley throws disapproving glances at

Ramsey, obviously dissatisfied with all the metaphors that Ramsey has mixed and scrambled. I follow Farley's antics, who, I conclude, gives the expression "looking at somebody down their nose" a new authentic demonstration.

When Ramsey is done, he turns the meeting over to Osgood.

Osgood pulls out a crumpled handkerchief and wipes his forehead.

He asks Farley to review each of the CSM members, give their background, strengths, weaknesses and how they should be dealt with.

Farley puts on his reading glasses and examines the piece of paper in his hand as if this is the secret map to the Holy Grail. He has a nasal voice and his hand is trembling slightly.

"Most of the members will be quiet and say nothing. Three people will ask all the questions. The internist is Fallon, from the University of Manchester. He is a decent chap, been around, but very tough. Always talks about safety."

"Have we talked to him?" Lansing asks. He blurted the word "talked" in a low and poignant manner, and what he means is, have we contacted him and tried to enroll him in our "incentive" program.

"I know Charles well, of course," Lang says. "I've spent many years in Manchester before moving to London. I spoke to him. He appreciates the need for a new therapy for diabetic patients, and as long as we can keep the safety profile acceptable, he should be okay."

"Perhaps we can offer him to speak for us," Lansing persists. This is a common practice for getting people to see your point of view. Have them travel the world on your behalf giving lectures. Neurovan would, no doubt, be frequently mentioned, in an appropriately favorable slanted light. All whims, lavish or not, will, of course, be fully taken care of.

"I also talked to Fallon," Osgood says, "but Fallon refused."

"Anything else we can do to whet his appetite?" Ramsey asks, looking at Joe.

Joe, who is writing something in a small black book, stops and looks up.

"What's his specialty?"

"I think rheumatology, but he's a general internist."

Joe scratches his head.

"He's editor of a textbook in internal medicine," Farley chimes in. Joe writes this down.

"Hmm. Maybe there's an interesting possibility here. Maybe we can help him publish it. Give honoraria to the authors so that they finish their chapters on time. Put them all in Majorca or Tahiti for two weeks so that they write and edit together."

Barnes leans forward.

"I like it, but isn't it too late? I mean, our meeting is in a couple of days."

Joe smiles.

"Yeah, but the committee will deliberate for weeks or months."

Barnes nods and Joe continues.

"We can ask him through some people I know. Very discrete and indirect. Gother isn't even mentioned until there's a clear deal in sight."

Joe is looking at Ramsey, asking for some signal. The nod that Ramsey gives him is barely perceived. Joe looks satisfied.

"See what you can do, Joe," Ramsey says and then turns to Farley.

"Who else do we have to worry about?"

Farley looks at the unholy list again.

"Then there's old Crawley. Stubborn as a bull. Knows his diabetes well. I spoke to him at a recent meeting. He's not convinced.

He simply refuses to buy the validity of our data."

"What does he say?" Barnes asks.

"He thinks the studies are uncontrolled and the changes that we see in the degree of pain are unpredictable and inconsistent. He wants to wait for the biopsy data."

My concerns exactly. I'm taking in this entire exchange wondering whether I'm missing something here.

I suddenly feel Dara's hand on my lap. She smiles at me and whispers, "what did I tell you? But that ain't all. Wait."

"We can't wait for that. Roger, you know this Crawley fellow, right?" Ramsey asks Lacoste.

"Sure. I already took care of everything."

We all wait for the details.

"Lansing told me that Crawley's daughter wanted to study in the US. I have arranged for her to get into Washington University. She's starting in the fall. Very simple."

"Well done," says Ramsey.

"In that case, I think he'll be okay," Lansing says.

"Who's the third bloke?" Osgood asks Farley.

"In many ways Raymond Henry is the most interesting. And potentially dangerous. He's a young pharmacologist from Leeds, an ambitious idealist. These are the worst kind. I can deal with a timid idealist or an ambitious pragmatist, but this is too much."

General laughter.

"He wants to save the world and he wants to be at the center of things. He's always extremely well prepared and asks a myriad of questions."

"I heard of him. He can't be educated with facts," Lansing says.

"So, what do we do?" Osgood asks. "He's good looking and single. They say that he's the second most eligible bachelor in England."

I'm not sure who's the first, but I'm not going to ask. Farley folds the paper and removes his glasses.

"We may get minor questions from just about anybody, but these are the three major players."

"Thanks, Professor Farley," Osgood says, "now let's go through the actual presentations."

Osgood gives an introduction about the importance of the disease and the product. Farley reviews the problems of diabetic neuropathy and the relentless pain and devastation that diabetic neuropathy can cause, ending his presentation by announcing, "here we have the first real hope for our patients. It may not be a cure-all medication, but many patients will benefit from its introduction to the British market."

Lang presents next. He talks about his twenty-three patients who took Neurovan, and not a single one of them had any safety problems. This is somewhat surprising, I think, but it's entirely possible that some centers have better luck than others with the liver problem. It is a random event, after all.

Roger Lacoste is next, and his presentation is just as brilliant as I remember it from Dallas. He comes across as very confident and his arguments and graphs are slick and overpowering. Ramsey and Barnes watch him with awe, and when he is finished they exchange glances, smiling broadly.

Lennox is next and his topic is, as usual, the safety of Neurovan. He quotes the small percentage of patients with abnormal liver functions, but doesn't mention the jaundice cases, let alone Mrs. Alberts's death.

I listen, but decide not to say anything. This is despite the fact that Lennox is actually reporting even less than he did in Dallas. I remember all the issues and concerns very well. Mrs. Alberts. The other possible patients. Dara's story. Tarrow and the consent form, and the missing lab values. Lydia and David. But I also remember my plan. Everything has its time and place. And this is neither the right time nor the place. If I want to stay on the project long enough to kill it completely, I have to show some discipline. But there's also a small part of me that isn't entirely sure about the evidence against the drug. Perhaps the Gother people are right after all. What if Dara and Lennox have some ulterior motive, some hidden agenda? Maybe I'm still a little drained from the jet lag and my feisty mood is taking a back seat.

"I'm surprised that you've not seen any jaundice cases to date," Dr. Mosby asks and I perk up, surprised. Is it possible that she wasn't informed, or is it a case of inadequate indoctrination?

I'm waiting for somebody to say something. Lennox, who is still standing in front of the group after his presentation, is examining his nails with great care and Dara looks at Barnes.

Barnes clears his throat.

"It's not surprising, if you consider the very careful screening and the frequent blood tests we perform during the study."

I am stunned at the blatant lie, but relieved that someone else delivered it. My relief is premature, though, because the next word I hear is my name.

"Dr. Holden," Dr. Mosby asks, "don't you think it's odd to have eight percent of patients develop liver function problems and nobody progressing to jaundice?"

She has a sweet voice that exudes sincerity.

All eyes are on me. I lean back to compose myself, to rapidly sort out my options. As I shift in my chair I can feel the envelope that Lennox gave me brush against my heaving chest. It's premature to break ranks with them, I keep telling myself. I'm about to wimp out, maybe, but my inner voice tells me that I'll get my moment. I hope my inner voice knows what it's doing. I decide to give them a dose of double-talk.

"It's surprising, yes, I agree. But different drugs may have different effects. It may depend on the mechanism of liver damage, of which we know very little. It is possible, but I have no way of predicting it, that as more patients are exposed to Neurovan once it's on the market, jaundice and death may rarely occur."

Barnes and Ramsey can't hide their satisfaction and they break into wide smiles. Lennox looks perplexed and Dara peers at me with disbelief. I look away.

Mosby writes down something and nods, and the meeting continues without any major discussions or controversies. Osgood rehearses what would be his final summary to the CSM:

"Based on these data, presented to you by some of the foremost British and American experts, ladies and gentlemen, we have concluded that Neurovan is a safe and effective therapy for the devastating complication of diabetic neuropathy. Our evidence is compelling, and we hope that you would grant us a license to market Neurovan in the United Kingdom."

When he finishes, Ramsey gets to his feet and applauds him, and after a few seconds the others join him. Lansing and Barnes are beaming and back slapping each other as congratulatory remarks fill the room.

Lacoste approaches me and extends his hand.

"Welcome to the team," he says with a smirk.

TWENTY TWO

An hour later, I'm in my hotel room, sitting on my couch, trying to analyze the events of the afternoon. By the time I'm about to finish my third Heineken, I feel in full control again.

A gentle tap on the door.

"Yes?"

"Can we talk to you?" Gerry Lennox asks.

"Sure. Come in."

The door opens and Dara and Gerry step into the room. Dara looks at me. I am slumped on the couch firmly gripping my bottle. I must look rumpled, with my collar open and my tie flying crookedly in the air, because Dara asks, "Are you okay?"

"Never been better. Please sit down."

The room's size is such that there's little comfort for three adults trying to relax and hold a normal conversation. Dara decides to sit down on the bed and Lennox sits on the other chair. They both look at me as if I was their only son, caught shoplifting at Sears, and they need to establish how could such a thing happen to their progeny.

"You acted strange," Dara says.

"You made so much fuss about these cases in Dallas, and how we should come clean and all that and now . . . " Lennox is searching for the right word.

"And now I chickened out. And you wanted to know where I really stood. Right?"

They both nod.

"Tell me, how come the Brits know nothing about the cases?" I ask.

"They do," Lennox says, "That is, everybody except the woman, Mosby. She is new to this. She was told to be ready to talk about drugs and the liver, in general."

"Really? And why didn't they speak up?"

"I assume that Gother has a hold of them in the same way they seem to have a hold of . . . " Lennox hesitates.

I chuckle.

"Same way they have a hold of me? No. Don't worry. I haven't changed my mind on your drug."

I hold the bottle to my mouth and lean back so that not a single drop is wasted.

"But let's be practical," I continue. "Had I said something, there would have been arguments. What to say, what not to say, how to say it. This way we can use the information at the most damaging time for Gother. We'll choose the time and place for dropping the bomb. This wasn't it."

Lennox scratches his head.

"So, will you bring it up at the actual hearing with the CSM on Wednesday?"

"That's also premature. I'll be kicked out and that'll be the end of my contribution."

Dara's face begins to brighten, and she smiles. Her perfect white teeth glisten inside her red full lips.

"Actually, the hearing is perfect," she says. "Imagine, you

standing up and declaring that there were three cases of jaundice that the company failed to disclose. Gother will be red in the face, Barnes and Ramsey will be fired for hiring you and then failing to muzzle you, and the drug will never see the light of day in Britain."

There's a long pause, as we're chewing over that idea.

"I'll get fired before Barnes or Ramsey," Lennox notes. "Remember, I'm the one who shows data without the liver cases."

"It would have been nice if you had another job lined up," I remark.

"I know," Lennox shrugs.

"I need to figure out a few things," I say. "First, I need to secure everybody's confidence at Gother. I also need more evidence, because so far everything Gother did was legal. We'll have to get them in the US. Nobody cares about lying to some foreign agency."

"Except for patients who will become sick taking the drug," Lennox says.

Lennox is pensive for a few moments, digesting what we've said.

"Only place where they're vulnerable is with the FDA. Notification. Not following regulations. Misleading consent forms," I think aloud.

"And we need to show that Barnes, Ramsey and the others prevented me from notifying the FDA. Otherwise, I am in the same boat as them," Lennox says.

He stands up and shakes his head.

"It's not easy, but we'll find a way," he says.

"Coming?" he turns to Dara. I notice that she isn't her bubbly self since she came in.

Dara slides out of the chair and stretches.

"Let's have dinner together," she says and looks at me.

"Okay."

"I have some work to do," Lennox says, "you kids can do without me."

"Work? Now?" I ask.

"I need to check my mail messages at the office. I monitor several clinical trials with thousands of patients taking our drug."

"You've got your laptop with you?"

"Always. Actually, tonight I may use the computer in the business center downstairs. They have dedicated phone lines, so everything is easier."

"Okay. Have fun. We'll see you tomorrow."

I look at Dara. The Heineken buzz is exhilarating

"Let's meet in the lobby at eight," I say and she nods.

Lennox waves to me and he and Dara leave the room.

I get up and stretch my legs. The conversation perked me up and my fatigue has all but disappeared. I flip on the remote on the TV when the phone rings. I pick up the receiver.

"Are you in a mood for a quiet room service affair?" Dara says.

I hesitate.

"I wish you hadn't used the word affair. Are you sure it's a good idea?"

"Positive," she says in her most velvety voice, "get me a steak, medium done and a bottle of Chateau Gabriel 1982 and I'll be there at eight."

"See ya later," I say and hang up.

* * * * *

I decide to go downstairs to clear my head. In the lobby there is the usual flurry of activity and I walk through it to the exit door and onto the street. It's still drizzling but I just raise my collar and go for a short walk. I make it up to Oxford street, a couple of blocks away, but then the rain intensifies and I have no choice but to dash back to the hotel.

I return through the lobby and start walking up the stairs. As I go past the first floor, from the corner of my eye I notice Larry Barnes. He's standing with his side to me, and his reading glasses are hanging on top of his nose as he's obviously reading something. I don't know why, but I have a sudden urge to find out what he's reading. I slip behind the column at a poorly lit area of the landing on top of the stairway and watch him. He's standing at the door of the business center, the light from within the center shining on him, and I have to assume that he chooses to read the paper right there because that's where it comes from. It could be a letter, a computer printout or more likely a fax.

It seems that Barnes takes forever to read what is only a single page.

Finally, he's done. He looks around and then enters the business center. I stay put for a few moments behind the column, waiting. After a short moment Barnes appears at the door and starts walking in my direction. In a quick motion I fall down on my belly and try to hide between the column and the other side of the corridor. I can hear his footsteps now and I bury my head between my arms and lie flat on the carpet. All I can think of is, what on earth will I tell him if he notices me? When he's about three feet away I suddenly hear a woman's voice calling: "Dr. Barnes, Dr. Barnes." He stops in his tracks, the tips of his shoes less than two feet away from my outstretched arm, and turns around. I raise my head. There's a woman coming out of the business center and running towards him in small steps.

"Here, you left your glasses behind, Dr. Barnes."

Barnes starts walking back in her direction and that's when I leap out of my hiding place and in two mammoth steps I get onto the stairway and run upstairs. At the top of the second floor, catching my breath, I look downstairs just in time to see Barnes saunter downstairs and disappear.

I wait a few long moments before returning to the business center. The first room is empty, but in the inner office I see a shadow behind a desk. I get closer. It's the woman who brought Barnes his glasses. She raises her head and looks at me, and I wonder if she saw my earlier jump.

"Can I help you?" she asks. She has dark skin and strong accent and I figure she's either Indian or Pakistani.

I give her my sweetest smile.

"Were you here when my colleague was down here, a few minutes ago . . . Dr. Barnes?"

"Yes," she says without expression.

My smile gets even wider.

"Thank God. Then you know about the fax he received . . . "

"What about it?"

She's suspicious, but my smile must be confusing her.

"Well, I'm his colleague and he sent me down to get him another copy of the fax he received earlier . . . "

She seems surprised.

"That's very strange."

I can feel my gums tighten, because of the strained smile.

"Why is that?"

"Because he asked me to shred it immediately."

I cover my face in feigned disbelief.

"Oh, my god. That's a terrible mistake. I hope you didn't do it."

She hesitates.

"Well, actually, I have."

I can't tell whether she's telling the truth, or lying to appear efficient.

"Are you sure?"

Another hesitation.

"Yes."

I don't know what's pushing me now.

"Please, could you check for me?"

She stands up.

"Okay. . . what is your name?"

"My name?"

"Yes, we keep records of all fax deliveries."

"Ramsey."

She glances at me, way too long for my nerves, and goes into another room.

I look around the office. There are several computers in the adjoining rooms, which otherwise seem deserted. I suddenly remember that Gerry Lennox said he might be working down here. We're on the same team, I hope, yet I wouldn't want him to spot me there right now. I poke my head in the various surrounding offices, but he's not there.

The woman returns from the other direction just as I wander back. She has a piece of paper in her hand.

"I found a copy of a fax to Dr. Barnes which arrived at 17:45 today. This may be what you're looking for."

I make a face like that must be it, and extend my hand to take it.

"Just a minute. What did you say your name was?"

"Ramsey."

She goes to a thick book in the corner of the office and starts thumbing through its pages until she finds what she's looking for.

"First name?"

"Leonard."

"Dr. Leonard Ramsey?"

"Yes, that's right."

She looks at me, then at the page, then at me again. Finally, she slams the book shut.

"Did you say you wanted your fax or the one given to Dr. Barnes?"

"Sorry?"

"There's a also a fax here in your name. It arrived the same time as the one for Dr. Barnes."

"I'll take them both, in case they're different."

She reaches to another bin in the corner and hands me a piece of paper. Then she also gives me what was the original fax. I thank her and am ready to leave.

"Make sure to call the operator, so that they remove the light from your message button on the phone."

"Thanks. You've been very helpful."

I leave the business center, papers tucked in my jacket.

I am no more than twenty steps out of the center, ready to walk upstairs, when I see Ramsey coming down the stairs opposite me. He sees me and smiles.

"Len," I say, and extend my hand to him. "I just want to congratulate you on a brilliant strategy. What a great meeting."

He continues to smile, but he's a little surprised and puzzled by my effusive outburst.

"Thank you. I was very pleased."

"Come, can I invite you to a drink? I'm in a mood to celebrate."

He hesitates.

"I'd love to. I just need to pick up something at the business center."

I put my arms around him.

"I'm sure it can wait. Come, humor me. Let's drink first, then you work, okay?"

He still hesitates. I need to change my tactics.

"I also wanted to run a couple of ideas by you, about Neurovan."

He looks at me, like why didn't you say so in the first place, I'm always open to business.

We go downstairs to the bar. It is a small bar with heavy burgundy furniture and red drapes, filled with dense smoke. We order two Johnny Walkers and sit on a couch in the corner. We chitchat for some time, he tells me how he loves to travel on company business. First class food, service, planes and hotels. He also likes to play golf, and he would invariably include sufficient time in his schedule to hit the course for an 18-hole game. We drink and laugh. I give him a few general ideas about how to better monitor the liver tests, he seems satisfied and almost an hour later he finally looks at his watch and departs.

I hurry upstairs to my room, and pull out the two faxes from my pocket. The fax to Ramsey is about some anti-arthritis drug Gother is working on, but the fax to Barnes proves to be quite interesting. With a prominent Gother logo in the corner, a dove carrying an olive branch covered with capsules and tablets, the note read: "Patient four in study 95-11, Vienna, Austria is getting worse and the natives are getting restless. Dr. Kunz believes that this is all related to our drug and he threatens to withdraw his support. What to do next?" I couldn't decipher the signature, but the name probably would have meant very little to me anyway.

I sit down and use the paper as a fan, pondering the significance of this new information. It all looks obvious and straightforward, but I try to figure out what Gother's reaction will be to this one. On the first patient, my patient, they try to delay and obfuscate. Information on the second patient, the woman in Miami, is only beginning to emerge. What will they come up with to explain away the third patient?

TWENTY THREE

It's about seven forty-five and soon Dara will be joining me. I'm sitting on the couch in my room watching TV, thinking about her while channel surfing absent-mindedly. Dealing with Gother on the Neurovan issue is a daunting challenge. Right now, Dara's imminent arrival is another one.

This is all wrong, and I know it. I shouldn't be alone with her, because stronger characters have succumbed to the temptations of the flesh. Even Oscar Wilde claimed that the best way to fight temptation is to yield to it. And I know down inside that if pushed enough, there's no way I could resist her advances. I am too flattered to just toss her away. The combination of her soft, long hair, innocent eyes, tall yet full figure is too much for any man. Add to that the stress of the meetings, the fatigue from the flight and jet-lag and the remoteness of my family. It's just too much.

I call room service and order dinner for eight thirty. Maybe by the time we finish we'll be too tired. Maybe she won't be in the mood. Maybe she'll have a headache. I feel confused and guilty. In advance.

I'm awakened from my daydreaming by the sound of the

phone. I pick it up, startled.

"Hi, honey. How are you?" Irene. Why is she calling now?

"I'm fine. I'm glad you caught me. I was just about to leave for dinner."

"How was the flight?"

"Just fine. First class is first class."

"And the rehearsal?"

"Went well. The Brits are top notch. Team is in top form."

A pause.

"You sound funny, Paul. What is all this talk about team? What do they think about the jaundiced patients?"

I look at my watch nervously. It's past eight and Dara is going to arrive any moment now. I have to be curt. And no way am I going to mention the fax. Wait a minute, Dara's late. Maybe she changed her mind about coming?

"Gother decided not to discuss it this time. It all happened after the submission of the written materials. Listen, honey, I really have to run now. People are waiting for me downstairs."

There's a tapping sound on the door.

"Paul Michael Holden, you didn't sell your soul to the devil, did you?"

"Of course not." I suddenly think about the large check I received, but realize it's the wrong time to mention it.

"Dada, dada," I hear Danny yelling.

"Hi, Danny. I love you."

There is a second knock, a little louder this time.

"Bye, honey. I love you."

Another pause.

"Paul, are you okay?"

She's sensing something, I don't know what or how.

"Irene, I'm fine. I just have to leave right away, people are waiting for me downstairs, that's all."

"Okay, okay. I love you too, Paul."

I hang up, dash to the door and open it. Dara is leaning on the door frame, long leg on top of long leg, head tilted, smiling. Her brown hair is long and curly, and a lock is covering her eye. Long eyelashes, white teeth, full lips.

"Hi. I thought you forgot about me," she blurts.

"I was on the phone. My wife. She called."

Stepping into the room, she runs her fingers down my cheek, touching me ever so lightly, and it makes me shiver.

"Marital love and fidelity. How sweet and admirable."

She is toying with me. She knows her powers and she is going to give me the test of my life.

"I ordered dinner. Should be here shortly."

"Good." She sits on the bed, tapping lightly on it as she does.

"Nice and soft. I like it, but they say it's not good for your back. I like it much harder."

She says this with her soft, bedroom hoarse whisper and folds her legs. I take a big gulp of air as her dress reveals white round flesh at the top. She's wearing a white dress, with the diagonal cuts of her open top emphasizing her ample bosom. I sit on the couch, mind racing, hoping for some supreme guidance.

"You know, Dara, I just realized that I hardly know you. Tell me something interesting about yourself."

I need to relax. I'm in unfamiliar territory. She gives me an oblique look.

"Oh, what's there to tell. I grew up in California, near LA. My father was in the service and we lived a few years in Germany. I always wanted to be a model. I actually did a few commercials while in high-school, but then my parents convinced me to get an education, so I went to Berkeley and studied biology and science. After school I did some more modeling, but I basically wanted some security and order in my life so I took this job with Gother.

Once in a while I get asked to model. I do a couple of jobs, but always come back."

"So, who'd you rather hang out with, the modeling folk or the industry characters?"

"Hmm . . . would you rather be stranded on a tiny island with poisonous snakes or a pride of leopards?"

"That bad?"

"The superficial vanity of the models is only matched by the endless greed of the executives."

"You must have received your share of proposals from both types?"

"That's what I like about you, Paul. You're so perceptive," she says, smiling. "Yes, I have, but there's nobody I like. I'm still looking."

"What are you looking for?" I say, and immediately regret it.

She gets up and turns on the radio near my bed. She dials for a moment and then stops. Soft elevator music flows into the room. She returns and sits down.

"What am I looking for? Somebody like you. Stable, smart, big, strong. It's a shame that all the right people are married."

"I understand you were married, too."

She raises her eyebrows.

"Who told you?"

"I'm not sure. I must have heard it somewhere."

She shrugs.

"It's just that very few people know about it. I don't particularly enjoy talking about it."

I can tell that her wheels are turning, maybe she's trying to figure out who dared tell me and what exactly I know. There's a shadow on her face now, as if her mood has suddenly soured, but as quickly as the cloud appears it disappears and she's smiling again. I remember Barnes telling me about a fight she had with her husband, the loaded gun incident. My mind wanders and I try to picture her standing over me, legs apart in a tight leather skirt, a pistol in her hand, ordering me around.

I'm startled back to reality by a loud knock at the door. A short dark skinny man brings us dinner. He pushes a cloth-covered cart into the room, all set up with elegant china and silverware for two people. The food is covered with large, round metal lids, and two bottles of red wine stand prominently in the center, like lighthouse towers watching over the food. I sign the bill and give the waiter an extra ten pounds as a tip. The man thanks me profusely and leaves the room, the door closing slowly behind him.

"This is wonderful, Paul," she says and gets up. The cart is placed and arranged in a perfect way for us both to sit on the bed and eat from there. I open one of the bottles and pour us each a glassful.

Dara lifts her glass, and I do the same.

"To a great evening," she says and winks at me.

I don't know what to say, I just mumble something to the same effect.

"You seem antsy tonight. Is anything wrong?" she asks.

"Well, I am a married man."

I put the white napkin on my lap, and she does the same.

"You didn't say happily married man."

"I am happily married."

"Nothing wrong with that."

Her face is only inches away from mine.

"How long have you been married?"

"Almost five years."

I arrange the food on my plate, ready to go to work with my fork.

"Have you ever had an affair?"

"No."

She makes a face like, yeah, right.

"Are you saying that an attractive man like you has never been alone with a woman in a hotel room?"

"Only once."

"Really? What happened?"

"You should know. You were there. In San Francisco."

"But, look at you. You . . . were an athlete, right? What, basketball, baseball, football?"

I'm taking large, quick bites from the steak. Dara is piercing the lettuce with her fork, but she doesn't eat it.

"Yes."

"You had your thrills, I bet."

"But it all ended when I got married."

"What a pity," she shrugs, and puts her hand on my thigh. "There's always the first time, you know."

"That's what they say." Her hand is warm and I don't push it away.

A pause.

"Anyway, the wine is terrific," I say.

She smiles and lifts her hand so that she can use it to feed herself. She starts eating slowly, taking very small bites. After every bite she puts down her fork and takes a sip from her glass of wine.

"Do you have any fantasies?" she asks.

"What do you mean?"

"You know, sexual."

If she keeps it up, so help me, soon I won't be responsible for my actions any more.

"Dara, I told you . . . "

"Relax, Paul, we're just two friends talking here."

I'm tense as a drum, and I take a huge swig from my glass of wine.

She continues.

"I'll tell you mine. I have two fantasies. The second one is in the ocean, in the water, just when the sun is about to set."

We're almost done with the first bottle, and I'm trying to decide whether to open the second one. Damned if I'm going to ask her about her number one fantasy. Now she's staring at me from up close, eyes wide open, the glass lightly touching her lower lip. Her soft smooth skin stretched underneath her high cheekbones is at a finger's length from my lips. I'm getting drowsy from the alcohol, or am I dizzy from the scintillating aroma radiating from her face? I know that I shouldn't do anything I might regret later but I want her so badly that it's painful.

"D'you know how long it's been since I've had a good man?"

"You mean . . . "

"I mean inside me. D'you know how long?"

I figure this is a rhetorical question, with no guesses invited.

"More than a year."

This is worse than I thought.

"Well, you should go out more often . . ." I joke.

I watch her as she puts down her glass and moves her face even closer. Next, our lips touch and she pushes me back on the bed. Soon, she is all over me, holding my body tightly with her thighs, pinning me down to the bed. For a few moments I'm participating, trying to sway and bend with her rhythm, both of us making the sounds of passion as our mouths and tongues are interlocked. But suddenly, I realize with unflinching certainty that I just can't go along. I sit up, and gently, but with great force, I move Dara away from me, lifting her slightly in the air before resting her on the bed. Panting, Dara watches me with disbelief.

"What's going on, Paul?"

"Dara, I just can't do it. I'm very sorry."

She looks at me for a long moment. I don't think I've ever seen a more perfect face or body, in magazine or real life.

"I guess you don't find me attractive?"

"Stop it. You know that's not true."

She gets up, straightening her crumpled dress.

"No. I'm sorry." She pauses, searching for the right words. "You're really something special, Paul."

I stand up. Towering over her, I put my arms around her shoulder.

"You're special too, Dara."

By now we have recovered our senses. The moment of passion came and went, at least for me, and we have our business-like faces on. But there's a visible shadow on her face, and her lips are pursed, and I don't know if she's fighting tears or anger.

"I'd better go," she says and moves away.

"You don't have to. I'm not sleepy at all." I don't know why I say that, maybe to soften the humiliation, which I realize she must feel.

"Neither am I. Still, I must go now."

She moves slowly to the door and turns her face to me.

"Thanks for dinner, Paul. The wine was stupendous."

And then she walks out.

TWENTY FOUR

I DIDN'T WANT IT TO END LIKE THIS. MAYBE I AM NOT READY FOR THE physical stuff, but we still have some other important things in common, things that we'll need to settle sooner or later. I prefer sooner.

I turn on the television and watch the tail end of the news, then some British sitcom, which I don't find particularly funny, then some old movie. I'm restless and wide awake.

It is almost eleven when I decide to call Dara in her room.

"Hi, are you asleep?" I ask.

"No. Watching some stupid old movie."

"I'm sorry."

"Not as much as I am."

"Are you ready to do some business now?"

"At this hour?"

"Yeah. I'd like to try and get into Gother's computer and work on some of the missing links. Besides, it's only after 2 p.m. in San Francisco," I remind her.

"Did you want to use the business center downstairs?"

"Yeah."

We're totally business-like now.

"I'm sure it's closed."

I straighten my shirt, and tuck it into my pants.

"If you don't want to go with me, it's okay. Just give me your new password, and I'll handle it myself."

"I'll come," she says, but there's very little enthusiasm in her voice.

"Good. Let's get the key from the front desk."

"Okay."

"Meet me there."

"Okay."

* * * * *

There are two clerks at the front desk on duty that night, and both jump to their feet when Dara appears. I stay near the stairway, in a dark spot, and watch her in action.

"How can we help you?" asks the taller of the two, as he proceeds to give Dara his most charming smile. Both clerks are in their twenties, and look like students.

"I'd like to use the business center," she says.

They exchange glances. That was hardly what they expected.

"Now?"

"Yes."

"I . . . we . . . don't have the keys here. The manager . . . "

A big white-toothed smile. She draws closer to them.

"Find the keys. Check with house keeping. Whatever. Find it."

They nod and then disappear through the back door. Dara starts pacing in the lobby, never looking in my direction.

After a few moments they return, grinning. The taller one holds a key in his hands and waves it pendulum-like above the counter as Dara approaches.

"It wasn't easy. I had to kill the guard to get it," he says, as Dara approaches the counter.

"Really?" she smiles.

"Yes, absolutely." His complexion is dark, with bushy hair and five o'clock shadow, but his features are chiseled, and he has the looks of a sly entrepreneur who's seen the rich and famous and would like one day to join their ranks. Now I watch him stretch his neck towards Dara, pointing to his cheek, but she just pokes his cheek with the key and saunters away. I join her and as we walk away, I can hear the tall guy blurt a loud "bugger" yelp.

We walk upstairs to the second floor. The business center is dark when we unlock the door and enter. l turn on the light and look around to scan the familiar surroundings. I point to one of the inner rooms were we have a better chance of working undisturbed. I turn off the light in the main office, then turn it on in the inner office, and close the door behind us. To a casual guest wandering by, the center would seem dark and empty.

I sit at the desk and turn on the computer. It's an IBM clone, and is driven by the usual and familiar Windows setup. After a few seconds, the screen displays a menu consisting of several icons. I click twice on the fax/modem icon and another menu appears, offering space for typing in the desired phone number to be reached.

Dara nudges me to move as she pulls up a chair in front of the screen and sits down. She types in the Gother number, and after a long pause, a menu appears asking for a password. She types it in quickly, but I still manage to decipher it as "CCIIFPA." I make a mental note by repeating it a few times in my head.

A moment later we are greeted by a cheerful logo— a white dove flapping its wings, and in its mouth is what looks like an olive branch with all the Gother products inscribed on its leaves. After flapping and flying, the dove disappears and another menu appears, a list of options. We study the categories carefully. 1. Clinical trials. 2. Meetings reports. 3. Study reports. 4. Manuscripts. 5. Correspondence. 6. Committees. 7. Licensing. 8. Miscellaneous. Dara gives me an explanation as to what our real options are.

"My password only gets me into 'clinical trials', 'study reports' and 'manuscripts.'" You need to be at a director level or higher to get into the others. I understand that some part of the "correspondence" file is available only for vice-presidents and above."

"Hmm . . . interesting."

Dara clicks on "clinical trials" and another list appears consisting of all the names of the drugs that Gother is developing. A few more clicks, and we find ourselves inside the Neurovan file, study no. 95-18.

"Okay. What now?" Dara asks.

"Why don't we look for the lab data on the liver tests of Mrs. Alberts," I suggest.

"Do you remember the date?"

"January 27."

"Any particular test?"

"Why don't we look at the transaminase levels." This is the most common and most important test that describes the damage, if any, to the liver, by any disease process.

"Why don't we," Dara says and clicks away. She knows that Tarrow's site is number 11, and I remember from the code breaking ceremony in Tarrow's office that Mrs. Alberts was patient number 004. A few more clicks, and on the screen appears the entire laboratory profile for patient number 004 blood tests.

It's in the form of a table, which includes dates and blood levels of transaminase for every particular date. According to the table, Mrs. Alberts had a normal liver profile on August 11, three weeks before she started taking Neurovan. It was normal also on September 30, October 27, November 24 and December 22. I press impatiently the "page down" key, eagerly anticipating the information on the January 27 lab test. After a few more seconds the results appear on the screen. Transaminases are normal. We search for some other liver tests but come up with the same results. Every liver test is here, and it is perfectly normal. Just like Tarrow told me.

"Damn," I say.

"I thought you couldn't find these results in Mrs. Alberts's chart, you know, that Tarrow gave you."

"That's correct."

There is a sudden shuffling sound from the direction of the door, and Dara looks at me. I put my finger to my lips, signaling for her to keep quiet. I turn the light off, and slowly open the door of our office. The entrance room is still dark, and through its glass door, the corridor outside also appears dark, and I can't see anything out there. Slowly, I go down on my knees and crawl toward the entrance. There is some motion outside the room, and I hear footsteps moving away from the door. I jump to my feet and swing the door open in a swift motion. As I do, I can hear somebody running and as I peek into the corridor I see a dark shadow disappear around the corner and to the staircase. I dash out into the corridor, but when I get to the corner the person has vanished without a trace.

I look around for a few seconds and return to the business center, where Dara is sitting in the dark room, only the green fluorescence from the monitor illuminating her silent shadow.

Of course. That green light, as weak as it is, was sufficient to alert the intruder when I opened the door. I come in and turn on the light and quickly shut the door. Dara jumps to her feet.

"What was it?" she asks.

"Somebody was standing outside the door, but he ran away when I came out," I say.

"Did you see him?"

"It was too dark."

"Who could it be?"

I shrug.

"Probably one of the guys from downstairs. He came after you for a tip." I wink as I say it, but Dara just turns her back to me.

"Seriously, Paul."

"Seriously, I don't have a clue."

"I don't like it."

Her face turns somber for a moment, and then she relaxes.

"It's probably nothing," she says.

"What do we do now? Do you want to continue?"

"Okay."

The tension lessens, and once again we study the screen with the table of the lab data still on display.

"So, d'you think that everything is okay with that lab entry?" She asks.

I hesitate.

"I guess so . . . wait a minute. Is there a way to tell when the information was entered into the computer?"

Dara moves the display up and down a few times.

"Here it is. The date was . . . February 18."

"That's interesting . . . let me see . . . February 18 . . . Mrs. Alberts got sick on the 17th, that is a day earlier, so the 18th . . . that was the day that Lydia and I visited Dr. Tarrow. You and Gerry came to Philly on the 19th, right?"

"Yeah. Seems like ages ago."

I am trying to focus on the screen.

"Can you find the previous date that information was entered from Tarrow's site?" I ask.

"No problem. Let me see . . . hold on . . . ah, here it is. Tarrow's site entered data pretty regularly, about every two months. September 22, November 24, January 31 . . ."

Dara stops in mid-sentence and throws a bewildered glance in my direction.

"Do you think what I think?" I ask.

"They were not supposed to enter the data until late in March, so why suddenly change the routine and enter new information only three weeks after the previous entry?" Dara closes her eyes and leans back in her chair, folding her arms behind her neck.

"Of course, maybe they just decided to enter the data when they found out that Mrs. Alberts was sick. You know, keep everything up to date, realizing that people might be looking for information . . ."

I am thinking aloud, as Dara goes back and forth on several of the data tables.

"Yeah. Makes sense. But . . . look here. On January 31, they entered all the results they had at the time, except for those liver tests. Why?"

"Very strange," I agree, "especially considering that the results were perfectly normal and unremarkable."

l look at the screen pensively.

"Okay. Now let me ask you something else. What's going on with the Austrian patient?"

I see no reason to mention the fax I found.

"What do you mean?"

"Well, you told me about some rumor of an Austrian patient, but then you said you couldn't find a single document to confirm his illness. Even Lennox refused to deny or confirm it. What's going on?"

"All I know is that our site monitor in Vienna, Brigitte, called and told Lennox about the case. She promised to send in all the information, you know, on the patient, lab data, and so on, but then the Philly . . . your case, came up, I traveled, off project, on project, you know the rest, so I never saw anything in writing about it."

"Can we check it out on the computer?"

"I don't think so. This is normally on the European database. It's all handled by our European research unit in Copenhagen."

"So the European study also has a different number?"

"Absolutely. I believe it's 95-11, but I'm not sure. In any case, I don't have the first clue about accessing the database in Copenhagen. It's usually done by our data people in Berkeley only when the study is over and it's time to analyze and report the results."

This is getting too complex, the tracing of a multi-national clinical study.

"Can you at least find out what the name of the investigator is in Vienna, or the name of the hospital. Something."

Dara is giving me a long look. I'm not sure myself why I think I need it, but one never knows.

"I can try," she says.

She clicks, screens come and go and finally she says,

"Here, I found it. This is the list of investigators for study 95-11. Do you want a print-out?"

"Sure."

I flick on the printer, and moments later I hold the list in my hand. With my pen I circle the name of Professor Helmut Kunz, University of Vienna. Next to the name there's a phone number, and I circle it twice, and then put the list in my pocket.

Dara yawns, quickly covering her mouth.

"This is not the way I thought we were gonna spend this evening, you know."

I put my arm around her, and she rests her pretty and tired head on my shoulder.

"We'll be fine," I try to console her, "nothing wrong with being friends, is there?"

"I suppose," she says without much conviction. I don't believe in it either. I don't think that true friendship is possible between two hormonally charged individuals like us. For now I am still comfortable with my decision, but who knows what will eventually happen if we keep bumping into each other.

I've just about had enough of this computer cat-and-mouse game and I'm ready to call it a day. There's just one more thing that whirls in my mind.

"Can we take another look at the earlier menu?" I ask and Dara sighs but obliges.

"Let's try this 'correspondence' file for a second."

Click.

A list of more than a dozen categories appears.

"Which one is only for the big honchos?" I ask.

Dara looks at me from the corner of her eye.

"Why?"

"Let's just say that I'm curious."

"I think it's the one called 'Corres. b.'"

"Let's try it."

"You're nuts," she says.

She double clicks the mouse on the "corres. b." line. A loud buzzing sound emanates from the computer, and we both jump back.

"Please enter your password," the message reads.

"Try yours," I suggest.

"It won't work," she says.

"Try it."

Dara types in her password, and another message, in bright green colors, appears.

"Please enter password number one hundred and six."

"What the hell is that?" Dara asks.

I scratch my chin.

"There must be some sort of password list that only the chosen few get," I guess.

"Yeah, I think I heard something about it," Dara says.

I yawn and look at my watch. It is almost two a.m.

"Boy, wouldn't it be fun if we could somehow land on this treasure island," I say.

"Why?"

"Don't you think that there's some pretty juicy stuff out there?"

Dara seems to perk up for a moment. I get up.

"Well, just find the right password and we'll know," I tell her.

Dara clicks on the mouse a few times, exits the communication program and switches off the computer.

"Yeah, wouldn't it be something," she says.

We turn off the lights, close the doors and walk downstairs to return the key. The registration desk is unmanned and we leave the key on the counter.

Upstairs, in front of my room, I say goodnight and insert the key into the door.

"No good night kiss?" Dara asks.

Before I can answer, she wraps her arms around me and plants a wet, open-mouth kiss on my mouth. I'm too tired to resist or maybe I just enjoy it, but we kiss for a long time. When she tries to inch her way with me into the room, I push Dara away, gently but firmly, and say,

"Dara. You're the best, but . . . it's time to say goodnight."

She half-smiles, and I can tell she smells victory, and well she should, because she came very close.

"Good night, Paul. And remember, I'm a sore loser. I'll get you one of these days, one way or the other."

"Sweet dreams, Dara." I smile.

TWENTY FIVE

Tuesday, March 9, London

THE NEXT DAY I SLEEP VERY LATE. WHEN I WAKE UP, AS SOON AS I
finish rubbing my eyes, I remember last night and feel a sudden
jolt. After washing my face, I stand in front of the mirror for a long
time in a disoriented daze. I'm not happy with what I did but feel
some silly pride for what I almost did. Luckily, I stopped in time,
and apparently nothing irreparable had occurred. My mind turns
to the puzzling lab data from January 27, the mysterious correspondence file and the unknown intruder outside the business
center. Finally, I decide that I need a break from these unsettling
and troubling thoughts and that I should just get on with my visit
to London.

Today I'm on my own because there's no rehearsal planned.
There's one short meeting scheduled for the evening, a "team
building" event. This is perfect, because I'm in no mood to talk to
the Gother people right now. I'm really in no mood to talk to anyone, but as soon as I walk out the hotel door I have the misfortune
of running into Roger Lacoste who suggests that we spend the
morning together, touring the city. His wife, Allison, is apparently

tired and prefers to stay in bed and feel sorry for herself. I make a face, but failing to come up with a quick excuse I reluctantly agree.

It's a cold day, with heavy dark clouds hanging above, but it doesn't rain and I'm grateful for that, because I love to engage in long walks in a big city. It turns out that Lacoste isn't a morning person, so we hardly exchange a word during our stroll to Trafalgar square where we enter the National Gallery.

We stand in the long hall, in front of Caravaggio's masterpiece, "The Supper in Emmaus". Christ, young and beardless, is blessing the bread after revealing himself to the disciples. I study the painting for a long time, admiring its clarity and beauty. Lacoste is standing silently next to me. All off a sudden Lacoste says,

"She's really something, isn't she?"

I turn to Lacoste, puzzled. There is no woman in the painting.

"Who?"

"This Dara. Don't you think?"

Last thing I feel like doing is talking to somebody about Dara. Not that day, not ever. Certainly not to Lacoste, certainly not in the National Gallery in London.

"She's okay," I mutter and move slightly to change my viewing angle of the painting.

"I was pleased to see that she was put back on our favorite project. This is what you wanted, isn't it?" Roger says, twirling his tongue against the inside of his cheek.

"We were just testing the system, back there in Dallas," I chuckle. "You sure impressed the hell out of me."

"You two look good together," Lacoste persists.

I want to tell him that I look great with my wife, too, but decide not to give him any opening. Instead, I give Roger a look, like what is he talking about and why is he bothering me, but I instantly decide to ignore him and open my museum guide.

"I want to see the other Caravaggio, a boy bitten by a lizard," I say.

Lacoste is obviously not interested in art, as he yawns and looks at his watch.

"I'm tired. I couldn't fall asleep last night and had to take a walk in the middle of the night. Anyway, I think I'll go back to the hotel."

"Okay. I think I'll just take a look at a few more things," I say, relieved.

Lacoste brings his face closer to my ear. He has to crane his neck, because I'm much taller.

"Be careful, my friend. Hotels are public places. Too public. The walls of the rooms are very thin. Remember that."

Lacoste gives me a parting look, lips pursed, eyebrows raised in a mockingly serious gesture, and then he departs.

I close the guidebook in disgust. I feel like kicking something but find nothing appropriate. I can't get myself to imagine what Lacoste and his Gother buddies might do with whatever information they have.

I suddenly lose my enthusiasm and interest in art and decide to leave the museum. I shove the guide in my pocket and as I do a piece of paper flies out and lands on the floor. I pick it up. It's the list that Dara and I prepared, the list of the European investigators, with Dr. Kunz's name and phone number prominently circled. I hold it for several moments between thumb and forefinger while I saunter towards the exit. There's a storm beginning to brew in my head—Austrian case, denials and caginess, no details anywhere, no documents, and but for an urgent fax landing in the wrong hands-one could wonder whether there was such a thing as a sick Austrian patient. Is there a third patient?

But I need to know, and it takes me a moment or two to figure out the only way to find out. As I walk from Piccadily Circus and up Regent's street I enter a travel agency, where I'm told that a British Airways flight will leave for Vienna at 1:20 PM, which is in exactly one hour. I purchase a ticket, despite the agent's warning that I have no chance of making it. Outside, I flag a cab and promise him an extra twenty pounds if he makes it to Heathrow, terminal 3, on time. Forty minutes later I find myself dashing out of the cab, and I even have time to make two phone calls: One to Dara, telling her about my trip, news that she accepts nonchalantly, and to Dr. Kunz's office, asking for directions and requesting a meeting at 5:30 that same evening. Kunz sounds like a jovial fellow, and he seems genuinely pleased that a liver expert who works with Gother will visit to help him deal with the situation. He gives me the directions three times, the precise building and the exact floor and room number, making sure that I get there without a hitch. At 1:18 I hand my ticket to the flight agent at gate 33, and moments later the MD-80 is climbing to 33,000 feet.

*   *   *   *   *

Same evening, Vienna, Austria

I'm definitely not ready for the snowstorm that greets our plane when it lands, and less so when I step outside the terminal looking for the taxi line. The temperature is 10 degrees below zero, and the wind is blowing hard, as if trying to impress a panel of Guiness world record judges. With my light raincoat and not a single piece of luggage, courtesy of a sudden impulse somewhere around Trafalgar Square, I'm not only frozen but also an object of curious looks by bystanders.

I've been to Vienna many times before, and most times I've just hopped on an airport bus and for a few schillings arrived at downtown Vienna without too much hassle. But it's already five-twenty, and it's snowing, and the taxi line is short, so I hop into a cab, telling the elderly driver that my destination is the "Algemeines Krankenhaus on 23 Spital Gasse." That's the General Hospital of Vienna and the main University patient facility.

The driver drives quietly for some time, but examines me often through the mirror. He finally can't hold it in anymore.

"Not ready for our snow, ja?" he chortles.

"Not really. This was an unexpected trip."

He watches me through the mirror.

"You sick or zomesing?"

"No, no. I'm a doctor. I have a meeting with somebody at the hospital."

He nods, but something still seems to bother him.

"Staying in Wien tonight, nein?"

"Yes, of course."

"There's a very nice hotel down from Graben . . . "

"Thank you, I'm all taken care of."

He shrugs, like suit yourself, but he's still not sure if I'm to be believed. Truth is, of course, I had no time to reserve a hotel. I'll try some of the better hotels in the center, Bristol, maybe Imperial, and depending on my findings, even send the bill to Barnes.

The snow has subsided somewhat by the time he makes a right turn off Wahringer Strasse to Spital Gasse twenty minutes later. One more block and he stops the car, in front of a gray building surrounded by a ten foot wall. The big sign "Algemeines Krankenhaus der stadt Wien" indicates that we've reached our destination. I get out, relieved that he accepted my American dollars, and slowly proceed to the narrow path that surrounds the first building. There's a booth with a guard, but I go left to a narrow passage, just as instructed by Kunz on the phone. The cobbled trail takes me uphill, next to several snow-covered elms, and it takes only one short minute before my socks swim in the wet slush. The cold wind is drilling into my bones and I find myself almost running. At the end of the passage, I take the staircase that leads to a large flat asphalt deck-like structure. Finally I reach a tall building on the right and fly through the double doors into the warm lobby. Next to the door there's a directory on the wall, and I catch my breath studying it for a moment. The department of internal medicine, where Kunz resides, is on the fourth floor, and I notice that the intensive care unit is on the 13th floor, red. I walk through the creme-colored hallway, which with its multitude of pipes reminds me of the belly of a submarine, locate the elevator and push the button for the fourth floor.

The elevator stops, and I change my mind. Maybe I should check out the intensive care unit first. I push thirteen. On the thirteenth floor I wander about for a few moments, until I reach the glass doors of the ICU. I hesitate. I don't look exactly like a local professor making rounds, so I remove my raincoat, button my shirt all the way to the top and push the doors open. Inside, I drop my coat on the first chair and proceed to the central nurses station. I'm pleased to find out that ICU's in Vienna look just like the ones back home—central monitoring area and eight patient rooms. Here they have a concentric arrangement, so that the medical personnel can see all the patients' beds from the central monitoring station. Two young nurses are busy studying one of the monitors, and I hear the whirring sound of the printer spitting out some information, ECG strip maybe. I scan the patient rooms quickly. Old lady, old lady, old man, young lady, young man, old man . . . I look again at the young man and take a deep breath. All I can see is the face: a tired face, eyes closed, breathing shallow, but the color is unmistakably dark yellow. This very young fellow, a kid practically, has jaundice.

"Gruss-Got. Suchen's sie jemand?" I suddenly notice the tall muscular man, in white coat, standing next to me.

I extend my hand, responding in English to his polite version of asking me what the hell was I doing there.

"I'm professor Holden, and I'm here to see professor Kunz."

Titles mean everything in the Germanic world, and certainly in this vestige of the Austro-Hungarian Empire.

The man gives me the up and down, from my buttoned-up shirt and khaki slacks to my soggy shoes and socks but says nothing.

"Professor Kunz is not here. His office is on the fourth floor."

His English is flawless. He moves towards the door and opens it for me. I notice his name tag:

"Dr. Fritz Reiber."

"Professor Reiber, I'm a liver specialist from Philadelphia. I believe the patient in room five is the reason for the invitation."

"Of course. I see."

He's probably too young to be a full professor and his tag proclaims him as a mere doctor, but I want some information from him. His face relaxes for a moment, but he still leans on the door to keep it open.

I pick up my coat, shake his hand and leave. He follows me with his eyes to make sure that I'm indeed going in the right direction towards the elevators. I do. On my way I briefly pass through the waiting room. In it, I see a man and a woman, sitting silently, holding hands and praying, with eyes closed. When I pass them, they briefly raise their eyes, but when they see me, they shut their eyes again.

On the fourth floor, from the elevator, I make a right, then a left; long hallway, double doors, and I'm in the department of internal medicine, in front of a closed door with the sign "Professor Helmut Kunz, Hauptarzt." I knock at the door, then open it when there's no response. I find myself in a small cubicle where a blond woman, mid-thirties, her back to me, is in the closet pulling out a heavy Loden winter-coat.

"Gruss-Got," she says, which is the common greeting in Vienna, meaning "God's greeting."

"Guten abend," I say, "I'm here to see Professor Kunz. I'm Dr. Holden from Philadelphia."

"Oh, yes, of course. But . . . " she looks at the wall, and I follow her gaze at the clock which reads 5:58. Furrows appear on her forehead. "Professor Kunz hasn't returned . . . "

"What? I came all the way from London. . . I made an appointment . . . "

"Ja," she interrupts me, "he had to leave but said he'll be back by 5:30, and now I don't know . . . "

I take off my raincoat and we both simultaneously look at my wet shoes and socks. "I'll wait, I suppose. Hopefully it won't be long."

"Here, you can wait in Professor Kunz's office."

I follow her into an adjacent office that would easily win first prize in every competition on neatness. Books and papers are arranged in immaculate order, all journals lined up like soldiers, and not a single piece of paper lying out of place. She points at the couch and I sit down.

"He's never late, never. When he's on rounds, nah, ja, naturlich, it sometimes takes much longer than planned, but I don't zink he's on rounds."

I scan the books on the shelf. Most are in German, but I recognize a few classical American textbooks in medicine.

"So, where did he go?"

She shrugs.

"He got a telephone around funf . . . , uh . . . five o'clock, and said he had to meet somebody . . . somesing really important . . . I don't ask . . . "

I look at her.

"Doesn't he carry a beeper?"

"A beeper? Ja, always."

"So, let's beep him."

She hesitates.

"He use beeper only for patient emergencies . . . "

I jump to my feet.

"Listen to me, please. This is an emergency. I came all the way from London just to meet with him, so b-e-e-p him, okay?"

She mutters something that sounds like "got in himmel" and "Americanen" but retreats to her office, picks up the receiver, dials a few numbers and hangs up. I'm back in her area, hovering over her, while looking at the clock, which reads ten minutes after six o'clock.

One, two, four minutes—no answer. The secretary has by now put on her coat and is fiddling with her gloves as she's slowly inching towards the outer door.

"Try again, please," I say.

"I must go now, wirklich. Is too late . . . "

"Please. Just once."

She obliges, and when there's still no answer a few minutes later she puts her gloves on.

"Please, Doctor, you can wait in his office. I don't know where he is, but surely he'll be here any moment."

I nod.

"Auf wiedersehen," she says and leaves.

I pace in the office suites for some time. From the window I get a good view of the low hanging clouds and the snow and slush covered street below. I can barely make out the pointed tower of the Votiv church which is less than half a mile away. Once in a while I venture into the corridor, but with the late hour and the storm outside, nobody's around.

I'm deeply frustrated and puzzled. Kunz was extremely pleasant and helpful on the phone and sounded eager to meet with me. An obviously well organized and punctual person, he must have good reasons for not showing up and not leaving a message. I'm not sure what to do now. There doesn't appear to be anybody around to talk to, as it's quite late. Besides, I have no clue as to who might be involved in caring for the patient, and since nobody knows me I can hardly expect any cooperation. Staying longer and catching the professor in the morning is out of the question because I have a flight at 7:50 a.m., and I need to be back for the CSM hearing.

By the time I decide to leave, it's close to seven. Before I do, I make a hotel reservation for the night. All the central hotels are full, so I settle for the "Regina," which is a little bit outside the downtown area, on the inner Ring, but less than a mile away from my current location.

I walk to the elevator, and on my way I run into the tall doctor from the ICU. He's wearing a heavy coat and hat, and is obviously on his way out. He nods in my direction as he rushes towards the elevator. I let him pass, and patiently wait for the next elevator. When it arrives, I take it down to the first floor, but when it stops at my destination, I press thirteen and up I go. This is going to be my last effort to turn around a wasted and ill-advised trip. It will surely cost me precious points with Gother, because I'm missing their "team building" dinner that night. I have no intention of mentioning my trip to the Gother brass, especially as I seem to have accomplished absolutely nothing.

I go directly to the intensive care unit. When I pass through the waiting room, I notice that the elderly couple is gone. I get through the glass doors, and put my coat down on the chair, just like before. None of the nurses is in the station, and as I look around I notice medical staff hustling about in the room of an old lady. They're engaged in animated conversation, seemingly exchanging pieces of paper and discussing some puzzling piece of information. Even if I wanted to obtain information on my jaundiced patient, this wasn't the right time. Maybe I can take advantage of the situation and grab the patient's chart? I look at the nursing staff, and they're still engaged in attending to the old lady's problems. One of the nurses raises her head and looks in my direction, but somebody shoves a stethoscope in her hands, and she turns around and approaches the old lady.

I realize that I don't know the patient's name, and without it I can't find his chart. I look in the direction of his room, but I notice that the curtain around his bed is half drawn, and I can only see the bottom of the bed, not his face. Slowly and casually, I exit the station and move towards my patient's room, but I take the long way around, so that I don't have to pass by the old lady's room. After a moment I enter the room. There's a chart attached to the rails of the bed, and I decide to look for his name there. This chart typically lists the fluid status of the patient, current treatments, medications, bowel movements and the like, but wouldn't have any of the information that I'm seeking, like whether he was on Neurovan, how long he had taken it and if he was on any other medications when disease struck. I pick up the chart and flip it open, glancing as I do at the patient, who moves and turns his face in my direction. An old man with a large bandage around his head, one eye open, is staring at me. My jaw drops.

I reach the nurses station just when one of the nurses arrives and we almost bump into each other.

"Was machen sie da?" She wants to know what I'm doing here. She's middle aged, dark hair, dark eyebrows, on the chubby side.

"Excuse me, I'm Professor Holden from Philadelphia, a guest of Professor Kunz."

She looks at me with suspicion.

"Er ist nicht da." She tells me that Kunz isn't there.

"Do you speak English?" I try.

"A little."

"In that room there," and I point, "was a patient with jaundice. I saw him an hour ago. Where is he?"

She looks in the direction of the room.

"The patient . . . brain surgery, not jaundice."

"I know that. But the other patient, where did he go? Was he transferred? Did he die?"

She raises her finger in mid air.

"Just a moment."

The other staff members return to the station and she goes to talk to them. They whisper in the huddle and then she returns to me.

"They think he was moved to another hospital."

"What?"

"Maybe they have found a donor. . . liver."

"They think? Maybe? God... when did all that happen?"

"Just . . . uh . . . before our shift."

"When did your shift start?"

"Sieben . . . uh . . . seven. We come at a quarter to seven."

While I was sitting on my thumbs in the office downstairs!

"Listen, is there somebody I can talk to, who has all the facts . . . "

She looks me straight in the eye.

"Well, I'm sure professor Kunz has all the information . . . "

"Kunz? Does Professor Kunz know about this."

"Yes, of course."

"Really? So they called him?"

"Nein, nein. Professor Kunz was here when they take him."

I take a step back.

"Here? In the unit?"

She nods.

"Are you sure?"

She chuckles.

"Nobody touch Professor Kunz patient if he not here."

God, this is so confusing . . .

I pick up my raincoat.

"So you know which hospital they took him to?"

She shakes her head.

"Can you please ask your colleagues?"

She makes a face.

"Dr. . . . uh . . . "

"Holden."

"Dr. Holden. I'm very busy. Why not call Professor Kunz?"

I put my hand on her arm.

"Please. And also, could you tell me the patient's name?"

She goes back to one of the other nurses, and returns a moment later.

"Nobody knows where they take him. Graz, maybe."

"Thank you. And the name?"

"Yes. Erika remembers. His name is Christian Hauptman."

She spells it for me as I write it down.

"How old is he?"

"Seventeen." This she knows immediately.

"When I came here earlier I saw a couple outside. . . do you know if they are related to this child. . . "

Erika walks closer and she overhears my question.

"Ja, his parents are here all time. . . Christian is their only child."

I thank her, we both bow slightly, and then we shake hands. I try to smile, but she looks as if a dark cloud has just crossed her face

* * * * *

I am in my hotel room for less than two minutes when the phone rings. I have removed my shoes and socks and, seated in bed, I'm rubbing my frozen feet to increase the circulation.

"Hello?"

"Dr. Holden, thank God I found you."

"Professor Kunz?"

How did he find me?

"I'm terribly sorry. I got tied up with a sick patient, we had to transfer him to another hospital . . . I just returned to my office . . . "

"So you were in the intensive care unit . . . "

"In and out. I understand we missed each other . . . "

"Is there any way we can meet now?"

A short pause.

"Uh . . . I'm afraid it's impossible now. We have guests from out of town and my wife will kill me if I'm late . . . "

Damn!

"Well, perhaps you can tell me some more about the patient," I straighten the scrap paper lying next to the phone and lift my pen, "you know, how long was he on Neurovan before his liver functions started deteriorating . . . "

"Excuse me," Kunz interrupts, "did you say Neurovan?"

I am still on my bed, hunched over the table, poised to take notes.

"Well, yeah, we are talking about Gother study 95-11 . . . "

"Oh, I'm not sure what you mean, but I don't have any liver cases on Neurovan."

I suddenly notice that his delivery is very slow and mechanical, and the joviality from our afternoon conversation is all but gone.

"Excuse me?"

"Neurovan, the anti-diabetic drug, from Gother?"

"Yes."

"Well, we have enrolled eighteen patients and we haven't seen a single liver problem."

"But I've been told by Gother staff . . . "

"Must be some misunderstanding. When you called I assumed you talked about another project . . . you know, we have so many clinical trials . . . "

And what about the goddamn fax? I realize I shouldn't tell him about it.

"Will it be too much if I asked you to fax me, to my home, the results of the most recent liver tests on your eighteen patients?"

A hesitation.

"This is highly unusual. Why don't you ask the Gother people to do that?"

I hurl the pen with all my might at the wall. Then I take a deep breath.

"Okay, right. And the patient today in the intensive care unit," I pull the crumpled note from my pocket, "Uh . . . Hauptman. What's his problem?"

"Oh, it's a sad and complicated case. Juvenile arthritis, alcoholism, stopped drinking, but received the wrong combination of drugs for his arthritis . . . you know, Voltaren and Vanuoren . . . and he's so young too."

Still very mechanical, slow staccatto delivery, despite the compassionate tenor.

Only one thing left for me to establish.

"Professor Kunz, are you all right?"

"I beg your pardon?"

"Is everything okay?"

"Of course. What do you mean? Again, I'm sorry about the whole situation. I had a crazy day and I'm sorry that your day wasn't very productive."

"Thank you, Professor Kunz."

I hang up and immediately dial Kunz's office number. I let it ring for two full minutes before hanging up.

TWENTY SIX

Wednesday, March 10, Vienna-London

NEXT DAY, I'M UP BEFORE SIX SO THAT I CAN CATCH THE EARLY FLIGHT to London. The experience of dressing up a showered body into dirty clothes is not particularly cozy, and reminds me of the wilderness camping trips of my summers in college. At least I should have enough time to change in London before the CSM hearing this afternoon.

I'm in the airport, at the counter, ready to board my plane when something good happens, the first on this trip. I'm informed that I've been upgraded to first class. They don't tell me why and I don't ask. This is a short flight, no big deal, but I'd rather digest and analyze last night's weird events seated in a wide and comfortable chair.

I'm in the aisle seat, first row. I sit down, next to a gentleman, whose only visible parts were his fingers holding up a newspaper. At least I think it's a man, judging from the big meaty fingers. I get a glass of champagne before I warm up my seat, and I gulp it down eagerly. After the second glass, just as we're ready to take off, I sense the beginning of a pleasant buzz, and this immediately dissuades me from thinking about the Vienna hospital and Kunz. As I lean back, I make only one mental note, one I've been making over and over in the last twelve hours: *Kunz was not telling the truth.* This was no misunderstanding: he knew what drug I was interested in because I told him over the phone, and I saw the fax that Barnes received with my own eyes. But the computer had no documentation. And Barnes denied it.

But I saw the fax. Did I see the fax? Did it say Vienna? And Dara was so convincing when she told me. And I saw a jaundiced patient, who, just by coincidence, was moved moments after I show up at the hospital. But why would Kunz lie?

My head is spinning and I close my eyes. A moment later, we are served breakfast. White cloth, silverware, fresh baked rolls and croissants, poached eggs and coffee. I open my eyes and straighten up, just as my neighbor folds the newspaper neatly, and lets the stewardess put the tray on his table.

"So, Paul, did you enjoy your stay in Vienna?" he says, and I turn to look into Joe Lansing's turtle eyes.

"Yes, wonderful," I say.

He looks at me, while spreading a heavy layer of butter on his roll.

"Are you okay?" he asks.

"Sure. Why d'you ask?"

"You look a little pale."

I'm sure he's right, because I could feel the blood draining out of my face, one drop after another.

"Must be the champagne and flying, so early in the morning." I try to smile.

I take a big bite from the croissant.

"So, what took you to Vienna?" I ask.

"Oh, I had some business to attend to. Marketing issues.

Planning launches in Europe. The usual stuff. It's hard work but it never bores me."

"So your trip was successful?" I munch on the roll.

"Better than I had any right to expect."

"That's great," I say.

I like Joe Lansing. All my encounters with him were sheer fun and delight, he being probably the best storyteller I've met. Loud and animated, he's the dream of every party thrower. Now he's eating very slowly, stooped over the tray, face calm and somber. I recall that he's not a morning person, so I don't expect any hilarious fireworks this time. But why did he go to Vienna? Is it a coincidence that he and I happened to be traveling to the same place at the same time? After all, we both had a free day in London, and it was a natural thing for him to take care of some business while over here in Europe. But . . . I remember his story about Kunz and his daughter, and how confident he and the others were that Neurovan was going to get approval for marketing in Austria. So I must conclude that the overwhelming odds are that he did visit Kunz this time.

"How about you, Paul? What took you to Vienna?"

"Excuse me?" I mumble, as he interrupts my private intersynaptic musings.

"Your trip, what took you to Vienna?"

"Oh, just visiting friends. I figured, I'm in London, why not hop over for a short visit."

"Uh-huh. Picked a lousy day to do it. That snow storm was something."

"I know. That was the only day I could do it, without missing the CSM meeting."

He looks at my clothes.

"You clearly weren't dressed for the weather."

"I'm a light traveler," I chuckle.

He takes a huge bite from his roll, swallowing it almost in its entirety in one fell swoop.

"So what d'you think about our chances today with the CSM?" he peers at me.

"I don't know. This is my first time. You're the expert. What d'you think?"

"It all depends," he grumbles, "on the experts. On guys like you."

He spits the word "experts" as if he was talking about poisonous snakes.

"We need you to guarantee the CSM that the liver is no problem," he proceeds, "can you do that?"

"We'll see." I say. Translation: I'll do what I have to do.

"That may not be good enough," he says, and his tone is unfriendly and ominous.

The stewardess fills my coffee cup and I take a long, hot, delicious sip. Then I lean back and shut my eyes. I open them abruptly, because Lansing is whispering something in my ear.

"Paul, don't ever take it upon yourself to visit our clinical sites and patients again. Ever."

"What?"

"That's my advice. Personal advice. I didn't hire you and I can't fire you. Barnes and clinical research did, and in that respect you're their problem. I'm just telling you: stop snooping. For your own good."

By now I'm sitting up straight in my seat. I can try and go on denying any snooping with patients, but what's the purpose?

"Is that a threat, Joe?"

"No. Not yet anyway. Let's call it friendly advice. Don't underestimate our determination to see Neurovan get to the market. That's all."

I watch his protruding jaw and beefy neck as he talks to me, and I wonder what he means exactly. I also decide to find out more about this peculiar, likely non-coincidence. I need just a little confirmation.

"How's Kunz?" I ask.

He shoots a rapid glance at me. I notice the knife in his right hand, the butter square in his left.

"You don't know?"

"Know what?"

"Well, you spoke to him last night, didn't you?"

"He was fine. I think he tried to avoid me."

Lansing is looking out the window, than back at me, window, me. He then breaks into a wide smile.

"Paul, Paul. I don't get it. You're such a smart man. What's the matter? You don't trust us? Ask us, and we'll give you all the information you need. Please, don't try to be a cowboy."

I smile back, but not without effort.

"Sure, okay."

I look down at his tray, and notice that the knife he has been holding is bent, almost broken, right in the middle.

* * * * *

Joe and I share a cab from the airport, but we don't communicate with each other. Instead, Joe and the driver discuss American football and its relationship—none—to British football, a game we call soccer.

In my hotel room I have just about enough time to shower and change before we have to leave for the CSM hearing. I feel calm and determined, looking forward to the upcoming new experience.

When I get down to the lobby, Barnes is pacing nervously, waiting for the last member of the team to show up. The taxis are waiting outside, and he obviously wants to be at the meeting site as early as possible. The last person to show up is Roger Lacoste and we split into groups of three per cab.

I'm in the back seat with Dara. In the front seat, Professor Lang, the British consultant, is shuffling his slides for the umpteenth time.

"Haven't seen you in a while," I say, "what are you up to?"

"Not much. How have you been?"

"Good."

"Seen any good operas lately?"

"Huh?"

"Heard any good Viennese music lately?" she continues, nodding and pointing with her head towards the front seat, like she's trying to tell me something in code.

"No. I was too busy." I finally get it.

"So, did you see our jaundiced patient?" she whispers in my ear.

"Yes and no. It's a long story," I whisper back.

Lang stops fiddling with his slides and turns to us.

"I think I finally got these blasted acetates in the right order," he announces.

"Great," Dara says.

"Are you sure this is the fastest way?" Lang asks the driver. They start discussing London traffic patterns at this time of day. Dara addresses me.

"I am so busy, you have no idea. Barnes just threw me one assignment after the other, you know, local company matters."

Her tone is now business-like. I fail to detect any signals of closeness, and though confusing, it is a welcome relief.

Lang and driver settle their differences, and Lang suddenly turns around and we all smile politely.

"When are you flying back?" I ask Dara.

"In a coupla days. I need to stay a few more days in London to help out with some office work. What about you?"

"I'm flying home tomorrow."

The trip to the huge cement office building on Langham street, where the meeting is to take place, lasts about twenty-five minutes, but we sit quietly the rest of the way.

*   *   *   *   *

The Commission on the Safety of Medicines, or CSM for short, is the body responsible for approving new chemical entities as drugs for sale in the United Kingdom. It is the British equivalent of the FDA, and has the reputation of a fair-minded yet tough and demanding scientific body. Unlike the FDA it only gets involved once all the clinical studies are complete, and has no say or interest in advising the companies what to do in advance.

Thursday, March 11, is the scheduled day of reviewing the new compound for diabetic complications, Neurovan. The committee consists of twenty-five or so members, and they are all seated alongside a table that's almost forty yards long. Members of the visiting company are always invited to sit at a desk placed on a stage hovering above the long committee table. A screen for viewing slides is erected at the other end of the table.

The visitors desk can only accommodate six people. Our group includes Osgood, the local manager, the two British specialists, Lang and Farley, and the presenters from Gother, Lacoste and Lennox. Barnes decides that he doesn't have to sit at the main table and that it's more important that somebody who can cover potential safety questions should be right there. I am the sixth man.

We cool our heels in a waiting room for some time, mostly engaging in small talk. When Lansing sees me, he grabs my hand with both of his, smiling, then pats me on the back, like Vienna never happened. I'm more reserved, but his gregarious nature is contagious, and I get more relaxed and mellow towards him.

At exactly one o'clock a young lady walks in and asks us to follow her. After several moments, one by one we enter the large meeting room. We, the six chosen presenters, walk up the stage and sit down behind the desk. Barnes, Dara, Lansing, Mark and the British liver expert, Mosby, sit on chairs set along the wall.

I sink into the extreme right chair and look down from the stage. All members of the committee are seated, and the chairman of the committee, Dr. Fallon, seizes the microphone in his hand. He's a gentleman in his mid fifties, with a head full of wavy brown hair, no graying whatsoever.

"Good afternoon, ladies and gentleman. We are here to review application number 21792, Neurovan, from Gother Inc. We have read the written materials and awaiting your presentation. Thank you."

The lights are turned down. Osgood starts with his introduction and then the Gother team proceeds to present all their results, exactly as planned. Lacoste is as brilliant as usual, and Lennox, in his slow deliberate delivery, gets the job done. The committee listens quietly. After Osgood finishes with his summary, requesting the CSM to approve Neurovan for marketing in the United Kingdom, the lights go on and Dr. Fallon mutters, "Thank you. That was truly an excellent presentation."

Such comments mean exactly nothing, a routine statement made after each and every presentation.

It's time for questions.

Raymond Henry gets up first. He's the young ambitious pharmacologist who has this burning need to always be at the center of things. Osgood warned the group about him.

He asks about the pain, the degree that it got better with the drug, why there were differences in the studies, and how pain was measured and so on. He's critical to the point of being obnoxious, but Osgood politely refers the questions to Roger Lacoste. Lacoste brings his head closer to the microphone and I watch with awe as he methodically destroys every last concern that Henry has. Roger asks for back-up slides numbers 411, 435 and 576 to make his points clear, and when he's done Henry sits down quietly, like a dog whose nose was rubbed in his own urine. He declines to ask more questions. Crawley, the diabetologist, who indicated earlier that he had a few questions, changes his mind and decides not to ask them. The statistician of the committee asks three benign questions about methods, and Lacoste brilliantly handles them too.

I notice that in the distance Barnes, who is all ears, becomes less tense and smiles at Dara who is seated next to him. It seems that the dangerous Henry and Crawley are satisfied, and I wonder whether the chairman of the committee and its main safety expert, Dr. Fallon, might also be satisfied and decline to ask any questions. Could it be that easy?

Fallon looks around, but no member seems to have any burning questions.

"Then it's my turn," Fallon says, and looks up to the stage where the Gother group is seated.

"I looked at the numbers of patients with minor liver problems and, while high, was not unusually so. What I fail to understand is how come there was not a single case of jaundice among your patients."

He just states it, like a rhetorical question. But he continues.

"I guess my question is, were there any jaundiced patients, I mean, that didn't make it into the written documents you had submitted?"

Osgood looks around, and nods in my direction, signaling that I should tackle this question. The microphone slowly makes its way to me, and I don't have too much time to think whether to lower the boom or to wait for another day. I clear my throat.

"Well, Professor Fallon, when I first saw the data I asked myself the same question. Apparently, there is an adjustment at the liver cell level that prevents the damage from becoming more progressive."

"So, Dr. Holden, don't you think that Neurovan has the potential to cause serious liver disease, eventually?"

Again, I'm ready.

"It's certainly possible, but so far my clear impression is that Neurovan is safe and effective."

Dr. Fallon runs his fingers through his hair and consults his notes. He has to decide whether my non-answer can be considered an answer. I look down at Barnes who can barely contain his glee. Fallon looks up at me, and I see immediately that he has no intention of swallowing the bait.

"Thank you. Perhaps . . . uh . . . just to make it clear for the record. Dr. Holden, to your knowledge, were there any cases of jaundice or liver failure in patients taking Neurovan?"

I lean forward and cup the microphone. Next to me, Lennox shifts in his chair. Down below, I notice that the committee members are beginning to relax, as if the meeting is just about over, and a "no" answer from me is a foregone conclusion. Dr. Fallon closes the notebook in front of him.

"Well," I say, but from the corner of my eye I see that Gerry Lennox is bending forward. All of a sudden I feel Lennox's muscular arm, wrestle the microphone out of my hand. Lennox brings his mouth close to the microphone. He seems to tremble slightly as he speaks.

"Three, Dr. Fallon," he murmurs, "we had three cases of jaundice."

*　*　*　*　*

There's a palpable gasp among the CSM members, who are suddenly brought back to life. Notebooks are reopened, papers shuffle and eager eyes are focused on all of us on the podium. A few moments later the meeting adjourns. Lacoste is the last speaker, taking charge of the proceedings. Without admitting for a moment that there were indeed three seriously ill patients, he goes into a long explanation how the causality of liver damage cannot be established with certainty when every diabetic patient takes so many medications, that liver changes are common in diabetic patients, that frequent monitoring of liver functions through blood testing would all but eliminate any danger and so on. His attempt at damage control is valiant, and I don't know whether it has any effect after Lennox's declaration. Fallon asks for a full review of the information for the alleged three patients, and explains that their decision on whether or not to approve Neurovan will depend on the outcome of this safety review. As we leave, we all shake hands with Dr. Fallon. I watch as he and Lang seem to have a long and friendly chat.

TWENTY SEVEN

BACK IN THE HOTEL, BARNES ASKS ME TO JOIN HIM AND LANSING IN HIS room. He shakes my hand, one of his hands holding my elbow, for a very long moment.

"Paul, I knew we could count on you."

He turns to Lansing, who is pacing in the room, his huge hands behind his back.

"I'm waiting for a call from management. I want you both here. But, Joe, we could still be okay, right?"

"You bet'ya." Joe stops his pacing and sits on the bed. "The public meeting is one thing, but privately we've done all the right things, you know, we have the right contacts. So despite Lennox . . ."

The phone rings. The Gother Inc. Lear jet is flying somewhere above Minnesota when the phone call comes through. Apparently the Gother brass, including president Dell and CEO Walnut are on their way for meetings in New York, culminating with a briefing of Wall Street analysts next week.

Barnes puts the call on the speakerphone, after telling Dell that Joe and I were also present. For a moment Dell listens to Barnes ranting and raving.

"He said what?" Dell barks into the receiver.

"Lennox blurted out the jaundice cases just when we were almost home free. That was the last question."

"Why? Goddamit, Larry, I thought you had it all under control."

Barnes has to yell because the connection is poor.

"It was a shocker. He said nothing at the rehearsals. I'm telling you, nothing. Everything went so well. Paul Holden was right on the ball, perfect answers, when Lennox blew a fuse."

"Larry, fire the sonofabitch," Dell screams.

"Okay, Carter, if you think so. But, this could be tricky . . . " Barnes says.

"Hold on."

A new voice emanates from the speaker.

"This is Dick Walnut. Barnes, any chance that the Brits might approve Neurovan anyway?"

"Excellent chance, Dick," Barnes says, "Fallon, the chairman of the CSM, told our guy Lang privately that everything is still open. They were impressed by the rest of the data, and once we take care of the three patients, they'll approve it."

Walnut speaks again. He has a raspy, irritating voice.

"Good. In any case, don't fire anybody. I'll decide who gets fired and when. Just get back to the office and we'll talk about it."

Walnut hangs up.

"Yes, sir," Barnes grumbles to the dialing tone.

"I'm dead meat, folks," he tells us. "I know these bastards. Right now Walnut is telling Dell to fire my ass as soon as the CSM reaches a decision. That Lennox creep just cost me my job."

* * * * *

Hours later we're in my room. Dara is slumped in the chair

and I'm on the bed. We each hold a bottle of Carlsberg from the minibar. Lennox is standing, his gaze fixed at the floor.

"I thought we had a plan, Gerry," I say. "We were going to get more incriminating information first and then act. Do the right thing at the right time."

"Maybe you had a plan," Gerry says, "but you've been acting strange lately. Like you've become one of them."

"But I said . . . "

"I know what you said. It's what you did, or didn't do that had me concerned," Lennox claims.

"What do you mean?"

"This meeting went so well that I saw Neurovan sailing on for quick approval, thousands of people taking it, hundreds getting jaundice and dozens dying. I just didn't want it on my conscience." Lennox speaks in a measured tone, like a man who has considered all the options and reached a final decision. Even if it means pain and suffering.

"But now, thanks to you, I've been branded as a liar in full view of my peers and the scientific world," I say.

"Not really. They'll all blame the company for not telling you. You're only an innocent consultant."

Dara purses her lips.

"Wait, Gerry. Paul did it because it wasn't the right time. Had Neurovan been approved, he would have raised hell with the CSM. Right, Paul?"

I am pensive. I can't really be upset at Lennox because he didn't follow my plan. He has a good point. Maybe I underestimated the difficulties in speaking out after a drug is sitting on shelves in pharmacies and selling like hot cakes.

"One problem I have," I try, "is that I don't know enough about the other two cases. Gerry, you've even refused to confirm the existence of an Austrian case for me. I asked you . . . "

"Listen, Paul," he interrupts, "this is a European situation. I don't monitor Vienna. They tell me only what they think I should know. And it ain't much, I assure you."

"So, if you're not sure about the case, why did you drop the bomb at the hearing?"

Gerry starts pacing in the tiny room.

"Well, you tell me, is there or isn't there a jaundiced patient in Austria?" he shoots.

"You're asking me . . . "

"Paul, I know about your trip . . . "

I look at Dara, but she shrugs.

"The trip was useful in many ways, but I didn't find any smoking gun. Kunz was first a no-show, then he called to tell me that it was a different drug that caused the jaundice in one of their patients. I don't know, he mentioned a couple of arthritis drugs."

I tell them briefly about the trip, the disappearing act of Kunz, transfer of the jaundiced patient and the phone call from a reappearing Kunz. I don't mention the encounter with Lansing.

"So, for all we know there's no third patient . . ." Lennox mumbles.

I decide to show them one of my trump cards.

"Well, except for the fax."

"What fax?"

I go to the dresser, and from under my underwear, I pull out the crumpled fax that Barnes has received.

I give it to Gerry, and Dara gets up so that they can read it together.

"Wow!" Dara exclaims.

"It doesn't say anywhere here that it's Neurovan," Gerry notes.

"What?" I get up.

I read the fax again.

"Patient four in study 95-11, Vienna, Austria is getting worse and the natives are getting restless. Dr. Kunz believes that this is all related to our drug and he threatens to withdraw his support. What to do next?"

"Well," I ask, "isn't study 95-11 a Neurovan study?"

"I'm almost positive," Dara says, "also, I don't think that Kunz would be involved in a second study. He's a diabetes specialist, isn't he?"

Gerry looks forlorn.

"God, so many question marks. We'll need to do better than that. I suppose we'll know for sure when our European company prepares the report for the CSM."

We all seem to be lost for words for a few moments.

"Anyway," Gerry finally speaks, "what drugs did Kunz blame for the jaundice in their patient?"

"Voltaren and Vanuoren."

"I know Voltaren, but I don't know the other one," Lennox says.

"Neither do I. Must be some generic German brand of something."

I take the fax and carefully fold it and shove it back into the drawer.

"What now?" Lennox asks, as if talking to himself.

"What's done is done," Dara says, "but . . . I don't think that our management is capable of forgiving."

Lennox shrugs.

"I just had to stop this madness before it was too late."

I get up, walk over to the surprised Lennox and give him a hug.

"You did the right thing. I'll do whatever I can to help you keep your job."

Lennox's face lights up.

"Thanks, Paul. And just so you know, I didn't do it for any high moral standards. I'm the medical monitor and I'm responsible for the safety of patients who take this drug. It's that simple."

Gerry Lennox picks up his jacket from the chair and walks to the door.

"I am tired. Good night," he says.

"Take care, Gerry."

He waves to us and leaves.

Dara sits next to me on the bed.

"He's finished," she says.

"Not yet, I still got a few cards left in my sleeve. They may need me for other things. FDA, for example."

"Well, anyway. At least the freight train named Neurovan has been slowed down," she says.

"You know, Barnes and Lansing think that the CSM may still approve it," I say.

"Sure. Despite what it seems, Lennox's disclosure is no big deal. Joe Lansing was and is very active. He is working on our famous trio from the CSM: Fallon, Henry and Crawley."

"Really?"

"I understand that he agreed to fund Fallon's textbook project. Crawley's daughter is coming to the US for training. Gother's expense."

"And Henry, the abrasive young pharmacologist? He seems like the toughest nut to crack."

"Joe told Barnes and me that he turned out to be the easiest to handle."

"How come?" I'm curious now.

"Joe wouldn't tell. All I know is that it has to do with Henry's being gay." Dara flashes a big smile.

"Tell me when you find out."

I stand up.

"It's been a long day. I'd better hit the shower and go to bed," I say.

"Okay," she says and gets up, bringing her face close to mine. The smell of her cosmic tease, or whatever the name of the perfume, is as intoxicating as ever.

"No, I meant alone," I say.

She gives me a kiss on the cheek, shorter and smaller than any of the previous ones. She moves away, her back to me. There's a short, awkward moment of silence.

"You're staying here for a few extra days, right?" I ask.

She turns around and nods.

"Then, I'll see you somewhere on the other side of the Atlantic," I murmur.

I look at my image reflected in the closet mirror and catch a glimpse of a tired face, but behind the fatigue I see calm resolution and determination. I'll do my best to make sure that Lennox's enormous gamble was not for naught. It won't be easy, because judging from Joe Lansing's ability to move around, pull strings and manipulate, I'm facing a corrupt, shrewd and insidious system.

* * * * *

Next morning, while standing in the long checkout line, I'm joined by Lacoste. As usual in the morning, Lacoste is in a foul mood. This morning, so am I.

"I hope they fire that cotton pickin' scoundrel, Lennox," says Lacoste.

"Why?"

Lacoste stares at me in disbelief.

"What do you mean why? What he did was despicable and treacherous. Could have ruined everything for his own company. And for us." He points at me and at himself.

"Best I can tell, all he did was tell the truth," I remark calmly, but I feel a knot tightening in my stomach.

A big blue vein appears on Lacoste's forehead.

"Holden, are you out of your cotton pickin' mind? We're talking billions for the company, millions to us, yeah, even you, and you'd give that up for . . . what?"

Telling him that money isn't everything would hardly have any impact.

"Lennox did what he thought was right," I say.

Lacoste doesn't have the ability to comprehend my kind of logic. He spits out his response in a rapid fire staccato.

"He told the truth. Truth. Empty word. What the hell is truth? Truth is relative and you know it. He doesn't know anything we don't, he has no more information than any of us, but he had to open his big trap."

I take a few steps as the line ahead of me moves forward.

"Anyway, this is between him and the company," I say.

"You bet. I'll talk to Dell and make sure they get rid of this squealing bastard."

I move closer to Lacoste, towering over his partially bare scalp.

"Roger, in my world, what Lennox did was right. And you're just a petty small-time crook asking for trouble."

Lacoste turns red in the face, and retreats in disbelief, jaws dropping.

"I don't know what's gotten into you. All I said was . . . "

I feel that I'm just about to lose it. I wave my index finger in front of Lacoste's nose.

"You better watch it, you little rat, because I'm going to be on your skin like leprosy. And if you try to pull off any of your shenanigans with Dell, I'm going to report you to your Dean and the American Medical Association."

Roger is no longer red, he's white as a sheet.

"I'll get you for that," he warns me. We stand chin to scalp for a few moments and he finally walks away, fuming. I stay in line, tension evaporating very slowly. God knows what characters like Lacoste are capable of when they're angry.

*   *   *   *   *

An hour later I'm inside terminal four in Heathrow, waiting for my direct flight home to Philadelphia. I'm in a relaxed mood, plenty of time before my flight. I spend several minutes in the British Airways lounge reading the daily newspapers, and munching on biscuits while drinking tea. When I'm done, I decide to roam the terminal, perhaps look for some last minute shopping items. Very few real bargains, but I like their wine and liquor selection. Just as I'm paying for a bottle of a thirty year old Taylor's Port at the duty free shop, I spot Dr. Larry Barnes in the distance. I pay and, without knowing exactly why, I start following Barnes down the long terminal. Barnes wears a white raincoat and carries a small brown briefcase. He walks at a fast clip, his pointed, shiny, elegant Italian shoes tapping and clicking as he does. He avoids the moving escalator and continues to walk parallel to it. I follow Barnes for several minutes, making sure not to get too close to him. At some point, he disappears behind a large column, and I increase my pace. When Barnes finally re-emerges, I notice that he is rapidly approaching what appears to be a young, tall, brown-haired woman. She wears a blue coat with its collar turned up covering the back of her head. He comes closer to her, and from the distance it seems that Barnes and the woman have touched each other in a familiar way. As I draw closer, Barnes and the woman start walking away, their backs turned to me. The couple arrives at gate number two and proceed to stand in the line, ready to board the plane. I start running, stopping only momentarily to check the destination of the flight leaving from gate two. The sign reads : "BA 179 to Nice." Just as I arrive at the gate, Barnes and the woman hand their boarding passes to the attendant. The woman goes first, and then turns around, awaiting Barnes to join her. And that's when I get a good look at her face. My heart skips a beat when Dara offers her arm to Barnes and they disappear, arm in arm, into the jetway.

After a few stunned moments I turn around to get my luggage and board flight 209 to Philadelphia. During the long flight home I keep reminding myself that the reason that I have to go after Barnes is because of Neurovan and not Dara.

* * * * *

When I emerge from baggage claim at the Philadelphia Airport, Irene and Danny are waiting in the car. It's an unseasonably warm March day in the Delaware valley, a muggy scorcher from out of nowhere in the waning days of winter. Irene is wearing her long brown slacks and a red-green colorful T-shirt, and with her hair tied in a bun behind her head she looks gorgeous. She gives me a short perfunctory hug, I don't know why, before Danny starts pulling on my pants and crying. I pick Danny up and we sit in the back seat together, Danny in my lap, with Irene looking at us through the rear-view mirror. There's a tiny shadow on her face, which translates into a queasy sensation in my stomach. We can't carry on any meaningful conversation because of Danny's babbling and screaming, but when we get home and Danny falls asleep, Irene makes a pot of strong tea and we sit next to each other on the sofa in the living room.

"So, how was it?" Irene asks, giving me a strange look.

"Honey, is anything wrong?" I inquire.

"Nope. So, tell me whether you sold your soul to the devil or not."

I'm taken aback a little, but I proceed to tell her everything. Or almost everything. About the rehearsals. About the Gother people. About the Vienna trip and Joe Lansing's threats. About the hearing and how I decided to say nothing for the time being, indeed, that I was willing to bend the truth when Lennox stepped forward and had his moment of truth. I explain how I decided to bide my time until hitting them will become more painful. I tell her how Lacoste is now on my shit list, and I'm on his.

"There's another patient with jaundice, dead, " she says when I finish.

"What?"

"There was a message on your answering machine from David Alberts. A young lady from Miami is apparently dead. He wanted you to call him."

"Dead? Jesus, that's Weissberg's patient," I say. "Boy, things are happening fast. Looks like I have less time than I thought."

I need to talk to David, to Lennox, and to Dara because we'll have to move on Gother quicker.

I suddenly remember something. I reach for the inner pocket of my jacket, searching for the $25,000 check, intending to give it to Irene as a present. She is staring at me obliquely, and I know something's wrong, so I pull out my empty hand from the jacket and wait for the shoe to drop.

"Did you get to do any sight-seeing while in London?" she asks.

"Yeah, I had some free time and I went to a few museums. The Caravaggios at the National Gallery are out of this world. Remember, honey, we loved it in our art book."

"Who'd you go with to the museum? Any other art lovers out there in Gother?"

"That philistine idiot Lacoste came for part of the time."

"Was that young woman there too, what's her name, Dara?"

"Yeah, she was there. I don't know why they send her everywhere. She really adds very little value to their program."

Irene is scrutinizing my facial expressions, but I just continue to talk matter-of-factly.

"You used to talk fondly about her," she remarks dryly.

"I did? What the hell is this supposed to mean?" I bark. I suddenly remember Dara and Barnes, arm in arm, getting on the plane to Monte Carlo.

Out of nowhere, she jumps up and waves a finger at me.

"You fucked her, you sonofabitch. How could you, you slimeball . . . "

She gets out of her chair and starts pounding my chest. She is screaming and wailing at the same time. I have never seen Irene lose her temper like this. I grab her hands in my fists.

"What the hell is wrong with you?"

"I'll tell you what's wrong with me. This is wrong with me." And she goes to the kitchen and comes back, handing me a crumpled piece of paper.

"What's this?"

"Read it, Casanova."

It's a printout of a very short message typed on a blank piece of paper, without any logo or address.

I start reading, but she yells,

"No, read it loud."

I peer at her and then I start reading it aloud.

"Irene Holden, ask Paul about his steamy Monday night in London. DL says thank you and hello."

"Where did you get it?" I ask.

"Came over the fax today."

"When?"

"I said today."

"I mean what time?"

"What difference does it make?"

"Tell me, when?"

"I don't know, it was here when I woke up."

This is not good.

"Sounds like a Gother job from London," I say.

"What's Dara's last name?"

She stops crying now, but speaks in an angry and hurt voice, which bothers me even more.

"I didn't do it, Irene."

"Answer me. What's her last name?"

"Lyons."

"DL is Dara Lyons. Right?"

"I don't know."

She knuckle dries her eyes.

"Why, Paul, why?"

"It's a lie, Irene. I swear to you."

"If you only stopped lying for one moment . . . "she says and starts crying again.

I start pacing the room. I always knew that Irene was the jealous type, but this . . .

"I'm going to get the bastard who did it. It's either Lansing or Lacoste, I'm pretty sure. I'm gonna get him, and break his neck, Irene, do you hear me? I'm gonna break his neck."

"Yeah, right, you big hero. You've been threatening to get the Gother people for so long, and what have you done? Nada. Zero. Zilch. You're a coward. I bet you stood up and declared their fuckin' drug safe and effective, in front of everybody in London. You sold your soul to the devil. And for what? For money and a fuck."

She's in my face now. She's never used a four-letter word with me before.

"Or were there many fucks. Did you do her in San Francisco too? And in Dallas? I bet you did, you miserable excuse for a human being."

I move away.

"Irene, you're losing your mind. But, you know, for all the crap I'm getting here now I'm sorry I didn't fuck her. D'you hear me? I'm damn sorry."

"Well, tell me then. Why would somebody make it up, huh, why?"

"Don't you see, they're trying to punish me for snooping in Vienna . . . no, this is just a warning, a blackmail . . . If I don't do what they want, they'll ruin my family life."

She's a little calmer, because she's listening to what I have to say. But she's not convinced.

"But . . . where there's smoke, there's fire . . . were you alone with her at all?"

"What d'you mean? Sure, I mean . . . we talked alone . . . we searched the computer together one night . . . in fact, that's what happened . . . somebody must have seen us in the business center."

She wants to believe me, I think.

"I don't know, Paul. Did you . . . touch her, I mean . . . kiss her?"

I hate it when someone's investigating my every action, especially a jealous woman on the verge of a nervous breakdown.

"No," I lie but I have no choice now, and I make sure that I lie loud enough, and I hope maybe this is not happening, it's just a dream . . . and I'm so tired . . .

"And if you believe an anonymous fax before you believe me, then maybe something is really wrong between us," I add indignantly.

But by the time I'm done, Irene is gone and she's in our bedroom and the door is slammed and I can hear her long, painful whimper.

I sit down, fatigued. I close my eyes and begin rubbing my temples, as they start throbbing. It's only five in the afternoon, but for my exhausted body it's really ten in the evening London time, and I want to sleep. Even a short nap would do, anything to eliminate the drowsiness and heaviness of my eyelids. But now I'm not going to fall asleep. I need to let Irene calm down first. Maybe we'll straighten this out tomorrow, but it won't be easy because Irene is nothing if not stubborn, especially when it comes to her possessiveness and its underlying insecurity.

I walk upstairs to use the phone in my den. I dial David's number and David picks up the phone after the first ring.

"What d'you know about the Miami patient?" I ask.

"Thirty one years old, has two small children. I'm told she had severe jaundice before she died. Husband fainted in the waiting room when he heard the news, they think maybe he had a small heart attack. They told me she was too sick for a possible liver transplant."

"How'd you find out?" I ask.

"Pure coincidence. I was calling all the Neurovan investigators for my articles, and one of them, in fact the last name on my list, a Dr. Weissberg, told me that the same morning one of his patients was admitted to the intensive care unit with jaundice."

I lean on the wall next to the phone.

"Do you have any information about the third patient in Austria?"

I give him the patient's name, age and so on, but mention that the local doctor managed to confuse me.

"Is this for the articles?" I ask when I finish.

"Yes. Listen, what are you doing tonight?"

"I don't know. I just got in from London and I'm beat . . . "

"Yeah, sure. I was just thinking, Lydia and Milo are here and we're all going out for some pizza, you know, nothing special . . . but I know you're tired."

Pizza and beer sound just like the right antidote for my tormented mood.

"I'm coming. Where are you guys going?"

"The pizza place out in Bryn Mawr. We'll be there in fifteen."

"It's a deal."

When I pass by our bedroom, I tiptoe. It's quiet and I think that Irene fell asleep.

TWENTY EIGHT

I GET INTO THE PIZZA PLACE JUST AS LYDIA, DAVID AND MILO ARE BEING seated in a corner booth. I scoot next to Lydia who gives me a warm peck on the cheek. She lost a little weight and looks pale, but the thick make-up does a good job of almost hiding it. I shake hands with the men.

"The big traveler is back," David says, and flashes his big gapped-tooth smile.

"Yep, it's nice to travel and it's nice to be back," I respond, but I think that I actually returned to hell.

"I told David not to invite you. I'm sure Irene wants you around a little after your long absence," Lydia smiles.

"I had a rough welcome. She thinks I had an affair in London," I blurt. I don't know why, but it feels surprisingly good to let it all out. I sense that I'm among friends.

There's a moment of silence.

"In case you are wondering, I didn't," I continue. "Somebody from Gother framed me. It's a long story."

I give them a Reader's Digest version of the CSM hearing and the Vienna trip. I leave out all the personal stuff with Dara,

Lansing, and Lacoste.

A young waitress appears and takes our orders.

"So, we still don't know for sure whether the Austrian case was a Neurovan induced problem?" David comments after I finish.

"Well, I'm fairly sure it is, but I can't prove it yet."

"How can you ever prove it?" Lydia asks.

I ponder the question.

"Well, we can look for the patient again—but that's not very practical at this time. Then, either we somehow get our hands on the patient's chart and lab numbers or we get a change of story from Kunz. I think he lied."

"Why?" David asks.

"Because he knew I came specifically to see him about Neurovan. And then there's the fax . . ."

"No, I meant why would he lie?"

"Oh, that I don't know. Pressure from Gother is my guess."

"David, maybe you should call this Kunz fella," Milo suggests.

"I could, but if he lied to Paul why would he tell me the truth?"

Milo shrugs.

"The human mind is a complex organ. Things change. Times change. Motivation and priorities change."

"How's your writing coming along?" I turn to David.

"Almost done. Actually, the first article is complete and should come out any day now. Tomorrow maybe."

"That was quick. By the way, what I just told you is off the record for your articles. At least for now."

I don't need my idle speculations or personal events in the newspaper.

"I've already mentioned the three sick patients. As I said, it's all done. I don't plan to make any changes, unless you find out more about the third patient."

"I'll keep you posted."

"Great. If you want, I can fax you a draft tonight."

"I'd appreciate it. Is it really juicy?"

"You'll have to judge for yourself."

The pizza's and beers arrive, and we start wolfing the food down.

"What else is new?" I ask, my mouth full between bites.

"Well, Jeff has submitted our lawsuit. It should have landed on the desk of the Gother legal department earlier today."

"It almost seems like a coordinated military assault . . . "

"It is, sort of."

"What about Mel Kraft and Tarrow?"

"We decided to leave Kraft alone. He's basically okay and Lydia feels sorry for him."

"And, no doubt," I say, "Jeff isn't sure how strong a case he has against him."

"That too," David chuckles. "Tarrow is a different story. We suspect that he screwed up, and probably falsified, the blood tests for my mother but we're not sure how."

"I know that there were irregularities in recording the data in the forms and entering them on the database at Gother. To prove it, I need to crack their computer system," I say. My jet lag is now catching up with me rapidly and I can barely keep my eyes open. The alcohol doesn't help.

Lydia is very quiet tonight. So is Milo, but I figure this conversation isn't really his cup of tea.

"I have a problem," Lydia says.

I look at her.

"Did I tell you that I was diabetic?" she asks.

"Yeah, I know that."

"Well, I have terrible pains in my feet and toes. It drives me nuts. They say I have diabetic neuropathy."

"I'm sorry to hear that."

"There's apparently nothing out there that works. They gave me some cream that actually burnt my skin. Then we tried all kinds of pills, I don't know, stuff they give for epilepsy, but nothing worked. I'm desperate, Paul."

"She lost some weight," Milo says, and puts his hand on Lydia's.

"There's a good expert out in Denver. A guy I know. Orville Morrison. We can call him first thing tomorrow morning," I offer.

"The guy I saw in Yale is also very good. Wrote the chapter on diabetes in the textbook. He ran out of ideas."

"Is your sugar well controlled?"

"Yes, but it doesn't seem to help."

Lydia looks me in the eye, and I can see that she's hurting as we speak.

"He wants to give me Neurovan," she says ruefully.

"What?" I shudder.

"He called around. He's been told that some people respond favorably. It's a small percentage but it's worth a shot."

I look at David and Milo in disbelief.

"This is insane."

They both look down as I speak, avoiding me.

"You've seen the risks," I go on, "you've seen what happened to your mother, the patient in Miami, and in Austria . . . "

Lydia's gaze is burning a hole in my face.

"True, but mom was on other medications . . . "

"Not at the time of her disease . . . " I protest.

"And the Miami patient, who knows, and maybe there's no Austrian patient . . . and every patient is different . . . "

"Paul, her pain is unbearable," Milo says.

This is too much for one day. I turn to Milo.

"So you'd let her take Neurovan . . . after all that's happened . . . "

Milo looks at Lydia. I turn to David.

"Paul, I don't know what to do," he says. "But she's an adult, you know."

Lydia looks suddenly so helpless and vulnerable.

"Fine," I say, "but Neurovan is not approved here. So you either enroll in a study, and I believe all studies have completed enrollment, or you get it in some of the countries where it was approved, like . . . I don't know . . . Ecuador . . . Turkey . . . "

I notice that all three are now giving me a strange look.

"We thought you might be able to get it for us . . . you know, directly from Gother . . . with all your connections."

"I really can't."

Lydia's green eyes are dull now, as if somebody hung a curtain across them. They're all laying a guilt trip on me with their gaze.

"Listen, I can't. My relationship with them has been too tumultuous. And after all the crap I've been giving them, my questions, snooping, I can't ask and they won't give. Besides, you've got a law suit pending. And the articles? How will that look? Blasting them on front pages across the country while your sister tries to obtain their product?"

A long pause.

"I haven't thought about it," David admits, holding a piece of pizza in front of his half-open mouth.

Another pause. We order coffee. Milo pulls out his pipe and sticks it in his mouth, unlit.

"If you insist on getting Neurovan . . . just call the Gother marketing department. They'll tell you exactly in which country to get it and how," I say finally.

"Okay," Lydia says tenderly.

"A real dilemma," Milo starts pontificating, "a lose-lose proposition. The need to make decisions without all the necessary information. Does the drug work on pain? No published data. Is it safe? Maybe for some, certainly not for everyone. What will the drug do to me, or you? Who knows?"

The coffee arrives and we all take our sips quietly.

"Unfortunately, Milo, I do know," I claim

Milo takes an imaginary puff from his pipe.

"Knowledge is worthless, unless it can be effectively communicated," he murmurs. "And to do so, one needs hard facts."

I take another long sip from the coffee, pensively.

"Paul, remember my mother's poem, the one David read out loud the other day?" Milo asks suddenly.

"How could I forget?"

"Well, what did you think it was about?"

"I like the part that goes: 'Stomach is throbbing like never before, and my eyes are cloudy hued like lawn.' It tells me she had jaundice for some time, possibly earlier than we think. There's no way that the January 27 lab results could have been normal."

David and Milo exchange glances.

"That's what we thought. I put all this in my article, though I'm on shaky ground with that," David says.

"I know. A poem is no proof. We made some progress on accessing their computers. Time is on our side," I promise.

I get up. I must be wearing a dogged look, because David asks,

"So, what next?"

"Turning on the heat, that's what's next. It's time for a little conversation with our favorite government agency. It's time to find out what the FDA knows and what they're going to do about it. We'll go from there. Keep the faith, lads."

They all get up and we hug. When I kiss Lydia on the cheek I get a wet salty taste in my mouth. Then I leave. I did my best to put a positive face on the situation, but my work is cut out for me. One thing I know. It'll be a frosty day in hell before I get Neurovan for Lydia.

*   *   *   *   *

I arrive home almost at midnight, 5 A.M. for my battered brain. Irene is in the kitchen drinking tea. I take one look at her dark, brooding facial expression and I know that the worst is yet to come.

I'm too tired for any meaningful conversation, let alone meaningless bickering. I just wave to her on my way to the bedroom.

"There's a message for you," she says.

I turn around and raise an eyebrow.

"Dara called."

"What?"

"She'll call again."

I don't like her ominous calm demeanor.

"Did you two . . . fight?" I ask.

"No. Would you like us to?"

This is not good!

I take off my jacket, and as I do I hear the envelope with Gother's check drop on the floor.

"I had a present for you," I say, "but I never had a chance to give it to you."

I hand the envelope to her. I know it's not going to make any difference, but I do it anyway. She looks at it without emotion. Then she opens the envelope, pulls out the check and studies it for a moment.

"Is this the price of your silence or of your sordid little affair?" she asks.

She could have used a four-letter profanity, but didn't. I wonder if it's good or bad. Probably bad because she's repressing.

I snatch the check from her hand and tear it into a thousand tiny pieces.

"Yes, it's the value of my affair."

I stagger to the bedroom, and fall flat on my face. I somehow manage to remove my shoes on the way.

TWENTY NINE

Friday, March 12, Philadelphia

FRIDAY MORNING I WAKE UP BEFORE FIVE O'CLOCK. ON THE TABLE IN the kitchen there's a little note. It's from Irene and reads: "Decided to spend the weekend with my sister. I need some time away. Talk to you next week. Maybe."

I know she took Danny with her. I am angry at this needless and mindless turn of events, but I decide to postpone my worries. I figure sooner or later she'll come to her senses. In the meantime I've got work to do.

I shave, shower, exercise and eat breakfast. Then I check all the notes I've made over the past couple of weeks, on paper, in the tape recorder and computer. From all the information, I prepare a list of arguments to use in my meeting with the FDA folks. Just as I finish the list, the fax machine whirs and David's article appears, a slow march of pages, for a total of more than forty. They are arranged in four parts, each part representing a separate newspaper article. I read each page carefully. It's a well written piece, chronologically describing the events of his mother's illness and death, putting it all in the context of the clinical trial. The scientific angle is somewhat weak, but the human and emotional side is strong. The language attacking Gother is direct and incriminating in nature. Gother is accused of every crime under the sun. From misleading and lying in their consent forms, hiding information and falsifying data to conspiring to deceive and ultimately hurt and kill innocent patients, all in the quest for the bottom line. He mentions all the major Gother players, giving full names and titles. He stops short of giving Dell's and Walnut's home address and phone numbers, and comes close to accusing them of genocide. If I am a Gother stockholder, I would dump all my stocks at the sight of this article. If I am the FBI reading this, I'd have a bunch of agents on a plane right now on their way to Berkeley to check this company out.

Attached to the article is a note from David, inviting me to a Gother stockholder's meeting next Monday at 1 p.m. in NY. I remember that Barnes had mentioned something about it when he communicated with Dell and Walnut aboard the Lear jet.

I fax David back: "David, your facts are correct (I think), but tone it down. Just my opinion. I'll go with you to NY. We can hop on the ten o'clock Metroliner."

It's around nine o'clock when I call Weissberg in Miami. He tells me more about his liver patient. A young woman, whom he describes as having been exceptionally attractive, diabetic for 18 years, complains to her husband that she's a little weak during breakfast, as she's about to send her two little kids to school. As soon as the kids are on the bus, she faints, and the husband carries her to the car and then to Jackson Memorial Hospital, the teaching hospital of the University of Miami. When she's admitted to the hospital she's yellow and confused. Her condition stabilizes, and things look up, but then there's a sudden deterioration, the liver practically stops functioning, she slips into deeper coma, bleeds from the gut and dies. The husband suffers a major heart attack, but Weissberg thinks that he'll recover. I ask about other medications, and the answer is nothing other than the usual Insulin injections that all young diabetics take. There's frequent beer drinking, but nothing out of the ordinary. He tells me that he seriously considers calling the FDA monitor, a fellow by the name of Aftaz. I encourage him to do that, writing Aftaz's name down as I do. I heard the name before, from Dara or Lennox, and calling him is next on my list of things to do.

I call the FDA office and make an appointment to see the medical monitor of Neurovan, Dr. Rashid Aftaz. I'm transferred from one extension to another three times but finally I get him. He answers the phone himself, and tells me to meet him in two weeks, but when I tell him that my subject is Neurovan and the liver, and he recognizes my name as a new advisory committee member, he says he'll meet me today at 2 p.m.

* * * * *

I take the train to Washington and from Union Station I hop on the local Metro train, the Shady Grove line. At ten minutes to two I'm walking from the Metro train station to the Park Lawn complex in Rockville, a Washington suburb where the offices of the FDA are located. It's a lot colder and breezier than yesterday, but the ten minute walk is brisk and pleasant. The FDA building is large, cold and gray, an austere office building with bare walls along endless corridors. After drifting in this huge maze for several minutes, I finally find myself in the office of Dr. Rashid Aftaz. He asks me to sit in front of his cluttered desk, while he seats himself behind it. He is a slight man in his late 40s, with receding hairline, chocolate colored skin, thick mustache and full mouth. His reading glasses are hanging from his neck, giving him a distinguished and scholarly demeanor. He gives the impression of enjoying the power he has, power I suspect he never expected, given his background.

A medical monitor like Aftaz, although not considered to be a top executive position in the FDA hierarchy, still wields a lot of power. If he likes a particular drug and recommends its approval, it usually sails through the advisory committee rapidly and gets approved. If he has any doubts, if he has any questions, if he isn't convinced by the results, a monitor can become very stubborn. Sometimes his questions can cost drug companies tens of millions of dollars, because he has the authority to demand new long, expensive clinical trials. It could also delay approval and marketing by many years.

Now he looks at his cluttered desk and takes a deep sigh.

"I try so hard, but I can never clear it. Every time I finish one thing, they bring me a new file. But I can't complain. It's all very interesting stuff."

He has a distinct accent, which is accentuated when he speaks fast, swallowing a few syllables in the process. He clears a small area on his desk and plants his elbows there, scanning my face for a few moments.

"So, you're an expert on liver diseases?" he starts.

"Yes, I'm on the faculty of Lincoln Hospital in Philadelphia."

"Oh, yes. It's a fine institution. And you want to tell me something about Neurovan?"

He leans back in his chair.

"Uh, Neurovan," he continues, as if talking to himself, "a wonderful concept. You inhibit one enzyme and you stop all diabetic complications at the same time—the eye, the kidney and the nerve. You know, we in the FDA helped design the studies that Gother is doing. People think that we're amateurs, ex-scientists, but sometimes we make very important contributions."

He smiles. "Maybe not big contributions. But still . . . do you know Dr. Lacoste?"

"Yes . . . "

"He's my mentor. I trained in endocrinology in St. Louis. The man is a genius."

"Oh, Dr. Lacoste is a . . . genius."

He leans forward again.

"Sorry for the distraction. Please, what is it you wanted to tell me?"

Now I'm starting to sweat, kicking myself for bothering with this meeting, but I proceed to describe my experience anyway. I avoid mentioning any names, but tell him about my being a paid consultant for Gother, which makes him raise his eyebrows. I give him the facts, in chronological order. Mrs. Alberts first. Lack of information in consent form. The constantly changing, and increasing, percentage of patients with reported elevated liver enzymes. When I get to the part about my suspicions that one set of data, from January 27, has been somehow manipulated, he stops me.

"What do you mean manipulated?"

I admit that I have no proof. It's just that they were missing from the initial chart, and that a computer printout indicated a possible later entry of data.

"These are serious charges, Dr. Holden. You shouldn't bring them up unless you are one hundred percent, no, one thousand percent, sure about the facts," he admonishes me.

As I mention the Miami case and Austrian case, he stops me again. This time he gets up and walks to a file cabinet in the corner and pulls out a heavy drawer exploding with documents.

"Dr. Holden, see this drawer? It's full of safety reports from Gother. There's nothing unusual about what you tell me. There may be some delay in sending information over, maybe they need time to sort it out. So what? We can be flexible sometimes, you know. But we know exactly what's going on, believe me."

"So you are not concerned about three patients dying because of Neurovan . . . "

He closes the cabinet and remains standing by the desk.

"Hold it. How do you know it's because of Neurovan?"

"Well, there's strong circumstantial evidence . . . "

He sits at the corner of his desk, feet dangling on the side.

"I talked to Dr. Lacoste about it. He assured me that so far, there's nothing unusual. I called the head of research at Gother, Dell, and he told me the same. The consensus among the experts is that the benefits outweigh any possible harm. In any case, we're monitoring the situation closely. If the drug is really to blame, we'll know exactly what to do."

I don't seem to get through to him. He just doesn't understand or care that if more people take Neurovan, more will die. Of course, I can't tell him everything that Dara told me about the inner workings of Gother, the selection of experts, the alterations of minutes of meetings, the rehearsal and hearing in the CSM, the attempts to buy CSM reviewers, my Viennese experience, Lansing's warning.

The phone rings and Aftaz answers it. He listens for a few moments, occasionally grunting something that sounds like "yes", and hangs up. He peers at me above his glasses.

"I assume, Dr. Holden, that you didn't notify Gother about your visit here?"

"No."

I have little doubt that Lacoste will find out while I'm still in the building.

"Why not?"

"This is really between myself and Gother."

"I see. But you are a paid consultant to Gother, right?" he asks again.

I decide that there's not much point in continuing this discussion.

"Dr. Aftaz, who's your superior at the FDA?"

He's off the desk, and goes back to his chair.

"Dr. Ness. Philip Ness."

I get up and he jumps up and we stand by the door.

"I hope you know what you're doing, Dr. Aftaz," I say.

"Interesting. This is exactly what I was going to say to you."

We shake hands and I leave. When I reach the end of the tortuous hallway I look back, and catch a glimpse of Aftaz still standing at the door of his office.

*   *   *   *   *

From the FDA I travel back to Union station where I catch the five fifteen train back to Philadelphia. It's half empty, and I doze off as soon as the train starts moving. But in that hazy zone that separates sleep from alertness, there's a swirl of thoughts that chases me every time I seem to slip into snooze.

So far, my deep involvement with this Neurovan project has led to exactly nothing. Trials are ongoing, the drug may get approved in several countries, including a major country such as England, Gother is flourishing, Lydia Alberts considers taking Neurovan, the only potential financial benefit is torn to pieces, and my wife left me for an affair I didn't even have! My first priority is to get my wife and son back. I know I should have done a better job of controlling emotions: mine and Irene's. This is too heavy a price to pay for the search for some elusive truth. I need to remove all her doubts about me, and then there's no reason why I can't get her back. I'll just have to say the magic words. Whatever they turn out to be.

As for the Neurovan story, I need a smoking gun, and I

haven't got one. From the way they talk at Gother, Barnes, Ramsey, Lansing, I know that ethics plays no role in their decision making or behavior. Lacoste is another living proof of the corruption, and I'll take care of him one way or another for the fax I think he sent Irene. But, living proofs are not enough. What I need is clear indisputable proof, preferably in writing, for something that will clearly indict Gother. I hope that Dara will come through during her travels with Barnes to the French Riviera. At least, I hope that's the reason for her surprising trip. Ah, who am I kidding? She realizes who's putting the butter on her bread, and it's Barnes, not me. Also, I haven't figured out how Lansing knew about my journey to Vienna. Who told him? Only two people knew about it—Kunz and Dara. Dara? Nah. She wouldn't. Must've been Kunz.

I doze off and again my mind is spinning. Kunz . . . Vienna . . . jaundiced patient . . . in bed one moment, gone the next . . . Kunz not showing up . . . Lansing's story about him taking Kunz's daughter to the opera . . . where was Kunz when I needed him? . . . patient . . . yellow patient . . . what's his name . . . yellow patient's name . . . I only had a short glimpse of him . . . his name . . . he has a Christian name . . . Christian, that's it . . . ah, who cares . . . why am I worried about his name . . . what matters is that he never took Neurovan . . . or so says Kunz . . . no, he took some other drugs . . . I know Voltaren . . . arthritis drug, can cause liver disease in a big way . . . so this settles it . . . wait, he took another drug. . . Vanuoren . . . I remember . . . I have good memory for names . . . Vanuoren . . . never heard of Vanuoren . . . strange name . . .

Suddenly, I'm wide awake. It hits me like a ton of bricks. Vanuoren has the same letters as Neurovan! I check it in my mind many times and I realize it's correct. A coincidence? I don't think so. A drug that nobody has heard of has the same letters as

Neurovan. Kunz was sending me a message, and I blew it. Why didn't he just say Neurovan, if that's what he meant? God, why? Maybe he couldn't talk because . . . because . . . somebody was with him at the time . . . Lansing? So why did he call? To tell me that the jaundiced patient had been taking Neurovan after all. Why was he afraid?

Is my imagination running wild with me? Am I on to something or am I on the brink of losing my senses? It's only been two days since my trip to Vienna . . . I figure there's only one way to find out. I get up and move to the end of the car where the pay phone is located.

I dig from my pocket all the papers and notes about the Neurovan affair, and fumble through them until I find the phone number of the hospital. I go through the international operator, billing the call to my telephone card. The phone rings, and within a few moments somebody answers it. It's close to midnight in Vienna, hardly the best time for getting critical information, but I have no choice.

"Hallo?" I hear a woman's voice and immediately I envision the chubby middle-aged nurse who was trying to help me while I was there.

"This is Professor Holden, and I'm calling about Christian Hauptmam . . . "

"Ach, ja, I remember you. My name is Erika . . . "

Erika. She's the other nurse who knew the patient's name.

"How's the patient?"

"He's in the other hospital, I think. Maybe you call in the morning and we look for telephone number . . . "

That's no help. It's time to try the long shot.

"Is Professor Kunz there?"

Long pause.

"Hello, Erika . . . "

"Ja, I'm here . . . you don't hear?"

"Hear what?"

"Professor Kunz died of heart infarct. How you say? Heart attack. Yesterday. He is tot . . . uh, dead."

"Are you telling me that Professor Kunz died of a heart attack?"

"Ja."

"How did it happen?"

"Very suddenly. He not come to clinic in morning . . . his daughter find him in bed."

"Did he make it to the hospital?"

"I don't know. He die very quickly."

"Was . . . was he sick before?"

"Nein. Nein. He always in excellent shape. Never smoke. Cholesterol very low. He ski a lot . . . climb mountains . . . everybody great surprise."

"So, you're sure this was heart attack?"

"Ja. Everybody say this."

I'm too stunned to think of anything else I might want to know.

"You Americans come to funeral, nein?" she asks.

"Funeral? When is it?"

"Montag . . . Monday."

I don't see how I could possibly travel to Vienna on such a short notice, or what good it is going to do. After all, I never met the man in person. But . . . something didn't sound right . . . what the hell did she say?

"Did you say Americans?" and I stretch the "s" into a long hissing sound.

"Ja . . . two Americans visit same day . . . I think maybe you together . . . "

"Who was the other American?"

"I don't know. Also, very big, like you. Big head. Brown hair, very short. Hair short, not man." She chuckles. "All Americans so big."

Damn!

"Somebody joke that Kunz see two big rich Americans he get a heart attack," she prattles on.

"Erika, is there another doctor there?"

"Ja, we just had a very sick patient. Many doctors here."

What was the name of that doctor who I kept bumping into while I was waiting for Kunz? I dig into my memory vault one more time. I can see him . . . muscles . . . white coat . . . straight hair . . . he had a name tag above his pocket . . . a very common German first name. . .

"Erika, when I was there I met another doctor. His first name was Franz . . . no, Fritz. Yes. Fritz."

"Ach, ja. Fritz Reiber. He is here."

Reiber. That's him.

"Can I please speak to him?"

There's another pause and I hear voices in the background. Finally,

"Doctor Reiber here."

"Yes. Hello. I'm Dr. Holden and a few days ago. . . "

"I remember you."

A deep voice, no particular warmth. Excellent accent.

"I am very sorry about Professor Kunz."

"Yes. He was my teacher. A very sad day."

The car is bouncing and shimmying and I wonder why on earth they can't give us a smooth ride, here in the East Coast of the greatest nation on earth, when it's so easy to achieve in every little country in Europe.

"Erika told me that he had a myocardial infarction?" I am using the precise term for heart attack secondary to blockage of the arteries that feed the heart.

"Yes, it looks like it."

"And you have no reason to doubt it?"

"No. I don't know what you're trying to say . . . "

"The day I came to Vienna was very strange. First, Kunz didn't show up for our planned five o'clock meeting . . . "

"He is very punctual. Sometimes things get so busy . . . "

"Then he calls me at the hotel and tells me that the patient . . . do you know the patient Hauptman?"

"Very little."

"Have you heard about a drug called Vanuoren?"

"Vanuoren?"

I spell it for him.

"No. What is it supposed to treat?"

"Arthritis."

"I have extensive training in rheumatology. There must be some mistake. This drug doesn't exist in Austria."

"Dr. Kunz told me that this patient suffered from liver disease induced by Voltaren and Vanuoren . . . "

"Of course. Voltaren can damage the liver badly, but the other drug doesn't exist."

It's time to stop beating around the bush.

"Was there an autopsy performed on Dr. Kunz?"

"No. This is not done in Austria in routine cases."

"Well, I'm telling you that there was foul play here and that an autopsy is absolutely essential."

"What?"

"I believe that Kunz was killed. Murdered."

I can hear the heavy breathing of Dr. Reiber.

"You have evidence for that?"

"I do. I want you to contact the pathologists and the local police to start the procedures. I'm sending you a detailed fax when I get home, in a few hours."

"I can't just tell them that somebody thinks that maybe . . . "

"Listen, Reiber, he was your teacher. You know he was healthy and in great physical shape. Somebody was upset at him and killed him. I don't know who or how, but we'll figure it out somehow. But we can't prove anything without an autopsy."

A long pause.

"Dr. Reiber, I think you owe it to this great professor."

Still pause.

"Dr. Reiber?"

"Okay, fax me the information. I'll see what I can do."

"Thank you."

I hang up.

I stagger back to my seat, fighting the swerving and shifting of the train cars until I reach my seat and slump in it. Finally, I fall asleep around Wilmington, which gives me exactly fifteen minutes of deep rest.

THIRTY

At home, no signs or messages from Irene. There's another message from Dara, just saying that she wants to talk to me, and confirming her plans to return home next week. There's also a message from my boss, Dr. Arthur Scott. It's been some two weeks since I took time off to pursue the Neurovan project, and he must be wondering how things are going.

I dial the number of Ellen, Irene's sister, but I get the monotonous message on her answering machine. I repeat the exercise every few minutes, but no luck.

Then I decide to call Art Scott, but this turns out to be a terrible mistake. I'm in bed on my back, while dialing his number at home. His son picks up the phone, and a moment later Art is on the line.

"Paul, how's it going?" he inquires.

"Pretty good."

"Making good progress, are you?"

"I think so, but I still haven't got the problem licked. More patients have suffered serious liver problems from this drug."

"Uh-huh. So what exactly have you found out?"

I don't like the tone of his voice.

"There's something going on, Art, you know, with Gother. I don't think they'll give up on their drug, not without a huge fight."

"Uh-huh. Actually, this is why I called."

"What is?"

"Gother. Their president, a Carter Dell, called me. He complained about you."

"Oh?"

"He said that you were acting strange, irresponsibly. Something about unauthorized talking to investigators, visiting and harassing the staff of an intensive care unit in Europe, then something about passing unauthorized information to the FDA, God knows what else."

Aftaz is faster than a rabbit.

"Hmm. Is that all, Art?"

I'm cruisin' for a bruisin'.

"He also mentioned something to do with adultery. In London."

I close my eyes.

"Everything's true, Art, except the adultery."

"Paul, they're pissed like you won't believe it."

"Sure, that's because I'm closing in on them and they're getting scared."

"Paul, I don't like this. I'm afraid your time is up."

"What are you saying, Art?"

"I want you back in the department Monday. Your assignment with Gother is finished."

I sit up in bed, rubbing my eyes.

"Art, you can't do this to me."

"I just did."

"But you gave me until the end of the month."

"That was before you stuck your nose where it doesn't belong."

"Art, they may have killed a doctor, one of the investigators."

"Uh-huh. Really? Have you notified the FBI?"

He's made up his mind and isn't taking anything I say seriously.

"Art, I beg you. One week."

"No."

"I'll be back at work Monday in nine days."

"No."

"Sorry, Art, but I have no choice. In time you'll understand."

I hang up, and I know he's fuming at the other end.

Bastards!

I can barely keep my eyes open, but suddenly I feel hungry. I throw two eggs into the frying pan, while at the same time dialing Ellen's number for the umpteenth time. This time the phone is answered and it's Irene.

"Hi," I start.

"Hi."

"How are you?"

"Fine. And you?"

"Okay."

"How's Danny?"

"Good."

"Does he miss me?"

"I don't know." A pause. "I suppose he does."

I use the fork to scrape the eggs off the buttered pan.

"Irene, please come home."

I hear a deep sigh.

"I need you, Irene."

Another sigh.

"Give me some time, Paul."

"I've a had a bad day, Irene. A bad couple of days."

She says nothing and I think maybe she's listening.

"I went to the FDA and they weren't interested. Then Art called and told me to return to work immediately because Gother complained about me."

I'm holding the receiver close to my face and I swear I can smell her L'Oreal sprayed hair.

"I don't think I can win this without you."

I take the pan off the stove and scrape the eggs into a plate. I pick a tomato from the refrigerator and look for a slicing knife, all the while holding the receiver between my ear and shoulder.

"So what did you tell Art?" she finally shows some interest.

"I told him to take this job and shove it."

"You didn't."

"I didn't, but came darn close. Bottom line is I'd better hurry."

I cut the tomato into nice regular slices, and then grab a roll and place it on the plate next to the eggs. I also open a bottle of Heineken and place it on the kitchen table next to the plate.

"I'll see you, Paul," she says and hangs up. The way she says it I know we'll be all right, eventually.

I eat my light dinner slowly while watching TV, drink my beer and go to bed. The house is eerily quiet as I turn the lights off.

*   *   *   *   *

On the weekend we get one of the worst snowstorms of the century—eighteen inches of white fluff parachuting to the ground and hugging it in a huge white blanket. Unprepared for this, I have to walk through deep snow and blowing wind to buy some basic food items. The entire trip takes me almost two hours, and when I finally stumble back into the house to take off my wet boots, I feel invigorated by the experience.

My mood isn't great, though. I am angry at not having Irene here, I miss Danny, and I'm upset at my boss and Gother. Lydia calls me to remind me about getting Neurovan for her from Gother and we fight over the phone, because I refuse, and that upsets me too. Most of all, I'm upset at the slow progress of my investigation.

I do find some time to fax Reiber a letter, describing the major reasons for my suspicions that Kunz's death may not have been accidental. It's not easy to convince myself, let alone Reiber, that somebody would kill Kunz to prevent him from reporting a serious adverse effect of a new drug, but the only way to find out is to perform an autopsy. Many chemical substances, some used as legitimate medicines, can lead to death-mimicking symptoms of a heart attack. The only way to find out is to check the body for the chemical, and any criminal pathologist worth his salt should know how to find it. I make a strong case in my letter and hopefully he'll show some initiative and get the autopsy done.

On Sunday, Dara calls. I'm in the shower when the phone rings. I grab a towel and pick up the phone in the dining room.

"Paul, finally," she starts.

I wrap the towel around my waist.

"Dara. Where are you?"

"Uh. . . I'm still in France. I plan to fly home in a coupla days."

"So, what's up?" I blow air on the frozen window, and it condenses at once.

"It's still busy as hell. How about you?"

"Everything is good."

I'm cautious, waiting to hear first why she calls.

"Gerry Lennox is on his way out," she tells me.

"What?"

"It's all unofficial, but rumor is he's getting sacked."

"Because of the CSM?"

"That's what I hear."

This is bad news. For Gerry, of course, but also for our battle. His insider status is invaluable for me.

"Who told you?" I ask.

"Oh, I've got my ways."

"I bet. Anything else you heard?"

"Rumor has it that you went to the FDA to complain about Gother. That's considered really bad form, you know."

"Not to worry. Tell your Gother buddies that the FDA has showed very little interest in my story. That medical guy, Aftaz, is he on your payroll too?"

"Paul, you sound weird. Is everything okay?"

I peer through the foggy glass to the snow-covered driveway.

"Irene left me. Somebody sent her a fax accusing me of having an affair with you."

Dara starts laughing like a hyena.

"Does that mean that you're free now?"

"Dara. . . "

"Just kidding, Paul. I'm laughing because you're such a klutz. You'd have been better off having the affair."

I don't answer.

"Paul. Let me talk to her. I'll tell her that nothing happened."

"She's not home. Some other time, maybe."

The snow seems to have tapered off outside the window, but the wind picks up.

"How's Barnes doing?" I can't help it.

"How the hell should I know?" she asks indignantly.

"I thought you went to the Riviera with him."

There's a beep in my ear, indicating a call waiting, but I decide to ignore it.

"Who told you?"

"I've got my ways."

"Paul, tell me who told you."

"I saw you two lovebirds at the airport."

"Listen, he asked me to help him on some project. You'll be proud of what I've accomplished with Barnes."

"I can't wait, Dara."

She giggles.

"Can it be, Paul? Are you jealous?"

I start pacing in the room, receiver in hand.

"I just don't like being lied to, that's all."

A long pause.

"So what happens now?" she asks.

"Nothing. I'm still working on stopping Neurovan. I'll tell you more when we meet."

"When will that be?"

She has this warm velvety voice and I don't want to end the conversation on a foul note.

"I don't know, but I'm sure it's going to be fairly soon. Call me when you get back to San Francisco."

A pause.

"Paul?"

"Yes?"

"Take care of yourself, do you hear me?"

"I will, Dara, and you do the same."

I hang up and stand for a few moments in front of the window. I drop the towel to the floor and watch the snow flakes float gently, yet with great purpose, until they hit the mountain of snow already on the ground. I'm still buck naked when the phone rings.

It's Irene.

"I just tried calling you. Who were you talking to?"

"I just came out of the shower. In fact, I'm still totally naked."

"Oooh," she smacks her lips. That's much better, I think.

"The snow is too much, so I'll try driving back tomorrow," she tells me.

"I'm going to New York tomorrow with David. We're going to a Gother meeting with the analysts."

"Okay. Then I'll see you when you come back, weather permitting."

"Great."

The rest of the evening I just slouch in front of the television. I can't remember the last time I had such a peaceful and quiet evening. I watch "The Guns of Navarone" on the old movies channel, joining it just when Anthony Quinn falls on his face feigning sickness, so that he can jump the guards and escape. I love every minute of it. When the movie is over I watch a brief interview with the new heavyweight boxing champion.

"If you were pitted against the strongest wrestler in the world, or the strongest player in the NFL," the interviewer asks the champion, "could any of them beat you?"

"One punch," the champion says.

"What?"

"That's all I need. One punch."

"Yeah, but some linesman in the NFL are three-hundred pounds, big, strong men . . . "

"One punch."

"You seem so confident . . . "

"One punch."

I turn the television off and proceed to bed. I sleep very well that night, for the first time in a long time.

*   *   *   *   *

Monday, March 15, New York

Different drug companies have different ways of communicating with Wall Street analysts. Some form special ties with one or two brokerage houses and then feed them periodic updates. Other companies announce every achievement as it happens, minor as it may be. This is done mostly to get a bump in the stock price. Gother has a biannual meeting with analysts who cover the pharmaceutical industry. This winter's meeting is held at the Waldorf-Astoria in New York. The Gother brass, chief executive officer Dick Walnut, chief financial officer Parfitt and chief operating officer Dunbar flew to the East Coast over the weekend in the corporate jet. Dell, the president of the research organization, is also invited. His role is to field medical scientific questions, should any arise.

When David and I arrive it's almost three o'clock, and the large ballroom is filling up in a hurry. David gives me an identification card marked "Press" and the security officer at the door lets me in. I look around. Several dozen well-dressed people mill about, slowly taking their seats. A long desk is positioned in the center of the stage, and seated behind the desk are four people. David and I find a couple of seats in the back and I sit down. I tell David that maybe we shouldn't be seen together here, and he walks away. I follow him as he finds an empty chair closer to the podium.

Richard Walnut, III, a tall lanky man in his early 60s, large forehead, short silvery hair and deeply wrinkled, tanned face, surveys the chattering crowd for several long moments. He looks at his watch and finally stands up. A gradual hush falls on the room. He walks to the microphone in the center of the stage.

"Good afternoon, ladies and gentlemen. It's a pleasure and a privilege to update you on the status of our organization. We have made great progress since we last talked and we can't wait to tell you all about it. We'll start with a short financial statement. Dan."

He motions to Dan Parfitt who stands up and gives a very brief presentation, discussing the company's debt, investment in research, sales, projected sales and profits, and so on. After him, the chief operating officer Dunbar talks about their worldwide organization, number of employees in each country, the expected growth in number, and so on. Finally, it's Walnut's turn to talk about the Gother portfolio and future plans.

Through colorful slides, he discusses every product, from the gleam in the eye of the lab researcher to products nearing approval for sale. He talks about medical need, diseases without treatment and how Gother's drugs can alleviate pain and suffering. Though he spends a relatively long time on every single project, he must be sensing some restlessness in the crowd. It is evident to most present that none of the products sounds particularly promising or exciting, as they are old drugs in new clothes, all based on well known and widely existing principles. No cures, no breakthroughs, just minor modifications of current drugs at best. He leaves Neurovan to the end.

"I'm delighted to tell you about the apple of my eye, Neurovan. As many of you know, we have invested close to 200 million dollars in its development and we're finally getting to the finish line. We have studies for every complication of diabetes, but the one that's almost done is for nerve damage, or neuropathy. Here we have the first drug that eliminates the terrible pain that accompanies this illness. It also prevents the progression of damage, so that loss of limbs can be all but eliminated. Its actions are based on interference with the main cellular mechanism that leads to cell destruction in diabetic tissues. We should be finishing the studies in the next few short months and submit a new drug application, or NDA, later this year. In the meantime, we are seeking, and receiving, approval in all major countries in the world."

He then shows slides depicting the severity of complications in diabetics, their number and potential sales of Neurovan. For neuropathy alone, he thunders, the drug could sell more than $1 billion dollars, because there is nothing else out there. He concludes by sketching out a general timetable for submitting an NDA for all indications.

The reporters take notes feverishly, and when Walnut finishes many hands shoot up. Walnut points to a young pudgy woman in the first row.

"Have the neuropathy studies been finished?" she wants to know.

"All patients have been enrolled, and most of them had the second biopsy."

"So you've analyzed all the data?" she persists.

"The studies remain blinded until all the information from the last patient is collected, entered onto the data base and verified."

Walnut looks at Dell, who nods. Dell looks a lot younger than I had imagined based on my brief telephone communication with him from Dallas. He is in his early forties, and his thick brown hair is sprayed and combed backwards, exposing a tall forehead.

"So how do you know that the drug will do all these wonderful things that you mentioned?" somebody asks.

"We have analyzed other smaller studies, and also we have a pilot study that was very positive," Walnut says and looks at another person in the audience.

"Is the drug safe?" comes a question from one of the front rows. I see a raised tape-recorder high in the air.

Walnut hesitates for a fraction of a moment.

"Based on all our information Neurovan is extremely safe and well tolerated. We did see a small number of patients with minor changes in liver functions, but these were reversible when Neurovan was stopped."

"Any cases of jaundice?"

Same man in the front, and suddenly I realize it's David Alberts asking all these questions.

Walnut looks around and flashes a big, reassuring smile.

"Adverse events are common in any large trial," he says. "The question is whether any of them are drug related, and our conclusion is a resounding no. Besides, I think we're getting too technical for this type of meeting."

"Perhaps the doctor knows the answer," somebody yells from the audience and an unflappable Walnut motions to Dell, who stands up and saunters to the microphone.

"To date, we have no confirmed cases of jaundice caused by Neurovan," he says with a smile.

"How about unconfirmed?" David asks. Finally Walnut shows signs of irritation, which he still tries to hide with a smile. He motions to Dell to ignore the last question, and Dell starts returning to his seat, when David mutters to the woman next to him, in a voice that carries through most of the room,

"Liars."

Dell stops in mid-step as if snake-bitten, but Walnut motions to another member of the audience. David climbs on his chair and announces:

"If you really want to know what this drug does read my series in your local newspaper."

He gets off the chair and storms out of the room. Walnut bites his lower lip as he listens to a new question about a different drug. I wait a moment or two and leave the hall. I catch up with David outside at the Park Avenue entrance.

"Come, I'll buy you a great Italian lunch," I grab him by the elbow, "there's this great place in Little Italy."

We're in a cab, but we're silent. By the time we're dropped off in front of "Angelo's" we're laughing hysterically.

"Did you see that smug Walnut, he looked as if he'd swallowed a frog," he says.

"You sure gave them hell," I say. We're both laughing but we're not sure exactly why.

"Do you still think that my article is too harsh?" he asks.

"Not really."

Sitting among the hundreds of wine bottles and in an authentic, bubbling Italian ambiance, I have one of the best pasta dishes in memory. And the tiramisu was made in heaven.

THIRTY ONE

I GET HOME FROM NEW YORK AROUND EIGHT. NO SIGN OF IRENE AND Danny, so even before taking off my coat, I call Ellen. She tells me that Irene took Danny and her son Michael to McDonald's for dinner.

"When is she coming home?" I ask.

"I'm not sure, Paul."

I don't like the sound of her voice.

"Everything okay, Ellen?"

She hesitates. Ellen and I always get along fine.

"She got a package today."

"A package?"

"Well, actually it was a large envelope. Somebody left it outside the door."

"What was in the package?"

"A picture."

She's telling me things in bits and pieces, so I have to drag it out of her.

"Dammit, Ellen, what the hell are you talking about?"

"They sent a picture of that bimbo you slept with, Dara . . . "

"Ellen, I didn't sleep with her. Do you hear me? I didn't. It's all a big lie."

She's not saying anything.

"Ellen, do you believe me?"

"She's a knock out, this Dara," she says.

"Ellen, you gotta believe me."

"It's Irene you have to convince."

I sit down.

"Ellen, what else was in the envelope beside Dara's picture?"

"Just a little note. 'Thanks for a great night, signed Dara.'"

"Bastards!"

I take my coat off slowly.

"Please tell Irene to call me when she gets back."

"Okay."

"Tell her I love her and miss her."

"Will do."

"Ellen, I swear to you . . . what else can I do?"

"Paul, just hang in there."

I get up trying to untangle myself from the coat.

"Ellen?"

"Yes?"

"That picture of Dara, was there anybody else in it with her?"

"No."

"So she was all by herself?"

"Yes."

"Is the picture in color?"

"Yes."

"Where is it shot?"

"All beaches look the same to me."

"Beaches? What is she wearing?"

"Nothing, Paul. Absolutely nothing."

I untie my tie and open my shirt collar.

"So, d'you think Irene's more angry . . . "

"I think she'd like to believe you, but she finds it very hard."

"So, please, don't forget to tell Irene that I called."

"Okay, Paul."

I hang up, and wonder if Dara's picture is a recent job taken at the French Riviera.

More importantly, I try to figure out how they knew where Irene is staying. A cold shiver runs down my spine and I enter the dining room to close the window. The temperature is dropping rapidly and will soon hit the zero mark.

I turn on the heating system and light a log in the fireplace. I make myself a strong hot tea, holding the mug tightly in my hands as I walk to the living room. I sit in front of the fireplace and close my eyes, slowly achieving a measure of complete relaxation. If I were more relaxed, I'd be asleep. My state of Nirvana lasts only for a few short minutes because the phone rings.

It's Milo. We chat for a few minutes about Lydia and her painful feet, but he's in his usual ruminative mood, and I am in a talkative mood and as it turns out he's visiting some friends not far from my house. I invite him over for tea and pastries. I'll supply the tea and he'll have to bring the pastries because my cabinets are empty.

An hour later the doorbell rings and Milo is at the door. He's got a pipe in his mouth and a dark-red scarf around his neck as he enters the house and shakes my hand. On his head he wears a checkered beret, which he removes. From the inner pocket of his coat, which he also takes off, he brings out a bag full of biscuits, scones and brownies. I show him to the living room and he collapses on the couch, scanning the surroundings as he does.

"Do you mind if I smoke?" he asks.

"Not at all."

He tinkers for a moment with the tobacco in his pipe, then lights a match and buries it in the tobacco. He inhales deeply and there's a flicker at the end of his pipe.

"Nice house," he observes, looking around.

"We like it."

We're at the uneasy juncture when the conversation has no direction or plan.

"Can I get you some tea?" I get up.

"Absolutely."

I go into the kitchen and return moments later with two steaming mugs of tea.

"Where's Irene?" he asks after the first sip.

"She's at her sister's. Should be home soon."

"You kids still fighting?" he asks. I now remember mentioning something about Irene at the pizza place a few days ago.

"She doesn't believe me. We were almost there, but they sent her another picture of my alleged co-conspirator, and now she's angry again."

"Who did?"

"I don't know. Has to be somebody associated with Gother."

"You're sure?"

"Who else?"

He puts down the cup.

"She's a lovely woman. I'm sure it'll all work out."

I get up to add more wood to the fire. I assume he's talking about Irene.

"She'll be sorry that she missed you," I say.

"Did you ever solve that Austrian case?" he asks.

I tell him about my figuring out the message that Kunz was trying to send me, about his untimely death and about my pursuit of a possible autopsy to find out how he died.

"You don't think that Gother is somehow involved?"

"Milo, I don't know what to think anymore."

We're both leaning back in our couches, pensive. He takes another long whiff from his pipe, looking around at the large rooms.

"Greed and Capitalism. The twins of the ever elusive search for distant dreams. Do you know what the definition of happiness is?"

I look at him.

"It's achievement minus expectations. One way to be happy more often is to lower one's expectations. It always works."

Milo is now surrounded by smoke and his calm soothing voice permeates the air from seemingly nowhere.

"Capitalism is the worst possible economic structure, except for all the others. The question is, where does equality and justice come into the picture? Can we survive as a society if more and more people make less and less, and less and less people make more and more?"

"That's called free market economy, Milo," I interrupt his rhetorical musings.

He waves his hand up and down in the air, cutting through the thick smoke.

"Rubbish. There's no such thing as free market. All markets are manipulated by governments."

I don't know that I want to engage in a deep economics-philosophical discussion now, but the soothing tone of his speech and the overpowering tobacco aroma sedates me and I'm happy to be with somebody like Milo in my tired and confused frame of mind. I say nothing for a moment.

"Forgive me, Paul. I have this uncontrollable habit, as I'm sure you've noticed by now, to break everything down in life into its smallest possible psycho-philosophical component."

He drinks slowly from his tea.

"What do we do with Lydia?" he suddenly asks.

Before I have a chance to respond he continues.

"She wants the medication badly, but I agree with you that it's more likely to harm than help her. But we've got to do something."

I have an idea.

"Let's give her placebo tablets."

"What?"

"When Gother made Neurovan tablets, they also had to manufacture placebo tablets that don't contain any active ingredient, but look and taste just like Neurovan."

Milo lights his pipe again for a long moment.

"Hmm . . . " he says, "placebo effect. She'll think that she gets the real thing and feel better just because of that. Now that's not the most honest approach . . . "

"In the Neurovan trials, almost half the diabetics feel better in the placebo group."

"And, of course, there are no side effects . . . "

"None."

"I like it," he concludes.

"The question is, will they give it to me."

We ponder the options for a moment.

"My only hope is to get it from Lennox. I have to do it quickly before he's fired."

Milo looks at me quizzingly. I tell him about Dara's report on the rumor. Coming from her, while she's with Barnes, it's more like a sure bet than a rumor.

Milo gets up and starts pacing.

"I read David's article," he says. "I can't get over what Gother is trying to do, and is doing, for the proverbial bottom line. For the most part, you've kept unruffled and extremely stoic about the whole thing."

"I always remember what Marcus Aurelius used to say . . . " I start.

Milo stops pacing and gives me a look, like who's the philosopher around here.

"Begin each day by telling yourself: Today I shall encounter interference, insolence, disloyalty, ill will and selfishness—all due to the offenders' ignorance of what's good or evil."

"Exactly," Milo smiles, "book two, section one. Do you know what else Marcus Aurelius said?"

Milo continues to talk while stopping to scan my collection of musical discs.

"In the life of a man, his time is but a moment, his being incessant flux, his senses a dim rush light. Where, then, can man find the power to guide and guard his steps?" Milo stops his recitation as if asking me for the answer.

"In one thing and one alone: Philosophy," I quote from memory.

Milo comes closer to me.

"I'm impressed, Paul. Tell me something, do you have some good brandy here?"

"Sure."

"Well why don't you get me a large one, get one for yourself and let's listen to the third symphony of Mahler. What do you say?"

I get us the drinks and set up the disc player for a magnificent evening of music, chat and relaxation. For the next hour I don't even think once about Neurovan or Gother.

It's after midnight when Milo is ready to depart, but it starts snowing again and I convince him to stay. I give him a blanket and he lies down on the sofa in front of the fireplace.

*   *   *   *   *

Tuesday, March 16, Philadelphia

Next morning I'm up early. I'm pleased to discover that despite the snow, my daily newspapers have arrived.

In the kitchen, over poached eggs and toast, the television tuned in to the local news, I turn to the Philadelphia Inquirer first, and down in the middle of the front page I see the headline of David's article: "A Deadly Cure." The italicized sub-text reads: "Part One: The Drug and the Patients." A boxed text informs me that this is the first installment in a series of articles, dealing with corruption in the pharmaceutical world. I read from top to bottom, and it's only slightly modified from the draft that I have seen. The first paragraph reads as follows:

"A few weeks ago I was paged at Dulles airport, Washington, D.C., just as I was ready to board a plane. I was told that my mother had become seriously sick. Instead of flying to San Diego I flew to Philadelphia, where I found my mother at death's doorstep. She had intense jaundice and was in coma. A few days later she died, and she was only 52. I found out that the cause of her death was a drug called Neurovan, manufactured by a company called Gother inc., head-quartered in Berkeley, CA. Neurovan is not approved for marketing, but is approved for testing by the FDA. She was in a clinical trial and paid with her life so that somebody else might benefit from this anti-diabetes drug. There's only one problem: the only thing that the drug has been proven to do is destroy livers in patients. So far there's no evidence of any benefits to patients with diabetes. Why is this allowed to happen? Why does the company continue investing in and investigating this poison? Why is the FDA silent? How many people will die before the company stops this madness?"

After that David describes the other cases, relying heavily on my recounts of conversations with Lennox and Dara. Lydia supplied him with information gathered from Tarrow. David did quite a bit of independent investigating, talking to various physicians and other experts in drug development and clinical trials. His discussion of diabetes and its complications, of liver disease and its consequences, are presented in respectable medical detail and accuracy. He also mentions at great length the concept of informed consent and how it's violated by the company, basically accusing the company of criminal negligence and attempting to purposefully mislead patients. He mentions my name only briefly, in the context of taking care of his mother. He doesn't mention Dara or Lennox, but he refers prominently to Tarrow. The scathing article concludes by promising more fireworks in the second installment, entitled: "Gother, the company, its people and morals," to be published next Tuesday.

The NY Times hasn't carried the story, and I wonder how many newspapers published it. David has mentioned something about syndication, so I'll have to wait and see.

Just as I finish, I hear some shuffling noises from the living room and Milo wanders into the kitchen. He's wiping water from his face with a towel.

"Boy, I slept great," he declares.

"Must be the brandy."

"You bet."

I pour him some steaming black coffee while he takes a look at the newspaper.

"David's article?" he asks.

I nod and point at it.

"What do you think?" Milo looks at me.

"Have you read it?" I ask.

"David showed me a draft."

"I'm troubled," I mutter. "This is too incendiary. David better watch it."

"Watch what?"

"I don't know, Milo. I don't rule out anything anymore."

"Violence too?"

"Anything's possible."

Milo takes a long pensive sip from the coffee.

"Very little we can do now. The cat is out of the bag," he mumbles.

"Unless David is willing to soften the next installment. . . "

"I doubt it. This has become an obsession with him, it's the mission of his life."

Milo gets up.

"Maybe we're just imagining things. Let's wait and see."

"Maybe," I agree.

"I have to go, Paul. I had a wonderful time."

We shake hands.

"Likewise."

Milo leaves. I watch him through the kitchen window as he climbs into his Honda, his scarf flying merrily about his face, and then as he slowly makes his way through the snow in the driveway. I follow his car until it disappears around the corner.

*   *   *   *   *

I spend the morning shoveling snow. Around noon, Irene and Danny return home. For a while, Danny and I are inseparable. He clings to my pants and follows me wherever I go, but eventually he decides that he also misses his toys so he goes to his room to play.

Irene acts and behaves business-like, as if there's nothing to discuss. No physical contact, barely eye contact. She goes out for grocery shopping, hustles about housekeeping chores, and in the evening moves into the kitchen to cook dinner.

After dinner, stomachs full with chicken piccata, spaghetti and chianti, we find ourselves at the table, in need of conversation. Perhaps not the soul-cleansing type, but communication nevertheless.

"I'm thinking of dropping the whole Neurovan thing," I begin.

She looks at me, puzzled.

"This thing has only caused trouble. Since starting this assignment, I've been bribed, threatened and blackmailed. I lost you, almost. And despite all that, what did I accomplish? Nothing. The first patient who died I know well, but I can't prove anything illegal took place. The second patient, in Miami, same story. The third patient, in Vienna, is surrounded by a lot of mystery and strange coincidences, but again, what proof do I have? I don't even know for sure that he was on this damned drug. I mean, is there a third patient?"

Irene is listening attentively. I go on.

"Where else have I failed? The drug may get approved in England, the FDA shows very little interest, Lennox is toast, Art is pissed at me and I may lose my job at the hospital. All this crap and all for nothing."

"You even tore up the $25,000 check," she reminds me. It's the first time that Irene's eyes smile a little.

Irene's shows more and more interest, and I can tell that she has not lost her feistiness and instincts for doing the right thing. I fill her on all the details, all the things that happened since our last civilized exchange. At the end, I show her David's first article.

"Maybe David's article will tilt the balance," she opines. "Gother just may go berserk after this one."

I shrug. Maybe she's right, maybe she's exaggerating.

"So do you want to drop the ball and return to work in the hospital?" she asks.

"What's today, Tuesday? Come next Monday, I'm either holding a smoking gun in my hands or a tube I'm shoving down a patient's stomach."

She nods. We sit for a few moments in that awkward uncertainty of whether a physical-sexual reconciliation is in order.

At the end nothing happens. Apparently, she's not ready yet.

THIRTY TWO

THAT NIGHT I CAN'T FALL ASLEEP. TOSSING AND TURNING, CONFUSED and weary, I follow the sun's rays as they emerge from under the window shades, slowly getting brighter as I begin to discern the familiar objects in the bedroom. Irene is in the bed next to me, breathing quietly and apparently oblivious to the tormented combat inside my brain, the struggle between the forces of drowsiness and wakefulness, neither winning nor losing, so that I'm left in a state of sluggish lethargy.

"Paul, it's for you," somebody yells, but I only mumble feebly, smacking my lips and hugging the pillow as if it's the last safety vest on the planet and I'm in the middle of the Atlantic Ocean.

Next thing I feel is somebody shaking me vigorously. I try to open my eyes, but the bright sunlight forces me to wince and close them again.

"Paul, you've got a phone call. Do you hear me?" I see Irene's face inches from my ear, as I'm slowly coming to.

"What?"

"From California. It's somebody from Moffit hospital."

"I'm not on call."

"Paul! Paul!" Irene slaps me lightly on my cheeks, "get up, for goodness sakes!"

Slowly, unsteadily, I remove the covers and open my eyes. For the first time I notice the cordless receiver that Irene is holding next to my nose. I grab it and bring it to my ear.

"Hello? Hello?" I clear my throat.

"Dr. Holden?" I can barely hear the soft feminine voice.

"Speaking."

"Uh. This is Margaret Dangerfield. I am Gerry Lennox's sister, and I am calling you about something terrible that has happened to my brother."

I jump out of bed. I can feel my heart pounding in my head and neck.

"To Gerry? What happened?"

For a long moment all I hear is sobbing sounds.

"He was just . . . uh . . . admitted to Moffitt hospital in severe coma."

More sobbing, this time loud and wailing.

"Oh, my God," I ask, "what's wrong?"

"He . . . he . . . overdosed on Valium. I think something happened at work . . . "

"Excuse me," I suddenly feel sick to my stomach, and I rush to the bathroom, phone in hand. I stop, leaning over the sink, taking deep breaths. I hear Margaret speak again.

"I didn't want to bother you, but he spoke so highly of you that I thought you . . . "

"How is he? I mean, do they think he's going to make it?" I start regaining my composure. Margaret also seems to calm down somewhat.

"They don't know. They pumped his stomach and everything, but they are worried because his bottle of medication was totally empty."

"When was he admitted?"

"Oh, about three hours ago. Patricia heard some weird noises from his room and . . . oh, poor girl!"

I move a few yards so that I can see the clock on the kitchen wall. 10:34. It's 7:34 in San Francisco, which meant that Lennox was admitted around 4:30. If he goes to bed late enough, say eleven, maybe they got him in time.

Irene comes to the kitchen and draws closer, watching my changing expressions. Overhearing my questions, she seems to understand what's going on, and her forehead becomes furrowed, eyebrows raised.

"Please, if he recovers, I know he'd love to see you. Anyway, could you come? I know that . . . " Margaret continues.

"I'll be there on the next flight. Hang in there. We'll all pray for him," I say, and Irene nods with approval. At least Irene is back in my corner, I think.

"Thanks," Margaret whispers and we both hang up.

"The bastards," I say, and proceed to my closet to start packing for the trip. By now I'm wide awake, cobwebs gone, sleepiness vanished and replaced by rage and determination.

Irene is watching me silently. I tell her what happened to Gerry.

"Why d'you think he did it?" she asks.

"This safety thing with Neurovan certainly put him in the dumps. On top of it, I think they fired him."

"The straw that broke the camel's back."

"Uh-huh."

While I stand with my back to Irene, getting shirts from the closet, she approaches me from behind and gives me a long smothering hug.

"I always knew that you'd do the right thing," she mutters.

I turn around and hold her tight against my body. She responds, and starts gyrating her belly against mine. Before we know it, her tongue pierces my mouth and twirls inside it with abandoned ferocity, and I reciprocate in kind, and we take our clothes off in a flurry of thrusting and pulling, and then we are on the bed, and she's wide open for me, and I'm inside her, muscling through with my thirsty masculinity. She moans and yells, and we climax in such vigor that the sheets are torn. And just as her back stops arching and I slide to her side, we hear a small voice next to us say:

"Dada, Mama," and Danny jumps right in between us, laughing and hollering in playful delight.

The phone rings. I jump up, covering myself with the ripped sheet, and rush out to the phone, leaving it to Irene to explain the event to Danny. I pick up the phone in the living room.

"Hello?"

"Dr. Holden?"

"Yes."

"This is Len Ramsey, from Gother."

"Oh, hi, Len."

"What the fuck d'you think you're doing, Holden?" He's yelling at the top of his lungs.

"I beg your pardon?"

"Pardon my ass. Who gave you permission to travel to Vienna, snoop around the hospital, talk to our investigator? Do you realize that the investigator died right after your conversation with him?"

"Really?"

"What are you, some sort of a smart ass?" Normally, he has a deep voice, but now it's high and shrieking. "And how did you find out about the patient in Vienna in the first place?"

"Listen here, Ramsey . . ."

"Don't lie to me Holden. I bet it was that no good fool Lennox. He almost ruined us in London."

"What is the purpose of your call?" I ask calmly.

"To tell you that you're finished, Holden. I'll make sure that you never publish or get grants again. That you never speak at scientific meetings again. That nobody ever hires you as a consultant again. Never, d'you hear me? Oh, and by the way, your consulting arrangement is finished. Canceled. Your check for the CSM deal will be sent to you."

"Are you done?"

His diatribe is actually more amusing than maddening.

"No, you're done."

"Good-bye, Ramsey," I say and hang up.

I shake my head as I walk towards Irene, who's in the shower now, but the phone rings and I turn back. I wonder if Ramsey is calling to add another insult, but it's Rubelli from the FDA.

"Dr. Holden, looks like your appointment to the advisory committee wasn't approved by my supervisors."

"I see."

"This idea of having a liver expert only for safety reasons did not catch on."

I have nothing to say.

"I bet you're relieved," Rubelli chortles, "most academicians would just as soon stay away from government bureaucracy."

"I'm sure. Did you know that I visited Dr. Aftaz the other day?"

"No. What did you see him about?"

"Doesn't matter right now. Thanks for the call, Dr. Rubelli."

I return to my room to finish up the packing. Irene watches me, toweling off after a quick shower. Rusty has now joined the festivities, as he and Danny roll on top of each other in our bed.

I tell her about the phone calls, pondering the significance of the extremely short time interval between them.

"Obviously, the Gother people figure they don't need you anymore," she sighs.

I try to pick a tie for the trip.

"No, they figure I can hurt them less if I'm no longer involved," I try to make sense out of all this. "More likely, they simply found out about my snooping in Vienna and didn't like it one bit."

"They figure you'd return to your hospital practice and teaching duties and forget about them and their drug," she dries her hair, tilting her head to one side. All she's wearing right now is the towel on her head.

I move closer to her. Suddenly everything feels right again between us.

"Well, they're sorely mistaken," I say, and kiss her on the forehead.

"You know," something suddenly hits me, "they probably think I know more than I actually do. They think maybe I got all the goods on them, that I actually found a gun with their fingerprints on it."

She hugs me for a long time.

"You'd better be careful," she says.

"Don't worry," I laugh. I suddenly remember Gerry Lennox, who's fighting for his life in a San Francisco hospital. "All I'm gonna do is visit Gerry. Hopefully I can help him somehow."

I finish packing, kiss Danny and Irene goodbye and leave the house with a suitcase and briefcase. I make sure to take David's articles with me. I figure they might be useful for something, I'm not sure exactly what.

* * * * *

Wednesday, March 17, San Francisco

This time I'm in economy class, since I'm no longer flying in the service of Gother. In the short time that I consulted Gother, I got used to the first class leg room that I needed to accommodate my long frame. This time I'm all squeezed, my knee deeply indenting the chair in front of me. Next to me are two teenagers, giggling and singing along with their portable CD-players. Needless to say, I can't doze off for even a minute during the five-hour flight.

I take a cab straight from the San Francisco airport to Moffitt hospital, the main hospital of the University of California campus. It's late in the evening and the air is cool and crisp, not a cloud in the sky. Half an hour later I meet Margaret Dangerfield outside Gerry's room in the Intensive Care Unit and we hug for a long time. She's too emotional for words and none are needed. We then both enter Gerry's room.

Gerry Lennox doesn't look too good. His face has a pale green-ish color and his eyes are closed. Two intravenous lines are feeding into his arms, which are covered with red blotchy dots. But he breathes peacefully and I conclude that he's asleep, not comatose.

"I think he's going to make it," I say to Margaret and she grips my arm forcefully.

"Did anybody from Gother call or send a card or something?" I ask.

Margaret shakes her head.

"Maybe they don't know yet," she says.

"Maybe," but I know they know everything. They have their ways of finding out.

"Did Gerry actually tell you that he was fired?" I ask.

"Yes. He was escorted to his car by two security men. He

---

wasn't allowed to return to his office and take his belongings. They promised to ship the personal stuff to his house."

"Bastards," I say.

"There was one call from France asking about him, but there was no message. I don't know who it was," Margaret suddenly remembers.

I nod, and look at Gerry, who just then opens his eyes. I lean forward to get closer to the bed. I grab Gerry's hand and squeeze it, but Gerry doesn't respond. Our eyes meet but Gerry gives no sign of recognition and closes his eyes again.

After a few moments I tell Margaret that I have to go and promise to stop back the next day.

It's close to midnight by the time I check into the Marriott hotel on fourth and Market. It's centrally located and has all the amenities required for my stay. I check in, and take the elevator to my floor. I hear the phone ringing inside the room while I'm inserting the key. I open the door and dash for the receiver.

"Paul?"

A woman's voice, somewhat distant.

"Yes?

"Boy, am I glad I caught you."

"Dara? How did you find my . . . "

"From Irene. Listen, I heard about Gerry. How is he?"

"I think he'll make it."

"Oh, that's great. I called the hospital but couldn't get any-body to tell me anything."

Dara. Last time I saw her she was boarding a plane in London with hairy Barnes. And she spoke to Irene. I hope the exchange went well and that no sleeping dogs were awakened.

"Where are you calling from?"

"Paris. We . . . I'm about to board my plane, direct flight to San Francisco. Barnes got a call about some article in the paper about

Gother. Is that the son of that patient who died in Philadelphia?"

"That's the one." I don't tell her about Ramsey's call, though I suspect that she probably knows about it anyway.

"So Dara, you had a productive trip, I assume . . . "

"I dreamt about you, Paul . . . "

"That's very naughty, Dara. Sleeping with Barnes and dreaming about me . . . "

"Shut up, Paul. It's not what you think. But I do have wonderful news."

"You getting married to Barnes?"

"Heavens, no, Paul. What's gotten into you? Have you been drinking?"

"No. So what's the news?"

"I got it, Paul."

I scratch my cheek with a bent finger.

"You got what?"

"The password, silly. The password." She whispers these last words and I'm not sure she says what I think she says.

"You got the password to the Gother computer, to that secret file . . . "

"Yes. I'll give it to you when I get there. You're gonna wait for me, right?"

"I'll be here, Dara."

"Good. Ciao."

I hang up. I almost forgot about the computer search. Why would Barnes give Dara the password? Maybe there's nothing secretive about the files after all.

Tonight I take an exceptionally long shower. I just let the water stream on my face and body, as my mind goes blank. I refuse to make any plans. From now on, I'll take events one at a time. Tomorrow I'll visit Lennox again, and then I'll wait for Dara and her password, for whatever it's worth.

THIRTY THREE

Thursday, March 18

NEXT MORNING I SLEEP LATE, BUT NOT AS LATE AS I HOPED FOR. THIS IS supposed to be the night when I finally cure my almost chronic sleep deprivation and pick up a large withdrawal from the sleep bank. The phone rings at least a dozen times before I pick up the receiver.

"Paul, what the hell is going on with that Alberts kid?"

"Huh?" I'm getting tired of the suddenly interrupted sleep phenomenon. The digital clock display flashes 9:27.

"This is Larry. Barnes. I had to cut my trip short because of that little asshole. Why is he writing this stuff?"

"Larry, stop bothering me. I'm no longer your consultant."

"So what? You know him well. You took care of his mother, didn't you?"

"What do you want, Larry?"

"Did you read the articles? Do you know what's coming next?"

"It's a free country. He can write whatever he wants."

I sit up in my bed and turn on the light.

"The articles are full of horrendous lies, fabrications and slander. We'll sue his ass, he won't know what hit him."

"Do this and you'll make it item number one on the nightly news."

Long pause.

"I want to tell you something in confidence," his voice is suddenly hushed. "Ramsey is flipping out. His call to you yesterday, was on his own. I advised against it. Dell doesn't know about it, and he may not approve it. I think you did a great job in London. I don't care about your going to Vienna. It's all bullshit as far as I'm concerned."

I make him wait a few moments before responding.

"What can I do for you, Larry?"

"I need a favor from you, and this time it's a big one. I don't think we've ever asked anything like this from anybody. Stop the publication of the Alberts articles."

I smile at the desperation in Barnes's voice and am going to savor this for all it's worth. Suddenly, an idea.

"Hold on a second, Larry. Let me get out of bed and sit by the desk here."

I jump out of bed and race to the closet. From my duffel bag I pull out the tape recorder that David gave me and push the record button and then watch the little red light go on.

I pick up the receiver again.

"I am at the desk, Larry," I say, "so how can I stop the publication?" I bring the tape recorder near the receiver.

"Talk to him. Explain to him the falsehood of what he's writing about. We're about developing drugs to help cure disease, and he makes us look like some two-bit crooks and villains. We're not the goddamned Mafia, for Chrissakes. Besides, tell him about the futility of all this. We have too many connections in the government, the FDA, Congress; we'll always prevail."

"Well, if you'll prevail, then what's all the excitement about?"

"I didn't say this isn't going to hurt us. There will be tangible damage."

"Larry, I could talk to him, but he's not going to listen. He's been working on this for some time, a lot of research, time, and money went into . . . "

"How much?"

"What?"

"How much money does he want for his expenses?"

I watch the recorder. The tape is whirling nice and slow.

"I can't speak for David . . . "

"One million dollars. One million even. You keep as much as you want. We'll open a numbered account for him wherever he wants. I suggest the Cayman Islands. Takes a few phone calls and two-three faxes."

"One million dollars?"

"You're right. He's giving up potential book sales. Make it two. In cash. Up front. We get all the hard copies, computer disks and notes for the project. We'll send people to take care of the hard disks. He sends us a letter promising never to publish any of it. He leaves on an extended vacation for, say, six months. Any place on the planet. On us. In addition to the two million."

I'm still not sure how desperate they really are.

"Make it four million and it's a deal," I say.

"Done," said Barnes, and I feel foolish for not asking for ten. Or twenty. Now I'll never now how much it's really worth to them.

I need to know one more thing.

"I can talk to him, but what if he turns down the offer?"

"He's a dead man, Paul."

The tone of his voice sends a sudden chill down my spine.

"What do you mean?"

"Just what I said. Keep it in mind when you talk to him. Tell him to fax the letter directly to my office. I'll take care of the rest."

"One second, Larry," I can't help it, "I have another suggestion. Why don't you just stop the Neurovan program? Your drug is killing people and does no good. Move on to something else. Try something that works."

"You don't know what the fuck you're talking about, Holden," he shouts and hangs up.

I hang up and I push the stop button. Then I rewind the tape and listen to the recording. It's loud and clear. I take out the tiny cassette and put it in the money belt I've been wearing recently during my travels. This is the same cassette that contains my conversation with Lacoste in Dallas and I figure it's time to protect its contents.

I tighten the belt around my stomach and get dressed in a hurry. I walk down to Market street and enter the nearest Radio Shack store where I buy a large tape recorder and several tapes. From the store I go to the nearest post office and buy three large padded envelopes and return to my hotel room. I spread my shopping items on the desk and sit down. I start by writing three different addresses on the three envelopes. First is my own home address. Second is my hospital address. The third is Dr. Gerald Lennox's home address. Then, using the new recorder, I slowly and patiently make four copies of the mini-cassette. I listen to each copy and, being satisfied with the quality of the recording, I insert one new cassette into a separate envelope. The fourth newly recorded cassette I put in a small compartment in my suitcase. The original mini-cassette I stick in my money-belt and the mini-recorder I put in the pocket of my jacket.

From my suitcase I pull out a copy of David's articles, walk downstairs and make three copies of each, return to my room and insert one copy into each envelope. The originals I put back in the suitcase. When done, I carefully seal the envelopes with scotch tape, trot back to the post office and mail all three envelopes, overnight express mail.

Back in the hotel, I pull out my address book, ready to make a few phone calls.

David Alberts is in, and answers the phone immediately. I relay to him the message from Barnes, but omit the part about David's life being endangered. When I mention the sum of money offered, David utters a loud whistle.

"Holy shit," he says, "they're really scared."

"Definitely. Question is, are you? You know, these thugs will stop at nothing."

"What are you saying, Paul? That I should take the money and run?"

"It's an option, you know." I didn't think he'd go for it, but at least he should consider it.

"Listen, Paul. If they're that depraved, you can't make deals with them. They may go after me even if I take the money. Besides, mother would have wanted me to play for the win."

"Okay, David."

"By the way, Lydia says hello."

"How is she? Is she still in pain?"

"She has her good moments. Milo told me about the placebo idea."

"What do you think?"

"I don't like it, but I don't know of anything better."

"It may be a lot harder to get the placebo than I thought. I'm on their shit list now and Lennox has been fired and is sick. But . . . I'll think of something."

A pause.

"Paul? Would you have taken the four million?"

"Not in four million years."

"That's what I figured," David chortles.

"One more thing, David. Who has copies of your upcoming articles?"

"Only the publisher of the Washington Post and you. It may have gone out to the other newspapers, but I doubt it. Of course, I have it on my computer and a few floppies lying around. Why?"

"Call the Post and tell them to safeguard the copies as if their lives depended on it. And you, stay near a phone. There may be new messages from our friends at Gother."

After we hang up I sink in the couch and close my eyes. I can't think of anything urgent I have to do. I have no intention of reporting David's decision back to Barnes right away. I also consider sending a copy of the articles and tape to the FDA, but decide to wait, because I figure there's more to come. Right now the Gother people are considering their options. With the second, more incriminating article coming out they have to do something right now. They can't afford to wait. It would be only a matter of time before a congressman is alerted and the FDA initiates a full investigation, with or without my prodding. Indictments of key Gother people might follow and the board of Gother will be called upon to find ways to salvage the company. So Walnut, Dell, Ramsey and Barnes have two options: agree to halt Neurovan's development or fight vigorously. I don't know which route they will choose, and the only thing left for me to do is sit and wait.

By now it's close to noon. I first shower and shave, then I get dressed and go downstairs to the mezzanine floor where they have a fairly decent restaurant. I order myself a hearty meal, real thick beefsteak and potatoes, and cap it with double cappuccino and chocolate truffles.

I return to my room and turn on the television. Flipping through the channels, I recognize the gaunt old professor philosopher whom I remember talking about life as a chess game back in

Philadelphia, just when Gother offered me the consultancy gig. He is at it again, speaking slowly into the camera, measuring every syllable.

"The end-game in chess is just like the end of life. Just as a game must end, so must one's life. It's just a matter of time. There are very few pieces left on the board, and so the options for moves are more limited than in the beginning of the game. But, alas, every option becomes more important. You can get away with a mistake here and there in the opening and the middle-game, but not in the ending. One sloppy wrong move, one miscalculated risk, one ill-advised adventure and the game is over and you're lost. And this is as true for life as for chess."

I prop my feet up on the ottoman, listening. I'm interrupted by the phone.

"Paul?" The voice is weak and raspy but I recognize it at once.

"Gerry? How are you?" I turn down the volume on the television.

"Much better," Gerry Lennox says, "in fact they're releasing me in a couple of hours. I guess I just had to sleep it off."

"That's great news, Gerry. Well, I suppose you have to take it easy for some time."

"Paul, really, I feel fine. I'm sorry about . . . everything. I heard you came to visit. Thank you."

"Not at all. Main thing is that you've recovered."

"They fired me, you know."

"Margaret told me."

"Just like that. Unceremoniously, like I haven't worked there for ten years."

"I know. Don't worry, we'll find a job for you."

A pause.

"So, what's new with you?" Gerry's trying to speak louder.

I tell Gerry about the upcoming articles, Gother's panicky and threatening reaction, Barnes's offer and its rejection. When I tell him about the FDA actions, I can hear him gasp.

"They sent somebody to threaten Aftaz. I know that. They have some goons, I think . . . they joke about sending something, somebody called Lucca . . . I don't know what the hell that means . . . but I always wondered if it was really a joke . . . listen, Paul . . . "

Gerry takes a deep breath. I can feel that he's trying to summon every last brain twitch to get his message across.

"You're right. They're panicking. That means that Dell, Ramsey and Barnes are meeting around the clock, planning, plotting, coordinating. Heck, Dick Walnut is there too. They don't know what to do. Walnut is shitting in his pants, and Dell is looking for a scapegoat. Barnes may want to bail out, but can't because he's in it too deep."

Gerry is rambling, and I begin to doubt if all synapses are properly wired.

"Paul, you've got to go there."

"Go where?"

"To our . . . their headquarters. They're meeting around the clock. Walnut is keeping everybody at work until David's article is stopped."

"So you think I should . . . "

"Get in there, somehow. In the evening. The night security people don't know everybody. I'll give you my card. No, no, maybe you should go in the morning. Then definitely everybody's going to be there. They'll be meeting in the executive conference room in the white building. But, I don't know when. Oh, God, this is so . . . "

There's a sudden pause.

"Gerry?"

There's no answer.

"Gerry?"

There's a woman's voice on the line.

"Dr. Holden? This is Margaret."

"Oh, hi."

"He's still exhausted. He needs some rest. Maybe you'll have a chance to visit him at home before you return to the East Coast?"

"I'll do that."

"Thanks for everything. Bye."

I close my eyes, leaning back in the sofa. Every so often I open my eyes and flip channels on the television set. News. Old black and white movie. Tom and Jerry cartoons. Old episodes of "I love Lucy." I begin to agree with Lennox, that sooner or later I'll have to confront the Gother brass in person, which means a short trip to Berkeley. But if Gother is really panicking, they can't afford to wait too long. I know that Barnes will call me to inquire about David's reaction to the offer. Maybe Gother has some other ideas.

THIRTY FOUR

I DOZE OFF IN FRONT OF THE TELEVISION, I DON'T KNOW FOR HOW LONG. Suddenly my head shoots up as I'm awakened by a soft tapping noise on the door. On the television screen Richard Widmark is seated on the ground as Robert Taylor hovers over him, holding a gun. I push the mute button and listen. Again, the tapping on the door, slightly louder. It takes me a moment to realize that no intruder would tap on the door before entering. I get up and walk towards the door. When I get closer, I hear a woman's voice: "For goodness sake, Paul, open the damn door."

I unbolt the chain and open the door. Dara shoots right into my arms and hugs me, standing on her tiptoes. With one hand I close the door behind her and bolt the chain again. She looks unkempt and her green dress under the raincoat is crumpled.

"Thank goodness you're okay," she says, her hands caressing my face.

"What do you mean? Why shouldn't I be okay?"

"Paul, what are you talking about? Don't you know what's going on?" Dara says, as she carries her suitcase to the center of the room. She takes off her raincoat, and runs her fingers through her long hair. She notices her image in the mirror on the closet door.

"God, I look terrible. I've been on planes for days nonstop it seems, and I must smell like a monkey's armpit."

She turns to me.

"I talked to Larry before coming here. There is a siege mentality at Gother, they are gonna fight this to the end. They plan to win. First they stop the articles, then with Lacoste's help, positive data from the studies, and pressure from the diabetic community, they'll get Neurovan approved by the FDA."

"So why should I be concerned?"

"They think that you supplied David with all the incriminating information. There are rumors of hired guns . . . I believe they use the code word Lucca for these kind of activities, but I never knew exactly what it meant. David should take the money and run. Drop the lawsuit too."

I move closer to Dara.

"So we should just give up?" I ask.

She sighs.

"That's the best for everybody. Paul, they would stop at nothing, and if you persist, it's a war. And in wars, people get hurt. Or worse."

"David has already turned down their offer. Article number two is coming out on Tuesday," I say calmly.

"Does Larry know that?" she continues.

"Not yet. I'm expecting his call."

I sniff a few times in the air.

"And you're right about your odor. Go take a shower, for crying out loud. I'll wait for you."

She thumbs her nose at me and turns her back.

"Okay. Could you please unzip my dress?"

Dirty, tired and all, she could still make it to the cover of

Playboy magazine. I wonder if she knows about the fax and picture sent to Irene. There's really no reason for her to know, unless Irene mentioned it to her.

I unzip her dress, getting a glimpse of a caramel colored back hugging the white stripes of a bra. Dara saunters towards the bathroom, her dress slowly slipping to the ground as she does. I turn around and sit on the couch in front of the television. From the corner of my eye I see her strip naked and enter the bathroom. She leaves the door open and I can see her turn on the water, get into the tub and stand underneath the powerful steaming stream.

"I heard that Gerry was doing much better," she screams to me.

"Yes. He called me."

"What?"

"I know. He called me," I holler back.

"Paul, I can't hear you. Don't yell, just come here."

I take a deep sigh, but then I walk to the open door of the bathroom. The steam is building rapidly around the showering Dara, and her image is now barely visible. It's very difficult to be just friends with this woman, I think, as I see her body move, twist and bend under the pounding water.

"Gerry has recovered completely. He is, in fact, leaving the hospital today and going home," I say.

"That's great news. Do you know that to punish him they made him report to me?"

"Really?"

"Can you believe the humiliation? He's a world expert and I, his boss, am barely a college graduate without experience. It was Ramsey's idea. Larry wasn't sure about it but went along anyway."

I wipe the splashes of water that hit my face with the back of my hand.

"I didn't think that Gerry was the suicidal type," Dara says.

"He must have been very tired and just longed for a long and peaceful sleep. That's what he told Margaret. He never thought of actually killing himself."

"I can understand that. Paul, come here. Can you do my back?"

"Huh?"

"C'mon, soap my back. No big deal."

"Bad idea, Dara."

"Paul, don't worry. I just need a clean back. Promise."

Right. And the wolf wanted Red Riding Hood to come closer only so he could see her better. Nevertheless, I walk in and come closer. She hands me the soap and turns her back to me. I examine the soap in my hand for a few seconds and then start soaping her back. Slowly, in round motions. Before closing my eyes I notice that she's definitely more tanned since I saw her last. I can't stop my mind from wandering, recalling all our previous encounters in hotel rooms in San Francisco and London. London. Airport. Riviera. Barnes. I stop the rubbing.

"How was Monte Carlo?"

"Vastly overrated. I lost one hundred and forty dollars in the casino. Did you know that you have to pay an entrance fee to play in the casino?"

"No. I didn't."

"And Barnes? How did he behave?" I ask.

She looks at me through the spread fingers of her hand.

"Oh, Paul, so you do care about me, don't you?"

"What makes you think that?"

"Your eyes, Paul. Your eyes."

She turns off the water, grabs the large white towel from the bin and covers herself as she walks out of the tub. My head is turned the other way.

"For your information, Paul, nothing happened between

Barnes and me. Most of the time he was too drunk to carry on a normal conversation. His idea of relaxing away from the office is drinking and gambling. Mostly drinking."

I leave the bathroom and go to the minibar. It's early afternoon, but all the talk about drinking and the showering make me thirsty.

"I need a beer," I announce, "want one?"

"Sure."

She comes over, still wrapped up in the towel, and I hand her an opened chilled Heineken. I take one for myself.

I sit down on the couch, and she sits on the sofa, crossing her legs, feet underneath her thighs. "You said you got the password," I take a long sip.

"Yep. He showed me his code book and I copied the pages with this week's and next week's passwords."

"I assume he doesn't know that you have it?" I ponder aloud.

"No way," she says and crosses her legs the other way. I take another swig and wipe my chin with the sleeve of my shirt.

"That's great. Next opportunity we jump into their system. We need clear, undisputed evidence."

She nods.

"What do we do now?" she asks.

I look at my watch. It's almost four o'clock. Before I can answer her the phone rings. I pick up the receiver in mid ring.

"Paul, I'm bailing out. I decided not to publish the articles." It's David, and he speaks very slowly, as if in pain.

"Are you okay, David?"

"I don't know. I guess so."

"What happened?" I ask.

"I . . . they . . . somebody came to my apartment and shattered my computer, took all my disks, notes, everything. I also think somebody tried to run me over."

"You think?"

"Well, I'm pretty sure. Have you contacted anybody from Gother since we spoke earlier?"

"No."

"Well, in that case, just call your buddies in Gother and tell them I'm folding. I've had enough. I am going to call the editor of the Washington Times and he'll withdraw it from all the syndicated newspapers."

I cup the receiver and say to Dara: "Somebody from Gother got to David. He was almost killed. He's bailing out."

I remove my hand and speak into the receiver again.

"David, what about the lawsuit. Are you withdrawing that, too?"

"I need to talk to my lawyer first. Maybe he can reach a quick agreement. I suppose that would be okay."

I'm hesitating.

"David, I'm not sure that they'll let you off the hook that easily. You'll have to sign a letter promising never to publish any part of the story and I'm sure they'll demand withdrawing the lawsuit too. You get nothing, but they still may be after you, because they know that you could destroy them any time, even after the drug is on the market. Especially then."

"I am not sure why they would care after I sign the letter. But even if they do, so be it."

Dara looks on pensively. I cup the receiver again with my palm.

"Dara, I have copies of the articles," I say. "I could publish them. Modified, perhaps, to give my own perspective of the cases."

I remove my hand and talk to David again.

"David, if that's what you want, I'll tell them, but only on one condition."

"What's that?"

"That as soon as you hang up you leave Philadelphia immediately. If you want, drive up to New Haven and spend the next week or so with Lydia. At least I'll know where to reach you."

"I suppose I could do that."

"Good. Before you leave, though, write a letter promising not to publish any material related to Gother and fax it here to the Marriott hotel. Okay?"

"No problem, Paul. I'll leave first thing tomorrow morning."

"David, you're leaving right after you fax me that letter. You're not spending another night in Philadelphia."

"Okay. I'll try."

"Don't try. Just do it."

"Okay, Paul, okay."

"I'll be waiting, David. Good night." I hang up.

Dara gets up, walks to the bar and grabs another Heineken.

"Paul, I'm telling you. Get out while you're still in one piece. Don't even think about publishing David's stuff."

"Dara, what's the matter with you? What happened to your fighting spirit?"

"I just have bad vibes. Very bad."

"I don't know, Dara. Let's play it by ear."

She offers me another bottle of beer, but I turn it down. We sit quietly for a moment.

"So, Paul, what do we do now?" she yawns.

"We wait."

"What are you talking about?"

"You go to bed now. I'll wait for David's letter and then call Barnes. We'll go from there. I'll probably have to visit Gother."

"Why?"

"We need to negotiate an end to this mess."

"What's there to negotiate?"

"Some sort of a settlement. They stop drug development of Neurovan, pay damages to David and the other families, and we stop campaigning against them."

Dara goes to the door and makes sure that it's locked and bolted. She utters another major yawn.

"Okay, what are the sleeping arrangements tonight?" she asks.

"You go to the bedroom, and I'll sleep on the sofa here."

"Are you sure?"

"Yes."

Dara walks away and I look at her closely. Sleepless and all, with her tanned skin, wrapped up in the white toga-like towel, brown eyes, long brown hair and full mouth she looks like a Greek goddess. In a sudden motion, she turns around and catches my stare.

"What's the matter, my dear Paul?" she asks sweetly, smiling.

"Nothing. Sleep tight. Tomorrow should be interesting."

She gives me the inviting finger motion.

"Don't you want to tuck me in?"

"Good night, Dara."

"Please, Paul, I've been so lonely . . . "

"I said good night, Dara."

Her smile disappears, and instead there's a cloud passing over her face, as she bites her lower lip. She turns around and walks into the bedroom, closing the door behind her.

THIRTY FIVE

Early morning, Friday, March 19

BY NATURE I'M A SOUND SLEEPER. THAT IS, WHEN LIFE IS FLOWING smoothly and I don't have a worry in the world. But it's been a while since I was in that peaceful state of mind, and now I must be worried, because I'm sinking into light sleep, then I wake up, only to sink into another round of shallow, dreamless slumber. But when the bright rays from the small flashlight travel through my pupil and land on the retina with a sudden excruciating impact, I know I'm not asleep anymore. I try to rise, but a heavy, muscular broad-fingered hand that surrounds my windpipe convinces me that staying prone would be the less painful alternative. The light prevents me from seeing the owner of that hand, and all I can do is utter a few dry agonizing coughs.

"If you resist, you die," the intruder whispers, "do you understand?"

I nod. I narrow my eyes as I try to look beyond the blinding light to see the face of the man, but I can't.

"Where is it?" the man asks.

"Where is what?" I manage to murmur, but the hand's grip

strengthens and the air stops flowing freely towards my lungs, and I cough and wheeze. I bring my hands in front of my neck and grab the offending fingers, attempting to peel them off my tormented neck. I realize that the man wears gloves, and after a short struggle I manage to unwrap one or two fingers. The intruder apparently decides to change tactics. He lets go of my throat and bounces backwards. I rise, only to notice a new shining object in the man's hand: a small gun, and the gun is pointing straight at my left eye.

"Give me the articles, all the copies, now," the man says, and I notice that the man has a foreign accent. Spanish or Italian, I'm not sure. I look at the man and all I can discern is that he is tall and his hands are huge. The man's face is covered with what looks like a black ski mask, and in the darkness I can't even see his eyes, only two dark holes.

I point to my suitcase, which is parked erect in the closet. Without taking his eyes off me for more than a split second, the man moves towards the closet and grabs the suitcase. He brings it back to the center of the room and turns it upside down in a quick determined flick of his wrist. Some clothing articles fall out and then a bunch of papers. A small metallic object that lands on the floor immediately attracts the man's attention and he picks it up. It's a small audio tape and the man holds it between his thumb and forefinger, trying to decide what to do. He looks at me, then at the tape again. Without words he puts the tape in his pocket. He picks up every clothing item and shakes it in the air. He does the same to my jackets which are hanging in the closet. From one of them my tiny tape recorder falls out, and he picks it up and puts it into his pocket. He then shines the flashlight on the papers, turns a few pages and then, with a swift motion, pulls out a match, lights it and holds it against the corner of the papers. In a few seconds, the papers are aflame and the ashes drop to the floor.

"Other papers," the man says.

"That's all I have," I mumble, and the man shines the light quickly in my face, trying to establish whether I'm telling the truth. He leans forward, bringing the gun closer to my face, when a beam of light suddenly permeates our room as the door to the bedroom opens and Dara stands at the threshold, rubbing her eyes.

The man turns his head towards Dara, and then quickly back to me, and I think that in the dark holes of the ski mask where a pair of eyes is hiding, I see a sign of surprise.

The man hesitates. He first moves towards Dara, his gun pointing in her direction. She utters a shriek, and he turns back to me, as I raise my head to get a better view of the man's movements.

Finally, seemingly having reached a decision, the man returns to me, sticks the gun in my nose and says, softly, "if the articles get published, I'll come back and pull the trigger."

He shoves the gun further up my nose, drawing a few drops of blood, and after a few painful seconds takes the gun out and speeds towards the door, opens it and dashes out. It happens so fast that Dara stands mesmerized, but as soon as he disappears, she runs quickly to me and holds my face in her arms.

I touch my nose and wipe the dripping blood drops, but then I jump up quickly off the sofa and dash to the door, fling it open and run through it to the hallway and towards the elevators. I stop to look around for a moment but find no signs of the assailant. I then run to the stairway, down two flights but there's no sign of the man there either. I walk upstairs slowly, return to my room and go straight for the mini bar. I pull out a bottle of Heineken and join Dara, who is lying quietly on the sofa, in a fetal position.

"I'm scared," she says.

"He's gone now. It's over. Relax." I sit next to her, and she moves her bent knees to make room for me.

"I told you they don't give up easily," she mumbles.

I'm shaking my head, trying to put all that's happened into some sort of perspective.

We sit without a word for a long time. I start ruminating aloud, in a soft voice.

"I suppose this is one of those situations in life when one thing leads to another. Small fibs lead to hiding information, to lies, to bribes, to cover up. The progression to armed threats and physical harm isn't that drastic."

Dara is listening quietly, nodding frequently. I look at her long tanned legs as they curve from underneath her robe, and she suddenly looks so small and vulnerable.

"So, what happens now?"

I run my fingers through my hair and fold my arms behind my neck.

"From their perspective, things aren't actually that bleak. After all, they have done several criminal things, but they think that we can't prove anything. If the drug gets approved in a large country, that'll prove that it's safe and effective. The articles are withdrawn and everybody's happy. David can't prove that Gother threatened him and neither can we. I have only one piece of evidence that I can use."

Dara's eyes widen.

"What's that?"

"I recorded the phone conversation today in which Barnes offered me money, for David, if he withdrew the articles."

"So that's perfect. You can offer them the tape if they resign quietly."

"I've missed the boat. That intruder found it and took it."

"Oh, my God," Dara sits up, "so now they know that you

recorded the conversation. That makes you much more danger-ous to them and they'll become more violent."

I scratch my chin.

"Could be. But they also must assume that I have other copies of the tape, and if I'm harmed, one of the extra copies may find its way to the police."

"Do you?"

"Do I what?"

"Have other copies?"

"In a very safe place."

"Okay, so you have the evidence that might finish them off."

I shake my head.

"Unfortunately, that's only partially true. They'll make Barnes the fall guy, blame him for everything, deny any knowledge of his actions and gladly toss him to the sharks. He may be finished, but the others will fight on."

"But, can't he then spill the beans on the entire compa-ny?"

"That's a risk that they may have to take. Don't forget, we don't know if the intruder will give the tape first to Barnes, who then has the option to destroy it, or to someone else, who may wait for the right opportunity to use it."

I get up and start putting my things back into the suitcase.

"What time is it?" Dara asks, yawning.

"Almost two."

Suddenly I have a brain cramp.

"Get dressed. We're leaving," I tell her.

"What are you talking about?"

"Let's get out of here. They may come back. I also want to go to a place that has a computer and a modem."

Dara gets to her feet.

"We can go to my place," she offers.

"I'm not so sure that's such a good idea. The man may have recognized you or something."

Dara suddenly shudders and moves closer to me.

"You know, funny you should say that. There was something familiar about that guy. I don't know, his physique, maybe his voice."

"Sounded foreign. A lot of foreigners in the clinical division at Gother?"

"Very few. A couple of Germans, a Belgian, two from India and a new clinical scientist from Spain."

"This guy definitely sounded Latin. Could be Spanish or Italian."

Dara shrugs.

"I can't tell. So, where do you want to go?"

I keep throwing clothes into the suitcase. Before I'm done, I stop and snap my finger.

"Do you know where Gerry lives?" I ask.

"Gerry? Sure. Last year's Christmas party was in his house. But he just got out of the hospital . . . "

I put on my shirt.

"I know, but he sounded okay on the phone today. Visitors may actually improve his mood."

"In the middle of the night?"

"There's no choice. Go get ready."

*   *   *   *   *

The doorbell must have rung almost a dozen times before we hear shuffling sounds and then somebody arrives at the other side of the door.

"Who is it?" Gerry asks.

"Paul. Open up quickly."

"Paul Holden?"

"Yes. Quick, Gerry."

Chain unlocks, key turns twice and door opens. Dara and I bolt into the house, and I dash to the window, pull its curtains apart and look to the dark street below. Cars are passing by, nothing unusual.

"What's going on?" Gerry asks. He is wearing a dark blue robe and brown slippers. Other than being a little pale, I reckon he looks fine, considering what he's been through.

"We were followed from the hotel by a guy who broke into my room and threatened me," I explain.

"Threatened you?"

I tell Gerry about the events in my room earlier that night. Gerry listens quietly without interrupting.

"Gother brass is desperate," Gerry concludes, "the articles must be pretty devastating."

We walk into the house, through the dining room to the living room. It's an old house. In the living room, nice dark flowery couches, piano in the corner, bar, two large brown speakers. An old grandfather clock indicates it's almost three. Gerry walks behind the counter.

"Can I get you anything?" he asks. He is all matter-of-fact, like we were a couple of old friends dropping in for an afternoon tea and a game of scrabble.

"I need coffee," Dara says.

"Yeah, same here. Make it black," I add.

Gerry comes out from behind the counter and walks past us on his way to the kitchen.

Dara sits down and I go to the window and look outside, up and down the street below. After a few moments I turn to Dara.

"Turn off the lights," I instruct her. It's impossible to see anything, looking from a lit room onto a dark street. Dara gets up, flicks the switch and suddenly it's pitch dark in the room. That's when I see the car and the silhouette of a man behind the wheel. It's a dark colored BMW coupe, two doors, and all I can discern about the man is his large head and large hands resting on the wheel.

In the darkness, I feel Dara's body next to mine. Next, I smell strong coffee and notice that Gerry is approaching us. We all look through the window, but the man behind the wheel just sits there without motion. He seems to be holding something near the side of his head. I strain my eyes. It's a cellular phone.

"I think that's him, and he's talking on the phone," Dara says, and I nod in the darkness. We close the curtains and Dara turns on the lights.

"Where does Gother find goons for such missions?" I ask.

I take a hot cup of coffee from Gerry and bring it to my lips. Dara and Gerry look at each other. Dara shrugs.

"There were some rumors about hired goons. The name Lucca came up a couple of times, but I don't know anybody who had actually seen this man or whatever Lucca stands for," Gerry says.

I take another sip of the bitter black coffee.

"Where is your computer, Gerry?" I ask.

"Upstairs."

"Dara, do you have the book of passwords?"

Dara nods and walks over to her bag, which she's left in the hallway.

"Let's go and see if we can get inside Gother's nerve center one more time," I suggest.

"There is a hidden file, for which we have recently obtained the password," I explain to Gerry as Dara returns holding a thick yellow book. Gerry just says, "follow me," and proceeds towards the stairway. At the top of the stairway, Dara suddenly grabs Gerry by the arm.

"Gerry, with all the excitement I forgot to ask you how you were feeling?"

Gerry smiles.

"I'm fine. I guess I just needed the sleep. I obviously overdid it."

"So you are completely okay?"

"Absolutely. The shrink at the hospital told me that I was the perfect picture of mental health."

We enter the den, Gerry leading. He sits down and turns on the computer. A few clicks of the mouse later, Lennox types in his password 'NNADII', and we're inside the Gother computer.

Recalling the other passwords from Gother I've seen, "TATALINC" and "CCIIFPA" it suddenly dawns on me that these are all anagrams of the words Atlantic, Pacific and Indian. I mention this to them.

"Brilliant," says Dara.

"Bravo," says Gerry, "but what does it mean?"

"Other than that these are all oceans, this is a totally useless piece of information," I say. "Let's continue."

Screen follows screen until we're staring at the list of categories. When we see "corres b." on the list, I tap Gerry on the shoulder. Gerry gets up and I slide into his vacated chair. Dara stands next to him, watching intently.

I click twice on the "corres. b." file. A loud beeping sound, same as in London, emanates from the computer, and a message appears on the screen.

"Please enter password number three hundred forty nine."

Dara thumbs quickly through the book.

"Anguilla-oratorio-destiny4," Dara reads and I punch it in.

"Thank you. Now please enter password eight hundred and seventeen."

"Julius-llama-instrumentalist," Dara reads and I punch it in again.

"Thank you. Now please enter your mother's maiden name."

I look at Dara and we both yell "damn" at the same time.

"Quick, how many people do you think have access to this file?" I ask and look at Dara and Gerry.

"In R&D, it's only Barnes and above. Ramsey, Dell and a couple of the other vice-presidents. In Marketing—who knows," Gerry says and Dara nods.

"Do we know anybody's mother's maiden name?" I turn around.

"Barnes? I don't know," Gerry says. Dara scratches the side of her face.

"Ramsey used to talk about his old mother living in Indiana. What was her name? What was her name?"

A beeping sound from the computer and I turn to watch the screen. A flickering message in bright red appears:

"Ten minutes to termination."

"What the hell is this?" I want to know. Next to the message an illuminated digital window displays "10:00".

"Oh, boy," Gerry says, "this happens when someone inside the company tries to get to the same highly restricted files. They give the outsider a warning to hurry up and finish."

"So that means that as we speak, there is somebody at Gother trying to get into the 'corres. b.' file?"

"Exactly. We'd better hurry up or else they could erase everything," Gerry responds.

"Why don't they just cut us off at once?" I wonder.

"I suppose it wasn't programmed that way," Dara says.

"It's all academic if we can't figure out somebody's maiden name," I say.

"Just try something," Gerry proposes.

I shrug and type in "robinson."

A beep and a message.

"The name 'robinson' does not belong to an authorized person's mother."

I type in "Smith" and "Barnes" but all I get is a beep and the same message. I raise my hands in sheer despair.

"What was Ramsey's mother maiden name?" I holler. I'm frustrated as hell. Finally we get the code book, and now this.

"Try Livingstone," says a deep voice with a foreign accent from the direction of the door, and I jump as if snake-bitten. Turning around, I stare into the barrel of a gun held by a tall masked man. A gloved hand hits the light switch and the room gets dark, except for the light coming from the monitor's screen. How the hell could he break in without any of us hearing a thing?

Dara and Gerry take a step backwards and the stranger turns and looks at them. He's standing at the doorstep and Dara and Gerry are a few feet away to his right. I'm at the computer approximately six feet straight ahead.

I can now take a better look at the man in the semi-lit room. He's six five, young looking, in his thirties, maybe, and he wears a black leather jacket and dark blue pants. On his face is a blue ski mask and on his hands the same black gloves. I swallow hard, remembering the pressure from these gloves on my windpipe. I also see his narrow eyes, green perhaps but I'm not sure.

"Go ahead, type 'livingstone'," the man says and waves his gun in an upward menacing gesture.

I hesitate.

"Do as he says," Dara blurts.

I turn my back to the stranger and type in the word "livingstone".

In the corner of the screen the digital display is at 8:11.

A pause, than a message

"Welcome, Dr. Leonard Albert Ramsey. Please proceed."

But by now I'm not paying attention to the screen. I'm busy

getting angry. I'm angry at how far Gother was willing to go to make money, how far they were willing to go to get a drug approved, how low they'd sink to save their cowardly yellow little skins. And I'm getting angry at myself for tolerating all that, for not standing up to them faster and in greater vigor, at having to suffer repeated humiliation at the hands of armed thugs.

With my right finger, visible only to Dara and Gerry I make a round motion sign, signaling to them to say something. Anything. Dara picks it up immediately.

She folds her arms across her chest and sets her feet apart.

"Don't I know you from somewhere?" she asks. Her voice startles the stranger who turns his face and the gun in her direction in a sudden jolt.

He looks at her, giving her the up and down examination. She has a short skirt and despite the hour and lack of make up she looks her usual voluptuous self.

I slide the chair slowly backwards.

"No," the man says.

"You are very tall. Where are you from?" she continues.

"Shut up!" The man says and takes a step in Dara's direction. I can't wait any longer. In a second, I'm on my feet facing the stranger, who exposes his left side while turning to Dara. I lunge forward, hands first, and push the man towards the wall with all my might. The stranger, surprised, is hit just as he's ready to face me. My blow sends him into the wall, head first, gun flying into the air, and he slumps on the floor, knocked out, gasping for air. I stand over the collapsed man and hit him on the back of the head with another huge blow from my fist. The man grunts a few times, and then stops.

I look around. Dara and Gerry, who fell to the ground when the fight erupted, stand up and approach me.

"Is he dead?" Dara asks.

I look at the man for a few seconds. His chest is moving ever so slightly.

"No," I say.

"Look," Gerry cries out, "two minutes left on the screen."

I rush to the screen. The line of "corres. b." is blinking. I click twice and a menu consisting of two dozen files appears on the screen.

"Quick, download them. We'll read them later."

Jumping from the title of the file to the "save" icon, I saved all the files to the hard disk. I barely finish saving the last file when the digital display hits 0:00, blinks and beeps for a few seconds and then the screen goes blank.

I let out a sigh of relief. I don't know what's exactly in the files, but at least now we have a chance to find out at our own pace.

"What are we going to do about him?" Gerry asks.

Dara and I turn to look at the slumped intruder. He hasn't moved, though he's obviously breathing.

"Let's take off his mask," Gerry says.

"Yeah," I say, "I'll finally get a chance to see his face."

I approach the man and bend over. I have to rotate his upper torso to reach for the mask. I put my hand at the man's neck and start pulling his mask off, when I feel a tremendous jolt in my face and neck as he kicks me with his right foot. I stagger back, holding my jaw, feeling faint, but can still see the man get up, take a quick look around and dash for the door. The last thing that I remember before darkness engulfs me is Dara uttering a loud shriek that she quickly muffles with her cupped palm.

THIRTY SIX

Darkness slowly lifts and I begin to see some light. Dara is hovering over my face with a wet towel. She applies it to my swollen jaw, and I wince as the pressure sends waves of agony up and down my neck. I try to sit up, but can't. For a few moments I just lie there.

"What time is it?" comes out of my mouth, I have no idea why.

"Almost four," I hear Gerry say.

It's obviously dark outside, so it must be still morning.

"How long have I been out?" I mumble.

"A few minutes." It's Dara speaking. "How do you feel?"

I sit up, and try to move my head and neck, up and down, then move my jaws to the side and do a chewing motion. It's very painful, but I don't hear any cracked bones rattle, so maybe I'll be okay. I hold on to the chair as I stand up. I feel wobbly, but overall not too bad.

"I guess the guy is gone," I state the obvious.

"He ran to his car and sped away," Gerry says.

"Did he say anything?" I ask.

"As he reached the outside door, he wagged his finger at us and said, 'nobody messes with Lucca'"

"So, this is the infamous Lucca," I say and Gerry nods.

"Wow."

I scan the room, and notice the large stack of printout paper scattered around the computer.

"Anything new there?" I ask.

"Yes. The top page had a message about an important meeting at seven this morning. All the big honchos were invited, and Walnut was copied so you know it's serious," Gerry replies.

I notice the unfinished mug of coffee on the window sill. I grab it and gulp down its contents. It's lukewarm, but very bitter, and I immediately feel more alert.

"I also called the office and spoke to Barnes," Dara tells me.

"What?"

"He confirmed the meeting. They are deciding whether to fight or flee."

"He told you that?"

"He said that the key is Alberts's articles. If they stop it, there's no problem."

"Did you tell him about the visitor?"

Dara looks at me like I was some demented fool.

"D'you think I'm crazy?" she scolds me. "I told him I couldn't sleep, and that I worried about the articles. I asked him if I could help."

This woman will never cease to amaze me.

"Don't you think that the visitor will tell him that he saw you with me in the hotel and here with Gerry?"

"Of course," she shrugs, "and when he does I'm finished."

"It was my idea," Gerry interjects.

"The call?"

"I just wanted to find out in which conference room they are meeting."

"The memo didn't say it?"

"No."

"What difference does that make?"

"We're lucky. They're in executive conference room A on the first floor of the white building."

I'm pressing lightly on my burning chin.

"Why is that lucky?"

"There is a perfect way to enter it and listen in to the conversation. There's a tiny projection room in the back adjacent to the conference room and it has its own separate entrance. It's down the hall from the side entrance to the building."

I take a good look at them.

"You're telling me all this because . . . "

"I think you should go and pay them a visit," Lennox says.

I ponder the situation.

"How will I get in?" I ask.

"We'll give you our identity cards. If they disabled Gerry's after he was fired, mine will get you in," Dara says.

"And the guards?"

"They are in the front. The side entrance opens at six for the early birds. There are, of course, cameras focused on the entrance, but they can't watch all of them at the same time. And besides, you just walk in using the card, make your way to the projection room and hide there. The entrance to the conference room is from a different hallway so you shouldn't run into anybody. Also, make sure you get there before they do. In the corner of the projection room you'll find a few chairs stacked one on top of the other. You can hide behind them very comfortably."

I start pacing the room. This all sounds right. I should be able to learn a lot from hearing the bastards make their plans. I also need to think about preventing or limiting the risks to my well being. What if I'm found?

"If you're found, and I don't expect them to be showing any slides in this meeting," Gerry's reading my mind, "just come out and bargain with them. They can't possibly hurt you in the building, with hundreds of people showing up for work."

"Besides, until all this is settled, they figure they still need you," Dara adds.

I feel a strange rush in my head, a sense of bewildered, uncontrolled excitement.

"Let me see the memo," I tell Dara.

She walks to the computer desk and returns with a piece of paper, which I take and read. It contains a very short message:

"Colleagues, let's gather at 7:00 tomorrow and discuss our options. Be there." It was signed "C.Dell" and it was addressed to Barnes, Ramsey, Lansing, Dunbar and Parfitt. R. Walnut was the only name on the CC list. There was no date or time.

"I'll go," I say.

Gerry leaves the room and returns with a small cellular phone in his hand.

"Take this," he says, "It has six hours of battery time."

I seize it and put it in my pocket.

"I'll need a taperecorder," I say. "Lucca took mine."

"No problem," says Gerry, disappears again and returns with a tiny recorder.

"Here. New batteries are in," he hands it to me. I test it briefly and shove it in my shirt pocket.

I walk to the phone and dial my home number. It's after seven in the morning in Philadelphia and Irene picks it up after a few rings.

"Hi, honey it's me. Did I wake you up?"

"Yes, but that's okay."

"I want you to take Danny and go back to your sister Ellen. Pronto. And please don't ask me why."

"Paul, are you okay?"

"I'm fine. Will you do it?'

A very short hesitation.

"Sure. Where are you?"

"In San Francisco. . . "

"Paul, I almost forgot. Somebody called from Vienna yesterday. Sounded very important. They're gonna fax you something this morning."

"Good. Wait one hour and then leave, whether or not the fax arrives."

"What should I do with the fax?"

"Memorize it, and then take it with you to Ellen's."

"I love you, Paul. Be careful, whatever it is you're doing there."

"I love you too," I say and hang up.

Dara looks at me for a moment, eyes narrowed, and turns away.

"What time should I leave?" I ask Gerry.

"It's about a thirty-five minute drive. You can leave around six. Take my car."

I look at my watch. I've got an hour and forty minutes before I have to leave.

Gerry makes me another strong coffee, and then draws me a map of the white building. I study it for a long time, until I know it almost as if I lived there my entire life. Dara spends most of the time skimming through the several hundred pages of the computer printout of file "corres. b".

THIRTY SEVEN

THE DRIVE FROM GERRY'S HOUSE TO THE GOTHER CAMPUS IN BERKELEY is uneventful. The traffic on the Bay Bridge is getting heavy, but it's 6:25 when I turn off the engine in Gerry's Taurus in a parking space south of the white building. A few cars are parked here, nothing out of the ordinary. From the car I spot the side entrance with the turnstile gate, but immediately I notice a slight inconvenience: a uniformed guard stands at the other end, presumably to personally greet the worker bees of Gother.

I wait in the car for ten minutes, until the volume of incoming workers is picking up. So instead of sneaking in alone, having adequate time to figure out the identity card routine, I decide to make my way in mingling with the crowds. I wear a tie-less white shirt and a blue blazer, and I'm relieved to see that mine is a common and appropriate attire for this place, just as Dara and Gerry promised. I wait for a group of four workers to form a line, three guys and a woman, and I join them as they approach the entrance. Exchanging smiles and small banter about the weather, I make my way to the door. I pull out Dara's card and being the fifth and last in the small line that has formed, I wait for my turn and pass the card through the detector, much the same way as one uses an ATM machine. At my first attempt nothing happens, except my heart rate approaches a hundred beats a minute: red light still on, turnstile gate resisting my push. The second time my swipe is better as the red light turns to green, I hear a loud click and the gate moves inward as I push. The guard watches with a bored expression, and as I pass him I smile and say "good morning." He says "good morning" and I turn to look for the corridor that leads to the projection room.

It's a short walk down a wide hallway, then two turns and I find the door to the projection room. I enter it, and to my surprise it's a lot bigger than I thought, but also a lot darker since it is windowless. In the center is the projector, supported by a tripod stand, with the lens directed through a small square hole into the conference room. On the walls there are two built-in bookshelves, with empty carousels and light bulbs, wires and the like strewn about. There's an old-looking armchair near the projector, which probably serves the projectionist, and in the corner I see the folding chairs. I peer into the conference room, now eerily empty. It's a lot fancier than the one I saw during my previous visit. The upholstery of the chairs is plush burgundy, the mahogany desk is impeccable, and the wall is hidden by a large bar surrounded by stools. Replicas of Monets and Renoirs adorn the other two walls. I move the armchair towards the corner, rearrange the chairs and slouch right behind them in the corner. If somebody walked into the room, they'd have to move furniture around to see me, even if they turned on the light. I take the taperecorder out of my pocket and place it on the chair, next to the armrest. Then I crouch in fetal position and check the time: 6:46. I wait quietly.

Ten minutes later there's a slight commotion and I hear footsteps in the conference room. Moments later more footsteps and human voices.

"Shit, I never ran so fast in my life," somebody says, and I recognize Ramsey's voice. He's huffing and puffing as he speaks.

"What's the hurry, Lenny?" another voice asks and this is without a doubt Carter Dell.

"I didn't want you guys to start without me. Last man in gets to eat all the shit," Ramsey says.

"Relax, man," Dell says, "everything is under control."

"Carter, are you outta your fucking mind? I hear rumors that Lucca is going berserk. Threatening, blackmailing, possibly hurting people . . . "

"Lenny, I want you to take some Valium right now. You're losing it, and I don't think our company appreciates it. Get a grip, Len."

"Is it true that one of our European investigators died suddenly?"

"I've no idea."

"And that Lucca situation . . . "

"Len, I said forget about Lucca."

The conversation ends. More muted voices, shuffling of chairs, and then silence. I slide my hand across and push the record button on the tape recorder. Suddenly I decide that hearing is not enough, and that I have to see the action. I move out of my hideout, get up quietly and position myself in front of the projector lens. I move very slowly and deliberately, making sure not to hit any objects in my way. I manage to get one eye in the viewing area and look inside the conference room.

Facing me, at the top of the desk and chairing the meeting, is the CEO, Richard Walnut III. He wears a bow tie, blue striped shirt, and his white hair is erect, as if he sped through a wind tunnel. To his right are the chief financial officer of Gother, Dunbar, the chief operating officer, Parfitt, and Dell. Sitting across from them are Ramsey and Barnes. I recognize Dunbar and Parfitt from the Wall Street analysts meeting in New York. There's another fellow in there, whom I don't recognize, seated next to Barnes. Except for Walnut, they are all in open shirts, looking informal, but the tension in the room is palpable. Ramsey looks crushed, slumped in his chair, eyes darting from one person to the next, like a deer caught in a car's head light.

"Is the door locked?" Walnut barks.

Barnes, evidently the most junior man in the room, jumps to his feet and checks the door.

"Yes," he announces, and returns to his seat.

Walnut throws a glance in my general direction, but says nothing, only swallows hard a few times.

"Where's Lansing?" he shrieks.

Ramsey, Barnes and Dell exchange glances.

"What's the matter, he doesn't know how to read his e-mail?" Walnut persists.

Dell coughs.

"He just got back from Europe and I believe he's on the road again."

"Did he notify anybody that he wasn't coming?"

Nobody has an answer.

"Never mind," Walnut mutters.

From his briefcase he pulls out a crumpled newspaper.

"Has everybody read this?" Walnut barks, pointing with a bony finger to the headline of David's article.

There are nods around the table.

"What about you, Len?"

Ramsey nods. Walnut ignores his nod and hands him the paper.

"Read it, read it," he bellows.

Ramsey looks around, uneasy and perturbed by the unwelcome attention he's getting. He puts on his glasses and starts reading it when Walnut yells again.

"Aloud. I want you to read it aloud. From the top."

Like an admonished school child he starts reading.

"A few weeks ago I was paged at Dulles Airport, just as I was ready to board a plane, and was told that my mother became seriously sick. Instead of flying to San Diego I flew to Philadelphia, where I found my mother at death's doorstep. She had intense jaundice and was in a coma. Who killed my mother?"

"Skip the mushy stuff. Next paragraph," Walnut screams.

"My mother was advised by her physician to enter a study with a new drug called Neurovan, manufactured by the Gother Company in Berkeley, CA. Supposedly this drug is a cure for diabetic complications, but in discussions with several experts in the field it became obvious that the basis for the promise is questionable at best, negligent at worst. However, all this is relatively minor compared to the safety profile of the drug. People got severely ill while taking Neurovan, but my mother didn't know it when she agreed to participate in the trial. Then, when the first signs of liver damage appeared in a blood test, the information was suppressed and the drug wasn't stopped in time. Other patients subsequently also became ill, but that information wasn't passed on to all patients and centers participating in studies. Here's a brief history of the other two very severe cases:

The second patient is a thirty-one-year old woman from Miami, Annette Delvechio. While preparing breakfast for her two little kids, she felt sick and threw up a few times before she was rushed to the hospital by her husband. She was diagnosed with liver failure and jaundice, and despite all the efforts in one of our top centers, she died a few days later after slipping into terminal coma. The third patient is from Vienna, Austria. A seventeen-year-old high school student, Christian Hauptman, is lying in a hospital terminally jaundiced and comatose, waiting for a possible liver donor. In all three patients there were no other possible causes for the liver disease, and Neurovan was established beyond reasonable doubt as the culprit. In addition, eight point three percent of patients developed a milder form of liver disease . . .

"St-o-o-o-o-p!" Walnut hollers and I retract my head, almost hitting the lens of the projector. "Is the information on these patients accurate?"

Ramsey looks at Barnes and Barnes looks at the floor.

"I'll have to check with the people in the field . . . "

"Check my ass, Ramsey. Why are you getting paid so much if you've got to check everything with somebody else? I'll give you the answer. I'll bet your annual salary and your hefty bonus and your zillion stock options that this is one hundred percent accurate! Anybody wanna bet?"

Dell and Ramsey exchange glances. Their faces suggest that the old man would be winning such a bet.

"Now that was easy. But now I want to know how the little prick obtained all that accurate information?"

Dell finally decides to take a chance and say something.

"He obviously interviewed people in the know. The physicians who treated the patients, maybe families, who knows?"

"Aha," Walnut pounds on the desk with his flat hand, "but where did he get the names of the patients in the first place?"

Walnut starts pacing in front of the group.

"How? How did he get that information? Is this information freely available to the public? Did he read about it in the Encyclopedia Brittanica? In Newsweek magazine? Did you post it on some bulletin board on the Internet? How?"

"No, but patients' consent forms usually contain such information, as does a drug brochure that investigators obtain before a study can start," Ramsey mutters.

"So, in the brochure there's specific information about patients, their names and everything?"

"Of course not."

"So? He got it from whom?" Walnut asks

"One of the investigators, no doubt," Ramsey says.

"Okay, maybe there's a clue in the article, huh, fellas? Dr. Ramsey, continue reading. Read! Read!" He rolls the letter 'r' in Doctor and Ramsey as if it causes him excruciating pain in the gums.

"According to one of the nation's most renowned liver experts, Dr. Paul Holden, from Lincoln University in Philadelphia, Neurovan is not a safe drug and many more patients are likely to die if the drug is approved."

"St-o-o-o-p!" Walnut yelled again, "do we know this guy?"

Ramsey inserts his hand in the collar of his shirt, trying to pry it even wider.

"Well, uh, yeah. He was one of our consultants."

"Was?"

"I got rid of him when he got too negative and too nosy," says Ramsey.

"I remember now," Dunbar suddenly chimes in. As the second in command he may be smelling some interesting career opportunities in this situation.

"Didn't we get him on one of the FDA committees so he could help us approve Neurovan in the US?"

"I called the FDA and removed him from the committee. Keeping him had a negative risk to benefit ratio."

"When did you dismiss him?" Walnut asks.

"Uh . . . a coupla days ago."

"Any of you meet him?"

"Well, Barnes did . . . " Ramsey decides to get Barnes involved. After all, Ramsey is the boss, and there's no reason for Barnes to just sit there and enjoy the show.

"Didn't you take him to dinner and offer him the consultancy when he visited Berkeley?" Dell asks Ramsey.

Ramsey's thin mustache starts twitching nervously. He doesn't need Dell on his ass, too.

"It's all clear now," Dell opines without waiting for an answer, "that sonofabitch Holden must have been the source of all the information for that Alberts writer."

"Bravo, Sherlock," Walnut says, clapping his hands mockingly.

"Barnes was assigned to deal with this consultant," Ramsey tries again.

"What's going on in your shop, anyway? That clinical scientist, Lyons, is taken off the project, then she's back. Lennox goes bananas in front of the CSM, then we have to fire him, and then he tries to commit suicide. You tell me Barnes this, Barnes that, but is anybody supervising Barnes?"

Walnut is addressing Ramsey as if Barnes isn't in the room. Ramsey decides on a slight tactical change.

"Carter, you did it," he says and looks at Dell straight in the eye.

Dell returns the favor with his most piercing look.

"Did what?"

"You put Lyons back on the project when Lacoste called you, and you wanted to demote Lennox and put her on top."

"Listen here, Lenny. You actually did these things. Lennox got crazy after you demoted him." Dell spits the "you" with great emphasis and relish.

"You told me to, you bastard," Len Ramsey yells and jumps to his feet.

"We had a meeting and we decided what's best for the company. The idea to put that bimbo over him was yours," Dell spits out the words in cool disdain.

"Shut up, both of you," Walnut shouts. "Ramsey, finish reading."

Ramsey picks up the newspaper and continues reading in a

quivering voice, still on his feet. A moment later, he decides to sit down after all.

"Not only did Gother endanger patients by not warning them about potential risks, but the drug apparently has almost zero probability to be effective. The diabetologist consultant for the Neurovan project has been misleading the company brass by painting unfounded rosy pictures to line his pockets. In the next segment we'll tell you about that "expert", Dr. Roger Lacoste, and about the fraudulent strategies that Gother uses to mislead the investment community."

Ramsey removes his glasses and puts the paper down in front of Walnut. He rubs his eyes with his thumb and forefinger and shifts in his chair.

"I need a drink," he says and moves towards the bar.

"Forget it, Ramsey," Dell says. "We need to think. All of us. What do we do next?"

"Wait a minute, Carter," Walnut says, "I'm running this meeting. First we need to gather all the information and then decide on a course of action."

Ramsey starts pacing about nervously.

"Ted," Walnut turns to the seventh man, the one I don't know. "You also have some wonderful news for us, so why don't you tell the group."

"Well, in addition to the article, David Alberts and his family are suing Gother for the death of Mrs. Dorothy Alberts. Named in the suit are Walnut, Dell, Ramsey and Barnes. They're asking for punitive damages in addition to pain and suffering."

"How much?"

"Twenty two point seven million."

"What are the charges?"

"It's a long list. It mostly deals with failure to notify patients about risks, misleading about nonexistent benefits, negligent monitoring, ignoring laboratory data, and all this is done willfully and maliciously with full knowledge and conspiracy of all the managers and executives at Gother."

Ramsey stops in mid-stride.

"Who the fuck cares about the lawsuit? We need to survive the damn articles first, don't you get it? God, I can't believe all this crap!"

"Okay, everybody, Len has a point," Walnut says and turns to the fellow named Ted, apparently the corporate legal counselor, "Ted, you can go now. We'll call you if we need you."

Ted gets up and for a moment I think he's maybe coming into the projection room, trying to leave through the back door, but he reconsiders, unlocks the front door and leaves.

"You two can also leave," Walnut motions to Parfitt and Dunbar, "I want to talk now to the R and D folks alone about the situation with Neurovan."

He looks at his watch.

"Come back in one hour," he tells them and they quickly rush through the door, following Ted.

My nose is on the wall, adjacent to the hole, as I watch Dell, Barnes and Ramsey, all getting up and starting to pace. Walnut sits down at the head of the table, watching them pensively.

"Larry, you've been awfully quiet," Walnut throws a glance at Barnes. "How about you do something for me. Call that expert of yours, you know, on diabetes, from St. Louis, what's his name, Lacoste. Let's have us a little chat."

Barnes gets the phone from the counter and brings it to the center of the desk. He digs into his back pocket and pulls out a tiny address book. He thumbs through it, moistening his thumb as he does, until he finds what he's looking for. He dials a number, then pushes the speakerphone button. A ringing sound, than a loud woman's voice rises from the desk:

"Endocrinology, good morning."

"This is Walnut, from Gother. Is Dr. Lacoste there?"

"I'm sorry, your name again . . . "

"Walnut. Richard Walnut. He knows me."

"Will he know what is this in reference to . . . "

Walnut jumps to his feet, as the three others can't hide a smirk.

"He'll have a pretty good idea," he screams.

A moment later, I hear a familiar, yet unpleasant voice.

"Dr. Lacoste here."

"This is Dick Walnut. I've got Dell, Ramsey and Barnes here, and you're on the speakerphone. We're talking about Neurovan and how to proceed. Give us an update, if you please."

"Perfect timing, Dick. Just got wonderful news through my contacts in London. The CSM is meeting Monday and is going to approve Neurovan. You can start collecting them bills there with the cotton pickin' queen of England staring you right in the face."

"So they have no concerns about the safety, the three liver cases?" Dell asks.

"Taken care of. They accepted our explanation that they are unlikely to be drug related."

"What if they call the FDA?"

"Taken care of. Aftaz, the medical reviewer, is in our pocket. You remember, I trained him, and he owes me a bundle."

"Anything else?" Walnut takes control again.

"We've started looking at the data from the current clinicals. Very early results, but so far looks fantastic. You've got yourself a blockbuster, my friend, do you hear me? You know, Zantac, the anti-ulcer drug from Glaxo, made two billion, that's with a bee, in one year. Neurovan will set the world record, I'm telling ya."

Barnes gets closer to Ramsey and raises his hand for a high five but Ramsey turns away. Dell looks confused.

"When will you finish your analysis?"

"Need a couple of weeks, maybe three at the most."

Walnut clears his throat.

"You saw the article by this Alberts fella?" he asks Lacoste.

"Yep. I'd like to wring the neck of that cotton pickin' sonofabitch, " Lacoste raises his voice, "can't you do something about him?"

"Like what?" Walnut asks and rolls his eyes, like he needs advice from Lacoste.

"You're the cotton' pickin' experts," Lacoste doesn't fall into the trap, "but if you ask me I'd start with that so-called liver expert, Holden. He's been feeding the kid all that information."

There's a knock at the door and Walnut motions to Barnes to check who is out there.

"Yeah, maybe. Listen, Roger, we got to go. Thanks for the info, and great job on the UK approval. We'll remember this come bonus time."

Ramsey turns the speaker off as Joe Lansing is let into the room by Barnes. I haven't seen him since the flight from Vienna and the London meeting. He has what looks like a bruise on his forehead, going down to his eye. His right hand is in his pocket, but when he extends it to pull a chair out for himself, I notice it's bruised.

"What happened to you?" Dell asks.

"I had a friggin' car accident on the Bay bridge. Some idiot rammed his pickup truck into the right side of my car. My head hit the damn windshield and my hand got caught in the shift stick. I'm lucky to be alive."

I take a long look at Lansing. The way he moves. His large head. His hands. I listen to his voice. And then it hits me, and as it does, a cold shiver runs up and down my spine. I recognize him. He is the intruder in the hotel and in Lennox's house. He is Lucca.

THIRTY EIGHT

INSTEAD OF SITTING DOWN, LANSING GOES BEHIND THE BAR AND PULLS out a bottle of vodka, and takes a big, long swig straight from the bottle. Ramsey is looking on and without a word, goes to the same place and grabs another bottle of vodka. He finds a glass and pours himself a hefty dose.

"What are we doing?" Lansing asks, staring at Walnut.

"We just got some good news from Lacoste. UK is in, data looks good on our trials there," Barnes says.

"I knew that," Joe spits. "What are we doing about that Alberts kid?"

"I offered him a bunch of money, like we said, but I haven't heard from anybody." Barnes is pacing now, hands behind his back.

"You called him?" Joe asks.

"No, I talked to Holden."

"Well, Alberts will agree to take the money," Joe says.

They all surround him.

"How do you know?"

"I know."

They exchange glances.

"C'mon, Lansing . . . "

"I'm tellin' ya, he'll take the money."

"Are you sure?" Ramsey can' t resist.

"Positive."

Walnut takes a deep breath.

"Wow, I guess that means we're out of the woods," he mutters.

"Not yet. Holden may still publish the articles. He has plenty of incriminating information."

"Like what?" Ramsey asks.

Walnut looks at Ramsey, then at Joe.

"Do I want to know what kind of information he has?" Walnut asks.

"I don't think so," Lansing says slowly.

"Well, what can we do to stop Holden?" Dell pipes in.

"I bet he'll take the money, just like Alberts did," Barnes opines.

"I doubt it," Lansing says.

"Why?"

Lansing rubs his sore forehead and winces when he touches the painful spot.

"Because he's a lot tougher, that's why."

"So what are you saying, that he got us?" Ramsey is fidgeting.

"Did you hear me say that he got us?"

"No, but you implied . . . "

"Implied my ass. Listen carefully, Ramsey. Did I say that he got us . . . "

"Not exactly . . . "

"Okay."

Lansing closes his eyes and leans back in the chair, as they all watch him intently.

"So what's left to do?" Walnut finally speaks.

Lansing looks around the assembled people.

"Perhaps, Dick, you should leave, if you want to maintain some plausible deniability."

"Hmm . . . " Walnut mumbles.

"What you don't know can't hurt you."

"Okay. I'll be back in thirty minutes. There's one thing that I want you to do while I'm gone."

He pulls out a white handkerchief and wipes his sweaty brow.

"Even if we stop the subsequent articles, and even if we win the lawsuit, we have been damaged by the first article. Damaged badly, and to pretend otherwise just ain't gonna work. We'll have to make some personnel changes in our clinical research and development group."

He looks Dell right in the eye.

"Carter, you decide. If you want to resign, I accept. If you want to handle it differently with your staff," and he points at the bewildered Ramsey and Barnes, "feel free to do so."

Walnut gets up and glances at the clock on the wall.

"Thirty minutes," he says, opens the door and disappears. Dell rushes to close the door after him.

"You can't fire me," Barnes says calmly, "without me you'll never solve the Holden problem."

Every time they mention my name, there's a knot tightening in my chest and stomach.

"Nonsense. We can handle him," Joe says.

"How?" Dell asks.

"Don't worry about the details. All I know is that he has a loving wife and a small child. That's usually enough."

I feel a little weak and lean on the wall for support. In the process, I knock the lens of the projector. It makes a slight noise. They stop for a second, look in my direction, then at each other.

After a long moment, a moment that seems like an eternity, they go back to their conversation.

"By the way, what's Lennox doing here today? I thought he was fired," says Lansing.

"He was." Barnes, who's been quiet for awhile, suddenly decides to exercise his vocal cords.

"So what's his car doing here?" Joe continues.

"Where?" Ramsey asks.

"In the side parking lot. I saw it when I came in."

"Maybe he left it here when he got the boot. Took a cab home or something."

"Maybe. Why don't you call security and have them check it out." Joe is clearly running things now.

Ramsey picks up the phone, dials, exchanges a few words and hangs up.

"Done," he says.

"So, where were we? Oh, yeah, Larry was explaining why he can't be fired." Joe is businesslike.

There's a swollen vein now on Barnes's neck.

"Besides," Barnes says, "I know too much. We're all in this together."

Lansing gives him a look that could freeze a lake.

"If I were you, Barnes," he hisses, "I wouldn't use that argument on your behalf. Ever."

Dell, who has been watching and listening to the exchange from the other side of the room, approaches Barnes.

"Barnes, you're finished. Done. We'll give you a nice package-say, three years of salary and you have to leave the country. Do you speak Spanish?"

Barnes lips begin to quiver.

"You know I do."

Dell inserts his hand into the inside pocket of his jacket, which is hugging the back of his chair, retrieves a thick folder and hands it to Barnes.

"One ticket to Santiago de Chile. Flight to Mexico City leaves at 4:27 p.m. today. Be there."

Barnes holds the tickets in his hand, unsure what to do. He then opens the folder and looks at the ticket.

"It's in my name, you bastard."

"Of course, in whose name should it be?" Dell responds.

Barnes walks around as if sleepwalking, then slumps into an empty chair. The cool efficiency must have impressed him. It sure impresses me.

"This, after everything I've done for you and the company. Years of devotion, I raised this Neurovan baby like it was my child. I got the studies going, got it approved in several countries, we . . . it's on the verge of making billions and now this . . . "

Dell stands next to him.

"After five years you can come back and look for work, if you want to . . . "

"But you said the salary package was for only three years . . . " Barnes whimpers.

"That's correct. Like I was saying, we'll give you terrific references, of course. And . . . don't ever call here and don't ever talk to anybody about Gother or Neurovan. Understood?"

"And if I refuse?" Barnes sounds like a broken man.

"I don't think so," Lansing says.

They are all calm now, almost bored with Barnes.

Dell walks back to his chair, inserts his hand into the inside pocket of his jacket and grabs another folder. Ramsey is watching, and when he sees the folder he closes his eyes and falls in the chair.

"Where am I going?" he snivels.

"Sydney."

"Australia?"

"Do you know any other Sydney? We know that you can't speak any foreign languages. And because you're more senior and married you get two tickets for tomorrow's flight. Quantas, non-stop."

"It's a great company," Lansing says, "best safety record among all the airlines."

Ramsey is fighting tears.

"But . . . I don't get it. Now that we're on the verge of victory. . . multi-billion dollar drug . . . Alberts articles will not get published. . . who's going to do all the work to get it approved in the USA . . . I know the FDA so well . . . "

Dell stops him.

"Ramsey, the first priority now is to handle this crisis. We need to clear all the safety blemishes of Neurovan . . . make sure things don't get out of hand."

"Think of this as a favor, not punishment," Lansing interrupts. "We're looking at many unpleasant moments, investigations, interrogations—God knows what."

"And once we're done with this . . . phase, we'll assemble a fresh new team and march on with the product," Dell adds.

"So, why are you staying here?" Barnes asks Lansing.

Lansing smiles wryly.

"I have nowhere to go. Besides, I love my job."

By now I'm shifting from foot to foot, as I'm trying to digest all that's going on. There's a sudden knock on the door.

"Who could that be?" Dell says and looks at the clock. "It's too early for Walnut."

He goes to the door and opens it. The sight of Dara walking in will be ingrained in my mind as long as I live. She's wearing a white blouse, upper button open, a blue long skirt and she is all smiles.

"Hi, everybody," she says, "what's up, guys?"

THIRTY NINE

"WHAT THE HELL ARE YOU DOING HERE?" DELL ASKS DARA. HE TOOK the words straight out of my mouth.

"I invited her," Barnes says without looking up.

"What for?" Dell inquires.

"She takes care of Holden for us."

"What's that supposed to mean?" Dell still doesn't get it, neither do I but a sneaking suspicion tells me that something is terribly wrong.

"Doesn't matter any more to me," Barnes says and starts to remove his jacket from the chair.

Dara walks briskly towards Barnes and stands by him.

"Why, what happened?"

"Larry has resigned from the company and I accepted. He's about to leave," Dell explains.

Dara plants her feet apart and folds her arms on her chest.

"What the hell is going on?"

"Listen, Dara, we have work to do, so if you don't mind . . . " Dell is showing signs of impatience.

Lansing yawns and addresses Dara.

"Okay, where is he?"

"Who?"

"You know who. Your buddy, Holden." Lansing says the word "buddy" with utter contempt.

"He's right here."

"Where?"

Dara hesitates, but only for a split second.

"In the projection room. He's been listening to your blabber the whole time."

As all eyes turn in my direction, I know I have less than a fraction of a second to act. If I make a run for it, I may only get as far as the security people outside the door, which, for all I know, may have been alerted by Dara. Besides, I need to finish what I started. Face to face. Like a man.

I take a few steps and open the door leading to the conference room. They're all staring at me.

"Good morning, Dr. Holden," Dell is smiling, "what a surprise."

I don't respond.

"Can we get you something? A coffee perhaps? Espresso? Maybe cappuccino?" Dell continues, oozing sarcasm.

"Maybe a good Viennese coffee, huh? With a large apple strudel. What d'you say, Holden?" Lansing asks wearily.

"That would be nice. I take my coffee with no sugar, lots of cream," I say. I look around, trying to decide if I should just sit down and act relaxed. I can't imagine them trying to hurt me in their own conference room.

Lansing is not smiling. After a moment, he stands up and closes in on me.

"Do you plan to publish the Alberts articles?" he spits the words in my face.

"Yes."

"And do you want to see your wife and boy . . . uh, little Danny?"

I can still nail him with a right hook, and maybe escape, but Irene and Danny. . .

"Sure. And I will."

Joe hesitates for a second. He then turns to the others.

"Why don't you all leave now. I have some private things to discuss with Holden. I don't think you'll find them particularly interesting."

Dell, Ramsey and Barnes scurry to get their belongings and leave in a hurry, with Dara following them.

"You can stay, if you want, Dara," Joe tells her, "you may want to see what happens to the guy you fucked."

He sits down, turning his back to me. When he turns around to face me, he's holding a gun and pointing it at me.

"Seems like the only way to stop you and save myself and Gother is to kill you," he says.

I look around the room. Dara is near the door. Lansing is a few feet away from me and I'm at least thirty feet from the door. If only I could get closer to the door . . . I decide to ignore him and talk to Dara. If he decides to shoot me, he can do it anytime.

"So, Dara, this is what it's come to," I say, "why?"

"Why what?"

"No, the question is not why, the question is when? When did you start working for Barnes and against me?"

She looks at me innocently with her beautiful hair and big brown eyes.

"It really doesn't matter now, does it . . . "

I get closer to her

"It matters to me a great deal."

From the corner of my eye I catch a glimpse of Lansing's face. He actually seems to enjoy my little conversation with Dara.

"I guess there's no harm in telling you. Larry . . . uh . . . Barnes promised to take care of me for the rest of my life. Financially, that is. I got a huge bonus for this . . . job. In the hotel, when you turned me down the third time, I really had no choice."

Lansing is laughing hard.

"Turned you down? What's the matter, big boy, things are limping a little, huh?"

I'm still looking at Dara. I don't want to get into a big discussion, all I want is to distract him.

"So you didn't fuck him after all?" he guffaws, looking at Dara.

"No."

"Oh, that's a real shame."

He suddenly notices that I'm getting slowly farther away from him.

"Hey, stop right there. Where the fuck you think you're going?"

I stop.

"I'm just talking to an old friend," I say.

This strikes him as being funny, because he guffaws again.

"Right, a real, good, old friend. Maybe one day she can knit you a little sweater, huh?"

Dara seems to be drained of emotion. The look of lust, desire or even friendship towards me, a look that I've seen so many times in her face is now gone. Instead, there's a cold indifference, a look that says nothing matters any more.

Lansing suddenly stops laughing.

"Look, Holden, you really have nothing on us, except the Alberts articles. Just forget about the whole thing and you'll live. We'll let Irene and Danny go free if you promise to stay out of Gother's affairs. All we're asking for is a promise."

I'm listening carefully.

"I'll take your word. You promise and everything's cool again. But if you publish, you die. You can't run away from us or hide for the rest of your life."

"He also knows about Kunz in Vienna," Dara states.

"What exactly does he have?" Joe asks.

"He was expecting some fax this morning. I don't know what . . . "

"Oh, that's nothing," says Joe, "we've got the fax. They found some Digoxin in his blood, but there's nothing that ties us to this incident."

Digoxin is a commonly used drug to treat heart failure. Given at high doses it's fatal.

Joe opens and closes his fist several times, as if trying to shake off some sudden cramp.

"Oh, by the way, Dara, did you find anything on the computer, you know, the 'corres. b' file?"

"Nope."

"That's good. So he really has nothing concrete on us."

They're talking to each other as if I don't exist.

"How do I know that you got my family?" I jump in.

"Just call Ellen, her sister. She'll tell you."

"Okay."

He brings the phone closer and pushes the speakerphone button.

"The number is 215-675- " I start.

"4332," Joe finishes dialing, and I realize that they know everything and I have no chance. The phone rings a few times and Ellen's voice comes on.

"Hello?"

"Ellen," I say, "is Irene there?"

"No, I've been trying to reach you, Paul. I got a strange call from Irene that she couldn't come and couldn't talk, and then I

heard a man's voice say, 'that's enough' and we were disconnected. I'm scared, Paul."

"How long ago was that?" I ask, but Joe pushes the speakerphone button and we're cut off.

"That proves nothing," I say.

"We've got her," Dara says softly, and when she says "we" I
know it's really over.

I walk to the chair at the top of the desk and sit down.

"Okay, Lansing, you win. As soon as Irene calls to tell me that
she's okay, from home, I leave for Philadelphia and you'll never
hear from me again. You have my word, and you know it's good
as gold."

Joe and Dara exchange glances.

"I don't trust him," Dara says.

Joe looks at me, trying to read my face.

"Ah, he's probably okay," he declares, still scanning my face
and body language "he's too much of a chicken to do anything,
because he knows that we'll get him. Right, tiger?"

I nod.

He picks up the receiver, dials long distance. After a few seconds he mumbles a few short sentences into the receiver, never
taking his eyes off me, and hangs up. He then looks at the clock
on the wall, which reads 8:35.

"She'll be home in twenty minutes and call you in thirty," he
says.

"I'll wait," I say.

Dara sits down on one of the chairs, Joe is across from her, a
bottle of Vodka in his hand, and I'm still in the chair at the top of
the long desk, my head resting on it. All I'm thinking about is
Dara. Her betrayal has completely deflated my resolve.

We sit in silence for a few moments.

"How big are you?" Joe suddenly asks me.

"What?"

"What, you're six-two, six-three, two hundred twenty pounds?"

"Yeah." I don't want to talk to the guy anymore. I just want to get the phone call and scram. I don't trust them, but I have no choice.

"I'm sitting here, and I'm getting more mad by the minute. You've been a pain in the ass from the start, Holden, and your face is so nice and smooth. Look at mine, look what you did to me in Lennox's house. Look!"

He pushes back his chair and jumps to his feet, startling me.

"Look, we've agreed to settle the whole thing. Now don't . . . " I try.

He pulls a gun from his jacket and aims it at my face. His hand is trembling and he starts laughing.

"Scared, huh?"

I get on my feet, as he tosses the gun to Dara who catches it in one swift motion, putting her finger on the trigger, ready to squeeze it if necessary.

I look at her.

"So, you think you have the guts to kill me?" I ask.

The muzzle of her gun is in clear sight, a few feet away. She's pointing the gun to an area around my neck and jaw. Her hand is steady and her facial expression displays total determination and concentration.

"Dara, shoot the bastard if he gets out of line," he says.

This is too much.

"You wouldn't dare . . . " I tell her.

"Paul, don't . . . " her voice is steady.

From the corner of my eye I see Lansing getting closer. He takes a swig from the bottle and puts it down.

"Come to papa, pretty boy," he shouts, and lunges forward. I try to duck, but his fist hits me at the left side of my neck as excruciating pain radiates to my head and shoulder. I turn and with my lowered head I charge into his upper chest, and with a loud thud he collapses on his back, with me on top of him. But he rolls to the side and I hit the floor, chin first, and he jumps on my back, his bent arm encircling my neck. I try to shake him off my back but can't, as the grip on my neck tightens. But there's something that distracts me first, and I think maybe he hears it too. There's some commotion in the distance, noise of people talking, feet rushing, and it gets louder by the second. Lansing raises his head trying to listen and Dara turns her head around, attempting to figure out what the rumbling noise is all about. Lansing decides to ignore the hubbub, and I feel the squeeze on my neck tightening. There's very little air now flowing through my windpipe, and just as the room is getting darker and darker, the doors of the projection room and the conference room burst open simultaneously and police officers, guns in hand, barge in. The first officer in the room quickly approaches Lansing and hits him on the head with his gun. Lansing's body slumps on the floor, still twisted in the holding motion he had on me. Dara yells and tries to run for it, but is immediately surrounded by a group of policemen.

It takes me a few seconds of coughing and gasping to recover my breath. I look at the policemen as they hustle about, searching the room and then I see a familiar figure emerging from the door and approaching me.

"I'm so glad we got here in time," Gerry Lennox says.

*   *   *   *   *

The phone rings and the room gets silent. Short hesitation, and Gerry Lennox is the first to pick it up. He listens for a moment and then hands the receiver to me, without words.

I get up slowly and grab the receiver. Dara, in the corner, has her back to me, pressed to the wall by a policeman.

"Hello?"

"It's me, honey, they told me to call this number . . . "

"Are you okay?"

"I'm fine."

"And Danny?"

"He's fine too."

"And you're home?"

"Yes."

"Alone?"

"Yes."

"Thank God. I'll see you tomorrow," I say and hang up.

The policemen are putting cuffs on Joe's and Dara's hands, while reading the standard stuff about their rights.

Gerry puts his arms around me.

"Let's go, buddy. Our work is done. Almost."

I look at him. He appears very calm, his ruddy appearance having returned to his face.

"I have two questions for you," I say.

"Only two?"

"Yes."

"Let me guess. The answer to the first one is that I suspected Dara for some time, but I knew for sure only when she called Barnes from my house. After you left she tried to call him, presumably to tell them about your being in the room, but she couldn't reach anybody. Then she got very nervous and left suddenly."

I smile, because he got it right.

"And the second question?" I tease him.

"The 'corres. b' file. I found the kind of memo we were looking for. A page was missing from the printout, and I figured Dara had tossed it away, so I printed it out again. Here, this is a copy for you."

He hands me the copy and I read it quickly. It's from Larry Barnes, and is addressed to Ramsey, Dell and Lansing, copy to Walnut.

"Gents, Given the current safety and efficacy data on Neurovan, it may be very difficult to get it to the market using conventional regulatory approaches. I suggest the formation of a special task force that would use creative persuasion and explanation techniques. Lansing will be in charge, and he'll have a completely free hand to pursue above goal. I also suggest to give this operation the code name 'Lucca'. If I get no response in 24 hours, I'll interpret this as a go recommendation. Please destroy this message immediately without making any copies."

I look at the date. It's September 18, that is, six months ago. I fold the memo and put it in my pocket.

A police sergeant approaches me.

"I need a few details from you and then you can go home. We'll ask you to come back for a more detailed questioning."

"Of course. Thank you."

He interviews me for almost two hours. He's especially interested in the final forty-eight hours in San Francisco. He wants to know when I met Lansing and under what circumstances, about the encounters with Lansing at the hotel and in Gerry's house and about the kidnapping of Irene and Danny in Philadelphia, no doubt by some of Lansing's sidekicks. He asks me about Dara's role in all this and I tell him I don't know. He pries into my relationship with Dara and I tell him just about everything. He takes copious notes and records my answers. I thank him for not taking me to the station for all the questioning and promise to return to San Francisco whenever I'm needed. A few minutes into my interview, I watch as Joe and Dara are taken away. As Dara is sauntering away, I see her perfect body sway from side to side. As she exits, she turns around and blows a kiss in my direction, and the officer no doubt wonders why.

When Gerry and I finally leave the building, I notice near the exit a body on the floor, covered with a brown wool blanket, being watched by two policemen. There's a red stain, about two thirds up the blanket. From underneath the blanket I notice one shoe pointing up, and I immediately recognize it as one of the shining Italian shoes of Dr. Larry Barnes.

FORTY

One week later, Philadelphia

WE'RE HAVING A PARTY IN OUR HOUSE TO CELEBRATE THE HAPPY ending of our ordeal. The arrest of Gother's top brass led to the halting of all activities of the company. The board was dismantled and a date was set for a congressional hearing about pharmaceutical practices in drug development. The events at Gother headquarters last week started the action, and David's articles—all of them published in the same issue last Tuesday—were the last nails in Gother's coffin.

I'm seated in my armchair in the living room, with friends and colleagues seated around, hanging on to every word that leaves my mouth. In the middle is a large table covered with all the goodies that Irene could prepare—from hors d'oeuvres to chicken and fish dishes, and tons of deserts. My boss, Art Scott, is here, as are some of my hospital colleagues; Steve Denker, who was the one who admitted Dorothy Alberts to the hospital, and the other docs who took care of her in the intensive care unit. All the Alberts children—Milo, David and Lydia—are here too. Milo is smoking his pipe, as usual, with the others sipping bottles of

Carslberg and Tuborg. Lennox came from the West Coast with his two lovely daughters, Patricia and Catherine, and his sister Margaret. I've also invited Mel Kraft, who seems just as wired and nervous as he was on the first day I met him at Gusti's.

"They asked me to write another article on the outcome and lessons of this affair," David says.

"Well," I respond, "you've got all the information you need."

"I have a bunch of questions," he continues.

"Shoot."

"What happened to Barnes?" he starts.

"He pulled out a gun and shot himself. In full view of all his colleagues. They're still investigating how he got the gun. There's a rumor that Carter Dell helped him find it."

"How's Lacoste doing?"

"He's still under investigation. They're trying to figure out if he's involved in some extortion scheme with the mailing of Dara's picture. He's definitely finished as a consultant."

"He'll probably be a major target of the congressional investigation on industry relations with universities," Milo adds.

"Also, the NIH is putting a hold on his grants and his hospital privileges have been suspended pending the outcome of the investigation," Art says.

Everybody in the room seems to have mastered all the details by now.

"But his buddy Aftaz, and Rubelli from FDA, were suspended pending investigation about their monitoring of the development of Neurovan. Also, the Aftaz-Lacoste connection is under scrutiny."

Irene comes by suddenly and gives me a big unabashed hug.

"I can't believe what you went through," she whispers.

I hug her.

"So, you guys ready for the big road show?" she asks. She's

talking about David and me going on Larry King and "Nightline" in a couple of days.

"Sure," David grins.

"Tell me something," Milo chimes in, "what was the deal with that Dara woman. Wasn't she the one that got you started in all this?"

There's no subject that preoccupied me more than this. Dara. Why? I close my eyes, and I see her in my bed in the San Francisco hotel, and then I see her standing at the doorstep of my London room, white blouse and feet apart, the symbol of elegance, warmth and tease.

"Yeah," I say, "somewhere in the middle there, she did a one-eighty on me."

"So you don't think that she planned it from the start, to somehow use you for the company's purpose . . ."

How many times have I wondered about this myself?

"No. In the beginning she really was upset at the company, she cared about those sick patients, and then something snapped. I think she was brainwashed by Barnes, maybe bought by him, during their trip to the Riviera."

I can't tell them that maybe she turned against me because I turned down her sexual advances. Twice, at least. Like somebody said, there's nothing worse than the vengeance of a woman spurned. Or words to that effect. Irene knows, but the others can only suspect.

"This was the shock of my life," Lennox leans back in the sofa. "I think that you're right about Barnes turning her around. I think that for a long time she really liked you."

He takes off his silver-rimmed glasses, blows air on them, wipes them with his shirt and puts them back on.

"I know she liked you," he says.

"What will happen to her?" Lydia asks. She told me earlier

that her painful foot had gotten better since she improved her glucose control with more insulin.

"It all depends on whether the others implicate her in any wrongdoing."

"She'll probably be a key witness, but there's a good chance she'll walk away scott free," Lennox says.

"What about the gun she aimed at you? Isn't that a crime?" Irene asks.

"Yeah, sure. Still, the main defendants are Lansing, Dell and Walnut. Ramsey is somewhere in Australia, maybe one of the islands, hiding, and for now he's safe. Depending on how much the others sing, he may be extradited back," I explain.

Milo blows a large puff from his pipe.

"Ah, prisoner's dilemma," he muses. "If you're Dell, do you rat on Walnut or Lansing? If you're Walnut, do you shift blame to Dell and Lansing? In theory, if all three keep quiet and say nothing, the better it is for everybody. But if somebody rats on you, you're better off spilling the beans on the others. Since you can't communicate with the others, what do you do?"

"They'll sing like nightingales," Lennox says.

"They may accuse you," Mel Kraft joins in.

"I'm sure they will. But, they can't pin the killing of the Austrian doctor on me, or the establishment of the Lucca taskforce."

"Isn't that something," Steve Denker says, "who would dream up a scheme like this to get a drug approved?"

"Barnes and Lansing," I say. "Look, it's actually simple. First, you build a frame of mind where the goal—getting a drug on the market and pocketing hefty profits—justifies the means. So you start with explaining, move to persuasion, then a little arm-twisting mixed in with bribing, then threatening. Every time you escalate, you up the ante. There's more to lose, but also more to gain.

Each step up the escalator doesn't seem to be a big step in itself."

"But murder?" Lydia asks.

"I think I may have contributed to this," I say.

"What?"

"Well, when they found out that I was poking around the patient in Vienna, Lansing got scared. Maybe Kunz threatened to bail out of the study, remove his support for the product, or maybe Lansing was just worried about what Kunz might tell me."

"We may never find out," Lydia says.

"Fritz Reiber told me that they are also investigating in Austria," I say.

"Are you sure that Lansing killed Kunz?" Mel asks.

I shrug.

"They found huge amounts of Digoxin in Kunz's blood. It wasn't a medication he was taking. Lansing has access to Digoxin—Gother makes it—and he was there. What can I say, he had a motive, an opportunity and the means."

"So Lansing was Lucca?" Irene asks.

"Yes, but he had some helpers. You met two of them, I guess." Irene shudders suddenly.

"Uh-huh. Looking back on it, they wanted to let me go and forget the whole thing more than I did. Their heart wasn't in their job. It's like kidnapping wasn't in their job description when they had joined Gother."

There's a pause as I get up to fill my glass of wine.

"Not only were they corrupt, but also dumb. To write a memo like they did . . . " Art just shakes his head.

Another thing that kept me awake at night, wondering.

"Yeah, but you know, if you just read that memo, it's fairly vague and innocent. It's only when you know what they did that the memo becomes incriminating," I say.

"And, come to think of it, Lansing actually helped us penetrate the Gother computer, when we fiddled with it in my house," Gerry says.

"I don't think that he was thinking about the memo at the time," I respond. "Or, he's a cocky sonofabitch, didn't think we'd find it and live to tell about it."

"Look," Irene cries, pointing to the television, "it's that professor philosopher you like so much."

In the corner, the television is on, but the sound is off. I reach for the clicker and increase the volume. The old gaunt man, whose name I don't even know, is looking at a chess board, with a few pieces scattered on it. The black king is lying on its side, signaling defeat for black.

"So this was checkmate. When the game is over, and the better player has won, there's a rush, a feeling of exultation and satisfaction. You've outsmarted your opponent. He made a mistake and you took advantage of it. If he doesn't make a mistake—could be tiny, sometimes trivial, but a mistake nonetheless—you can't win. Plain and simple. Before you conclude, you sit down and analyze the game move by move, trying to understand why the opponent played the way he did, and explaining to him your brilliant strategy. You find the mistake he made and try to improve on it, in case you play again."

The professor gets up and starts putting the pieces, one by one, into the box.

"You won, but be humble. Remember, at the end of the game the mighty king and the lowly pawn go into the same dark box."

He looks directly at us, straightening his glasses.

"And this, folks, is the end of the game."